Disturbers Row

Dennis Domrzalski

ISBN: 978-0-9851813-5-2

Library of Congress Control Number: 2021919048

Illustrations by Dan Florentino

Logan Square Press

ALSO BY DENNIS DOMRZALSKI

I Got Stinky Feet Volume One: Open Air Asylum

I Got Stinky Feet Volume Two: Fools, Losers and Idiots

Raped: Memories of a Catholic Altar Boy (With Larry Monte Jr.)

A Poet's Dilemma

To my fellow Disturbers and all the fun we had.

CONTENTS

CHAPTER 1

Room 204

"DISTURBERS ROW!"

The five boys in the classroom's back row didn't respond to the two words, which were an order that they leave their seats and walk quietly to the enclosed cloakroom at the room's front end to get their jackets and sweaters, or "wraps," as the nun called them. Instead, they sat and laughed amongst themselves, proud of their refusal to obey even the slightest order that the old, wrinkled, angry nun gave them.

"Disturbers Row!" Sister Mary Zita spat out with even more than the usual contempt she had for the five, who were driving her crazy with their lack of respect for her authority. They were brazen and bold, disrupted her classroom to no end and shamed the very idea of what seventh grade, Catholic schoolboys should be. They were challenging her again by refusing to get their wraps for the lunch hour dismissal, and as she half sat on the front edge of her wooden desk at the front of the room, Sister Zita made ready to respond to the challenge by grabbing her favorite weapon off the desk: a four-foot-long, rubber-tipped wooden pointer.

That Zitabug, as they called her, was getting angrier, made the boys laugh out loud. Those laughs seared her ears. She considered them a direct assault on her role as a representative of God and was even more determined to wipe those taunting smiles off their twelve-and-thirteen-year-old-year-old faces. They stayed in their chairs, reveling in the glory that they knew would soon be theirs.

"Disturbers Row!"

They stayed put and laughed harder. That was enough for Sister Zita. The old nun, pointer in hand, launched herself off the desk and hobbled, half bent over, as best she could, across the wooden floor and past the rows of Room 204's good kids: the kids who always did their homework, never talked in class and always obeyed her orders, the kids who succumbed to authority's every effort at control and who made the Disturbers sick.

The five had once sat amongst those annoying, properly behaved kids, but they could never keep their mouths shut and they couldn't help but bust out laughing every time Zita gave an order or even spoke. The poor woman couldn't pronounce "geography," she called it "gergerphy." She used silly phrases like "Mister Big Stuff," and "You are as bold as brass and even bolder than that" to try to embarrass kids who goofed off in class, and she said "D'wuhh?" every time she tried to say "What?" or "What did you say?"

And so, within the first few weeks of classes at Our Lady of Grace grammar school on Chicago's northwest side, Sister Zita had identified the five—Gary Kolba, Dave Ruchinski, Bob Kurkowski, Richard Bozeman and Dennis Domrzalski—as problem students, put them together in the back row and labeled them "Disturbers" in an attempt to shame them into conformist behavior. The move had the opposite effect. The boys wore the title "Disturber" as a badge of honor and felt it compelled them to be even more disruptive and antagonistic than they already were.

It had long been that way for Sister Zita. She was old—at least sixty or so, but exactly how old was a mystery—and had long ago lost the ability to control a classroom. For the past ten years the rowdier boys who went to OLG prayed to get Zita as their seventh-grade teacher. If they did, she obliged their rebellious instincts by making them Disturbers.

There had been some legendary Disturbers in the past—Steve Domrzalski, Frank Hopkins and Tommy Tamkin—who brought disturbing to new heights of rule-breaking, disrespect, scholastic irresponsibility and contempt for classroom decorum.

They were heroes in the neighborhood, and the current batch of Disturbers admired them. But they were individuals. They had acted alone and separately and were never able to bring the full concentration of their combined prowess to bear on the hapless nun.

This year's Disturbers were different. There were five of them who had the benefit of history, and who knew that Zita would soon be retiring. They were fully aware of the opportunity they had to become the greatest group of Disturbers in OLG's sixty-year history. To claim that coveted honor they realized that they not only had to take disturbing to a new level, but that they had to disturb as a unit, as one.

That they did. During those first few weeks they had all already been beaten several times by Zita—slapped by her dried, scaly hands, cracked with the pointer and clubbed with the "rung of a chair," a foot-long, half-inch-square, solid piece of wood that formed the cross-supports for the legs of their wooden classroom chairs.

The beatings fueled their desire to do even more harm in the classroom and made them heroes to themselves. With every back of Zita's hand, with every punch from her bony fist and with every thump from her chair rung they laughed harder and disturbed more.

When Zita attacked—disciplined—one, the others stormed into action and raised ruckuses in other areas of the second-floor classroom. Sometimes they antagonized other students, sometimes they ran around the room screaming and laughing and stomping their feet, and sometimes they raced up to Zita and taunted her. No matter what they did, it always worked. Zita would stop beating her original target to chase them, and what had started out as a small-scale disturbance usually turned into a classroom-wide riot.

It was happening again. Zita, the four-foot-long, standard-issue nun's rosary dangling from her belt, and the starchy stench of her full-body, black and white linen habit smelling up the room, was charging toward Disturbers Row.

At least she thought she was charging. To the Disturbers, she was limping slowly and taking forever to get to there. That annoyed them because they gloried in the attention that a battle with her brought them from Room 204's other thirty-seven students, especially the girls, most of whom giggled when these riots erupted.

Zita was at row three, approaching the Disturbers from the classroom's left side. The boys held their positions and laughed louder. As she hit row four, the five-foot-tall nun began raising the pointer that she held in her right hand. The Disturbers started talking to each other, pretending that they hadn't heard her earlier order and that they didn't see her heading back toward them.

SISTER ZITA

The pointer rose high into the air as Zita crossed row five, just a few steps away from Disturbers Row. Still the boys held and pretended not to see her. She walked another two steps and then—Crraaack! The pointer came down and slammed on the wooden top of Kolba's table-like desk. Zita hadn't meant for that. She had swung with the intention of smashing Gary's arms as they lay folded across the desk, but at just the right moment he had jumped out of his chair and run to the other side of the room, denying the nun the satisfaction of inflicting physical pain.

The other boys had done the same; they had reacted instantly to avoid Zita and her pointer, and she was angry. She shuffled slowly across the back of the room, trying to get to the side where the Disturbers had fled. But the Disturbers were long gone; they had scattered and were all over the room. Kurkowski was already at the front of the room rummaging through the drawers in Zita's desk. Ruchinski had Roger Krask, one of the nun's perfectly behaved pet students, in a headlock in row two. Bozeman was assaulting another of her pets, Bernard Heller, in row three, and dumping his books on the floor. Kolba was marching around the room, stomping his feet on its wooden floor and shouting, over and over, "We don't have wraps, we have jackets!"

THE DISTURBERS

Bozeman had crawled to row five, where he crouched down behind, and readied for an assault on Thomas Dodkin, who annoyed Zita with his habit of loudly blurting out anything that was on his mind. It never mattered to Dodkin what subject was being taught. If it was spelling class and he had something to say about religion, well, he just shouted it out, always to the amusement of his classmates.

Bozeman wound up for his assault on Dodkin by raising his arm behind his back as far as it would go. His right hand held a weapon. Then he swung the arm forward with full fury and— "Aggghhhhh!" Thomas Dodkin shrieked so loud the world could hear. He jolted up into the air, plopped back down in his chair and wailed again while grabbing for his right buttock with his hand. Bozeman had stabbed him with the pointed end of a steel geometry compass.

Bozeman had let go of the weapon when Dodkin jumped into the air, and now he tried to grab it as it dangled from his victim's ass. Dodkin writhed and wiggled, instinctively trying to shake the weapon from his body, all the while screaming that he had been hurt. Bozeman grabbed and missed. He grabbed again and missed, and finally, on the third try, he got hold of the compass and—"Aggghhhhh!" Dodkin screamed as Bozeman withdrew the two-inch-long steel point from his flesh and scurried away.

The entire room exploded with laughter, talking and shouting—even the good kids laughed—and Zita now had a general insurrection to put down. She was furious, believed that it was another one of Dodkin's improper outbursts, and wobbled toward him as he got up and stood next to his desk.

"You think you're Mister Big Stuff, don't you, Mister Dodkin?" Zita sneered as she raised the pointer. "You want attention just like they do? Well, I'll give you attention!"

She began flailing away at Dodkin with the pointer and landed six or seven quick blows to his back and shoulders. The poor boy was no Disturber and was dumbfounded that he was being beaten for having been stabbed. He saw neither the humor nor the opportunity for glory in the situation, and he slumped down into his chair and covered his head and face with his arms to protect them from Zita's repeated blows.

"But Sister," Dodkin cried after she had hammered him with another ten blows, "somebody poked me with something and it hurt real bad. I think I'm bleeding."

"Oh, poor little baby," Zita said with a sneer that said she didn't believe him. "Where is the little owie?"

"On my ass!"

Whack! Whack! Whack!

Zita went after with the boy with a fury that impressed even the Disturbers, and in just a few moments Thomas Dodkin was sobbing.

"But Sister!" he kept crying in feeble attempts to gain her sympathy. "But Sister!"

"Don't 'But Sister' me!" Zita huffed as she continued to pound the boy. "You keep quiet in my room. Speak when spoken to! Otherwise, mister, you *will* get the back of my hand!"

"But Ster!" shouted a voice from the opposite corner in back of the room, "Sterrr?"

Zita wasn't prone to answer to the name of "Ster," which was the Disturbers' disrespectful shorthand for "Sister," and which infuriated her. But this was a desperate situation, so she acknowledged the summons:

"D'wuhh?"

"Ster! I saw what happened. Thomas is right. Someone poked him with something. I think it was a compass! I think he's hurt real bad. He might need an ambulance! If he doesn't get to a hospital soon, he will die!"

The voice belonged to Dave Ruchinski, one of Zita's chief antagonists and a Disturber for whom the old nun had mixed feelings. She hated Ruchinski's unceasing efforts to humiliate her, and knew he was a Disturbers ringleader, but she didn't think that the boy riled her on purpose. After all, he had a somewhat angelic face, blond hair and a pretty smile, and he could be nice when he wanted to. No, she figured he was mildly retarded, as she thought were many of the working-class Polish, German, Irish, Italian and Scandinavian children she taught.

"So, mister pretty boy," she said with more than a hint of sarcasm, "It's so nice of you to help. So sweet of you. So tell me, mister, who did it?"

"Well, Ster, I only saw their outline and so I couldn't make out who it was," Ruchinski said, feigning breathlessness and intense interest in identifying the culprit. "But I saw their outline and I know that it was a big person."

"How big?"

"Not real big, but pretty big. Pretty real big."

"Was it a boy or a girl?"

"It was a boy, Ster. I think, anyway. But maybe not. Boys don't wear dresses. I think he had a dress on, so it couldn't have been a boy."

"What color was the dress?"

"Purple, Ster!"

"No one here has a purple dress."

"You're right. It was green!"

"No one here has a green dress." Zita was right, of course, because no one in the school wore what the nuns considered garish colors. All the students wore uniforms: the girls white blouses and dark blue plaid skirts, and the boys, dark blue pants, white shirts and solid blue clip-on ties.

"I think it was white!"

"Maybe it was yellow, sweetie."

"Exactly, Ster! It was yellow. But Ster, I don't think it could have been a girl. I mean, I really don't think so."

"Why not, pretty boy?"

"Because she had a beard!"

The entire class convulsed with laughter, even Thomas Dodkin, and Zita knew that, once again, she had been beaten. She was furious and determined to exact a terrible revenge on at least one of the Disturbers for her humiliation and started lumbering toward Ruchinski. Then Thomas Dodkin blurted out through his tears:

"Sister! It was Dennis! He did it!"

"D'wuhh? Mister Ruchinski, is that true?"

"Ster, I definitely saw it, and I cannot tell a lie. Dennis did it," Ruchinski said while laughing about the situation into which he has just put his fellow Disturber.

That was the perfect answer for Zita. She might have had mixed emotions about Ruchinski's disturbing, but she knew that Domrzalski's disruptions were the purposeful work of a mean-spirited youth who was out to get her and who was beyond redemption. In fact, he had come from a family of Disturbers. His oldest brother Wally had disturbed her class in 1962. It was his class that had given her the humiliating name of Zitabug. His brother Steve had been a Disturber in 1965. He was a fiercely rebellious youth who had set new standards of contempt for her. Now it was 1966 and she had another disturbing Domrzalski in her room, and she finally had the reason she needed to pay him back for all the pain, suffering and humiliation his brothers had caused her. If his parents were set on breeding Disturbers, well, she was determined to beat this one silly.

Already in the short school year she had almost blurted out that Dennis was just like his brothers. But she knew it wasn't true. Wally, although a sneak and a liar, wasn't a career Disturber who was determined to disrupt her class every day. He reacted to opportunities and responded well to beatings. Steve, although a whirlwind of mischief in the classroom, usually calmed down once he lashed out at her and vented his anger. Both seemed relatively normal. But Dennis, a skinny, angry-looking kid with short brown hair and thick, black-rimmed glasses, was bitter beyond his years. He had started kindergarten in 1959 at four-and-a-half years old, and most of his classmates were six months to a year older than he was, which at that age, was a significant difference.

Dennis was smaller than his classmates, which made him feel insecure and stupid, and had been a shy, sullen brooder who was, as the saying went, afraid of his own shadow. In first grade he barely learned how to print because he was too afraid to raise his hand to ask questions about the subject. In second grade he crapped in his pants because he was too scared to raise his hand to ask to go to the bathroom. It took the scared kid until third grade to work up the nerve to raise his hand to ask or answer a question. He was also a little slow, or a slow learner, the nuns said. Sister Mary Concepta, the second-grade nun, had smelled the problem that day and had called the frightened boy to the front of the class, where she quietly asked him, "Have you had an accident?"

Figuring she was talking about a car crash or something, he answered in the negative. The nun, angered by what she thought was a deliberate lie, lost her temper and shouted so the entire class could hear:

"You've had an accident! Go to the lavatory and clean up!"

His classmates knew exactly what that meant, and they giggled and laughed at the shy boy with the leaky bowel. The embarrassment had seared itself into his memory, and he had vowed to someday get even, if not with that nun, with anyone who wore the black and white habit of the Dominican Order. And so, through the discipline of ceaseless and solitary brooding sessions, Dennis had programmed himself to be a human torpedo whose guidance system was permanently locked onto nuns in black and white habits. Although he really bore no ill will or personal animosity toward Zita—he actually felt sorry for her—Dennis operated under the code that drove many a Catholic schoolkid: antagonize and humiliate them as they have humiliated you.

He had busted out of his shell in third grade, and now, as a Disturber, he was fully prepared to live that code.

"Maybe Mister Domrzalski forgot his dress today," Zita said, chuckling proudly at her sarcasm. She wheeled and turned to the boy, who had been standing in the back of the room shooting spitballs at the good kids through a plastic ball-point pen tube during the riot.

"No, Ster! I haven't forgotten it. It's in the cloakroom. I'll just go get it and show it to you," Dennis replied with a smirk. "I think it would look good on you!"

Zita hated being outwitted, especially by a twelve-year-old, and she advanced on Dennis, while her hand that gripped the pointer twitched uncontrollably with a sense of pleasurable anticipation at being able to whack the boy.

"You think you're Mister Big Stuff, don't you?" she snarled. "Well, I'll give you wearing a dress in my room!"

"But Ster! I haven't even worn the dress!"

"Why not? Afraid they'll call you a sissy?"

"No, Ster."

"Then why?!"

"Because you won't let me go get it."

"No back talking to me, you little—"

9

Zita always started mumbling when she got to the point of calling the boys names. They swore that she swore under her breath, something that, if it could be proven, would have been a devastating embarrassment to the nun.

"Please, Ster. No swearing. God is listening," Kolba, who had run to a side of the room, said with mock concern. "He's in this classroom, you know. He's everywhere and he can hear you. Please, Ster, set a better example for us."

Zita was torn. She hated Domrzalski and wanted to crack him a few times, but she also despised Kolba for his smart aleck ways. He was the wittiest of the Disturbers, and she couldn't abide it.

"Get to the back of the room, Mr. Kolba," Zita said, hoping to trick him into moving next to Dennis.

"Why, Ster?" Kolba asked, knowing that she wanted him there so she could beat them both at once.

"So I can pray for you two together," Zita said. "It's more efficient that way."

"But Ster, I don't want to stand next to Dennis."

"Why Gary? Are you afraid to stand next to a boy who wears dresses?"

"No, Ster."

"Afraid that you'll get caught up in his pretty boy ways?"

"No, Ster."

"Then why?"

"Because Ster, his dress went out of style four years ago, and I don't want to be near someone who is so unfashionable. It's embarrassing."

Zita went berserk, and fueled by her outrage, she nearly ran to Dennis, shoved him against the back wall and started savaging him with the pointer and punching and scratching him with her free hand. Dennis escaped her grasp and ran to a side of the room to flee. But Kolba and Kurkowski blocked his way and pushed him back toward the nun. He ran to the room's other side, only to be blocked and pushed back by Bozeman and Ruchinski.

Zita pounced on him again. The beating lasted several minutes, during which Dennis and the other Disturbers laughed the whole time. It ended when the school bell rang, signaling the noon hour and lunch time. The nun had no choice but to let him go as the children raced out of the classroom.

Dennis was bruised, and his arms, neck and cheeks were scratched and bleeding slightly, but he was in heaven.

So were the other Disturbers.

CHAPTER 2

Working Up an Excuse

THE KIDS POURED out of the two-story, red brick school building that had been built in 1910 and into the bright sunshine of a late September day. More than a thousand kids went to OLG, which had classes from kindergarten through eighth grade, and except for a hundred or so who stayed for lunch in the school's basement auditorium they—those whose mothers stayed home to raise families—were on their way home for lunch. They fanned out from the school at Ridgeway and Altgeld avenues to the neighborhood's streets: Lawndale, Monticello, Central Park, Wrightwood, Diversey, Hamlin, Avers, Springfield, Harding, Fullerton, Schubert, Pulaski, Drake, St. Louis, Belden, Parker, Palmer, Kimball and Armitage. Some had only a couple of blocks to walk, while those who lived at the limits of the parish's boundaries had a five or six block journey past the rows of wood frame and brick two-flat houses, three-story brick apartment buildings, and an occasional, single-story brick bungalow squeezed onto twenty-five-foot-wide lots, fifteen or sixteen buildings to each side of a block.

They took one of two routes home: Altgeld or Fullerton. Those on the Altgeld route headed north on the sidewalks out of the school building and wound their way home east or west. The Fullerton kids headed south, and many had to cross Fullerton, a main street, to get home. At Fullerton and

Ridgeway, to stop cars, trucks and buses, and to shepherd the kids safely across the four-lane street, stood a massive Chicago Police Department crossing guard by the name of Angie, a loud, brick of an Italian woman with dark hair whose mere presence in the middle of the street set drivers slamming on their brakes out of fear of running into her and damaging their vehicles.

Angie had a police department whistle to get motorists' attention, but she rarely used it. She preferred instead to whistle through her fingers, shout for cars to stop, or her favorite, to simply lumber into the middle of traffic to stop it.

ANGIE COULD STOP TRAFFIC

The kids had learned which route to take home on their first day of kindergarten, that is, if their parents or someone else had told them. Many a four-and-a-half or five-year-old kindergarten kid panicked that first half day of school when they were told get into either in the Altgeld or Fullerton lines. Some hadn't been told, and some, because of the stress of that first day away from home, blanked out and forgot which line to join.

Mike Macewich, who lived above a tavern on the corner of Wrightwood and Pulaski, learned what terror was that first day of school when he was asked, "Do you go home by the Fullerton or Altgeld Route?"

He was five, had never been around the block by himself and didn't even know what Fullerton or Altgeld meant. He picked Fullerton, which was the wrong choice, and he was the last kid standing on the sidewalk on Ridgeway in front of the school waiting for his older sister to pick him up and walk him home. She had looked for him in the Altgeld group of kids, which had huddled together about a half block away from the Fullerton group.

As the other kids in the Fullerton group got picked up and it seemed that no one was coming to take him home, Macewich started to cry. The nun who was guarding him normally would have slapped him for such a transgression, but even she started getting nervous when every other kid had been picked up and the four-foot-tall, skinny Macewich was standing there by himself crying and feeling abandoned. His sister eventually looked down the block and found him, but he had already been traumatized. For many years afterwards, Macewich trembled when he heard the name Fullerton, and for a long time he avoided the street altogether.

The Disturbers didn't live near each other, so they split off in different directions at lunchtime and after school and walked or ran home with other kids in their class.

Dennis usually made the five-minute walk down Altgeld with John Klosk, one of 204's good kids; Stanley Polit, a 204 kid who, although a little nutty and strange, was never strange enough to be a Disturber; and Jim Masciola, a stout, rebellious kid who threw back at the nuns all that they threw at him, and who, had he not been in a different seventh-grade class, would have been an official Disturber.

Masciola lived on Harding down the block from Dennis. The two had been friends and comrades in adventures, petty theft and borderline anti-social behavior since first grade.

"Nice scratches," Masciola said to Dennis as they walked on the sidewalk past the parish rectory on the corner of Hamlin and Altgeld. "Zita?"

"Yeah."

"Cool."

Masciola, like every other OLG seventh and eighth grader, knew Zita well. The seventh and eighth grade classes were conducted high school style where different teachers taught different subjects and the students changed rooms. Zita taught geography, spelling and religion; Miss Donatello, a stocky, humorless, mean, dark-haired woman with a slight mustache, science and math; Sister Frances DeLasalle, a large, beefy, nun with a powerful punch, art and history; and Sister Mary Yvonne, a stern, mean, disciplinarian, English, reading and writing. The Disturbers had extra time with Zita in the mornings and afternoons because she was their homeroom teacher.

"How'd it happen?"

Dennis told the story quickly and without embellishment—Disturbers were proud that their stories needed none—leaving Masciola jealous.

"Damn. You're so lucky. You guys have all the fun. I just wish I had her for home-room."

"Yeah, but if you came home with scratches like this, your old man would beat the crap out of you.

"Yeah, I know. But still. Hey, but what'll your ma say about the scratches?"

The question hit Dennis hard. Like most kids his age, he lived for moment, for the immediate attention and approval of his friends. He never thought ahead or about the consequences of his behavior. When he taunted Zita he thought only about being hit by her and of the attention and admiration it would bring him from his friends. He never considered what it might mean for him grade-wise, or how his parents would react to news that he spent a good portion of his day at school—at a school they paid good and scarce money for him to attend—disrupting classes and being a little jerk.

Like all parents in the neighborhood, Dennis's were raised during the Great Depression when jobs were scarce, existence itself was threatened and when people dropped out of high school in order to work to help support families. They clung to their jobs, frowned on any kind of risk, even that of talking in class, and were respectful of authority to the point of submission. Most parents who sent their kids to Catholic schools were especially mindful of religious authority. To them, nuns were a breed of superwomen who were smart enough to do arithmetic, spell correctly and teach, strong enough to knock the biggest kids around, disciplined enough to not smoke or booze, imbued with special grace from God, and most importantly, shrewd enough to know when and how badly to beat up their kids. In their minds, nuns—even the young ones—were grandmothers made perfect by God, and parents had absolute faith in the nuns' judgments and decisions regarding the kids.

The kids, especially the Disturbers, saw things differently. They hadn't yet had their youthful honesty, inborn skepticism and rebellious instincts educated and indoctrinated out of them. To them, the nuns were very strange. Even many of the girls thought it odd that a group of women could live together by themselves, pray constantly and find happiness in singing hymns.

Many of the boys saw that the nuns were even meaner than their fathers. They were quicker to smack them across the face than their dads were, and the nuns acted like their only joy in life was beating up kids.

It's not that the boys frowned on the idea of beating up children; they just wished that they could be the ones who administered the blows. In third grade, Dennis and Kolba so wanted to beat other kids up that they asked how they could apply to become nuns.

The request alarmed the sisters, who immediately tried to thwart any type of unholy or abnormal behavior in the boys. They brought the two before the parish pastor, Monsignor Francis Flavin, for an inquisition in the parish rectory. For more than forty minutes the white-haired priest, who sent tiny droplets of white spit flying from his lips when he talked, questioned the two about their home lives, what they did for fun, how they entertained themselves, and if they had any "special" daydreams, fears or secret hiding places.

The line of inquiry, especially about the secret hiding places, troubled Kolba, who figured the nuns and priest were after his secret stash of comic books, a paving stone that he had dug up from a city street, boxes of light-anywhere stick matches, an old cigarette lighter, a can of lighter fluid, ballpoint pens he had stolen from Saxon's hardware store on Fullerton, a magnifying glass that he and his friends used to start piles of leaves and sticks on fire, old firecrackers he had found on the street after one Fourth of July, scissors, a couple of rusty pocket knives and other stuff. Gary's stockpile was hidden under boards in the three-foot-wide gangway between two garages down his alley. Dennis had a similar hoard that he kept under cardboard boxes in a junk-strewn field next to a factory a few blocks from his house.

"We're going to give you boys a few minutes to think about this," Monsignor Flavin said sternly that day as he and the nuns left the room in an effort to apply silent pressure to the youngsters.

The boys didn't need to think, though; each instinctively knew what they would say when the inquisitors returned. To make sure, Kolba mentioned the plan:

"I know where Gronski and Kowalski hide their stuff—"

"Yeah, and I know where Klosk and Pateras stash theirs," Dennis interrupted.

"If they want stuff, we'll just tell them where the other guys' hiding places are," Kolba said. "That'll get them off our backs."

The nuns and Flavin returned, and the questioning resumed.

"Well, young men, for your sakes, I hope you have thought good and hard about this," Flavin said.

"Yes Father, we have," Kolba started. "We do have secret hiding places. Mine is—"

The boys then proceeded to reveal the location of the other boys' stashes, and they were proud of themselves for having been so clever.

Angered by what he thought was an intentional misinterpretation of his questions, the monsignor shouted:

"Now boys, I'm tired of your games and your disrespectful ways. I want answers, and I want them now! You know that only girls can become sisters! Why? Why in God's name do you want to become nuns?"

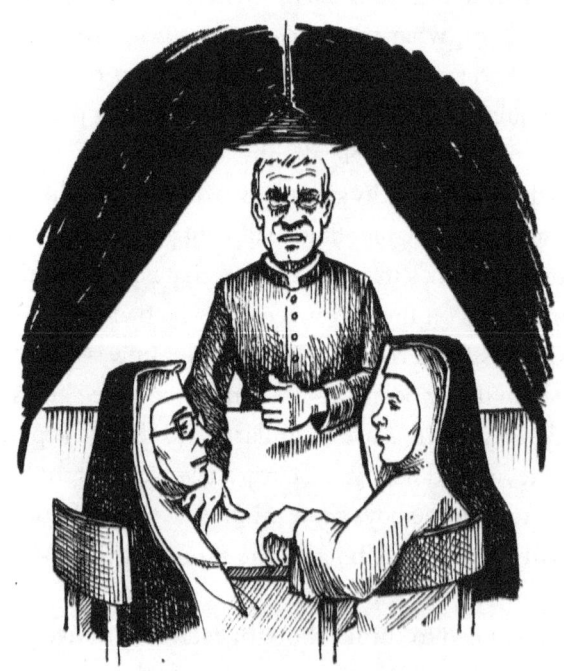

BOYS CAN'T BE NUNS!

"That's easy, Father," Dennis said eagerly and without thinking. "We want to become sisters so we can beat kids up every day and not get in trouble for it! That seems like a good job!"

Kolba laughed and agreed with Dennis, and in an instant they were being slapped around by the nuns and priest.

"Shame on you boys! Shame! You'll go to Hell for thoughts like that," the school's principal, Sister Mary Vitaclaire, yelled as she pounded Dennis's back with the undersides of her forearms. "It's two week's detention for you two! Get out of here!"

"This isn't fair," Kolba said as he and Dennis, wobbly from the beatings, carefully picked their way down the steps of the rectory's brick and concrete front porch, "they've got these good jobs and they won't let boys have them. I don't think we should give up, though."

"We won't," Dennis offered. "Someday, no matter what, we'll be nuns and we'll beat everybody up."

Yes, the nuns were mean, often too mean, but the kids had no recourse. When a nun said a kid was a monster in class who needed severe discipline, there was no question from the parents that it was true and that the nun was probably shading things slightly on the kid's behalf.

So now, Dennis had a problem. His mother would see the scratches and the blood when he walked in the door, and she would know instantly that he had been acting up in class again and gotten the beating he deserved. She could excuse a couple of disruptions, after all, that's what boys did, but idea that he was now misbehaving on a permanent basis troubled and saddened her, and he knew that she would have to do something about it.

"I don't know. I'll just go to the washroom and clean up real fast. Maybe she won't see," Dennis said in response to Masciola's question about the scratches.

"I don't think it'll work. Those are pretty big scratches."

"I'll say that we found a cat on the way home and we picked it up and that it scratched me in the face."

"She won't believe that. No cat's going to come to us and let us pick it up."

"I'll just say I got into a fight."

"Then she'll ask with who, and call somebody's ma to see if it's true."

"I'll say I got into a fight with you."

"Yeah, and then when she calls my ma, my ma'll beat me up for fighting."

"I could say that Marty jumped us looking for money and that we had to fight him off," Dennis said, referring to Marty the Bum, a frail, dirty, smelly drunk who shoveled coal in some of the neighborhood's apartment buildings.

Marty was a real bum. He had no job other than the occasional work he got shoveling coal into building furnaces. He slept on railroad tracks and in coal bins, which was why he was always dirty and blackened. He scavenged for food in garbage cans and dumpsters in the alleys behind restaurants. He stunk of urine and excrement. He barely talked, shuffled along the sidewalks because he never had the strength to lift his legs, and he spent the little money he made on cans of beans, which he always ate cold, and bottles of cheap wine.

"I'll just say that Marty jumped us."

Are you nuts? She'll call the cops on him and then we won't have anyone to make runs for the older guys," Masciola said, referring to Marty's true value to the neighborhood; he was the kids' pipeline to alcohol. The kids would give Marty money and he would shuffle off to a tavern to buy beer and wine. The kids tipped Marty enough so he could buy himself a pint of sixty-cent wine. And although it always seemed to take forever when Marty was sent off on a beer run, the man was reliable. He always returned with the beer, and he always got the order right.

"I got it. Just start climbing that tree," Masciola said as he pointed to a large cottonwood in the grass just beyond the sidewalk.

"Why?"

"Because. You can say that you were climbing a tree and when you were halfway up you lost your grip and slid down and scratched your face. And if you get your shirt and pants dirty and full of bark, it'll make it seem like it's true."

That sounded like a good idea, and Dennis got about a third up the trunk and then slid down, pressing his face against the bark in an effort to pick up a few extra scratches.

It worked. His white shirt and blue pants were dirty, his hands a little bruised and his face scratched a little more. Dennis now had an excuse for the scratches, and he was relieved except for one thing.

"Why am I going to say I was climbing a tree?"

"I don't know," Masciola said as they reached the alley between Harding and Springfield where Dennis split off to go home. "Think of something."

"I'll try," Dennis said as he sprinted down the alley to his house.

CHAPTER 3

His Ma Isn't Fooled

"HOME, MA!" DENNIS yelled as he burst up the six grey wooden, back porch stairs of his family's three-story, two-flat frame house on Harding Avenue and into the kitchen of the small first-floor flat.

He hadn't needed to announce his arrival home for the sixty-minute-long lunch break because his mother, Florence, was always in the kitchen when he, his older brother Steve, and his younger sister Barbara came home for lunch. Florence always had sandwiches or hot dogs or soup on the Formica-topped kitchen table ready for the kids, who always rushed right to the food.

So when Dennis, his head down and eyes pointed to the kitchen's patterned, light-blue linoleum floor, rushed right by the kitchen table and straight into the washroom that was off the hallway that led from the kitchen into the dining room, Florence Domrzalski knew that something was going on.

The boy quickly pulled the wooden door shut, groped for the light switch on the wall, flipped it on and stared at himself in the mirror that hung on the wall above the small, white porcelain sink.

It didn't look good. The scratches were prominent, red and on both sides of his face. There was some blood, but not a lot. Maybe, he figured, soap and hot water would turn his entire face red and hide the scratches. He turned on the hot water faucet and hurriedly splashed his face. He grabbed the bar of white hand soap from the clear plastic receptacle that hung from the wall, soaped up his hands and washed his face for a good minute. He rinsed with hot water, grabbed a towel, tried rubbing his face raw with it, and when he thought that had been accomplished, looked again in the mirror.

This time it wasn't so bad. His face was pink, and although the scratch marks still ran down the sides of his face, they blended in with his reddened skin and appeared to be less visible than before. He wasn't totally confident that he had disguised Zita's beating and the fact that he had once again been tormenting the old nun, but he felt better about the situation than he had a few minutes earlier.

"What's to eat?" he asked with a contrived cheerfulness as he left the washroom and took a few quick steps into the kitchen. "I think I'm pretty hungry."

Dennis was the first of the kids home for lunch and he took his usual seat at the end of the kitchen table that was next to a wall. Although a skinny kid, he still had to squeeze, as he did for every meal, around a wooden kitchen cabinet, into a chair at the long end of the table, and into the tiny space between the table and his chair. He pushed the table out a little toward the middle of the kitchen, pulled his chair out back toward the wall, placed one hand on the table and the other on the nearby countertop as if on a set of parallel bars, bent his knees, lifted himself off the ground, swung his body back and forth a few times and dropped himself into the chair.

The salami sandwich on white bread, slathered thick with yellow margarine and cut in half on his plate looked delicious, as did almost any food to a growing twelve-year-old. He took a huge bite out of one half of the sandwich, and while chewing furiously, held the remains of it in front of the plate and inspected the rounded bite mark for the traits of a Florence Domrzalski sandwich: his teeth marks were bitten into the thick layer of meat and into the way-too-thick layer of margarine.

"You went a little easy on the butter today, huh, Ma?" he said, knowing that no matter how many times he kidded her about her habit of putting too much margarine on sandwiches, she would never change.

Florence sat at the opposite end of the table and chuckled to herself. She was raising four children, had been making lunch sandwiches for fifteen years and knew exactly how much margarine, or butter, as they called it, to put on sandwiches. No matter what the kids thought or said, she always put the same amount on a sandwich. And even though it was a lot, it was the correct amount and belonged on those slices of bread because, well, she said it did.

LUNCH

"Your face looks a little red. Did you run home?" she asked, trying to gently draw out the truth. "Or maybe you've got a fever? I'll have to get out your winter jacket."

Dennis had to think fast because he knew that she would make him take a winter jacket back to school, and probably even his rubber winter boots, too. He wouldn't wear them to school and subject himself to the ridicule of his pals, but he'd have to leave the house with them on and then go through the trouble of stashing them somewhere on the way to school. And if he did that, there was a good chance that one of the many bums who worked as part-time janitors in the neighborhood apartment buildings would find them. If he came back without them, he'd be in big trouble.

"Ma, it's seventy degrees out," he said, hopping to make her realize that it would be ridiculous to wear winter clothes in September.

"It's a cold seventy," she snapped back.

Dennis had expected that answer. It was his mother's stock answer whenever she thought the children weren't dressed warmly enough. He had heard some version of it a million times before, it seemed: It's a cold seventy or a cold eighty or a cold ninety. Never though, did she use the argument in reverse and tell the kids it was a warm fifty or sixty and that they should wear lighter clothes than what they had put on. He decided to challenge her on it.

"How can it be a cold seventy? Seventy is seventy! You never hear the weathermen saying it's a cold seventy. It's just the temperature, and the temperature is what it is."

It was a powerful and logical argument, and an argument that Dennis knew, from the little science he had absorbed in school, was unassailable. A temperature was what it was. Even the nuns would scoff at the idea that it could be a cold seventy. The skinny youth knew he had his ma, and he waited for her to concede his logic and admit defeat.

"Oh! You're just so silly," Florence said with a slight laugh and wave of her hand in dismissal of his argument. "What do they teach you at that school?"

It was always that way with Florence, a forty-year-old woman who worked hard at keeping her home clean, meals on the table, the laundry done, the rugs vacuumed, the beds made and the husband and children off to work and school. Like most working-class, Depression-era kids, she had dropped out of high school to get a job and help support her family of seven kids. What she lacked in formal education she made up for with common sense—loads of it. And when she knew she was right—which was all the time—she laughed and dismissed challenges to her authority and logic as silly.

It worked every time, and it worked this time. Dennis had nowhere to go with his argument. He dropped it, hoping his ma would forget about making him wear a jacket to school on a seventy-degree day.

Dennis knew that Florence wouldn't drop her inquiries into his reddened and scratched face. He had been thinking of holding the tree-climbing story in reserve. He really liked the being-scratched-by-a-cat story, but knew his ma wouldn't believe it, and so, with the threat of having to wear a winter jacket back to school on a late summer day, he decided to preempt the round of questions that were sure to come.

"Me and Masciola were climbing some trees on the way home and I lost my grip and fell down one of them. Scratched my face, and uh, guess I got my shirt dirty."

"Climbed a tree? Which one?"

"One of the ones by the apartment building on the corner."

"Those are big trees. How high did you get?"

"About halfway up."

"Why did you climb it?"

"Jim said there might be a bag of money up in one of the branches. Just wanted to see."

"A bag of money?"

"Yeah."

"How would he know there was a bag of money in the tree?"

"I, uh, I don't know. He just said there was."

"What kind of bag?"

"You know, a brown paper bag."

"It rained yesterday. Do you think that money got wet?"

"Naah. The leaves kept it dry."

"Who put the money there?"

"Jim said it was one of the bums, maybe Marty."

"Hmmh. How much money did he say was up there?"

"A couple a million bucks."

"A couple million dollars and you only got halfway up?"

"I was hungry. Wanted to get home."

"Will you go back for the money?"

"Yeah. After school. Or maybe tomorrow."

"You don't think anyone else will find it?"

"Naah. It's pretty high up there. No one will see it."

"What if the wind blows it down and somebody else gets it?"

"I, uh. I don't know."

"Maybe you should go back for the money right now. We could use it."

"After school, Ma. It'll still be there."

"You sure you're telling me the truth?"

"Yeah!"

"Okay, but your father's going to be mad about your clothes. That shirt is ruined."

Dennis knew his ma didn't believe the story, but he also knew that her inquiry was over and that she wouldn't need to learn the reason for his scratched face. He savored his triumph with a large bite of the salami sandwich and a big gulp of milk from the glass in front of his plate. He was about to take another huge bite when his brother Steve bolted up the back stairs and into the kitchen.

"Heard Zita beat the crap out of you just before lunch," he said with a sinister laugh. "Heard she scratched your face real bad."

Steve knew exactly what he was doing; he was snitching off his younger brother, and he took great joy in doing so. The two were twenty-three months apart, and although they were brothers, they often acted like sworn enemies. Steve was more muscular and stronger than Dennis, and he pushed his sibling around a lot. Dennis hated it that his brother was stronger, and he plotted to someday get even with him, going so far as to develop an "enemies list" that contained only one name: Steve Domrzalski.

In their younger years, Steve had teased his brother remorselessly. He gave Dennis the name "Stinkpot," which their cousins took up and used to endlessly ridicule the budding Disturber. He constantly told anyone who would listen that Dennis was crazy. When on vacation at the family cottage in Wisconsin, the young Dennis wet his bed, and Steve proclaimed that the stained bed sheet drying on an outside clothesline was a "Map of Japan." In the mornings before school, Steve shoved and elbowed the younger boy away from the bathroom sink and mirror they were supposed to share when washing for school. The two fought over books, food, milk, candy—over pretty much everything—and Steve won every battle. Their greatest fight occurred on their Aunt Helen's eighty-acre dairy farm in northern Wisconsin one summer when the two were assigned to feed the chickens in a decrepit, wooden chicken coop.

Their mission was to take two large coffee cans full of eggshells, throw the shells on the ground and then crush them with their shoes. The insecure Dennis was pitifully eager to do the job. He wanted to do it correctly to gain just an ounce of approval from his aunt, or anyone else, because he so craved approval and attention.

That morning, Steve emptied his can of eggshells and crushed them. Dennis was about to empty his, when Steve yanked the can out of his hands— stole it, really—threw the shells on the ground and stomped them himself.

Young Dennis was beyond furious. He threw a violent temper tantrum, stomped his feet, screamed, foamed at the mouth, and in an act of unmitigated fury, cocked his right arm, clenched his fist and threw a punch that was intended to crush his brother's skull and send his brains oozing to the chicken coop's floor. In the ensuing battle Dennis's right wrist somehow plunged into the coffee can's sharp edge, splitting open his skin and sending a torrent of blood all over himself, his brother and the chickens.

Yes, Steve was often the enemy—he had just proven it again by revealing the run-in with Zita—and Dennis glared and silently vowed to get revenge, even if it took a couple of weeks.

As Steve flew past the kitchen table to the bathroom to wash his hands, Dennis got the look from his mother that he dreaded. She wasn't angry, just sad. Her eyes trained on his and said she was heartbroken that he had lied and that he had caused the good sister such pain and aggravation.

"The sisters are there to teach you," Florence said in a soft, sad voice. "They're just trying to help you and educate you. God doesn't want you to torment her."

"I know, Ma."

"You know you'll go to Hell if you keep this up."

"Uh huh."

"Do you want to go to Hell?"

"I don't think so."

"You'd better not want to. Have some respect for the sister."

"I will, Ma," Dennis said as he dejectedly took another bite—this time a small one—out of the sandwich. "I will."

"You promise?"

"I promise."

After finishing their sandwiches and milk, Dennis and Steve bolted from the kitchen table, down the hallway and into the living room to turn on their 18-inch, Zenith color TV set. The two fought over who would pull the knob switch out to turn on the set. The vacuum-tube TV powered up slowly, and in thirty seconds or so, the dark screen flashed to life, and they were watching the city of Chicago's favorite noontime TV show, Bozo's Circus on WGN-TV, Channel Nine.

Ringmaster Ned hosted the live show that was broadcast from noon till 1 p.m. from the station's studio in Chicago. Bozo the Clown had a bulbous, orange nose, white face and a partially bald head what was framed by a wild fringe of orange hair that stuck straight out. The show was fun for kids, but adults enjoyed it too. It seemed like every kid who went home for lunch in the city stayed in front of their sets until the end of the show's Grand Prize Game, which had kids standing in front of a five-foot long board with pails nailed to it in a row.

The object was to toss white ping-pong balls into the pails, starting with the first in line and going to bucket number six. They were awarded a prize each time they successfully got the ball into a pail, and the prizes got better as the degree of difficulty increased.

Almost every kid got the ball into buckets one and two. Quite a few made the third one. Very few made four or five and almost no one made the sixth. If a kid did get the ball into the sixth pail, Bozo, Ringmaster Ned, the audience as well as the kid and the parents went wild. The kid got a big prize, and everyone was happy.

Dennis and Steve waited for the Grand Prize Game. That day it was short as the little boy made it only to the second bucket. After that, Steve shut off the TV and they ran for the back door and back to school for afternoon classes.

CHAPTER 4

Smoking and Pagan Babies

THE PROMISE THAT he had made to his mother was one that Dennis had no intention of keeping as he met Masciola in the gangway of his house. The youth, embittered by the constant teasing he had endured from the mouths of his brothers and cousins, had turned into a twelve-year-old cynic. It wasn't just the teasings, fights and the eggshell incident that had turned him sour and resentful. He had been born that way. At least that's what he thought. Florence had always explained away his sullen behavior to relatives by saying he had been born a sad baby.

It wasn't just that, either. He had tried to believe—he had wanted to believe—in all the goodness and holiness of the world, but several years back his faith in goodness, angels, prayer and God had been permanently shattered.

"Pray and you will receive," one of the parish priests had instructed Dennis and his classmates in a religion class. "If you pray to God with humility, you will get what you ask for. God answers all prayers."

So Dennis prayed and prayed and prayed some more for BB guns and knives. Every night for three weeks straight he got down on his knees, folded his hands, bowed his head and sent his supplications skyward that the weapons would be under his bunk bed in the morning. He wanted powerful guns to use against birds, rats and neighbors' windows, and long, sharp knives to do who knows what.

Every morning Dennis leaped out of bed and checked under it, only to find that his prayers were never answered. He resigned himself to knowing that his prayers would never be answered, and that he was, for some reason, an outcast in God's eyes.

HIS PRAYERS WERE NEVER ANSWERED

When he met Masciola for the walk back to school, Dennis was in high spirits.

"Whadja tell your ma?" Jim asked as they walked out the Dennis's small backyard to the alley.

"That I climbed the tree."

"What'd she say?"

"She asked me why I climbed the tree."

"And?"

"I said because you said there was a bag of money in the branches."

"She believed it?"

"Not really. She asked me how much you said was in the bag."

"And?"

"I said a couple million bucks."

"Whadda you nuts?"

"She bought it until Steve came in and said that Zita had gotten me. I had to promise that I'd be nice to Zita."

"That ain't gonna happen. We don't change rooms this afternoon. You got her all afternoon. You guys'll have a blast."

The alley wasn't their normal route back to OLG. Usually, they headed east on Altgeld Avenue for the four-block walk. They used the alleys to engage in behavior that the nuns decried and warned would, without question, send them directly to Hell—no pre-Heaven penance time in Purgatory whatsoever—cigarette smoking.

Jim had stashed smokes in a bag next to a garage down the alley. He had to hide them, for if his parents ever found out he was smoking they would have beaten him senseless. He didn't dare be caught with cigarettes at school because the nuns would beat him and then call his parents, who would beat him again. Dennis and Jim found the stash under a chunk of busted-up concrete: a couple of packs of Kools and Marlboros. Kools were a strong, menthol smoke, while Marlboros were strong and harsh, and made the youths, when they smoked them, feel tough, strong, grownup and cool.

It was easy for them to get cigarettes, even though the law said no one under eighteen could buy them. Nearly every restaurant in the neighborhood had a cigarette vending machine in its lobby, and no one cared when kids plunked their forty-five cents into the machines. It was another sale and more money for the cigarette companies, the vending machine owners, and the restaurant owners, who got a percentage of the sales for allowing the machines in their stores.

Grownups used to send kids to stores with money and notes, requesting that the proprietors or cashiers sell the kids cigarettes. The hand-written notes were short and usually said something like, "Please sell my son (nephew, niece or daughter) a package of (brand name) cigarettes. Thank you. Mr. or Mrs. So and So."

If the kids couldn't get cigarettes from the vending machines, they could always forge a note from their parents and get them that way. Although that could backfire, especially if the kids forgot what brand their parents or uncles or aunts smoked—the cashiers knew everyone, including their brand of cigarettes—or if the adults had already been to the store that day to buy smokes.

Dennis and Jim took two smokes apiece—a Kool and a Marlboro—out of the packs in Jim's stash, replaced the damp and crumpled cigarette packages under the concrete and walked to their favorite smoking spot: a basement landing in the backyard of a house whose owners it seemed—even the wife—were gone during the day.

Sitting on a concrete step that led to the basement, Jim lit his Marlboro with an Ohio Blue Tip strike-anywhere wooden stick match and cupped the match in his hand as Dennis leaned toward him to light his Kool. They took big drags on the smokes, inhaled deeply and let the smoke out of their lungs with a relaxed easiness that showed they had been smoking for quite a while.

"What are you guys gonna do to Zita?" Jim asked as he took another drag.

"I don't know. We've got a spelling bee. That ought to be good for some laughs and a beating or two. But I think we're gonna get some of our stuff back. She steals our rulers, protractors, pens, compasses, lead pencils, erasers—everything—and she's gonna hold a sale next week to sell it to fifth and sixth graders. We're gonna distract her so Dave can get the stuff out of her desk drawers. Basically, we're gonna steal it back."

THEIR AFTER-LUNCH SMOKES

"How does she steal it?"

"Every time she catches us goofing off or talking, she takes something and puts it in her desk. I've gone through three compasses. She's got a bunch of Dave's stuff. She's got stuff from all of us."

"You guys oughta call the cops on her."

"Yeah, right. They'll laugh us out of the place. And then they'll call our parents and we'll get our asses kicked. It's better if we just steal it back."

"Yeah, but that ain't stealing. You're just recovering your stolen property. That's how you need to look at it. I mean, where do these nuns get off taking stuff from kids? That ain't very holy or Christ-like."

"Yeah, but I think that's why they got into this religious order stuff, so they could legally beat up kids and steal our stuff. But this gives me an idea. I'm gonna use it against her. It'll be a blast."

"What's she gonna do with the money if she sells it?"

"Use it for pagan babies."

Pagan babies were one of the biggest things at OLG and all Catholic schools. For a mere five dollars, a school, kid or group of kids could "buy" or adopt a pagan baby, that is pay for a baby in some far-off land, usually an undeveloped country, to get a Christian name and to be baptized into the Catholic faith. The nuns loved the program, and individual nuns and schools competed to see which classroom or school could buy the most pagan babies. The nuns put coffee cans on their desks, one marked "Boys," and the other "Girls," and encouraged—actually demanded—that the kids fill the cans with change brought from home. It was a difficult and agonizing mandate for most of the kids, as they came from working-class homes where the fathers worked in factories and didn't earn much, and the mothers stayed home. Most families were on exceedingly tight budgets and watched every nickel. They didn't eat out, bought groceries once a week, shoes for the kids maybe every six months, and new clothes once a year. They didn't have extra money, especially for pagan babies.

The kids were torn. They knew their families didn't have extra change to throw around—they were already required to put change in offertory envelopes and deposit them into the collection basket at Sunday masses—but they also knew that the nuns would look, and behave, disapprovingly toward them if they didn't fill those pagan baby coffee cans with nickels, dimes and quarters. The nuns, the kids knew, kept track of who brought change to school for the coffee cans. Those that contributed regularly were looked upon favorably by the sisters.

The nuns encouraged the boys and girls to compete to see which group could adopt the most pagan babies. None of the pupils had ever seen a pagan baby. No one knew where they were or where they came from—although

Africa was a pretty good guess—and no one ever knew if all that money really went to buy pagan babies or if the nuns kept it. Kids and classes got certificates of adoption once they bought a pagan baby, and the chance to name it themselves. But to some young cynics, the nuns could have printed those certificates in the convent. And there seemed to be no real accounting for the money and no independent proof that it actually bought pagan babies.

The Disturbers, and most of the other boys in class, except for Zita's pets, made their contributions in pennies, a move that infuriated Zita and the other nuns.

"This is a disgrace," Principal Sister Mary Vitaclaire angrily scolded the class a week before, after Zita had told her that mostly pennies were being put into the Boys' can. "If you can't be generous with your money, you will go straight to Hell. You are selfish, and your selfishness isn't funny; it's sinful. These children are starving for the word of God and for the holy sacrament of Baptism. This money will help convert them to Catholicism. It saves these children for Christ. Can you imagine a child not being baptized in the name of God?

"I expect that starting tomorrow there will be nickels, dimes and quarters in this can. There will be no more pennies. If I catch any of you pupils putting even a single penny into these cans, there will be consequences. I also expect that within a week, this can will be full. If it isn't, there will be severe consequences. Am I understood?"

She was understood by every pupil except the Disturbers. All raised their hands at once after Vitaclaire had finished with her threats. The mass show of hands angered the principal. Her pale face twitched, and she glared at the boys in the back row, who held back their laughter.

Vitaclaire glared for a few moments. She didn't want to acknowledge the troublemakers and knew that doing so would lead only to a challenge to her authority. But the boys were acting politely, and to not call on at least one of them would have raised questions among the good students as to her holiness and ability to treat everyone with respect, compassion and love.

"Mister Ruchinski," she spat out, "apparently you have a question."

"I do, Ster," Dave said as he rose from his chair.

"You will address me as 'Sister,' young man, or you will be down in my office forthwith."

"Yes, Sister," Dave replied, knowing that a trip to Vitaclaire's office meant a real beating, a beating that inflicted real pain, a beating with large, wooden paddles, steel-edged rulers and tosses into the office's walls. Vitaclaire was twenty years younger than Zita and full of rage and anger, and she vented it on OLG's troublemakers.

"Well, Sister," Dave started with a serious face and an attitude that tried, but failed, to strike a perfect balance between insolent smart aleck and respectful diplomat, "we were told that contributing to the pagan baby fund was voluntary. Now you're saying that we have to? Seems to me that 'voluntary' means just that, and that forcing us to come up with money makes it not voluntary. We've been taught that God's grace comes to people who freely give and who give without having to. By forcing us to buy pagan babies, aren't you denying us the grace that comes with voluntary giving? I'd hate to think that you would commit the awful sin of preventing us from getting God's grace. I don't think he'd like it."

The other Disturbers knew as they sat in their chairs holding back their laughs that Dave had her—he always did. Anyone who used just a little logic had them, for the nuns' proclamations of holiness and love never matched their actions of authoritarianism, anger, bitterness and physical violence. They were easy targets.

They were also angry and resentful targets who brooked no challenge to their God-given right to be correct one hundred percent of the time, especially when it came to their own authority.

Vitaclaire's lips became thin and white, her face stiffened, and her brown eyes simmered with hatred as they glared menacingly at Dave.

"Mister Ruchinski," she said coldly and without emotion, "come up here."

Dave shuffled slowly to the front of the room, trying to delay the inevitable beating.

"Faster, Mister Ruchinski," she snapped.

Dave complied, reached the front of the room and stopped as he faced the nun.

"Stand next to me," the principal snarled as she yanked Dave's arm and pulled him around to her right side. Dave stood facing the class, his head slightly bowed.

"Stand up straight," she ordered.

As Dave raised his head, Vitaclaire lectured the class:

"This is an example of what you do not want to be and how you do not want to act. Mister Ruchinski will never amount to anything in life because he is a—"

"He's a communist, Sister!" Zita blurted out. "They're all communists back there. Each and every one of them, communists!"

It was one of Zita's favorite lines, one she thought would bring instant shame, disgrace and self-hatred to whomever she applied it. The United States was in the midst of the Cold War with the Russians and Red Chinese, and from kindergarten on, OLG kids were taught that the Devil and communists were one. Communists hated all religions, especially Catholicism; they didn't believe in God, and they were out to torture and murder all Catholics. So were the Chinese. Father Fu, an OLG priest, had been tortured by the Red Chinese, the kids had been told. So had hundreds of other priests. The nuns never let a day go by where they didn't remind the kids that the Red Chinese cut out priests' tongues, yanked out their fingernails with pliers, denied them Holy Communion, tried brainwashing them into denying God and left them in cold, dank dungeons to rot and die.

It was true, of course. Father Fu had been tortured, and the communists had it in for Catholics and all religions. But global politics didn't mean much to seventh graders, and for the Disturbers, being called a communist meant nothing.

"Yes. I know they're communists, Sister," Vitaclaire replied. "They're also infected with the Devil's evil. They are—" she paused a moment for effect, and with the class waiting in fearful anticipation of her verdict, snarled, "sinners!"

A gasp went out from the class's good kids and true believers. It was as if Vitaclaire had sentenced Ruchinski and the Disturbers to death, and, of course, an immediate trip straight to Hell. The kids squirmed in their chairs, terrified by the fact that Satan's accomplices and Hell-bound sinners were right there in their Catholic school classroom.

Vitaclaire wasn't done. She paused again, eyed some of the good kids with an all-knowing and warning glare, waved an arm, and in a voice that implied there was absolutely no hope for redemption, said sternly:

"Unrepentant sinners! Their souls, children, are as black as coal and even blacker than that!"

That was too much for some of the kids, especially Roger Krask and Karen Drokowski, the biggest teacher's pets the world had ever known. Roger, a puffy-faced and slightly awkward kid with light brown hair and an eager-to-please personality, was awash in wholesomeness. He smiled at the nuns, laughed at their corny and safe religious jokes, constantly did extra credit work, studied, got As, excelled at math, wrote short stories with religious themes, worked for months on legitimate science projects, was a Boy Scout, and always said things like, "Sister, we're so blessed to have you teaching us. There's enough of God's grace in you for a million people to get to heaven!"

Karen was worse. Every time the class made its bi-weekly trip to the school's small library, she checked out five or six books, always making sure to let Zita know how many and what titles she had picked. Karen then prepared—and there was no requirement for this—written book reports on every book and gave them to Zita, who always smiled approvingly. What was worse, and what made even some of the good kids cringe, was that Karen often invited nuns to her house for Friday night suppers and Sunday afternoon dinners. Those invitations were accepted, and every nun in the school spoke highly of Karen and her "blessed family."

Vitaclaire's pronouncement that the Disturbers were unrepentant sinners was a shocker. Roger buried his head in his hands, began to cry, then lifted his head and raised his right hand to ask a question.

"Yes, Roger? What is it?" the principal asked.

"Maybe, Sister Mary Vitaclaire, if we all pray as one for them they can be saved. Satan and sin are no match for prayer."

"Unfortunately, Roger, there are such things as lost causes. They are extremely rare, extremely rare, and Mister Ruchinski and those other hoodlums are indeed lost causes. Your generous spirit, though, has not gone unnoticed."

Karen, who had also started crying, raised her hand and was acknowledged by Vitaclaire:

"Sister? Maybe if we bathe them in holy water the devil will flee their blackened souls."

"Holy water, Miss Drokowski, is for holy people. It would be a sin to waste good holy water on these communists. Your kind thoughts, though, commend you to Jesus."

Dave knew his time was up and he braced his body for the blows he knew were coming. Vitaclaire, however, had another short speech to give. She loved and lived for these moments. Beating up smart aleck seventh graders and making examples of them to the class—examples that would frighten all but Disturbers into submission to her and Christ's authority—was her specialty, and she always made the most of these moments.

"Mister Ruchinski, have you no compassion and love for pagan babies?" she asked. "Of course you don't," she said before he could answer. "We're just going to have to instill it in you, aren't we?"

Before Dave could answer, Vitaclaire grabbed his left ear, spun him around, marched him three long steps to the room's front blackboard and slammed his forehead into it.

"We are going to teach you to love," she shouted as she pulled his head back by the ear and slammed it forward again. "And to understand that Sister Zita is God's representative here on Earth! Do you understand that? Are you learning what love is?" she asked as Dave's head hit the blackboard a third time.

Dave's head bounced off the blackboard three more times before Vitaclaire let go of his ear. As he wobbled back to his desk, Vitaclaire made sure that the impression she was trying to make had permanently sunk into the pupils' minds.

"Is there any question that these cans will voluntarily be filled with change within a week? Is there any question that Our Lady of Grace will voluntarily buy more pagan babies than any other school in the Archdiocese of Chicago?"

Only five hands raised—Disturbers hands. Although they knew that the principal would be enraged at such defiance, and that the beatings they got as a result would be ten times greater than what Dave had received, they raised them in support of their battered brother Disturber.

Vitaclaire was furious, but secretly she welcomed such rebelliousness because it gave her another chance to go to bat for God with her fists. She coolly eyed the raised hands and selected her next target.

"Mister Kolba? You don't understand what I just said?"

"No Sister, I do understand, and thank you for helping us. I have a question, though—"

"What is it?" Vitaclaire spat out before the boy could finish. "It had better be an appropriate question."

"It is, Sister. I was wondering, why don't the pagan babies and their families ever write or call us? Or visit us? Are they not grateful for our generous contributions? We could buy them pizza if they came here."

Before Vitaclaire could stammer for Gary to sit down, Kurkowski leaped up out of his chair to further torment the nun.

"Sister, I was wondering, if the boys buy a pagan baby, can we name it Joshua, or Abraham, or Levi, or Solomon and send it to public school? I think it would be nice to give a pagan baby a Jewish name."

It was hell for the next fifteen minutes as Sisters Zita and Vitaclaire hacked, pounded and punched their way through Disturbers Row. No one was spared, after all, they had all raised their hands to make some disrespectful remark. Dave was beaten again, and Kurkowski was bashed repeatedly with a pointer and rung of a chair for his blasphemous comment. When it was over, the Disturbers were bloodied but still defiant.

❧

"That pagan baby stuff is a joke," Jim said as he let more smoke out of his lungs. "They tell us you can't buy and sell people—slavery is wrong—and yet they force us to buy pagan babies. You know what I say? We should just let pagans be pagans. It's a neat sounding name: pagan."

"I'm not even sure what a pagan is," Dennis offered as he lit his second cigarette. "Seriously, what the hell is a pagan?"

"They're the people who worship golden calves and who invented Halloween."

"Then they can't be that bad."

"They're not. They got it pretty good. I mean, they don't believe in God, got no religion, don't have to go to church, don't have to not eat meat on Fridays, don't have to learn hymns, can get married as many times as they want, don't have to get confirmed, they can swear and steal all they want and burn down people's houses. And get this, because they ain't part of any religion, they don't have to feel guilty about breaking rules because they ain't got no rules. They never have to go to confession because, to them, the stuff they do ain't a sin."

"You'd think they'd be able to raise their own kids, though, huh?"

"They can. It's just that the pope and the nuns don't want them to. They want everybody on Earth to be Catholic because it's the one true religion. They want to take over the world. And that means that we adopt every other religion's babies and turn them into Catholics."

"You know what we should do? We should convince all the Jewish and Protestant teachers to put cans on their desks and ask for money to buy Catholic babies. There's got to be lots of Catholic babies out there that people in other religions want to baptize as their own. That'll get the nuns, huh?"

"Jesus. You're talking about starting a war, man. If something like that happened the nuns and priests would go and kill all those Jew and Protestant teachers. They can't have other religions adopting Catholic babies. They'd call that kidnapping."

"You gotta think that not all those pagan parents want their kids to be Catholics."

"They probably don't. But to the nuns that just means they're stupid and uneducated. They think that, deep down, everybody wants and needs to be Catholic. And they figure that those who don't just aren't smart enough to know it yet."

"Can you imagine if we got a pagan baby, raised it and then taught it to smoke? That'd be funny, wouldn't it?"

"It'd be pretty funny if you want to die. The nuns would kill you for that. They really would."

"True. But the cool thing is that they'd then be charged with sins. They'd have giant black blots on their souls. It's a sin to kill."

"Not if it's done in the name of God."

"Next time Vitaclaire comes up I'm gonna use the Halloween thing on her. And you know what I'm gonna ask her?"

"What?"

"If since the pagans invented Halloween, do pagans get more candy on Halloween than the rest of us? Do they get more candy than Catholics?"

They laughed loudly at their cleverness, and Jim lit his second smoke. He was inhaling a deep drag when what they always feared might happen on their smoking outings occurred.

"Who's down there?" a woman's voice shouted. "Who is smoking down there? Who is smoking in my basement?"

They'd been discovered!

The guys dropped their smokes, bolted up and ran for the alley. But another thing they feared also occurred. The woman, who was looking out her first-floor, back-porch window, had seen them as they ran to the alley! At least she had seen their backs.

"What school do you boys go to?" she demanded. "What school do you go to? I'll find out!"

CHAPTER 5

Hunt for the Smokers

DENNIS AND JIM were out the gate and into the alley before the woman could say more, and they ran until they were a block away.

"She didn't see our faces," Dennis said confidently. "We'll be okay."

"Yeah. I think so, too," Jim replied. "And if we have to, we can come back and paint Gronski's or Gusftason's name on her garage. That'll make it look like they were here."

To make sure they'd be okay and that they wouldn't smell like cigarette smoke at school, Jim took from his pockets his customary, post-smoking kit: a small bottle each of Jade East cologne and Listerine mouthwash. They splashed the cologne over their hands, especially the two first fingers that usually held the cigarettes, and a little on their faces, and rinsed their mouths with the Listerine.

"No one will ever guess," Jim boasted. "Just to make sure they don't, take this."

It was added insurance against the stench of tobacco smoke: two sticks of chewing gum. They chewed furiously as they walked out an alley, on to Ridgeway and to a parking lot just off Fullerton Avenue that served as one of OLG's lunchtime playgrounds for seventh and eighth graders. They found some pals, played basketball, told each other dumb jokes and waited for the bell to ring to send them back to the classrooms.

The hand-held bell was wrung by a patrol boy—boys who had volunteered to be mini-traffic cops at some of the streets near the school, and who wore white and orange patrol belts on their upper bodies to show their official authority—and when it sounded, the kids in the lot formed lines and started off through a short alley and then turned north on Ridgeway and marched a half block to where they would enter the school through the building's two arched wooden front doors.

Dennis had always loved that lunchtime walk back to class, but not because he liked school. He hated it and was a lousy student. It was just that the two-story red brick building reminded him of the Alamo in Texas. He had seen the movies of how Jim Bowie and Davey Crockett had beaten off the Mexican army as its soldiers tried to scale the fort's walls. He imagined himself and the other Disturbers firing rifles through the school's front windows at invaders, pouring boiling oil on them and standing on the roof furiously clubbing enemy soldiers with the butts of their rifles and using their Bowie knives to gut their foes. There were always plenty of enemies—kids from other neighborhoods, public school kids, and the most hated enemy of all, the good kids, although he knew that the teachers' pets would never be bold enough to fight. In his mind he saw great battles and heaps of blood-drenched dead enemies in front of that school. That always made him feel extremely good about life.

Dennis was daydreaming about tossing scores of enemy soldiers off OLG's roof when the line of students came to a sudden halt. The kids started speculating about why they had stopped.

"Maybe the school's on fire and they're gonna send us home for the afternoon," fellow Disturber Richard Bozeman, who was in line in front of Dennis, turned and suggested.

"Yeah. Maybe the janitors are all dead. They'd have to give us a couple of hours off for that," Dennis added. "Or maybe someone sprayed the place with poison. That'd be worth at least an hour off."

"Or maybe," Rich speculated, "they're gonna make us go into church to sing hymns. I'd rather do math than sing hymns. I hate singing, and I hate hymns."

The kids didn't have to speculate further. The reason for the halt was being whispered kid-by-kid down the line.

PLEASANT DREAMS

"They're checking the boys' hands to see who's been smoking," a kid in front of Rich turned and reported. "Some lady called the office to say she saw two guys in our uniforms smoking in her yard. They're checking our hands for nicotine stains and smelling them for smoke. And they're checking everybody's pockets for cigarettes. Who do you think it was?"

"I'll bet it was Gronski and Gordy," Dennis said, cracking a little smile. "It had to be."

He was talking about Ken Gronski and Ken Gordy, two classmates who were sometime Disturbers. They goofed off a little, and when they did, Zita made them sit in the back with the Disturbers. But unlike real Disturbers, they didn't like sitting in the back row. And when put there, they tried to behave so they could return to their regular seats. In the eyes of the Disturbers, this was disgusting and disgraceful behavior. The Disturbers couldn't understand why any kid would want to be good and wholesome when being just the opposite was so much fun. So, as a way of punishment for not subscribing to the creed of creating mayhem whenever and wherever possible, the Disturbers, whenever they had the chance, accused Gronski and Gordy of doing things the nuns, and probably the rest of society, found immoral, objectionable and un-Christlike.

Masciola was particularly skilled at putting the blame on Gronski. Once when he, Dennis and Kolba started a small fire next to a wooden garage by Monticello, Masciola, knowing that the owner would be looking for evidence as to who tried burning the garage down, pulled from his pocket a small bottle of silver model car paint, a thin paintbrush, and wrote on the garage, "Ken Gronski was here."

That their accusations against Gronski and Gordy were always false filled the Disturbers with pride. No one else, they knew, was bold enough to make such reckless and irresponsible charges. And no one else got so much pleasure out of seeing innocent kids get in so much trouble for something they hadn't done.

Dennis wasn't at all concerned about the news that the nuns were on the hunt for him and Masciola. He was confident of his pal's genius and post-smoking precautions, and sure that the cologne would overpower any evidence of their smoking. Masciola was ten places ahead of him in the line, and if he passed the inspection, all would be well.

The nuns were furious and determined to find the smokers and beat out of them the Devil's insidious and hateful evil, and into them God's loving and saving grace. Vitaclaire, Zita, Sister Mary Francis DeLasalle and Sister Mary Yvonne were standing near the school's front steps and yanking boys out of line. They weren't gentle. Each boy, except for some of the teachers' pets, was violently grabbed by their ears or hair, pulled out of line and pushed and screamed at.

"Smoking is the Devil's work, you worthless good-for-nothings!" DeLasalle bellowed at the boys. "You will never amount to anything in life! Where did you get those cigarettes?"

DeLasalle was OLG's toughest and meanest nun. At five-foot-nine and an easy two hundred and fifty pounds, she could have been a wrestler, and probably had been a wrestler in a former life, the Disturbers figured. Born and raised in Wisconsin—most likely on a dairy farm where she put in seventeen-hour days wrestling lumbering Guernsey cows—she was beefy. She might have even been muscular, but no one, except if they had been hammered across the back and upside the head by her massive, ham-like forearms, ever would have known it because she was clad head to foot in her strange-smelling white and black linen habit, and her physical features were a mystery.

Her hero, she proudly instructed her students over and over, was the Green Bay Packers football team's legendary and ferocious middle linebacker Ray Nitschke. Every OLG pupil, even the good kids, knew that DeLasalle's real dream was to race headlong into kids, just like a linebacker, and smash them into the ground so hard that they would never get up. She ached for the chance to do just that on that clear, September afternoon, but knew that she couldn't just body slam a kid to the pavement in broad daylight with women who lived in apartments and houses across the street from the school watching out their front windows. However, DeLasalle was determined that some of those young boys were going to feel God's furious wrath. The instrument of that wrath would be her forearms and her meaty fists.

SHE ACHED TO TACKLE KIDS

The boys were yanked out of line. Matthew Bork, a tall, heavy, sensitive kid—in third grade he was taller and weighed more than the lay teacher—who was usually polite to the nuns, and who laughed at their unfunny, religiously tinged and moralizing jokes, was one of the first. Bork lived south of Fullerton and hung around with Ray Pagentini, Mike DelGallo, Mike Guadagno and others on that side of the busy street. He was, as were most of OLG's kids, normal. He wasn't a saint, talked a lot, at times craved the nuns' approval, and at other times was mildly rebellious. He didn't try to gain the nuns' favor, nor did he try to torment them. He was an altar boy, played baseball and football with his pals after school, roamed his neighborhood with them and played silly jokes on them. By seventh grade he just wanted to graduate, get out of there and get on to high school.

Yvonne and DeLasalle both jerked him out of line. The beefy nun grabbed a clump of his hair and his right ear, while Yvonne gripped his left arm and gouged her fingernails into the back of his puffy neck. They yanked him backward at once, and the toes of his shoes left the ground. He would have fallen and split open his head on the pavement had the nuns let go.

Sister Yvonne released her grip, but not DeLasalle. She kept hold of the boy's hair and ear while Yvonne, her face nearly nose-to-nose with poor Matthew's, screamed:

"Where did you get those cigarettes? Don't lie, Mister Bork! God, mister! God is listening! And if you lie in the presence of God, if you lie to God, you will never be redeemed. Now tell us, or you *will* get the backs of our hands and more!"

Bork couldn't tell them because he didn't smoke. He never would have smoked because he just didn't want to.

Matthew's history of nonaggression toward the nuns, though, hadn't saved or protected him from their wrath. Like every other human child, he talked in class. In first grade, he had the dreaded Sister Mary Thomas Edward, an older, terribly embittered nun, who, like the other nuns, took her anger out on the kids and who could not abide the fact that six-year-old children talked.

Bork was one of OLG's kids who, because his mother worked during the day, stayed at the school during the lunch break and ate in the school's basement, which was called the school hall. Some remodeling was underway in the hall, and so for several weeks that year the kids ate their lunches, which were brought from home in square, tin, brightly colored lunch boxes or brown paper bags, in their classrooms at their desks.

Sister Thomas Edward recruited spies from her first-grade charges to tell her who talked during class or during the lunch break. It was insane, of course, for anyone to think, expect and demand that fifty first graders would keep perfectly quiet during the thirty minutes they had to eat lunch, but Thomas Edward had such insane expectations and demands.

Like every kid in the classroom that day, Bork talked. He knew he had been ratted on after the lunch break and playground recess was over when Thomas Edward walked to up his desk and angrily secured to the tops of each of his ears a plastic, spring-loaded clothespin. The clothespins firmly gripped the boy's soft ear tissue and made him wince with pain. Sister Thomas Edward was pleased. So, apparently was the girl who had snitched Bork off to the nun.

Sister Thomas Edward had, for some reason, developed a particular dislike for Bork. He was, even in first grade, a large, fast-growing chubby boy. One morning Bork arrived at school late from his five-block walk. He had stopped at principal Vitaclaire's office to explain his tardiness. The stern nun understood the reason for it and excused the tardiness with a note that Matthew was to present to Thomas Edward.

When Matthew arrived at his first-grade classroom, Thomas Edward was angry and demanded to know why he had been late. Bork sheepishly handed the nun Vitaclaire's note that exonerated him. He felt relieved that he would not be punished.

Thomas Edward read the note to herself and angrily dragged Mister Bork, as she called him, to the side of the classroom where she reached down and lifted the wall-sized blackboard, which was on rollers, up to reveal the cloak-room in which the kids' sweaters and coats hung on two rows of metal hooks, one higher than the other. The nun lifted the six-year-old up by his waist and hung him by the back collar of his jacket on a hook on the top row. He was short enough so that once on the hook, his feet did not touch the ground.

While the nun was hanging him on the coat hook, the terrified Bork cried out so all in the class could hear, "I poked my eye!"

THE PENALTY FOR TARDINESS

Bork hadn't poked his eye, the nun had, inadvertently, with one of her angry fingers. She was pleased that one of those fingers that every day fondled the beads of her sacred, four-foot-long rosary had managed to inflict additional injury, pain and humiliation on the six-year-old.

Sister Thomas Edward sneered that no pupil would be late for her class and slid the blackboard down so that Matthew dangled in darkness from the hook. He hung there and cried most of the morning, while his stunned classmates, who could hear his whimpering through the blackboard, were too terrified to concentrate on their schoolwork. Those whose lapses of concentration were too great were warned by the nun that they would be next for a cloakroom hook.

~

Bork was scared as he stood in front of the inquisitors who were determined to catch a smoker.

"I...I...I," Matthew stammered without being able to put together a sentence. The boy was terrified, and his soft, trusting blue eyes revealed yet again the horror of betrayal that many of OLG's good kids felt. There was no pleasing those nuns. Their anger, bitterness and resentment were so great and so in need of victims that they would turn even on their pets.

But they had no pets, really. Every kid, no matter how submissive, had the capacity for independence and rebellion, and thus was a potential target, a potential vessel for Satan's evil who at some point would need to be beaten and reformed. To the good sisters, there was no point in waiting for that rebellion. Since the potential was there, beatings needed to be administered right then and there, and in advance of expected sinful behavior.

"You will speak in complete sentences, or you will not speak at all!" Yvonne snarled at the boy. "Tell me where you got those cigarettes, or you *will* be sorry!"

"But...but Sisters," Matthew stammered through tears. "I don't smoke."

"Have you ever thought of smoking?" DeLasalle bellowed, "because if you have, you, mister, are in big trouble!"

That stunned Bork, although it should not have. The nuns and priests always used guilt and the potential for sin against the kids to intimidate them into submission. How could he be punished for something he had merely thought about, he thought to himself through the pain of his hair being pulled even harder by DeLasalle.

"No! Sisters. No! I've never even once thought about smoking," the boy cried.

"But you will, won't you?" DeLasalle barked.

"How can I know what I will think?" Bork asked, a hint of a human's instinctive resentment at being bullied and betrayed now starting to assert itself.

"No back talking!" Yvonne snarled. "You will not back talk to Sister DeLasalle! Am I understood?"

"Yes, Sister," Matthew whimpered.

"Mister Bork, I just don't believe you! You're just like the others, and you will get what you deserve!" Yvonne shouted as she began to pound Bork on the sides of his head with her open palms.

The beating lasted no more than thirty seconds, but it seemed like an eternity to Matthew. When it was over, the nuns inspected his hands for nicotine, or tar stains, and sniffed his hands for any telltale sign of smoke. Finding none, they shoved him back into line while admonishing him to never again act like a hoodlum.

The kid was broken. He trembled and cried. He tried to hide his tears but couldn't. Many of the kids in line, especially the good kids, were shaken and stunned at the treatment Bork had received. If he, someone who had tried to obey the nuns, could be threatened and beaten, it could happen to them as well. They waited their turn to be falsely accused of having even thought about smoking.

Their next victim was Lawrence Yager, a thin, quiet kid who in his eight years at OLG had never purposely caused anyone any trouble. That was Lawrence's misfortune, as it made him an easy target for the sisters of the Dominican Order.

In second grade, Lawrence, whose deep brown eyes neither sparkled nor flashed anger, and whose closed-lip smile was tinged more with sadness than with hope and happiness, ran across Sister Mary Concepta, a young, good-looking nun who showed mercy and extended compassion to no one, not even to scared second graders who had never disrupted her class, and who never would.

Lawrence looked like most of OLG's second-grade boys, that is, he looked like a young old man. His short brown hair and pale skin were framed by two fully-grown ears that were attached to a head and face that were at least fifteen years away from full size and maturity. He rarely spoke in class and seemed to, well, no one knew. He was a mystery, but a quiet and non-threatening one.

One day, Lawrence began crying in class. Concepta noticed the boy's tears and ordered him to the front of the room where she demanded of the scrawny, scared boy:

"Mister Yager, why are you crying?"

Lawrence was terrified and could answer the angry young nun only with more tears.

"Why are you crying, Mister Yager?" she demanded again.

Lawrence trembled. Never before in his short, Catholic schoolboy career had he been called to the front of a classroom. He had never done anything wrong. He bothered no one and wanted no one to bother him.

"Why are you crying?" the nun demanded again.

Lawrence again answered with more tears, and this time, convulsions. Concepta was enraged, but as she always did, maintained a calm demeanor.

"Well then, Mister Yager," the nun said with a slight smile, "if you are going to cry in my classroom, I'll give you something to cry about. Since you think crying is so much fun, you are going to cry like you have never cried before."

With that, the nun pulled Lawrence onto a small, two-foot-high wooden stage at the front of the room, picked up a round, olive-green, metal waste-paper can from a corner, placed it on the floor in the middle of the stage and ordered Lawrence to sit on a small wooden chair in front of it.

"If you won't stop crying in my classroom, you will truly cry. Now, Mister Yager, you will fill this can up with your tears. And you will not go home until it is filled with tears," Concepta calmly told the terrified boy.

Lawrence spent that afternoon sitting in front of the garbage can wringing his clenched fists over his eyes hoping to squeeze whatever tears he could into it. Normally, many of the kids—even second graders—would have laughed upon seeing one of their classmates so humiliated. But no one laughed that afternoon at poor Lawrence. Those young minds knew that their classmate would never be able to fill the can with tears—especially if it leaked—and they sensed the shocking impropriety of the situation and the nun's uncompromising depravity. At some point they had all been sad at school and cried, wanting only to go home and be with their mothers instead of with the child-beating nuns.

CRY, LAWRENCE, CRY!

As Lawrence stood in line in front of the school, DeLasalle and the others accused, berated, slapped, punched and told him to never even think about even lighting a match.

Next in line was Andy Collins, an enthusiastic and happy kid from a family of eleven. His older brothers and sisters had gone to OLG, and the stories they told had long prepared him for the nuns' brutality.

Collins had been in the first-grade room when Sister Thomas Edward hung Matthew Bork on the coat hook. Even though he was six, Collins was horrified by the deed and began a long mental process that would lead him to fantasize about nuns in a way that, had they been able to read his mind, they would have sent him directly to Hell.

Collins had also been in Sister Concepta's room when she ordered Lawrence Yager to fill the small garbage can with his tears. The obscenity of that punishment further helped crystallize the boy's fantasy.

As he stood in line waiting for his hands to be inspected, Collins remembered two run-ins with Yvonne, one in second grade, and the other just a week earlier that had seared into his mind a permanent hatred of all nuns and a desire to someday do them harm.

Second grade was when the OLG kids made their First Holy Communion—everything was holy to the Church. The kids were practicing for that special day in OLG's upper, or main, church. Collins and his classmates were kneeling on red velvet knee pads at the church's white marble communion rail that curved around the front of the altar.

Collins's hands were folded and reverently pressed together, fingers perfectly aligned skyward, thumbs crossed, back straight and rigid and eyes closed. He was eager to please and imagined how the bishops and cardinals who would administer the sacrament would admire his piety, and after the ceremony, track him down and personally ask him to model for the next Vatican calendar, and how his picture, with his perfectly folded hands and angelic face, would be plastered on every holy card in the Archdiocese of Chicago.

Collins stuck out his tongue, practicing to receive the Body of Christ, and then, whack! Yvonne slapped him on the tongue, scolding the shaken second grader that he was supposed to wait until the priest arrived with the precious host before sticking out his tongue.

A week earlier, Collins had been in the parking lot off Fullerton Avenue that served as the playground for the seventh and eighth graders. The bell ending the lunch recess had rung and the kids were forming lines to walk the half block back to school. Stuck under a chain-link fence on one side of the lot was one of the basketballs the school provided the kids to play with. Collins saw the ball, bolted from the line of kids and ran to rescue it. Suddenly, as if out of nowhere, Yvonne appeared before him.

"Is that your ball?" she demanded.

"No, Sister," he replied.

It was just what Yvonne wanted to hear. Almost before Collins had finished answering, the nun cocked her right arm and slapped him hard across the face. The boy told himself that he had deserved no punishment for attempting a good deed, and from that moment on he had only one desire for nuns: that they be tossed off building roofs into alleys so he could hear their broken rosary beads rolling down the concrete pavement.

Collins's hands passed the inspection, but apparently not well enough because Yvonne found reason to slap him across the face.

COLLINS HAD A DREAM

Behind Collins was John Klosk, a star student and math and science whiz who had never purposely caused trouble in his eight years at OLG. Klosk was so good at science that he was routinely picked to represent the school at city-wide science fairs. His conscientiousness and love of school hadn't saved even him over the years. In first grade in Sister Thomas Edward's room, Klosk had gotten the clothespin punishment on his ears and lips.

Warren Litka, who sat behind Klosk in first grade, had said something to the budding math star. Klosk turned around and told his classmate to be quiet, as it was forbidden to talk in class. Thomas Edward saw that it was Klosk who was talking and clamped the clothespins on his ears and lips.

In second grade, Klosk nearly incurred Sister Concepta's wrath when she caught him drawing a turkey on a sheet of paper. The turkey had a pouch, complete with a penis, from which it peed. Concepta saw the boy's drawing, grabbed it off his desk and from his hands, crumpled it up into a ball and told him:

"Mister Klosk, draw something like that again and I will wash your mouth out with several bars of soap! Am I understood?"

NO TALKING IN MY ROOM!

Klosk's hands also passed the inspection. He wasn't hit and was allowed to walk up the concrete steps at the school's front entrance and into the building.

As the other boys reached the front of the line near the school's entrance, many of them trembling, they held their hands out, palms up, to be inspected and sniffed by the nuns, and some of OLG's lay teachers, including Miss Donatello and Miss Laffey, a stocky, humorless lay teacher who liked to bang kids' heads together.

More boys were yanked out of line and screamed at. None, though, went through what Matthew Bork and Lawrence Yager had. It wasn't necessary to beat the other boys. The nuns had used Matthew and Lawrence as examples, and most of the kids had gotten the message and were by then sufficiently intimidated, terrified and docile.

Not so with Masciola. He calmly and confidently held out his hands for inspection. DeLasalle was the inspector. She didn't like Masciola. Neither did the other nuns and lay teachers. But they were wary of him. They sensed, correctly so, that he would fight back—even swing at them—if pushed too far.

They also knew that his parents, although respectful of their authority, weren't cowed by it. They would beat their own son if necessary, which they often did, but they were tough, practical Chicago Italians who had long ago come to realize that missing a Sunday mass or two, or challenging the nuns' beliefs and decisions, wouldn't send them directly to Hell.

DeLasalle smelled Masciola's hands. The stench of the cheap cologne was overpowering, and she was suspicious.

"Going on a date, Mister Masciola?" DeLasalle sneered.

"No, Sister," the boy replied in a cheerful and confident voice.

"Then why the cologne? Covering up cigarette smoke, are you?"

"No, Sister."

"Then why the cologne? And no back talking!"

"Because, Sister, I wanted to smell nice."

"For whom?" DeLasalle, who was ready to explode, demanded. "For whom?"

Masciola lowered his head as if embarrassed—he was a decent actor—then raised it, and with widened eyes that he had managed to glass up with the beginning of a couple of tears, said:

"Sister, for Jesus. He's everywhere, and I just wanted to be at my best this afternoon for Jesus."

The nuns were furious, enraged and ready to beat Masciola senseless. The slight tremble in DeLasalle's voice betrayed her absolute fury and the rage she felt at being bested by a twelve-year-old-boy. How she wanted to beat him.

She couldn't, though. He had answered perfectly, and she knew that if she admitted her humiliation, which beating the boy would have done, the other kids would have known that she had been bested, and her authority would have been weakened. She couldn't have that.

"Move on, Mister Masciola," DeLasalle spat out. "Move on!"

Seeing that his partner in sin had escaped detection as a smoker, Dennis was relieved that he would get through, too, but he was nervous as well. He was a nervous kid. Everything gave him the shakes—homework, being called on in class and even having to make telephone calls to order pizzas.

In fourth grade when the kids had to present and explain their annual science projects to the class, Dennis was terrified that he would be called on and made to stand in front of his classmates and talk. He never raised his hand in class and never volunteered anything. It's not just that he was shy. He felt he was dumb, didn't know the material, whether it was science, math or English, and that everyone would laugh at his stupidity. So he had slunk through school being deathly afraid of not knowing the material, afraid of being called on, expecting to be laughed at for not knowing what he was supposed to, and being afraid to raise his hand to ask the teachers or nuns for help. He had tried to be The Invisible Pupil.

He was going to be called on, eventually, by the teacher, Miss Sturgis, because she called every student up to give a ten-minute presentation during the week it took to get through all the kids and their science projects. But Dennis slumped in his desk, hiding behind the kid in front of him, hoping he would never be seen and that Miss Sturgis would somehow forget that he existed.

She didn't forget. Of the fifty kids in class, Dennis was the very last called. He had sat there those four days, ducking and slouching and hiding, and had put himself through an entire week of nerves and agony. By the time he had to make his presentation, he was so sick and exhausted from nerves and fear that he could do nothing but stand in front of his classmates and laugh. He couldn't explain his science project—an electromagnet made by coiling wire around a large nail and connecting the two ends of the wire to a dry-cell battery—other than to say, "if you put a penny between the two battery terminals, it gets hot."

The class laughed at his ineptitude and fear. Then, the final humiliation came when Dennis, standing in front of the class that Friday morning, looked over at Stanley Polit, who was standing next to him holding the science project's poster. All the other kids had nice, almost professionally made posters to go along with their presentations—all with straight lines, neat writing and a draftsman-like look to them. Not Dennis. His had been hastily drawn longhand with a black felt marker. The outline of the battery was crooked and jagged, and the lines representing the wires from the dry cell to the nail were squiggly things that looked vaguely like corkscrews.

Dennis glanced at Stanley, a bloated kid with a round face, ruddy cheeks, thick, black-rimmed glasses and a lost, bewildered look, saw how ridiculous and inept his poster looked and his science project was—compared to what other kids had done—and in a final rush of humiliation, fear and nerves, busted out laughing.

He laughed and convulsed and laughed some more and doubled over and heaved and laughed and laughed and laughed. In his mind, he had never seen or heard anything so stupid and inept, and as he stood in front of the room presenting the worst science project the world had ever seen, he realized that he was the one who had concocted it, and he laughed at his own ineptitude.

When Miss Sturgis ordered Dennis to stop laughing, he laughed harder. Soon the entire class was laughing, some of them with, but most of them at Dennis. He was possessed and so embarrassed that nothing could stop his laughing.

Miss Sturgis sternly ordered him back to his desk, and Dennis laughed all the way back to it. The teacher had the last laugh, though. She gave the boy a D-minus for the project.

Dennis stood in line waiting to have his hands inspected. He was a boy who had gained the swagger of a Disturber and the confidence and defiance of someone who challenged authority, especially the mindless authority wielded by the nuns, but wasn't quite free of the anxiety and fear that had imprisoned him for so long. He was defiant, but a little scared, and by the time he held out his hands to be inspected and sniffed, they were shaking.

DeLasalle instinctively sensed a culprit and her next victim.

"Are we afraid of something, Mister Domrzalski?" the nun asked in a raised voice. There was a glee in her voice as well. It was perfectly clear to her that she had the smoker, and she knew this boy wasn't as clever or as quick thinking as Masciola, and that made her happy. She wanted everyone to know that she had triumphed, and she spoke again, this time in a voice so loud that it boomed up and down the street in front of the school.

"You stink like cologne, too! Clever way to cover up the cigarette smoke, isn't it, Mister Domrzalski?"

The boy said nothing, knowing his silence would enrage DeLasalle.

"Isn't it, Mister Domrzalski?" the nun huffed.

Again, he failed to answer.

"Mister, I am talking to you!" she said, her voice nearly a scream. "You are not deaf and dumb! Do you understand me?"

All he could think to say was "No," and he calmly uttered the one-word response.

"No! I'll give you no," DeLasalle shouted as she raised her right arm and prepared to pound the boy's face with her open hand. "I'll give you back talking to me! Now tell me who you were smoking with. Was it James Masciola? Don't lie, because God sees everything that you do! He knows! If you lie, you will go straight to Hell when you die!"

That was one of the nuns' favorite lines when they wanted to force a confession, whether legitimate or not, from a student. It usually worked. God knew and saw everything, the nuns preached relentlessly, and there was no hiding from him or Hell.

Liz Hamm knew that and so wanted to avoid Hell that she now wrote on both sides of any piece of scrap of paper because of the threat of going to Hell she had received from a nun in second grade.

One day Sister Concepta had seen Liz throw a piece of lined loose-leaf paper in a trash can. The nun retrieved the paper from the can, inspected it, saw that Liz had written on only one side of it, and launched into a tirade that permanently scarred the girl.

"Miss Hamm! Why are you wasting paper?" the nun screamed at the seven-year-old. "Paper is made from natural resources, and wasting even ounce of a natural resource is a sin for which you will eternally burn in Hell! You must write on both sides of a sheet of paper. Do you want to burn in Hell?"

The girl was so stunned and scared that she sat in her desk and whimpered, unable to answer the question.

"Do you want to burn in Hell?" Concepta screamed again. "Answer me now or you will go straight to Hell. Are you going to waste paper again and go to Hell?"

"No, Sister," the girl whimpered through tears.

"Are you ever going to waste paper again? Ever?"

"No, Sister. I will never waste paper again. I don't want to go to Hell."

"You had better mean it, young lady, because if you ever again waste another piece of paper you will wind up in Hell with every other sinner. Now write on the other side of this paper," Concepta snarled as she threw the sheet of paper on the girl's desk. Liz furiously wrote on the other side of the paper and always did so after that day on every sheet or scrap of paper she had.

The nuns never wasted a chance to solemnly inform the kids that they would someday die. God, the nuns said, saw, heard and remembered everything that everybody ever did, and when it came time to go to Heaven, Hell or Purgatory, God would be in front of you reminding you of every lie you ever told and every sin you ever committed. Even if a kid hadn't done what a nun was accusing them of, once that line was spouted, they confessed.

Dennis sometimes thought about it. Part of him believed that God did see, hear and remember everything. And for a while, when he was younger, he tried to be good and not tell lies or sin. He long ago had given up on it, though, because every time he told the truth to the nuns or his parents—whether it was about shoplifting, starting fires, not doing homework, not going to mass, or getting other kids in trouble—he got a beating. He rarely got beaten for lying, because, he figured, no one knew he was lying. If he told the truth after denying something, they would know that he lied, and would beat him twice as hard for lying. No, for Dennis and the other Disturbers, lying was the safe and the right thing to do.

This situation about smoking was no different, and the boy wasn't about to risk the awful and painful consequences of telling the truth to a nun, especially to one who had her arm cocked and was ready to pound him senseless.

"No," Dennis started as he stared at the nun. "No, Sister. (The Disturbers never referred to DeLasalle as Ster. They knew she would beat them for it, and they knew that her beatings hurt.) It would not be a very clever to try and cover up the smell of cigarette smoke with cologne."

The answer confused DeLasalle, and she lowered her arm. The boy was safe for now from being beaten.

"Why is that?" the nun barked.

"Because, Sister, in your wisdom, of which God has blessed you with in abundance, you would see through it. Wearing cologne would be admitting that you smoked, and no one would do that. You're way too smart to be tricked like that."

Dennis was pleased with his "of which God has blessed you with in abundance" remark. Kids didn't talk like that, but Dennis, who observed people and read a lot, could sound like an adult if he wanted to.

DeLasalle couldn't hide or control her growing fury, and she barked again: "Then why? Why are you and Mister Masciola—she spat that name out slowly and contemptuously—wearing cologne?"

"Because."

The angry nun grew angrier. All nuns and lay teachers at the school—and just about every adult in the neighborhood—went berserk when a kid spouted that one-word answer to an inquiry. Dennis knew exactly what the nun would scream at him in response, and she did:

"'Because' is not an answer!"

It wasn't an answer, and Dennis and the other kids knew it. They also knew that any time they wanted to drive an adult crazy, they could answer an interrogation with that word.

It worked. DeLasalle was enraged. Now she was the one who was shaking. Dennis was calm. He knew he had her, but he also knew he was taking a huge risk. He was gambling that she would be paralyzed and exhausted by her rage. If she wasn't, she would beat him and probably kill him, or at least put him in the hospital. That would have been worse than death, he figured, because he would have gone to a Catholic hospital run by nuns, and well, they would not have been kind to him.

DeLasalle raged again:

"'Because' is not an answer! You will speak in complete sentences, and you will answer honestly. Am I understood?"

The boy said nothing. The nun screamed as loud as she could:

"'Because' is not an answer! Why are you wearing cologne? Tell me now, before I—"

Dennis was perfectly calm now. He had the nun, and he knew it. He affected a puzzled and bewildered look. He knew the nuns and teachers thought he was "slow," or mildly retarded, and he used it against the behemoth who raged before him. He blinked slowly twice, tried to look stupid, tilted his head and said slowly:

"Because."

It was, as the kids would say, history for Sister Mary Francis DeLasalle. She exploded with such a string of insults and vituperations against the boy that several windows in the homes and apartments across the street from OLG slammed shut. The women who were home couldn't bear the nun's insults.

The nun raged and raged, screamed at the boy that he would go directly to Hell, that she would take him there and that he would never amount to anything in life. Finally she was spent, and as Dennis had hoped, had no energy with which to beat him.

"Get to class," DeLasalle stammered. "You! Yoooouuuuu!"

She couldn't put together a final sentence. For an instant, Dennis thought of saying something like, "Sister, please speak in direct and complete sentences. After all, you should be setting an example for us."

He didn't say it, though. He knew that would have been pushing things too far. He had beaten the beast, was a hero to the other kids and was in heaven. And besides, they weren't changing classes that afternoon and he and the other Disturbers would be able to torment Sister Zita all afternoon. It was going to be fun.

CHAPTER 6

Derailing Trains and Shutting Down an Airport

ENNIS AND MASCIOLA were heroes to all the students who had seen or heard about their remarkable performances. No one had ever flustered and outwitted DeLasalle like they had. Dennis's colleagues in Disturbers Row were proud and envious.

In the back row, Dennis told the full story as the other guys pulled their chairs near his desk, all of them ignoring the fact that the school bell had rung to start afternoon classes and that Sister Zita was beginning to conduct a spelling class.

The story needed no embellishment and Dennis offered none. Ruchinski, in one of his usual attempts to enhance his reputation by belittling the accomplishments of others, proclaimed loudly that Dennis had acted timidly and that he himself would have challenged DeLasalle more directly.

"I would have accused *her* of smoking! And I would have demanded that she kneel and confess that sin to every student individually!" he proclaimed with a bluster that made the others laugh. "Then I would have said, and I would have pointed my finger right in her face, I would have said, 'Ster, you are going straight to Hell!'"

"Yeah, right. You've never called her 'Ster' once this year," Richard Bozeman said in a challenge to Ruchinski's boasting. "You're a chickenshit. All you ever do is play nicey-nice to her. You're a liar."

Bozeman was no chickenshit. He was a true Disturber, a boy who disturbed in and out of class. That summer, just a few weeks before school had started, Richard decided that he wanted to derail one of the many commuter trains that ran in Chicago.

He had gotten the idea when the guys were walking along the Milwaukee Road railroad tracks that angled through the neighborhood just west of Pulaski Road. Ever since the first or second grades, when they could wander the neighborhood after school and on Saturdays, the boys had played on and near tracks. Always they put rocks, nails and coins—anything they could find—on the tracks and waited to see them smashed and crushed by the trains. Adults always warned them to never put coins on the tracks because they could derail a train. There was always a hope in each boy's immature mind, though, that their rocks and nails would really cause a derailment. They had no idea what that would have meant for the passengers, and they didn't care.

The guys had been walking along the tracks near Wrightwood Avenue when Ruchinski looked down near a rail switch box and saw a key lying at the bottom of a slatted wooden box next to the switch. His hand was small enough to fit between two of the rotting slats, and he retrieved the key, a bulky metal thing that was similar to the skeleton keys used on old locks. The guys figured the key was official because the letters "MWR RR" were stamped on the ring on its top.

On the switch box was a kind of heart-shaped metal lock, and the guys just had to see if the key worked. It fit. Ruchinski opened the lock and a three-foot-long metal handle popped up to a ninety-degree angle. The kids realized they had opened a railroad switch box and that they could move the switch, which would have routed trains onto a rail spur that angled down a slope onto and across Wrightwood into an area with a bunch of factories.

Ruchinski put all his weight on the handle and the track moved! He had worked the switch! He was both thrilled and terrified because he knew that if a train suddenly came along, especially a commuter train that ran at high speeds, it would be directed off the main track onto the spur and onto Wrightwood and it would crash and people would die.

"Shit, we gotta get this thing back in place. This could derail a train!" Ruchinski said.

"No. Just keep it open and let's get out of here," Bozeman said. "It's just a train. It'll be fun to derail one. Just keep the thing open."

Ruchinski recognized the insanity of the proposition and he decided to immediately return the switch to its proper position. He worked the handle, and, to his horror, it barely moved! He tried again, and again it hardly budged. He wasn't strong enough to get it back into the correct position!

"Holy shit," he said nervously. "We're screwed. I mean, this thing won't budge. If a train comes, goddammit, it'll crash and we'll be blamed."

"So what. It's just a train," Bozeman said.

"But what about the people on it?"

"Screw 'em. It's their fault for being on it."

"You're crazy!"

"No I ain't. Gimme the key and let's get out of here."

Ruchinski would have none of it. He told the other guys to help with trying to get the switch and track back in place. Four of them leaned on the lever and pushed with all their terrified might, and after a couple of tries the thing finally moved and slid back into proper position. Ruchinski snapped the lock shut and the guys pretty much flew off the tracks and headed to Dennis's basement a couple of blocks away.

HE WANTED TO DERAIL A TRAIN

Ruchinski still had the key, and when they had calmed down, Bozeman demanded it.

"Gimme the key! Gimme the damn key!" Bozeman insisted.

"Why?" Ruchinski asked.

"Cuz I'm gonna derail a train."

"No you're not, you nut!"

"Yes I am, and don't call me crazy or I'll kick your ass."

"I called you nuts, not crazy. Now shut up and stop it."

Bozeman didn't stop, and the rest of that day and for a few weeks afterwards he kept asking for the key so he could derail a train.

Ruchinski and Bozeman had known each other since first grade and they had had many adventures together, their greatest coming in fourth grade when for an hour or so on a Saturday afternoon in the spring they shut down all air traffic at O'Hare International Airport, the busiest airport in the world.

Ruchinski had gotten it into his head that he wanted to see jetliners and visit the airport's control tower to chat with the air traffic controllers. He loved maps and studied them, plotting and planning imaginary trips around the city and elsewhere. He had pored over a map of the city and found the most direct route to the airport, which was on the city's northwest edge. So early on a Saturday morning in May they got on their twenty-inch bicycles and headed for the airport, which was at least ten miles away.

They took Milwaukee Avenue, which angled through the city's northwest side, stopping a couple of times to buy sodas and nibble on the peanut butter and jelly sandwiches they had brought along. A couple of hours later they got to Higgins Road, which skirted the edge of the airport. From there they turned north and eventually saw a grassy field. Since there were no fences, they went into the field to finish their sandwiches. They stopped at a small creek and played with the frogs, and they could see the airport's tower in the distance.

They rode along a little more and suddenly they saw what looked like the straightest and most beautiful concrete road in the world, and so they decided to get on it and pedal to wherever it would take them. They had never been on such a smooth road before, and they thought it neat that giant jet planes were roaring overhead and pretty close to the ground.

Suddenly, a Chicago Police Department paddy wagon, its light flashing, screeched to a halt along the side of the road in front of the kids and a cop stuck his head out the window and shouted angrily, "Follow me!"

The two obeyed and they eventually found themselves in the airport's police station where a police captain angrily explained to them that they had bicycled onto the airport's main runway and had shut down air traffic.

"What on earth is wrong with you kids? You could have gotten killed. They've had to divert all the planes off that runway and all those planes are circling around in the air wasting gas and time and everything else!" the captain roared. "The guys in the tower want to kill you two! You've just shut down the world's busiest airport! Do you have any idea what that means? The world's busiest airport! Are you kids crazy? Your parents are going to give it to you two, and you deserve it!"

SHUTTING DOWN THE WORLD'S BUSIEST AIRPORT.

The captain continued chewing the kids out, and pretty soon Bozeman was crying. Ruchinski was unnerved, his lips were quivering, and he was about to cry. The cop kept up his harangue, making the kids feel worse, and he was about to give them another blast of "You two are in big trouble" when Ruchinski jumped out of his chair and shouted:

"You bully!"

Stunned at being confronted by a fourth grader, the cop asked: "What did you say?"

"You bully! You're a bully!"

The captain's only response was to throw up his arms and say "Ahhhhh!"

The cops called the kids' homes and Bozeman's parents got in their car and headed for the airport.

Ruchinski's parents had left home that morning before he did and were on an all-day excursion and weren't home when the phone rang. His sister, Joyce, who was four years older, answered. She obviously couldn't pick her brother up, so she called her older sister, Pat, who lived with her husband in a suburb of the city that wasn't too far from O'Hare, and they drove to the airport.

A cop who had some sympathy for the kids walked them to a cafeteria in the airport and bought them ice cream sundaes, which the kids devoured while waiting for their rides to arrive.

Never one to quit on a task or goal, and not comprehending the enormous trouble he had just caused for the world's busiest airport, Ruchinski asked the friendly cop:

"Do you think we can go up into the tower now?"

"Young man," the officer said while smiling at the kid's boldness, "I don't think you want to go there right now. Believe me."

By now, word of the kids' exploits and the fact that they had brought O'Hare International Airport to a standstill was on the radio news. Ruchinski's older sister and her husband heard the reports while they listened to the radio on the drive to O'Hare, and they couldn't believe what they were hearing. Two kids on bicycles had shut down the world's busiest airport!

Bozeman's parents arrived first and were briefed by the cops about the situation, and they were not happy. They put Richard's bike into the car's trunk, shoved him in the back seat and yelled at him all the way home.

Dave's sister and her husband arrived and drove him back to the neighborhood. Once home, Dave, still needing more adventures, told his sister Joyce that he was going out to play, as it was still light out.

"Oh no you're not. And when Ma and Dad get home, they're going to hear about this," Joyce said.

A while later, Dave's parents returned. Joyce ratted her little brother out. They had left the house happy; they'd had a fun day and they returned happy, and when Joyce told them all that had gone on, they smiled and did nothing.

Monday morning at school, Dave and Richard met up and Dave noticed that his partner was carrying a pillow, or cushion on which to sit.

"Hey Boz, what happened? I mean, what'd your parents say?" Dave asked.

"Oh my god! I got the beating of my life!" Bozeman said. "My dad took out a big fat belt and he beat me and beat me, and I'm swollen all over! It was the worst beating of my life. My ass hurts. What happened to you? Did you get beat?"

"Naah. Nothing happened. My parents came home, my sister told them what happened, and they didn't do anything."

Richard was pissed that Dave hadn't gotten a beating, but there was nothing he could do about it. From that day afterwards, Bozeman's parents always referred to Ruchinski as "David O'Hare," the kid who had shut down the world's busiest airport.

CHAPTER 7

Threats from the Principal

A S HE SAT in the back row listening to Ruchinski's boasting, Bozeman remembered Ruchinski's reluctance to derail a commuter train. Now he used it against the kid who called himself the King Disturber.

"You were afraid to knock out that train in the summer. Sissy. If you can't derail a train, how would you say that to DeLasalle? You wouldn't."

"I would have because I'm the boldest man here. You guys can't match me," Ruchinski huffed.

The argument would have continued had not Sister Vitaclaire barged into the classroom, full of authority and anger. The Disturbers scrambled back to their seats when the principal walked in and they listened as she stood motionless in the front of the room and icily addressed the class, her pale white skin whiter than usual and her arms stiffly at her side.

"Smoking, boys and girls, and you hoodlums in the back, is wrong! We know who the smokers are, and we want them to come forward and confess. Confession is good for the soul. It cleanses the soul of sin's evil blackness. If by the end of today the guilty ones don't confess, well, they will be in big, big trouble." She paused briefly and then snarled: "We know who you are!"

The kids thought she was finished there. Then, almost as an afterthought, she blurted out:

"They will be in trouble, not only with God, but with me!"

That hit some of the kids hard. Being in trouble with God was no big deal, because as far as they could tell, he just wasn't around. If he was, he was invisible, and he was supposed to be all-forgiving. As they understood it, all one had to do with God was confess, ask forgiveness, be done with it and be free to goof off some more.

Being in trouble with Vitaclaire was a whole different proposition. She was meanness itself. Unlike the other nuns, she didn't bellow or shout. She had a stern, icy demeanor that made some of the kids think that she would have enjoyed being tortured, and that as a lover of pain, she needed to dispassionately inflict it on anything that breathed.

Several of the kids who truly feared the nuns were rattled. Four of them were about to raise their hands and confess to having smoked cigarettes when they hadn't. Just as they were about to, Ruchinski raised his hand.

Vitaclaire glared at the boy. She didn't want to acknowledge him or ask what he wanted. But she knew the other children were waiting to see what would happen, and so she called on him.

"Mister Ruchinski, are you ready to confess?" she snarled. "Where did you get the cigarettes?"

The Disturber started to answer, while sitting in his chair, which was a sign of disrespect that was not tolerated by the nuns.

"Stand up when addressing me or you will be sorrier than sorry, mister," the nun said in her emotionless way. "I am not impressed by you, and I will not hesitate to acquaint your head with this blackboard again, as I have in the past. If you force me to do it again, you will not walk out of this classroom. Am I understood?"

"Yes, Sister," Ruchinski said as he stood up.

"What is it you want?"

"Sister, I just wanted to say that smoking is bad. It is the worst thing anybody could ever do. It is pure evil, Sister. The Devil's work. I don't smoke. I never will. And I want to say that me and these other guys back here, we will—"

"It is, Mister Ruchinski, 'These other students and I will.' When you speak to me you will speak properly, and in the English that we have spent so much time teaching you.

"Yes, Sister. My fellow students, the Disturbers and I, will be happy to conduct an investigation into this matter and get to the bottom of it. We will deliver the smokers to you, complete with their evil cigarettes and with the names of everybody else in this school who has smoked, who is smoking, or who ever will smoke! To show how serious we are about finding these unholy sinners, I move that we appoint Dennis as the lead investigator! If anyone knows who was smoking, it's Dennis!"

That short speech got the self-proclaimed King Disturber the laughs and attention he craved. It also got him called to the front of the room where, Sister Vitaclaire, as promised, reacquainted his head with the blackboard.

ARE YOU LEARNING WHAT LOVE IS?

CHAPTER 8

More Threats

VITACLAIRE WAS LYING, the Disturbers knew. The nuns always betrayed their frustration at not knowing which kids had misbehaved by threatening, "We know who you are!"

It was their unsubtle strategy to bluff the young minds into submission and into confessions. They cared little who confessed, just so long as someone did, and so long as they had another body to beat. And if their tactics of intimidation elicited some false confessions and the innocent were whacked and humiliated, so much the better. That would teach those pliable young minds to bend, mold and submit themselves to authority. That was what Catholic school and teaching was all about, they thought.

Ruchinski wobbled slowly back to Disturbers Row, his eyes a bit moist and his face wearing the pathetic look of someone who wants desperately to believe that they have just done something clever and important, but who knows deep down that they've just acted foolishly and hurt themselves. There was defiance in that face, as always, but it was tinged with hurt and desperation; the desperation of someone who wants out of a situation where those who are in control are crazy and abusive.

As Ruchinski sat down, Kolba raised his hand. This time, Vitaclaire immediately called on him, for she knew the boy would say something that would give her justification to hit him.

"Mister Kolba, apparently you have something meaningful and respectful to add?"

"Yes, Sister, and that is this: It seems to me that, uhhh, that uhhh, that. It seems that you should, I, mean, if you think about it—if you really think about it—and sometimes these are really hard things to think about, ummm—"

Kolba was babbling. It was a tactic the Disturbers used to infuriate the nuns, for they despised incoherence and improper English; despised it because they believed in perfection, but most of all because it reflected poorly on their teaching skills. They would brook no hint that they were not teachers made perfect by God.

"Mister Kolba, if you insist on talking like an idiot, I will oblige you and make immediate arrangements for you to be sent to Dunning," the nun said.

That was another threat the nuns and other adults made to kids. Dunning was the name of the city's insane asylum on the far northwest side, a public institution where crazy people were locked up. As far as the kids knew, no one who went to Dunning ever came out.

If an adult thought a kid's laughter was inappropriate, particularly if the kid was laughing at that adult, the older person would end it by threatening, "Keep laughing that way and you'll wind up in Dunning, and I'll take you there myself!"

The Disturbers weren't afraid of Dunning; they thought it would have been fun to go there, at least to visit. They also knew that the threats were hollow. They doubted that any adult could just take or send them to Dunning. Even at their young ages, they sensed that there were giant bureaucracies that needed to be engaged, and that being sent off to Dunning would take at least a few weeks. To them, a few weeks was an eternity.

Kolba wasn't cowed by the threat.

"I'm sure I will do well there," the boy shot back with as serious a tone as he could muster.

Most of the room erupted in laughter. It was a brilliant retort and an instance where even the good kids relished the idea of a kid outwitting a nun.

Most secretly wished they had the courage to challenge Vitaclaire's authority as Kolba just had.

SMARTEST STUDENT AT DUNNING

Vitaclaire fumed. The entire class had laughed at her! A thirteen-year-old kid, a kid who had no respect for her authority as God's representative on Earth, had humiliated her. Was there no end to the insolence of these ignorant working-class thugs, she thought to herself? Was there no respect for her authority? Was there no end to Satan's scheming?

She determined that there would be an end to all three, and maybe more. She wanted to give the boy an opportunity for more reasons to clobber him.

"Gary, you will be Dunning's star student. You will be their star student for the rest of your life," the nun shot back. "Now, whatever were you trying to say? If you need a translator to put your incoherence into English, we will help. Mister Krask, Miss Drokowski, Mister Heller and some of these other pupils have learned to speak. Tell us if you need help, dear."

"No, Sister," Kolba replied, knowing he had a beating coming and that he had to talk quickly in order to get in his smart-aleck lines. "I just think that if you know who the smokers are, you should tell us right now. We need to know so we can stay away from them. We do not want their sinful ways to rub off on us.

"Besides, Sister, as God's representative, you have a duty to confront them now!" He shouted that last word for effect, and effect he got. The class laughed again, and Vitaclaire calmly walked to Sister Zita's desk and purposefully and lovingly picked up the wooden pointer with her right hand.

"If they're not confronted now, Sister, they will continue to smoke and sin. The faster that they are confronted, the faster they will be forgiven and filled with God's grace," Kolba continued. "I would hate to think that you, when you had the chance to stop a sinner from sinning, refused to. I think that delaying someone from receiving God's grace would be a sin!"

That was it. Kolba had committed the ultimate sin of accusing the nuns of sinning, and for that there was no forgiveness.

"Come forward, Mister Kolba, and let's see what God has in store for you," Vitaclaire demanded.

Gary obeyed and slowly shuffled to the front of the room. Vitaclaire was patient. She waited until he was next to her and stood facing his classmates. The nun said nothing. She walked in back of him to get to his left side, paused as if she were going to give him one final admonition, and then, without warning, began whacking him with the pointer across his left shoulder and back.

The boy endured the beating in silence. That infuriated the nun even more. He was refusing to acknowledge that she was hurting him. That she couldn't take, and she whaled away with an intensified fury. The beating was ferocious. When it was over, the boy bore purple welts on his bare arms where the pointer had hit. Vitaclaire was nearly out of breath. She had enough left, though, to address the class.

"Is there anyone else here who thinks that Mister Kolba was funny?" she demanded. "If so, please speak now."

No one did.

"Are there any other of you hoodlums in the back row who want to say something?"

No one did.

"Good. I expect the smokers to come forward. If not, every one of you in this class, because you all know who they are, will pay for it. I expect perfect behavior the rest of the afternoon."

CHAPTER 9

A Crazy Spelling Bee

THE TWO WOUNDED Disturbers were in no mood for perfect behavior, nor were their three colleagues. There would be no changing of rooms that afternoon, and the Disturbers relished the idea of tormenting Zita until the 3:15 bell rang to end classes for the day.

Zita had kept silent when Vitaclaire had threatened the class and hammered the two Disturbers. She mostly kept out of it when the principal came up from her first-floor office to restore order in the classroom.

This time, while Vitaclaire had lectured, Zita snarled out twice that all the Disturbers were smokers.

"They get their cigarettes from communists, Sister, from communists, and the Devil. They all deserve the back of your hand," she said after Ruchinski had been beaten.

Now, even though Vitaclaire had left the room, Zita was in full glory. She was thrilled that the two had been taught a lesson, and envious that she had not done the teaching herself. She was also full of retributive zeal.

"There will be no back talking this afternoon. None!" she declared as she slammed the pointer in her hand on the top of her desk. "If there is, Sister Vitaclaire will not hesitate to come here again and attend to the troublemakers. Nor will I hesitate. We are going to have a spelling bee. I want the girls on that side of the room, and the boys on the other. Now move!"

It was a poor choice in terms of positioning the kids, for Zita had ordered the girls to the classroom's left side, which was framed by windows that looked out into a small courtyard between the school and Our Lady of Grace church.

The boys were ordered to the room's right side, which had a room-length blackboard with a wooden ledge that held too many sticks of white chalk to count. The Disturbers knew what to do with the chalk; they dropped the sticks onto the floor and ground them into powder with the heels of their shoes.

"Ster!" Kurkowski shouted after the chalk had been crushed. There is something on the floor, and it is staining our shoes. I don't think we can stand here, Ster. It's ruining our shoes. For all we know it might be acid! Acid, Ster!"

The other Disturbers feigned horror at the word, and although they were scattered throughout the string of boys lined up against the blackboard, they shouted together:

"Acid! Acid! We're going to die! Our feet will dissolve! Steeerrrr!"

"I'll give you, Mister Kookowski," Zita snarled, purposely mispronouncing the boy's last name, "disrupting my classroom! You think you're big stuff, don't you?"

"No, Ster," the boy replied. "It's just that this acid is burning our feet! Please, Ster, let us go to the bathroom so we can wash the acid off our feet! Steeerrr! It hurts!"

Zita had lost the ability to control a classroom, but she wasn't a total fool. She knew the Disturbers were trying for an insurrection, and she wasn't going to oblige them.

"Surely, Mister Kookoski, you, Mister Big Stuff, surely a little acid won't hurt a bold man like you, will it? You're not a sissy, are you, sweetie?"

That shut Kurkowski and the Disturbers up for a while, and Zita finally managed to get the spelling contest between the boys and the girls going.

The girls, none of whom were real troublemakers, enjoyed the contest and took it seriously. They tried to correctly spell the words. So did most of the boys, and the Disturbers despised them for it.

The game also seemed rigged. The girls appeared to get easy, one-and-two-syllable words, while the boys, especially the Disturbers, got harder ones. A few words had already been given out and correctly spelled. Carol Booza got "priest," while Bernard Heller gleefully spelled "Catholic."

It was Kurkowski's turn, and Zita asked him to spell "communist, as in, all troublemakers are communists who will go straight to Hell."

They boy stood silent for a moment, then stroked his chin as if in deep thought, repeated the word, and started:

"Communist is spelled, let's see, communist. It sounds like a bad word. Communist. Ster, could you give me a hint? What does it start with?"

"D'wuhh? Mister, D'wuuuuuuhhhhh?"

"Ster, that's a hard word, and I could use a hint. What does it start with?"

Kurkowski was trying his best to start another insurrection, but Zita would have no part of it.

"That's for you to figure out, sweetie. If you can't spell the word, then you'll have to sit down."

"No, Ster. I can spell it. I just need some help." Then he looked down the line of boys and asked loudly:

"Anybody know how to spell communist?"

Dennis replied in as loud a voice:

"I know how to spell it! But, but it's such a bad word that I don't think we should! We shouldn't be using that word in this classroom. Steeerrr! Please don't make him spell such a terrible word! Pleeeaaasssse!" he yelled in mock terror that got much of the room laughing.

"Bob, don't spell it! Don't even say that word!" Ruchinski yelled from down the line. "It's just too terrible!" Then he slumped to the floor as if he had fainted. The other Disturbers followed, and the laughs grew louder, even from the girls.

Zita, now greatly annoyed, tried to remain calm as she sat on the edge of her desk.

Bozeman joined in the fun. "Ster, if you make him spell that word—that word!—we will have to report you to the authorities! Can't you change the word to 'America' or 'saint?'"

"And if he doesn't spell the word, he will flunk spelling and be held back at the end of the year," Zita sneered. "So, Mister Kookowski, spell it now, or you will fail everything."

"But Ster!" Kolba shouted. "God might strike him dead for spelling it, especially if he spells it correctly!"

"Then, Gary, this classroom will have one less commu—I mean, one less troublemaker. Now spell the word or sit down!"

Kurkowski picked himself off the ground, again stroked his chin as if in deep thought, and began:

"Communist. Communist is spelled, and I think this is right. I hope it's right! Communist is spelled. Ster? Can I check a dictionary?"

The laughter was loud and constant by now, and Zita was losing her temper.

"Spell the word, you little—"

"Communist is spelled. Communist is spelled." Kurkowski paused here, stroked his chin again for effect, and said loudly:

"Communist is spelled, Z-I-T-A!"

The room exploded with laughter. Zita lost it. She lurched off her desk, grabbed her pointer and stumbled after her tormentor. It was no use, though. The boy was too quick and agile for her. She could have spent all afternoon chasing him and she would not have caught him.

She had managed to get to the boys' line. By then, Kurkowski was on the girls' side of the room trying to flirt with anyone who would flirt back. Frustrated, Zita found Dennis and whacked him a few times with the pointer.

"That's for being acquainted with Mister Kookowski," she huffed. "Beware of who you associate with."

"But I don't associate with him, Ster. He's just my friend," Dennis said. "I don't think I've ever been associated with anyone."

That got him another whack across the arm.

Zita hobbled back to her desk, perched herself once more on its front edge and continued with the spelling bee.

Kurkowski, who had been ordered to sit down, did so, but not at his desk. He decided to make a spectacle of himself by combining the tabletops of three desks in the classroom's middle row and reclining on them, facing Zita, so he could see if she decided to come after him again.

Whenever the girls were given words, the Disturbers raised their hands, stomped their feet, made a general ruckus and shouted that they knew how to spell it. When the girls began spelling, the Disturbers shouted:

"Wrong! Wrong! Wrong! You can't spell! Hey Ster, why don't you give us such easy words?"

It went like that for fifteen minutes. Because of the ruckus and the constant interruptions, very few words actually got spelled. But enough of them did to show that the girls were easily winning the contest. Half the boys had already sat down for failing to spell correctly.

One was Ruchinski, who botched the word "hoodlum." Another was Bozeman, who, when told to spell "theology," angrily blurted out:

"I don't like that word. I don't even know what it means!"

"Well then sit down, you little—" Zita snarled.

"No!" Richard roared back to the laughs of the boys. "Ster, sitting down hurts my—"

He hinted that he was about to use a word that was forbidden in Catholic schools, and that got the boys, and some girls, laughing even harder.

Zita wasn't laughing. Just a hint of what the nuns considered profanity was enough to infuriate her. Then she caught herself, and fired back at the boy:

"What, sweetie? Does it hurt your brains?"

Zita was in her personal heaven. She had embarrassed—at least she thought she had—a kid, and nothing made her happier. If those boys were going to torment her, she would torment them back, physically, verbally and emotionally.

Bozeman wasn't embarrassed, though. The nun's witticism flew right past him without so much as nicking him or even ruffling his hair. He stared at her blankly for a few moments, not knowing that he had been stung. That made Zita angrier and more determined to do him some emotional harm.

"Well, sweetie, where are your brains? Because I haven't seen any anywhere!"

"I don't have any today," Bozeman said.

"Why is that?"

"Because I left them at home."

"D'wuhh?"

"Yeah, Ster. I left them at home because in this class—" He paused here to let the anticipation build and to let the nun twist a little.

"D'wuhh?" Zita demanded. "D'wuhh!"

"Ster, I don't know what 'D'wuhh' means. Please tell me what it means."

The boys were rolling with laughter. Some now were sitting on the floor, their backs against the wall, an act of disrespect and defiance that was driving Zita crazy.

"Stand up!" she shouted to the boys. "Stand up in this room!"

A few of the boys got to their feet. But not the Disturbers who remained in the contest. Dennis, Kolba and Bozeman reclined on the floor, yawned and pretended to go to sleep.

"Stand up, I said!" Zita shouted.

Kolba sat up, rubbed his eyes as if tired, and said from the floor:

"Why should we, Ster? There's nothing important going on here."

Zita was near popping a blood vessel in her head, but she managed to control herself.

"I'll deal with you later, Gary. But first, I'll deal with Mister Bozeman. Why did you leave your brain at home?"

"Because, Ster," the boy replied, trying to hold back laughter. He paused again, and then, as Zita was about to launch herself off the desk, he shouted out:

"Because in this class you don't need a brain!"

Zita lurched forward, grabbed her pointer and shuffled to the line of boys, intent on swinging the pointer with uncontrolled fury. At that, Kolba jumped to his feet and shouted:

"Ster! I want to spell! I can spell!"

That stopped the nun cold.

"Well, Gary, that's a surprise. How many words can you spell?" Zita asked with a sarcastic grin.

"Four million!" Kolba shouted. "Actually, Ster, four million two hundred forty-seven thousand one hundred and three!"

Every kid in the class roared. Things were out of control. Zita knew it and tried to reestablish her authority.

"Well, Gary, we'll see about that. Spell 'magazine!'"

"Yes Ster! That's easy. It's one of the first words I learned!"

"And you learned it when, Gary?"

"When I was six weeks old!"

"And how did you learn it?"

"Well, Ster, my mother didn't have any blankets to wrap me in, so she tore out the pages of a magazine and rolled me up in them. She even covered my face. I couldn't see much, but I do remember seeing the word 'magazine.' That was the first word I learned, Ster!"

"Then prove it!"

"Yes Ster! Magazine, as in, 'Ken Gronski stole a magazine from the dime store yesterday.' And, Ster, that's the truth!"

"Get on with it, Gary."

Kolba stroked his chin, raised his eyes to the ceiling, stroked this chin again and repeated the word, all to the disgust of Sister Zita.

"Spell the word! You little—"

"Magazine. M-A-G."

The boy paused and stroked his chin.

"Spell it!"

"M-A-G." He paused one last time for effect, and just as Zita was about to lurch forward toward him, he yelled out:

"WXYZ!"

It was bedlam in the room. Everyone howled. Zita was enraged. She ambled toward the boy, pointer in hand and arm raised.

"D'wuhh?"

"WXYZ!"

Zita tried to spring to the boy, but all she could do was shuffle slowly. It didn't matter, Kolba was going nowhere. He stood his ground, waiting to glory in the coming attack. It came. The nun whaled at him with the pointer. He covered his head with his arms and hands. She swung harder. At one point, when she was exhausted from beating him, Kolba peeked out from behind his hands and shouted one more time:

"WXYZ!"

The nun lost it. She dropped the pointer and swung at Kolba with her scaly, bony hands. She had no strength left, so Kolba lowered his arms and let the nun's ineffectual blows fall on his face, head and neck.

"Ster." he said when she paused to catch her breath. "Are you angry at me for something?"

She was. The beating went on. Her blows caused no harm, the class howled, the Disturbers were envious and proud, and Gary was in full glory.

STER, ARE YOU ANGRY ABOUT SOMETHING?

CHAPTER 10

He Eats Pencils!

KOLBA'S SPELLING WIZARDRY ended the spelling bee. When Zita began beating him, the other Disturbers flew into hyper-Disturber mode. Bozeman began shooting spitballs as fast as he could tear little pieces of paper, roll them into balls small enough to fit into a pen tube and shoot them at any moving target. His favorite was Zita herself, and he got her several times. Another favorite was Daniel Kowalski, a kid with a pale, emotionless face who fascinated the Disturbers because he ate wooden pencils.

At least he chewed pencils—gnawed them vigorously. No one knew why, and no one cared because it was exciting to be associated with someone who did something so crazy. And seeing Kowalski chew up pencils for no apparent reason was different, fascinating and exciting.

Kolba first discovered Kowalski's talent when he stopped by his house after school one day. They lived across the alley from each other, and Kolba wanted to go out and goof around. He saw Kowalski sitting on a swing on his home's front porch. Gary walked up the six wooden stairs, asked Dan what he was doing, and then saw that he was angrily chewing up a pencil.

"He was chewing it like it was a sausage, and half the pencil was chewed down," Kolba breathlessly reported to the Disturbers the next morning at school. "I asked him why he was eating a pencil, and he just stared at me. He didn't say anything. I asked him if it tasted good, and he didn't say anything. Then I asked him if there were any beavers in his family, and he took big bite out of it! I couldn't believe it! He was eating a pencil, eraser and all!"

"We need to use him," Ruchinski said. "You know, we could make him our official pencil sharpener. Or we could study him. Maybe he's from another planet. There's got to be other people out there. Maybe he's a Martian or something? If he's part beaver we can sell him to the circus or something. Was he eating anything else?"

"Naah. Just the pencil."

"Well, let's just give him a couple of pencils and see what happens."

That they did, and when they checked Kowalski's desk later that week they found five pencils chewed half-way down.

THE HUMAN BEAVER·

Kowalski was neither a good kid nor a Disturber. He seemed to associate with no one and showed no emotion other than a simmering annoyance and bewilderment with everything. When hit with spitballs, he looked around for the shooter, appeared befuddled as to why someone would shoot at him, and stared blankly into the distance. He neither complained nor laughed.

Another favorite target was Gerald Mayer, a good kid who was good out of shyness and fear, not because he wanted to curry favor with the nuns. He seldom spoke, but he did get scared when hit with spitballs, and he always tried to duck after the first hit, and that made him a favorite target as well.

Kurkowski had gone to the second row where, before some of the kids had returned to their desks, he took out their books and dumped them on the floor.

Ruchinski was at Zita's desk, going through its drawers, looking for stuff—pencils, compasses, pens, protractors, rubber bands, paper clips, staplers, rulers and other things she had confiscated from the Disturbers.

The nun loved taking things from the Disturbers. She thought it proper punishment for their disrespect. Plus, she had a grand plan: when she had accumulated enough of it, she would sell it to students in the lower grades. Ruchinski was about to take two handfuls of confiscated material from a drawer when Zita saw him. She let Kolba go, picked her pointer off the floor and limped toward Ruchinski, saying nothing and hoping the boy wouldn't notice her. She had planned—hoped and prayed—for at least one mighty whack across his back.

Like all Disturbers, Ruchinski had an instinct for a Zita surprise attack. It helped that many of the kids started howling and laughing as Zita tried to sneak up on him. It also helped that the nuns' heavy linen habits had a distinctive odor, and that the wooden heels of their black leather nun shoes clunked on the wooden floor, both of which announced their presence well in advance. Ruchinski smelled Zita as she shuffled toward him. He also saw her out of one eye, but went on going through the desk drawers, pretending nothing was amiss.

Zita shuffled closer and raised her arm. The pointer was high in the air. She moved closer, hoping that just once her surprise could be complete and she could swing the pointer with enough force to injure her tormentor. One more step, and the arm came forward, and, nothing!

Ruchinski was well out of range before the pointer whiffed though the space his back had just occupied and slammed onto the top of her desk.

The class roared. Ruchinski, off to the left front corner of the classroom, feigned shock.

"Sister Mary Zita," he scolded her. "You should tell me when you're going to hit me with the pointer. It's not nice to sneak up on people. You could hurt them like that."

ZITA STOLE THEIR STUFF

Of course she could have hurt him. That's what she was aching for. She was too tired, though, to chase Ruchinski, and so she shuffled to the front of her desk and perched herself on its edge.

Kolba collapsed to the floor as if he was hurt. Dennis ran to him, pretended to be concerned and exclaimed: "Sterrrrrrrr! I think Gary's hurt! He's not breathing! He might be dead!"

"Hmmh. Maybe we should call Mister Letart," Zita replied.

The class roared. Mister Letart was OLG's janitor. He could do plumbing, burn trash and mop floors, but dealing with a medical emergency, well, the kids knew how totally ridiculous Zita's suggestion was. They also knew that the old nun had called Dennis's bluff and had gotten one over on the Disturbers. Zita was pleased that she had gotten a laugh. It wasn't just Disturbers, she thought, who could get the kids going.

"But he's the janitor! What good will he do? I think we need an ambulance," Dennis shouted with a feigned breathlessness.

"Well, sweetie, at least he'll be clean for the ambulance. If he's hurt, then he'll get detention. No one hurts themselves in my classroom."

"But what if he's dead?"

"Then he won't be promoted to the eighth grade because he will have missed all his assignments. And he'll go straight to Hell because he will have missed Mass."

Not wanting detention, Kolba rose to his feet and walked back to Disturbers Row.

The riot was waning. The protagonists and antagonist were tired. Disturbing took a lot of energy, and, at times, even the Disturbers tired of it. Seeing he would get no more from Zita, Ruchinski walked back to his desk as well.

CHAPTER 11

Hairspray, Makeup and Whoring

THE DISTURBANCE HAD taken a lot of time, so much that everyone was surprised to see that it was time for the afternoon recess, or as the Disturbers said, time to go to the john.

The kids from all six seventh and eighth grade classes shuffled out into the school's main corridor where they stood in line—girls in one and boys in the other—to use the bathrooms at one end of the hallway.

The morning and afternoon recesses were both fun and frightening times for the kids; fun because they could talk, although they were supposed to stand silently in line, and because they could exchange information with kids in the other classes; and dangerous because it left them open to inspection and torment from the nuns and teachers of the other classes: Sister DeLasalle, Miss Donatello and Sister Yvonne.

For all the trouble they caused her, the Disturbers and other kids appreciated Sister Zita. She was old, crazy, wrinkled and gnarled, and she beat them, but she wished them no lasting harm or real serious injuries. In many ways, she enjoyed the game as much as they did, and she relished playing it. When she got the class to laugh at the Disturbers expense, Zita was as happy as the boys were when they embarrassed her. There was an underlying sense of mutual respect and of the game. In so many ways, she was, as they were, a kid. It wasn't so with

DeLasalle, Yvonne and Donatello; they were truly mean people who had no problem with doing real and lasting physical and emotional harm to children.

As they formed their lines in the hallway, many of the kids figured there would be trouble. The two smokers hadn't been caught, and the mayhem in Zita's room during the spelling bee was heard all over the second floor, especially by Donatello, DeLasalle and Yvonne.

One look at Yvonne leaning with her back against one edge of the open doorway to her classroom, her hands folded and hidden inside a pouch at the waist of her habit, told the kids that trouble was indeed at hand. The nuns always hid their hands in those pouches when they were angry, and when they did, the kids prepared to be terrorized.

Yvonne calmly and intently surveyed the kids like a witch who was certain she would have a victim, but who was taking great joy in making those potential victims squirm. She had fifteen minutes and was in no hurry.

There were strict rules about these recesses. No more than two kids were allowed in the bathrooms at one time. The nuns wanted no talking in the lines or bathrooms. They wanted no horseplay, no fun, no plotting against them, no gossiping, no laughter, and most importantly, no talk about crushes the boys had on girls or the girls had on boys. Attractions that the boys and girls had for each other infuriated the nuns. They believed those natural urges were sick and that those who had them were sinners—loose and evil women, and perverted boys, they called the kids who let their fascinations with the opposite sex be known. The kids were expected to silently, quickly and efficiently expel their waste and return to the lines.

YVONNE ON THE HUNT

It never went that way, though. The kids were human, and their natural tendencies to talk, laugh, gossip and have fun couldn't be suppressed, even by loud and constant threats that they would go straight to Hell for acting normal.

Once, when Kolba was being berated, beaten and threatened with Hell by DeLasalle for laughing in class, he shot back:

"If Hell is full of kids who laugh, I'd like to go there. I will go to Hell, Sister."

That earned him a second and more intense beating and the threat that his parents would be called to the school. That was the threat that terrified the kids. They could deal with beatings and damnations from the nuns; those seemed temporary. Sometimes the nuns could be nice, even compassionate and forgiving.

But their parents, especially their fathers, were different. The "old men" as the kids called them, were often bitter, depressed and all too willing to take their anger out on their kids. They were blue-collar, working-class men who worked in factories, foundries or for the city. Some were cops and firefighters. They had been born during the Great Depression, and many hadn't finished high school. They married young and had lots of kids—four children seemed the average. Those were kids that many of the men really couldn't afford. They were always short of money, and they were angry because of it. Many hated their jobs, and because of their lack of education, they felt trapped in them. Many saw their lives as bleak and hopeless. Some were alcoholics who beat their wives and their children. It was the neighborhood's dirty secret that many of the men were drunks and wife beaters.

The nuns and priests knew it. When parish women came to them for help, for a way out of the beatings and abuse, they were counseled to pray. Some were told the beatings were their fault because they hadn't been good wives. Others were told that the beatings were their cross to bear, their suffering for Christ that would get them to Heaven. Some were told that the violence and abuse was normal because that was just the way men were.

Most of the women accepted those explanations. They were devout Catholics who believed that the nuns and priests were imbued with the wisdom and grace of God and knew better than they did on just about everything, including marriage, sex and raising kids. They never dared think of questioning or challenging that authority. Most had even less education than their husbands, and even if their instincts told them that those explanations were twisted and crazy, they didn't know how to challenge them. They had been raised to believe that women had a very limited role in life—to marry, have plenty of children and make sure that hot food was on the table when the husband arrived home from work. Their role was also to wash dishes, do laundry, shop for groceries, sew, clean house, iron and make no complaint when the husband wanted to make another baby. Very few of the women worked outside of the home, and so their social contacts were limited to relatives and neighbors—women who were just like them.

Fathers were bitter enough with their feelings of hopelessness and despair and the jobs they didn't like, and they hated to be bothered with calls from the school about their kids. It was one more annoyance and problem they didn't need. So, when they were called to school, they often took their anger out on the kids in front of the nuns. Many boys and girls were beaten by their fathers while the nuns looked on with approval.

When Kolba was asked that day by DeLasalle to repeat his smart-aleck line about wanting to go to Hell, he considered the consequences—one of the few times he did—and wisely kept his mouth shut.

The boys had already broken the recess rule of no more than two kids in the bathroom at once. Six were in the small room, and they were talking and laughing and engaging in something the nuns hated: combing their hair in front of a small mirror over the bathroom's sink.

The boys loved to comb their hair. Most slopped their heads with hair lotion or grease. Wildroot and Brylcreem were the big brands, and the kids always put way too much on. They loved it when the grease caked up on the comb after it had been run through their hair. Winter mornings were especially fun for those guys. They never wore hats when they walked to school, not even in sub-zero weather, and they loved it when the grease on their hair froze. They never wore scarves either—that looked sissyish to them—because they thought that their faces, turned red by the bitter cold, looked tough and manly.

DeLasalle heard the commotion and charged into the boys' bathroom. She and Yvonne and the female lay teachers always did that, never mind that there were boys at the urinal. Kenneth Gordy was running a comb through this hair. He paid the price for his vanity. DeLasalle seized the black comb from his right hand, grabbed the back of his white dress shirt with her left hand and dragged him out of the room into the hallway in front of the boys' line.

"Hair, Mister Gordy, is to be combed but once in the morning, at home and before school. Is that understood?"

"Yes, Sister," he mumbled quietly. He and other boys often mumbled to the nuns because it angered them. It was just another way of setting them off.

"I did not hear you, Mister Gordy. Speak up!"

"Yes, Sister," he mumbled again, this time with his head bowed so as to make it even more difficult to be heard.

"Mister Gordy, do you know what hair is for?" DeLasalle bellowed.

"To keep me from being bald?"

"No. It's to be pulled like this," DeLasalle yelled as she grabbed the boy's short hair and dragged him by it down the row of boys. "This," she continued in a loud and angry voice, "is what happens to boys who comb their hair in school. You get your hair pulled by me! Do you think you're so handsome or special that you must keep combing your hair?"

"No, Sister."

"Then why were you combing your hair? Why?"

"I don't know."

"You don't know?"

"No."

"Good! Because you are going to stand next to this wall, on one leg, until you do know why!"

With that, DeLasalle, her hand sill grasping the boy's hair, flung him against a wall and ordered him to stand on one leg until he could explain why he combed his hair at school. The boy complied, bent his left leg at the knee and lifted it slightly off the floor.

"If that leg touches the floor, or the wall behind you, Mister Gordy, you will be in trouble," DeLasalle roared.

The boys in line laughed. Some were envious of Gordy. He had been punished, he hadn't succumbed to DeLasalle and he was getting what they all desired: attention.

Several of the laughers got attention: whacks across the back of the head from the beefy nun as she rumbled up and down the boys' line expounding on the sinfulness of combing one's hair in school.

VANITY IS A SIN·

Yvonne cracked a slight smile when DeLasalle yanked Gordy by the hair. Hair yanking was a favored technique of the nuns and lay teachers. It caused a decent amount of pain and a great degree of humiliation. The boys didn't mind being hit with pointers, fists, open hands or forearms, but they hated being dragged around by their hair.

While DeLasalle charged back into the boys' bathroom, Yvonne, who had been calmly surveying the line of girls for a victim, pounced. She had had her eye on Lillian Cornell, a tall girl with blond hair and a wonderful smile who the boys thought was beautiful.

Lillian had irritated the nuns since the first grade when she did what all kids do; she talked in class. That first time she was caught engaging in normal human behavior went badly for her. The first-grade nun, Sister Mary Thomas Edward, shot a few rubber bands at her, threw two pieces of white chalk at her and then made her stand in front of the room all morning while sticking out her tongue.

Lillian was a born gabber, though, and that early punishment, which was meant to make her fear and obey authority, had no lasting effect. She talked and laughed throughout her OLG career and was criticized and hit for it. Now, in seventh grade, as she was beginning to bloom into a young woman, Lillian, like the other girls, was developing more interest in boys.

The boys' and girls' interest in each other had begun in the fourth and fifth grades. The boys had started showing off to the girls by fighting with each other or by hitting the girls and pulling their hair. The girls had begun taking interest in their appearance. They used perfumed soaps, ratted their hair, and occasionally used hair spray and makeup, and they wrote and passed notes to each other about the boys they liked.

In fifth grade, the contact between the sexes was little more than holding hands at Koz Park while ice skating in the winter. The girls held pajama parties, which some boys crashed by hanging outside the girls' apartments or houses and trying to peep at the pajama-clad budding beauties through the windows and making noise.

By seventh grade, the bolder and more aggressive boys began to try to feel up the girls every chance they got, whether at the park, on their front porches, or in the cloak rooms in the front and sides of their classrooms.

Lillian and many of the other girls had been wearing makeup and using hairspray since fifth grade. The nuns hated both makeup and hairspray, and they hated the girls who used both. To the nuns, makeup and hairspray were signs the girls were engaging in womanly behavior. They were horrified by it and determined to stomp out any and all unholy behavior.

Already during the school year Lillian had been accused by the nuns being a loose woman. She and her friends had ditched Sunday mass one morning and were standing outside the church when DeLasalle saw them. The nun was enraged that they weren't in mass, which was mandatory for OLG kids, and warned them they would go to Hell for cutting mass. She also accused them of waiting for boys, which was bad enough. But waiting for boys outside of church on a Sunday morning, and waiting to lure them into unholy activity after church was beyond sinful.

DeLasalle wanted to beat them, but since she technically had no authority over them on a Sunday, she opted for a more damaging course of action. She went to the convent and wrote a letter to Lillian's parents in which she accused the girl of trying to lure boys into sin outside of church, which, in DeLasalle's mind, amounted to being a whore.

"As you know, missing Sunday Mass is a mortal sin that will lead to Lillian burning eternally in the fires of Hell!" the letter said. "I shudder to think which of God's punishments awaits Lillian and her friends for their whoring, and whoring outside of church!

"It is a known fact that children follow the example of their parents. It would be uncharitable of me to conclude that her sinful ways are the result of parental example, and I fervently pray that is not the case. Scripture tells us that those who lead children astray, even if by unintended sinful example, will also burn forever in Hell.

"It is also known that, in attempts to be popular, children fall in with the wrong crowd. It is up to the parents to prevent this from occurring, and if, unfortunately, it has occurred, to immediately rectify the situation.

"I pray that you may find the strength to immediately put an end to Lillian's sinful behavior and return her to God's loving grace.

"If I may be of further assistance in saving Lillian's soul, you may contact me at the Convent. Yours in a loving Christ."

It was a typical Catholic letter in that it used eternal damnation, which all Catholics were taught to fear, and which most believed in and did indeed fear, blatantly suggested that the parents were to blame for Lillian's sinful behavior, and that they would all burn in Hell forever unless the parents and Lillian changed, repented and obeyed the nuns' rules.

The note served only to enrage Lillian's parents, who were some of the few adults in the parish who weren't cowed by the nuns or priests. Lillian's mother knew her daughter was a budding beauty, but also knew she wasn't the incipient whore DeLasalle said she was. She also knew that it was highly unlikely that a seventh-grade girl growing up in blue-collar neighborhood in Chicago in the 1960s was whoring around and selling her body. A return letter was sent in which DeLasalle was chastised for making such accusations against a nice girl.

The letter enraged DeLasalle, who passed it around the convent. She wanted all to know that the Cornells weren't yet broken, and that Lillian would have to pay for her parents dismissing her authority.

Yvonne had read the letter and was enraged by it, and now she saw her chance to make Lillian pay, for the girl had committed two sins; she was wearing makeup and she had used hairspray.

Yvonne grabbed the girl's left arm, yanked her out of line, rubbed her face with her fingers and yelled: "What is this? Makeup! Makeup! Miss Cornell, what are you thinking of doing? What do you think you are? Don't answer because I already know. You little—"

Slut and whore were the words she had in mind, but she caught herself and readied for a second accusation.

"And this," Yvonne said as she ran her fingers through the girl's stiff hair. "Hairspray! Hairspray! What kind of floozie are your parents raising? What kind of unholy sinful little tramp are they raising?"

She dragged Lillian into the girl's bathroom, turned on the water in the white porcelain sink, pulled a coarse washcloth from the pouch in her habit, lathered it up with a bar of white soap from on top of the sink and went furiously to work scrubbing the makeup off Lillian's face. The job was done in a few minutes, after which Lillian's face was raw and red. Then Yvonne yanked the girl by the hair and shoved her head under the sink's faucet. She lathered her hair with the bar soap and cleansed Lillian of hairspray and sin.

"You will never wear makeup or hairspray again! Never!" she said as she shoved the girl out the door with her hair dripping wet. "Now get back into line."

She followed the girl back to the line and announced to the girls: "Miss Cornell thought she would play beauty queen and floozie. Wearing makeup is a sin. So is using hair spray. So is thinking about boys! This is what sinners get!" she finished as she pushed Lillian back into the line.

CLEANSING THE HARLOT OF SIN AND HAIRSPRAY

None of the girls believed Yvonne or the other nuns when it came to makeup, hair spray and boys. Although their young minds couldn't articulate why, they knew that the nuns were wrong and crazy. After all, most of the kids had two parents, a mother and a father, meaning, a girl and a boy, and sometimes they even saw their parents kiss each other. If boys and girls getting together was so evil and sinful, why was everyone in the neighborhood married, they wondered? And, why, and how, did they all manage to have kids? A rhyme that was always on Masciola's lips came to their minds:

> My Bonnie lies over the ocean.
> My Bonnie lies over the sea.
> My daddy lies over my mommy,
> And that's how they got little me.

CHAPTER 12

An Idiotic Penalty

THE AFTERNOON RECESS was over, and the kids—all except Ken Gordy—filed back into their classrooms. Gordy had tried to walk back into room 204, but DeLasalle stopped him with a slap across his face.

"Mister Gordy, did I not tell you to stand here on one leg?" the beefy nun demanded.

"Yes, Sister," the boy muttered.

"Then why did you put your leg down? Did I give you permission to do so?"

"No, Sister."

"Then why did you disobey my order?"

"Because, Sister, I thought—"

"You thought nothing, mister, nor will you think again. Am I understood?"

"But I don't want to miss class; it's geography."

"Class, Mister Gordy, is not for dandies who comb their hair in school. Now you will stand here on one leg until I say otherwise. And you will not, mister, shift legs. Am I understood?"

"Yes, Sister."

Room 204's door slammed shut, DeLasalle lumbered off to her classroom, and Gordy was left in the hall by himself, standing on one leg. He thought, after

DeLasalle had entered her classroom and closed its door, of putting his leg down and standing on both feet, but he knew that Miss Donatello and Sister Yvonne would stick their heads out their classroom doors and make sneak inspections, and if he were found to be standing on both legs, or on his left leg, he would be beaten.

Although Gordy had relished the attention he got for combing his hair in the bathroom, he was not laughing at having to stand in the hall on one leg by himself. The hall was deserted and silent while classes were in session, and being made to stand in the hall by oneself was, to the kids, something like solitary confinement. There were no buddies to talk to and laugh with, and no one to heap praise on you for your boldness. As companionship often leads to boldness and a carefree attitude, especially when pals are stoking your ego, urging you on and congratulating you, solitude sometimes has the opposite effect. You are alone with your thoughts of self-doubt, and the praising brays of your buddies, even though they came just minutes before, are a distant memory.

Gordy stood in the hall alone, afraid that his parents would be told of his hair-combing insubordination and thinking that his young life had come to an abrupt and horrible end. Had he been back in the classroom the Disturbers would have assured him of how unjust it was for him to have been punished for trying to look nice, and that even the most slavishly-respectful-of-nuns'-authority parents would see the idiocy of a child being made to stand on one leg in the hall all afternoon for combing his hair.

The moment the Disturbers hit their desks in the back row, and before Zita could mumble "Gergerphy lesson," the boys had gone into action to show support for Gordy. They whipped their eight-inch-long black barber combs out of their back pockets and, sitting in their chairs, began combing their hair in the most obvious ways, all so Zita could see them.

"You've got two hairs out of place. You look like a slob!" Ruchinski said to Kurkowski in a voice loud enough that the entire class could hear.

Kurkowski feigned shock, bolted up out of his chair and walked quickly to his left and the bank of windows that looked out onto OLG's small courtyard. He pretended a closed window was a mirror and began posturing and combing his short brown hair.

"God, I look like a pig. I can't be such a mess for gergerphy class! Ster! Do I look all right?" he shouted as he turned toward the front of the room and Zita, who was sitting in her chair behind her desk.

"You look fine, sweetie boy, as pretty as a girl," Zita spat out. "Just keep combing your hair, sweetie, and you'll get prettier by the moment. You are so pretty."

"That's good, Ster. If I keep combing, someday I'll look as pretty as you!"

The class let out a roar, which infuriated Zita. But she was determined to ignore the boys so as to not start another riot and she let the remark pass.

"Gergerphy class!" Zita said as she raised her old and creaking body out of her chair to stand. "Get out your gergerphy texts."

The Disturbers had no intention of participating in gergerphy class. They tried to never participate in any of Zita's classes. Kolba slid his chair backwards on the wooden floor, hoping the chair's four legs would make noise to further disrupt the class. He stood up, slowly slid his chair forward and began whistling and walking back and forth across the back of the room while combing his hair.

Zita could ignore that the boy was walking across the back of the room, and she could ignore that he was combing his hair, but she could not abide his whistling, which was forbidden at OLG.

"Mister Kolba, are you trying to be as pretty as Mister Kookowski?" Zita shouted to the boy.

"No, Ster," Kolba answered, continuing to pace and comb his hair.

"Then what are you doing?"

"I'm combing my hair and whistling, Ster."

"You will not whistle in my room!" Zita said, her anger building as she shuffled to the front of her desk. "What are you, a boy Lothario?"

No one in the class knew what a Lothario was, and certainly the Disturbers didn't. If they had, they would have all started whistling.

"Ster, what is a Lothario?" Kolba asked.

"Something you'll never be," Zita said with a suppressed smile.

"But Ster, you just said I was, and now you said I ain't. You just contradicted yourself."

"'Ain't', Mister Kolba, is not a word!" Zita yelled. All the nuns and lay teachers at OLG hated that word. Using it at any age and in any class was grounds for a beating. "It is not in Webster's Dictionary, and it never will be! You will use proper English in my classroom!"

Zita knew that she was once again losing control and so, before Kolba could shoot back and scold her for uttering the word ain't, she asked:

"Why are you combing your hair, sweetie?"

"Because I have an appointment after school, Ster, and I want to look nice for it."

"With whom is the appointment? Principal of the reform school?" Zita replied, chuckling again at her own wit.

"No, Ster. That's tomorrow!"

"Then who are you meeting with that you must comb your hair in my classroom?"

"With my barber, Ster. I'm getting a haircut after school, and I want my hair to be perfect for the barber. He's fussy and won't cut my hair if it's messy."

Zita grabbed her pointer, which was always on the top of her desk, and lurched forward into the attack down the room's left side. Although it was Kolba who had infuriated her, Kurkowski, who was still at the window combing his hair, was closer. She set out for him.

Bozeman and Ruchinski, who all the while had been combing their hair at their desks, launched into action. As Zita shuffled to the back of the room, they ran in the opposite direction to the front, stood in front of the class and started combing each other's hair.

The laughter that erupted from the class forced Zita into an about-face. She boiled with rage as she saw the two boys combing each other's hair while laughing and posturing. She reversed direction and started making her way to the front of the room where she hoped to savage them with the pointer. Two boys together made for a more productive beating as she could get both with one swing of the stick.

Dennis stood up and shouted: "Ster! Ster! Ster!" to get Zita's attention. "Sterrrrrr!"

The nun wheeled around and sneered, "What?"

"I know how to stop them, Ster!"

"How?"

"Make them go bald. Bald people don't comb their hair because they ain't got none!"

In the meantime, as Zita had approached him, Kurkowski fled to the room's other side, slid into the third row, leaned with an elbow on Lillian Cornell's desk and combed his hair.

Lillian stifled an embarrassed giggle, then dug into her desk, retrieved a comb and began combing her hair.

"You look so pretty," Kurkowski told her. "As pretty as a girl."

It was insanity again; Zita had no idea who to go after. She was, in fact, exhausted, not just from the afternoon's circus, but from decades of having been the butt of seventh graders' jokes and their disruptive and disrespectful ways. As she tried to keep the present riot from escalating to an even more ridiculous level, she prayed silently that the boys would for once show her some respect. After all, she thought, she was trying her best to educate them so they could go to high school, maybe even to college, and get good jobs and not be bums. She cared about the kids and wanted them to be educated. It's just that they never wanted to cooperate. Nor, she thought, did they ever consider that their disturbing and interrupting precious class time kept the other students from getting the full value of the education their parents were paying for and that she and the other nuns tried so sincerely to give. She thought they were selfish.

As she wobbled to the front of the room, Zita had decided to give up for the afternoon and sit down and hope that the riot would subside on its own. For that afternoon, she was beaten. She thought of sending one of the good kids to Yvonne's or DeLasalle's rooms for help from those nuns, but she recoiled at the idea because it would show once again that she was incapable of controlling a classroom. She knew that the other nuns had begun to question whether she should still be teaching, and she did not want to give them any evidence that that was the case. She loved to teach, and she loved the classroom when the kids behaved.

The problem for Zita, though, and the Disturbers, was that the laughter caused by their disruptions drifted down the school's second-floor hallway and into Yvonne's and DeLasalle's rooms. If those nuns heard too much laughter, they would bolt to Zita's room and punish the troublemakers.

That happened now. Yvonne became alarmed at the braying that came from Zita's room, which was across the hall from hers.

"I will be back in a moment. Bury your heads in those books. Any disruption while I'm gone will be severely punished," Yvonne told her class as she headed for the door to check on Zita.

The riot had begun to lose its steam as the Disturbers were themselves tired from laughing so long and so hard. Dennis sat down, and Kurkowski had started to make his way back to Disturbers Row. Kolba had stopped whistling but still paced the back of the room. Ruchinski and Bozeman, seeing that Zita had sat down and was no longer interested in doing battle, and that the class had stopped laughing at their hair-combing demonstration, had pocketed their combs. They were just about to start back to Disturbers Row when the round brass doorknob to Room 204's door at the front of the classroom spun around and the wood and glass-windowed door burst open. Yvonne walked in slowly and deliberately, saw the two Disturbers standing in front of the class and Kolba standing in the back and demanded:

"What goes on here? What is the meaning of this?"

There was a moment's hesitation. Bozeman, who was not quick-witted, had no idea how to respond other than to insult the nun, which he opted not to do. Ruchinski, a student and practitioner of the absurd, was thinking desperately of a believable response. He had none.

"What is the meaning of this?" Yvonne demanded again.

Kolba responded:

"Sister, we're having a contest to see who can name the most state capitals. We're the last three left standing."

It was semi-believable because it was geography class, Yvonne knew that. But to think that Disturbers were the three finalists in a class-wide academic contest made the nun realize that she was being defrauded. Sister Mary Yvonne went on the attack.

"Why the laughter, Mister Kolba? What is so funny about state capitals?"

"Nothing, Sister. It's just that some of us got some pretty easy ones wrong, and Dennis just got the easiest one wrong."

Kolba had just put his fellow Disturber on the spot, and Yvonne instantly took advantage of what she considered a huge blunder and an opening.

"Mister Domrzalski, stand. What state capital did you fail to properly identify?" she asked.

Dennis stood slowly, gripped the edge of the top of his desk with his fingers and said calmly:

"Illinois, Sister. I got that one wrong."

Although Yvonne believed she was being had, that answer left her helpless because it was so believable. The answer was consistent with Dennis's unremarkable academic career.

"So, mister, what did you answer?" she asked, still looking for an opening that would allow her to administer a beating.

"Kaskaskia, Sister. Kaskaskia."

Yvonne did not know what to think, for the answer showed some knowledge.

"And why Kaskaskia, mister?"

"Because, Sister, it was Illinois's first capital. I got it confused with Vandalia and Springfield. Kaskaskia and Vandalia were the capitals before Springf—"

"That's enough, mister," Yvonne said in an obvious fluster. Then she reversed herself and continued:

"In what year, mister, was Illinois admitted to the Union?"

"Sister, in the year 1818."

The nun was startled. She simply could not believe that Dennis knew anything at all. While he did poorly in school, Dennis read on his own, read what he wanted to and read at his own pace. He actually knew a number of things.

"And where did you learn all of this, mister?"

Dennis paused for effect, for he knew the answer would infuriate Yvonne, and then delivered the blow:

"Sister Mary Zita, Sister. She's a very good teacher."

There was nothing Yvonne could do. She considered asking Ruchinski and Bozeman to name some state capitals but decided against it for fear that they just might get one or two correct and leave her humiliated. She wasn't quite done, though, and decided to exact some revenge on Dennis.

"Mr. Domrzalski, failing to know the state capital of your own state is an embarrassment. So that you will never forget, you will go home tonight and write one thousand times: 'The state capital of Illinois is not Kaskaskia or Vandalia, but Springfield.' It will be handwritten, mister, and on Sister Zita's desk in the morning."

Dennis was angry. He hated penalties. The nuns loved them. From first grade on they liberally gave penalties to students, and those penalties always involved handwriting something fifty, a hundred or five hundred or more times. In second grade, Dennis constantly had to write out the multiplication tables. He got in so much trouble and had so many penalties, that he learned how to multiply.

Yvonne was angry, but she managed a stiff smile to the class and said, "Carry on students," and left the room. In the hall outside the door, she reminded Kenneth Gordy, who was still standing on one leg, that he risked terrible punishment if he dared put the leg down or that if he leaned his back against the wall for support.

Zita was relieved that she hadn't been caught. She relaxed and the class returned to a semblance of normality, which was shattered briefly when Zita asked Dennis what he knew about Cuba.

The Caribbean island had been the focus of Catholic school children since the Cuban Missile Crisis four years earlier. The nuns and priests denounced Cuban dictator Fidel Castro at every opportunity. Dennis read books about World War II, as well as weekly news magazines that detailed the Cold War the United States was engaged in against the Soviet Union. He had long believed that he had the solution to the Cuban problem and was honestly thrilled when Zita asked him his thoughts about the communist island.

"Ster, all we need to do with Cuba is hook it up with ropes or cables to two of our aircraft carriers, start them up and tow Cuba to the middle of the ocean where it will sink," he said earnestly and without the slightest attempt at making a joke.

"Oh sit down," Zita commanded.

The large round clock on the classroom's front wall above Zita's desk soon showed it was three in the afternoon, and just fifteen minutes away from dismissal for the day. At three, Zita stopped her gergerphy class and the students shoved their books into their desks. Zita told one of her pets to stick his head out the classroom door and tell Kenneth Gordy to come in and take his seat. The youngster, embarrassed that he had suffered such a humiliating and solitary punishment, shuffled to his seat in the fourth row with a bowed head.

The students made ready to get their wraps from the cloakroom and head home for a couple of hours of play before supper and homework.

Zita always called the students row-by-row to get their coats and jackets, and it was always an event for the Disturbers, who always stomped their feet as loud as they could when walking to the cloakroom at the side of the room. Before she began calling the rows to get their jackets, Zita called Dennis up to her desk. He walked to her as slowly as he possibly could in an attempt to annoy her further.

"Faster!" she demanded at one point. "Otherwise, mister, I will double your penalty."

Dennis had no stomach for having to write something two thousand times, but he maintained his oh-so-slow pace because he already had a plan on how to deal with the penalty.

"Yes, Ster?" he asked loudly upon reaching her desk where she sat in her chair. Turning to the class and announcing in the loudest voice she could muster, Zita said:

"Ignorance will not be tolerated in my classroom or in this school. You should have known in first grade the capital of Illinois. Your ignorance reflects poorly on your mother and father, the United States and this school. So that you never mistake the capital of this state again, I am tripling Sister Yvonne's penalty. Three thousand times, mister! Three thousand times!"

Many in the class gasped. While they believed that the Disturbers deserved their punishments, they did recognize that the nuns often crossed the line between punishment and rank abuse. They knew that a three-thousand-line penalty due the following morning was impossible, even if one prayed for help.

Zita wasn't through. She rarely missed an opportunity for revenge, and she wasn't about to here. She stood up from her chair, and with a wave of her right arm to the class, she announced:

"And it will be printed! No penmanship. I want it printed and all in capital letters! And if it is not on my desk in the morning, you will not be promoted to the eighth grade!"

There were more gasps. Printing took much longer than writing, and the kids knew that Dennis's situation was hopeless and that he could never complete the penalty. They also believed in Zita's threat of flunking Dennis for the year because she and the other nuns regularly, and with great amusement, threatened the kids with being held back.

The flourish was pure Zita. She loved large numbers and dishing out impossible and ridiculous penalties. Years earlier she had demanded of a group of troublemakers that they count the raindrops falling from the sky during a thunderstorm. No matter what number they reported, she said it was incorrect and imposed further penalties.

Hoping to aide his fellow Disturber, Kolba stood in front of his desk and shouted to get Zita's attention:

"Ster! Sterrrrr!"

"What is it now, Mister Kolba?"

"Ster, I know that Dennis deserves a long penalty. But I think this is too much."

"Why is that, sweetie?"

"Because Ster, if he has to spend all his time on the penalty, he won't be able to go to church with me after school."

"Church! Mister Kolba?" Zita asked, angered by his brazen lie.

"Yes, Ster. We were going to go to church right after school and pray six rosaries for the poor and six to end communism and so that all communists die."

"That's nice, Gary. You'll just have to pray his rosaries for him. God will appreciate your extra effort."

"But Ster, that's eighty-seven rosaries," Kolba replied, deliberately misstating the number in order to anger Zita.

"Sit down, Gary, before I call Sister Yvonne in here to see what she says about your math skills. Mister Domrzalski will have his penalty on my desk in the morning, otherwise you will all be held back at the end of the year."

Dennis calmly shuffled back to Disturbers Row. When Zita called on them to get their jackets, the five stomped their feet the hardest and loudest they had ever done.

Dennis walked home after school with Masciola and John Klosk, who lived on Springfield. Klosk was a good kid who sympathized with his friend, but who didn't have much of an imagination or any rebellious instincts.

"How are you going to write that three thousand times? That's impossible," Klosk said.

"I ain't gonna write it three thousand times," Dennis answered.

"Maybe we can find a mimeograph machine. You just write one page, and we copy the others on the machine," Masciola said.

"Or we could just set my house on fire, and that would give me an excuse to not have to do it," Dennis said.

"Or," Masciola added, "you could just say that communists stopped you on the way to school and stole it from you. They hate communists, so it might work."

"That's pretty good, but then they'd probably call the cops and they'd be hunting everywhere for communists. And why would a communist steal a penalty from me?"

"Because they hate Catholics and will do anything to get at us."

"That's a good idea, but I've got a better one," Dennis said as Klosk peeled off at Springfield and he and Masciola continued on Altgeld.

They stopped and sat against the wall of an apartment building at Harding and Altgeld and Dennis told Masciola his plan.

The plan had been inspired by Dennis's oldest brother, Wally. Four years earlier he had been in Zita's class and had gotten into trouble one day for shooting spitballs at Bruce Paizk, a chubby good kid who obeyed the nuns.

Wally had been shooting Paizk from behind from three rows back, and the tiny pieces of spit and rolled up paper had been hitting him on the back of the head and his neck. Annoyed and scared, Paizk turned to see who was shooting at him. Just as his head turned, one of Wally's spitballs hit him on the cheek just below his right eye.

"Sister! Sister Mary Zita!" the kid screamed. "Sister!"

"What is it now, Mister Paizk?" Zita demanded.

"Mister Domrzalski is shooting spitballs at me, Sister."

"Mister Domrzalski, is that true?" Zita huffed.

"Yes, Ster!" Wally replied, not even trying to hide his crime.

"Why is that?"

"Because, Ster, I don't like him," he answered defiantly.

At one level, Zita appreciated such brazenness. It was rare that a trouble-maker so boldly took credit for misbehaving. But she also recognized that such boldness was outright and open defiance. That a kid wasn't afraid of her, or of any nun or lay teacher, was the worst there could be. Kids who made excuses and tried to hide their crimes knew fear and could be controlled. Those who admitted them weren't afraid and couldn't be controlled.

And Wally Domrzalski couldn't be controlled because he had hated the nuns since his second day of kindergarten in 1955. He had walked to school with his mom. The family lived in an attic apartment on Drake Avenue near Diversey, about a half-mile away from the school, and the long walk was traumatic enough for the five-year-old. When his mom left him at school the day before, he, as did every other kid, cried and wondered why he was being left alone with strangers. He had never seen a nun, and when he saw the nun in front of the room with her black-and-white, body-length habit that obscured all but her cheeks and eyes and nose, he was terrified. He thought she was a giant bug that was going to attack and eat him, and he wanted out of the classroom. But the doors were locked, and Wally had to endure the terror of being away from his mother for the first time and of being stuck in a room with a giant bug.

Most kids wanted out of the classroom on that first day of kindergarten, and many tried to escape and run after their mothers as they walked away from the school, many of them crying as well. The moms were as saddened to have to part with their children as the kids were. As far as anyone knew, the only kid to get out after lockdown was Jack Scully, who accomplished the feat in 1958 when he squeezed out a door before the nun could grab him. Jack ran after his mom, shrieking and crying and seeking deliverance from the terrible fate of being stuck in a classroom with a nun. He caught up to his mom, who wiped the tears from his eyes with a thin cotton handkerchief, took his hand, turned around and promptly delivered him back to the scary classroom.

After getting over his initial terror that first day, Wally made a few friends and had fun playing on the slide, merry-go-round and other stuff in the classroom. The bug-like nun hadn't eaten him, and he felt a little better about being in school.

His second day was different. The kids were playing on the slide and other stuff when the nun rang a bell, signaling the end of their play time. Wally was climbing up the slide when the bell rang, and figured he'd slide down it and get back to his table.

He figured wrong.

The bell, according to the nun, meant an immediate end to play time. When it rang, the kids were supposed to stop whatever they were doing, put down whatever they were playing with, and walk quietly back to their tables. Sliding down after the bell had rung was a violation of that rule, and the nun yelled at Wally and told him that his crime, which had lasted all of three or four seconds, would be punished by two weeks of having to sit at a table by himself during play times. For the next ten days of school, when the other kids played and laughed, Wally sat by himself. Kids teased him, and he felt confused, angry, sad, humiliated, alone, friendless and like a freak.

He had never forgotten that humiliation, nor what had happened to him in fourth grade when he was preparing for confirmation. All of OLG's fourth graders were in church one afternoon, going through how and where they were to walk to the church's communion rail where they would kneel and where their foreheads would be smeared with oil by a bishop in a pointy hat and funny looking robes who would dip his thumb in a cup of oil and make a cross, or some other symbol with it on the front of their heads and declare them Soldiers of Christ.

Preparation for confirmation had taken months of studying and memorizing answers to questions about Catholic doctrine. Knowing the answers to those questions was important, the nuns said, because while the kids were kneeling at the communion rail waiting for their heads to be slathered in oil, the bishop might pop a confirmation question to them. If they got it wrong or couldn't answer, well, the bishop would shake his head in disgust, refuse to anoint the kid, and move on to someone who knew the answer.

Kids' extended families—aunts, uncles, nephews, nieces and grandparents—would be at the ceremony, and being passed up by the bishop for being stupid would have been humiliating to a kid and his or her entire family. As the kids knew from talking amongst themselves, confirmation was worth at least fifty dollars in cash gifts, stuffed into confirmation cards from the relatives. Blowing a question from the bishop and not being confirmed could mean the loss of decent money.

Wally and his buddy, Joseph Mendrick, sat next to each other on the varnished wooden pew telling each other jokes. They repeated a little song that was popular at the time with the kids:

> Whistle while you work,
> Hitler is a jerk,
> Mussolini bit his weenie,
> Now it doesn't squirt.

The two laughed themselves silly at the rhyme and figured they were cool for knowing such a racy song and for reciting it in church.

Sister Mary Dennis, a thin, humorless disciplinarian, saw Wally laughing, walked to his pew and called him out into the aisle.

"Young man, what is the meaning of this?" the nun demanded.

"Of what?" Wally responded.

That was not a good answer; it infuriated the angry nun who determined that she was going to be more severe with the boy than she had initially intended.

"You were laughing, mister. What was so funny?"

"Nothing, Sister."

That was Wally's second wrong answer and it got him slapped across the face.

"What was so funny?" the nun demanded.

"Joseph made a joke, that's all."

"What was the joke?"

"I don't remember."

"I want to hear what was so funny. Either you tell me what the joke was, or you will stand here the rest of the afternoon and all evening. What was the joke?"

Wally, figuring he'd be killed if he repeated the actual rhyme, muttered the first line as softly as he could.

"What? I can't hear you?" the nun scolded. "Say it louder!"

He repeated the line a little louder, hoping it would satisfy the nun. It didn't.

"Say it louder! I want to hear the whole thing!"

After more aborted tries, Wally repeated the entire rhyme.

The nun was furious. She yanked one of the boy's ears so hard that he thought it had been ripped off his head. He instinctively reached for the ear with one of his hands.

"Don't you dare raise a hand to me!" the woman of God warned him while slapping him with her other hand. She released his ear, curled her long, skinny fingers around the short hair on top of his head—those fingers were skinny enough to grab even the shortest of hair—and yanked his hair so violently that he thought a clump of it had been torn off his scalp. The pain was intense, and the boy reached with a hand to the top of his head.

"Do not, mister, do not raise a hand to me!" the nun said as she slapped him again. She released his hair, slapped him twice more, said, "Your father is going to hear about this," and ordered him back to his place in the pew.

Joseph Mendrick was spared an interrogation and the hair-pulling and slapping that his pal had received, but he was shaking as much as Wally was.

Fearing that Sister Mary Dennis would call his father, and that he would get a beating, Wally went straight home after school and raced up the wooden stairs to his attic where he hid out for a few hours behind an old door that leaned up against the inside of the building's pitched roof.

Zita knew that Wally's boldness had to be punished in a big way. If it wasn't stopped immediately, he might encourage other kids to openly challenge her authority, and that could not stand. She announced his punishment:

"For that, Mister Domrzalski, you will write two thousand times: 'Spitball shooters are condemned to Hell.' It will be on my desk in the morning, otherwise you *will* get the back of my hand and then some."

Although he was defiant and hated authority and challenged it head-on, Wally was smart and clever and knew how to outsmart the nuns. He had no intention of doing the penalty. He also knew that cleverness was often more effective than outright defiance. He counted the lines on his loose-leaf paper, divided that number into two thousand and determined that he needed eighty-four one-sided pages. He wrote his penalty lines on three sheets and numbered them one, twenty-seven and fifty-four. Then he gathered three pages together, went to the basement where his dad had an industrial-style stapler, stapled the pages and then used a screwdriver to remove the staple.

He got to school early the next morning and put the three sheets of paper on Zita's desk before she got into the classroom. Once class began, Zita saw the sheets, examined them and called Wally to her desk.

"Mister Domrzalski, I told you to write this out two thousand times. There are only three sheets of paper here. What is the meaning of this? Why have you refused to hand in this penalty?" Zita demanded as she waved the sheets in his face.

"I did do it, Ster," the boy pleaded. "I put it on your desk before class. There were eighty-four pages stapled together. Look Ster," he continued, pointing to the holes where the staple had been, "someone took the staple out and took all the pages. Someone's trying to get me in trouble, Ster. Look, you can see, here's page fifty-four."

Zita had been tricked. She could do nothing but wave a dry, crooked, bony index finger in the boy's face and sneer:

"You, mister, are the sneakiest of the sneaky, and even sneakier than that. Get out of here."

Dennis told Masciola, "I'm just gonna do that, you know, write out three sheets, make staple holes in them and put them on her desk. She fell for it once."

"Yeah, but she'll kill you if you do that. I think she'll remember," Masciola replied.

"I know, but I ain't gonna write that three thousand times. How am I supposed to do that?"

"I don't know. See you later," Jim said as they parted and went home.

Dennis printed three pages of his penalty, numbered the pages one, fifty-five and one hundred twenty-five, which was the last page, took them to the basement, stapled them and ripped the staple out. The next morning he put the three sheets on Zita's desk when she was distracted and not watching.

She eventually saw the sheets, took them up in her scaly hands and had an inner explosion when she realized that Dennis had pulled the same trick that his brother had pulled four years earlier. Knowing another riot would ensue if she challenged the boy, she let it go and said nothing.

Back in Disturbers Row, the others spent their morning religion class asking Dennis about the penalty. He explained what he had done, and they speculated about how severely he would be beaten, especially if Yvonne found out.

"They might kill you. I mean, really kill you," Ruchinski said breathlessly while trying to scare Dennis. "You're in big trouble, I mean, really, really big trouble. All I know is if I were you, I'd be scared, I mean really scared."

Ruchinski's attempt at upsetting Dennis went nowhere. The boy knew that Ruchinski was an instigator who had no morals. He didn't care what he instigated, or against whom, or who his troublemaking might hurt. All that mattered to him was doing something to someone whenever possible.

Dennis laughed at Ruchinski, which made the self-proclaimed King Disturber angry. Ruchinski hated it when his attempts to instigate failed or were ignored, and now he was stung by Dennis's laughter, which he took as a direct assault on himself.

"I wouldn't be laughing if I were you. Why do you think it's so funny? I mean, we're talking big trouble, especially if Yvonne finds out," Ruchinski said in another attempt to rattle his fellow Disturber.

"Maybe Zita believes me. Besides, what can they do to me, shoot me?" Dennis replied. His lack of fear made Ruchinski even angrier, and the boy lashed out in the only way he knew how.

"Sister? Oh Sister Zita," Ruchinski shouted from the back row while raising his hand. Zita guessed that something was amiss because Ruchinski had referred to her as Sister, and not Ster. His politeness indicated that he was up to no good.

"What is it, Mister Ruchinski? Is there something wrong?"

"No Sister. Nothing is wrong at all. I'm just making sure that Dennis turned in the penalty you gave him, all three thousand lines of it. I just want to make sure that he obeyed your orders, Sister."

While Zita hated Dennis, his Disturber brothers and his Disturber-breeding parents, what she hated more was a kid who was so self-centered, insecure and selfish that he needed to get others in trouble in order to make himself feel important. Zita knew a no-good sneak when she saw one.

"It's so nice of you to be so concerned. Mister, that is none of your business. Yes, he turned in the penalty. Now sit down and keep quiet."

"But did he turn in all of it, Ster? I mean all three thousand lines? That's a lot of writing to have to do in one night. I don't think anybody could do that in one night. I mean, three thousand lines?"

Before Zita could order Ruchinski to sit down and shut up, Kolba sprang to his feet and to Dennis's defense.

"Ster, I know that three thousand lines are a lot and hard to do, but not if you have God's help. Yesterday after school I prayed and asked God to help Dennis with the penalty. Ster, nothing's impossible with God."

"Thank you, Gary," Zita sputtered. "You're correct, nothing is impossible with God's help."

Ruchinski, angry that he was being challenged by a fellow Disturber, struck back:

"I think Sister Yvonne should see the penalty since she's the one who assigned it. I think she needs to see all three thousand lines. And I hope it is three thousand lines, and not two or three lines short. That would be bad. I'll go right now and ask Sister Yvonne to come and look at the penalty if you want me to, Ster."

Now Kurkowski jumped to his feet to defend Dennis and smack down Ruchinski.

"Ster, Sister Yvonne already knows that Dennis did the penalty. God has already told her. You sisters are always praying to God, and I'm sure he always answers your prayers. I'm sure he's always talking to youse."

Ruchinski couldn't abide the challenge to what he considered his authority as the self-proclaimed King Disturber, and he shot back at Kurkowski:

"I think we should ask Sister Yvonne if she knows that Dennis did his complete penalty. That's how we'll find out if God talked to her about this stuff."

Now it was Bozeman's turn to put down Ruchinski. He stood in front of this desk in the back row and addressed Zita:

"Ster, Sister Yvonne knows that Dennis did the penalty."

"How's that?" Ruchinski shouted to the fourth Disturber who had challenged him. "How?"

"Because God talks to her. If Dennis hadn't done the penalty, Sister Yvonne would have known and would have been in here already. The fact that she isn't in here is proof that Dennis did it."

Ruchinski still wasn't finished. "I don't believe it. We should ask her to take a look at it," he demanded.

Now Zita had the opportunity to embarrass and challenge Ruchinski as he had so often done to her.

"Well, sweetie, since you're the one who is so concerned about this, maybe you should be the one to tell Sister Yvonne that you don't believe that God talks to her," Zita said. "I'll go get her, and you, sweetie, can tell her in front of all of us that you think God ignores her."

That got a laugh from everyone in class but Ruchinski, who slumped into his chair beaten. His fellow Disturbers had turned on him, Zita had bested him, and he had failed to get another human being into trouble.

CHAPTER 13

Saving Naked Ladies

THE REST OF the day was quiet for the Disturbers. Dennis was grateful that Zita hadn't made a big deal out of the penalty assignment—Yvonne would have slapped him silly had she discovered his ruse—and the other Disturbers were glad that Ruchinski had been embarrassed.

Dennis walked home with Masciola and Klosk after school in the afternoon. Klosk was astonished when he heard of Dennis's penalty ruse. It was something that he would never have dared trying, and he was almost in shock that someone would have put himself so at risk by challenging any nun's authority and orders.

Masciola was thrilled that the deception had worked and was proud of his pal for having been so bold to have tried it. They had been friends since first grade and had always encouraged and supported each other in their ideas and schemes.

By second grade the two had been roaming their Logan Square neighborhood at will, walking and running to Kozciuszko Park, or Koz Park, as everyone called it, three blocks away, after school and on weekends to play baseball or just goof off.

By third grade they were crossing Pulaski Road, a busy street lined with grimy brick factories, to play at a sloping grassy knoll at the Milwaukee Road railroad tracks a block west of Pulaski. The knoll sloped upward from a small asphalt driveway toward the tracks that ran diagonally through the city from the northwest to downtown, five miles away.

To the two boys, that knoll and an empty, junk-strewn lot two blocks away that was surrounded by factories seemed like wilderness in the tightly packed city where home lots were only twenty-five feet wide and almost everything was concrete, brick, asphalt and perfectly mowed tiny lawns.

The grass on the knoll was never mowed and grew thick and high, causing kids to call it The Prairie. Any empty lot that wasn't taken care of or mowed was called a prairie by kids and adults.

When they strolled into that tall grass and climbed the knoll, Dennis and Jim were in a different place. To them, they were on the vast and empty grasslands of the Great Plains, the thick, dark, Indian-infested forests of the Northeast, the towering mountains of the American West or the battlefields of every war America had ever fought.

In the winter they were George Washington and the troops at Valley Forge fighting the British while walking barefoot and suffering from frostbite and hunger. Many a time they pretended to lop off a blackened, frostbite-ravaged toe or two. They pretended to eat bark, soup made of grass and dirt, dead horses and pieces of their stinking, shredded uniforms to stay alive.

Sometimes they were Confederate troops in the Civil War, charging the Yankees with their homemade Confederate flag and sticks they pretended were muskets, complete with bayonets. They shot, clubbed and bayoneted their way to glorious and bloody victories, leaving behind battlefields strewn with thousands and thousands of enemy corpses. They never lost a battle, they gloried in their heroics, and their imaginations never deserted them.

The empty lot by the factories was as much fun. To the boys, every one of its broken beer and soda bottles, rusting coffee cans, discarded TV sets, bricks, chunks of concrete, lumber, baby strollers, paint cans, car tires, rags, dirty blankets, newspapers, magazines, nails and other assorted garbage was an adventure and had a story behind it. The blankets, they imagined, had been left by starving Indians a hundred years prior as they tried making their way to their reservations out west.

The baby strollers had been dumped by kidnappers who had snatched babies and who the boys would hunt down and capture, while saving the babies. There were holes dug throughout the small lot, and to the boys they were foxholes from which they aimed machine guns and cannons at charging German and Japanese soldiers. The sticks they used as machine guns, and the coffee cans as cannons, as they mowed down and slaughtered each and every enemy combatant. No prisoners were ever taken.

One winter Jim and Dennis made a tent out of a couple of filthy brown blankets and two-by-fours in the lot and pretended they were Indians who were fighting off starvation and freezing while hatcheting, scalping and generally slaughtering pioneers and farmers.

They started a small fire inside the tent. It wasn't to keep warm, it was just that they liked playing with matches and starting fires. Once in third grade, the two walked the neighborhood's alleys after school. They got all the way to an alley by Monticello Avenue, six blocks away, and started a fire in front of a garage. While they were watching the blaze and enjoying their fire-making efforts, a woman's voice rang out from behind a fence:

"I see what you do! I see what you do!"

Startled, the budding arsonists did the only thing possible when caught starting fires: they ran like hell. They had to, because getting caught starting fires would have meant big-time punishment from their dads and from the nuns, who somehow would have found out.

They raced down the alley to Altgeld and then sprinted west down the sidewalk as fast as they could. The woman opened her gate and walked to Altgeld where she faced the backs of the fleeing kids while shouting, "I see what you do! I see what you do!"

When they were three blocks away, the boys turned around, figuring the lady wasn't chasing them and that they were safe. They were right, but when they turned to look back, the woman was still on the sidewalk looking at them and apparently still shouting, "I see what you do! I see what you do!"

⁓

The fire inside their tent quickly started the tent itself on fire, and the boys did the only thing they knew how to do in such a situation: they ran like hell.

THE BUDDING ARSONISTS·

Once, in the lot, the two and Dennis's older brother Steve found a discarded TV picture tube. Fascinated, the three maneuvered it into one of their foxholes and began throwing rocks at it. The first few rocks bounced off the tube's front glass and made a high-pitched ringing noise that intrigued the boys. Then Steve lobbed a brick at the tube and, KABOOM! There was a massive explosion. The picture tube had imploded and vanished. The boys didn't stick around to look for its pieces. They were scared, figured someone would catch them and call the cops and their parents. They ran like hell.

They didn't run too far, though, just down to Wrightwood and a block further to where the railroad tracks that crossed the street veered into a two-block-long industrial area that contained the Stewart's Private Blend coffee company, a foundry that made railroad car wheels and other railroad equipment, and Salt Mountain, a giant hill of salt that the city's bus and subway department, the Chicago Transit Authority, had stockpiled behind a bus barn to melt ice and snow on city streets in the winter. It was easily twenty feet tall and just as wide, and to the kids it was as white as snow and a place to play guns and army, mountain climbing, skiing and anything else their minds could think of. If it was army they were playing they'd crawl to the top, firing their pretend guns in attempts to dislodge enemy troops. Once victory was secured, they'd dig foxholes with sticks or their hands, settle in and pretend to repulse counterattacks by thousands of enemy soldiers. After those victories, they'd lie flat on the salt and then roll themselves down the mountain, pretending to be army tanks. As skiers they tried to cause avalanches, and as coal miners, they tried digging mining shafts into the dense salt.

One Saturday, Steve Domrzalski and his pal Dave Hojnacki came across an old, hand-operated railroad car that was sunk into the dirt and weeds a few feet from the railroad tracks. They were fascinated by it and imagined themselves getting the car onto the tracks and pumping their way across the country.

They spent several hours pushing and pulling the wood and steel contraption and strained their bodies trying to budge it out of the weeds, all to no success. They weren't discouraged, though, and made plans to come back the following week. Over the next several weeks the boys used two-by-fours, bricks, ropes and anything else of use they found to dislodge the car and get it onto the tracks. At one point, while using boards and bricks as a lever, the car moved a few inches and the boys hooted and screamed with joy and excitement that they would soon be on the railroad and traveling free and easy. It never occurred to their young minds what would happen if they did get the car onto the main set of tracks and a train came at them. All that mattered was getting that car onto the tracks. That three-inch victory was the only one they had after hours of working on it every Saturday for a month, and the two moved on to other adventures.

The foundry provided some of those adventures. After railroad car wheels and other parts were cast, they were set outside on blocks of steel or concrete to cool. The kids would walk between the rows of cooling steel while pretending they were hiking through baking deserts and other hot places. Some theorized that the area was as hot as Hell, and that if they were sentenced to Satan's underworld home at the end of their lives, it wouldn't be so bad.

The industrial area was littered with discarded machinery, tools, supplies, wooden boxes, metal cans and other junk that made great hiding places for the kids' stuff, including cigarettes, matches, BB guns, knives, rocks, railroad spikes and anything they didn't want their parents to know they had. The older guys hid naked-lady books and the half-drunk pints of wine or half pints of whiskey or vodka the neighborhood bums had gotten them.

Jim and Dennis's favorite game at the grassy knoll was battling Indians. They'd creep through the grass on their hands and knees and pretend to be on a ridge from which they could look down into an Indian camp. Their whispered conversations usually went something like:

"Jim, what do you see?"

"A bunch of Indians."

"How many?"

"Not sure. Ten or fifteen thousand."

"What are they doing?"

"Dancing around a bunch of poles in the ground."

"Yeah, I see. Those aren't poles, they're stakes, and they've got people tied to them. They're gonna torture or burn them to death. We've got to rescue them."

"Yeah, but we've got to figure out who the prisoners are. You got your binocs?"

"Yeah, here."

Dennis would pretend to hand Jim a pair of binoculars, which he put to his eyes in the form of the thumbs and fingers of his hands curled together to form two circles. After peering through the binocs for a moment or two, Jim would whisper:

"They're all women and they're all naked, dozens of 'em. They've got dozens of naked ladies tied to those stakes and they're going to burn them to death. We've got to rescue them!"

"But there's only two of us."

"So what. We can take 'em. Can you imagine how happy they're gonna be when we rescue them?"

With that, the boys would rise up out of the grass and charge the Indian camp while firing their pretend rifles, brandishing pretend swords and screaming that the good guys were on their way, that all enemies would die hideous deaths and that the women were saved.

They'd hack and shoot their way through all ten thousand Indians, leaving not one alive, and then untie the naked women from their stakes. And what did they do after rescuing those grateful naked women from being burned to death? They went home to eat supper.

The two never knew what to do with all those naked women once they had rescued them, but at least they knew that they should have been rescuing women and that those women should have been naked.

THE NAKED LADIES WERE GRATEFUL

CHAPTER 14

Crucify Him!

THEY HAD OTHER adventures. In fourth grade, Jim had assured Dennis that they would both get the full grace due them as a result of their confirmation and becoming Soldiers of Christ.

The two had become skilled at shoplifting, especially pens from Saxon's, a hardware and all-purpose store on Fullerton, as well as ice cream bars, soda and potato chips from Harding Drugs at the corner of Harding and Fullerton.

The drug store was on the street level of an eight-flat apartment building that contained retail space on Fullerton. The store was laid out in a way that made it easy for the young shoplifters to steal. The cash register was in the back of the store, while the soda cooler, ice cream freezer and potato chip rack were in the front, next to the entrance. The boys had their stealing routine down. They'd both walk into the store, one would get ice cream and the other sodas and they'd both grab a bag of chips. Then they'd race out, run north on Harding and into the apartment building's hallway, which wasn't more than thirty feet from the drug store's entrance. They'd walk up the stairs to a landing where no one could see them and devour their stolen snacks.

On the evening of the day before they were to be confirmed, Jim and Dennis had shoplifted ice cream, soda and chips from the drug store. Dennis was worried that because of their shoplifting they would be denied God's grace at their confirmation the following night. The kids had been told during confirmation classes that if they had any sins on their souls at the time of confirmation they would not get the expected and promised grace.

Dennis was looking forward to that grace, which he thought would blast him all at once, change him immediately and turn into a supercharged Soldier of Christ. He daydreamed about going to war on Christ's and the Church's behalf and tormenting and killing Indians and anyone else who wasn't Catholic and who refused to join the church, especially the hated and dreaded communists.

He did have some worries. He knew that stealing was a mortal sin and that his soul—which he thought of as a kind of brightly shining sun or moon inside his chest—was now totally black with sin. He feared being denied that grace and asked his shoplifting partner about it.

"We're supposed to get all this grace at confirmation, but we won't get it because we've got sins on our souls," Dennis said. "What we gonna do? We ain't ever gonna get this grace."

"Yeah we will," Jim replied, taking a huge bite out of his pilfered ice cream sandwich, "but not right away. That grace is gonna be held back until we go to confession. Once we confess that we've been stealing, we'll be forgiven. And when we're forgiven all that grace will hit us at once. It's kind of like we've got it in reserve. So don't worry about it, just go to confession."

"Wow. Okay. That's all we gotta do?" Dennis replied in obvious relief. "Jeeze, we should go steal some more stuff. If all we gotta do is go to confession, that's a pretty good deal."

One of their greatest adventures also occurred in fourth grade and was inspired by the Catholic Church and the nuns.

One Friday, while Jim and Dennis were walking home for lunch, Daniel Bernas, a kid who lived two doors down from Dennis, and whose dad raised pigeons in a space underneath his home's covered back porch, wanted to walk with them. The two agreed at once that they didn't want to walk with Daniel, who merely wanted someone to walk with and talk to. They told the kid to get lost and that he couldn't walk with them. When Daniel persisted, they crossed the street to the other side of Altgeld. Daniel followed, which annoyed them.

To show their annoyance, Dennis and Jim crossed back to the other side of the street. Daniel followed, at which point the two boys ran to get away from the kid who wanted their company and friendship. They parted at the alley between Springfield and Harding with the words that Daniel would need to be punished for trying to be their friend.

On the walk back home after school in the afternoon, Daniel again tried to walk with the two boys. They grew even more annoyed and determined to make him pay for wanting their company. They discussed and agreed on the proper punishment, and at the alley parted with the words, "See you back here in fifteen minutes."

After changing into their play clothes, which were old, worn-out school clothes, or hand-me-downs from their older brothers that didn't fit well, Jim and Dennis met at the alley and started on their plan of terrible retribution. They went to Dennis's basement, which was loaded with his dad's tools and building materials—hammers, nails, wrenches, vices, pipe cutters, screws, screwdrivers, pliers, levels, straightedges, saws, hand and electric drills, rose clippers, hedge shears, rope, string, wire, electrical tape, light bulbs, rakes, shovels, oil, grease and pretty much everything a man needed to take care of his home. They took a hammer, saw, garden spade and a pocket full of nails and began roaming the alleys for what they needed most: lumber.

There were plenty of discarded two-by-fours and other wood by the fifty-five-gallon metal garbage cans that stood guard to people's back yards by the alleys. The men in the working-class neighborhood were tireless workers who did their own home repairs and remodeling. Dennis's dad, George, had transformed their wooden, two-flat frame house that had been built in 1886 into something that resembled a modern 1950s home.

George Domrzalski had smashed the old coal furnace in their basement to pieces with a sledgehammer one summer, hauled the debris out to the garbage cans, paid the garbage men five bucks to take it away and installed a new, natural gas furnace and a system of water-heated radiators. Another summer, his dad and uncles took sledgehammers to the back yard's sidewalk, ripped it out and poured a new one.

The home at 2511 N. Harding as originally built was a fire hazard. The old-fashioned electrical wires were wrapped in cloth, not rubber insulation, and not housed in metal conduit. That was fixed one summer when George and Dennis's Uncle Benny ripped out all the old wiring, installed new wiring in conduit and replaced the house's old fuse box with a modern circuit-breaker box.

As if he didn't have enough work at his job building airbrushes at the Paasche Airbrush factory near Clybourn and Diversey avenues, George decided one summer to enclose the home's wooden back porch. Again, relatives were called in, and in a couple of weeks they had sheathed the entire back porch area with wood, windows and siding.

When George got tired of his old garage, he took a sledgehammer to its wooden walls and concrete floor and paid the garbage men to haul it away. He didn't build a new garage himself, though. In a rare moment of what his kids considered sanity, he actually paid for a new, two-car garage to be built.

George had torn out much of the first-floor apartment's plaster and oak china cabinets and woodwork and replaced it all with plasterboard and modern, fake-wood paneling. He remodeled the kitchen and bathroom, installed new cabinets, built a modern pantry and new closets, laid down new linoleum, tiled the bathroom, installed glass-block windows in the basement and did his own plumbing. In the backyard he chopped down trees, dug up rows of hedges, mowed grass with a push mower and replanted grass every year. When he wasn't working on his own house, George helped relatives fix their homes.

Within thirty minutes, Dennis and Jim had all the wood they needed, and they dragged the pieces to the front lawn of the apartment building at Altgeld and the alley where they set to designing, sawing and hammering. In another half hour they had completed their masterpiece: a cross. The two kids, in the finest Catholic tradition, were going to nail Daniel Bernas to a cross.

The plan had been hatched on the walk home from school that afternoon when Daniel had again tried to walk and talk with them.

"I can't stand this kid," Jim said.

"Neither can I," Dennis added.

"We gotta do something to him."

"I know, but what?"

The words came without hesitation out of both of their mouths at once: "Crucify him!"

That seemed like a perfectly logical solution to the boys. They were in their fifth year at OLG, and every school day of those five years they had sat at their desks and gazed upon large crucifixes affixed to the walls above the nuns' and lay teachers' desks. It was the same when they went to mass on Sundays, except more so. In church they were confronted by huge crosses everywhere with Jesus nailed to them. Their religion books and their Sunday missals, with the Stations of the Cross, always showed Romans nailing Jesus to a cross. Jesus was always in excruciating pain and agony on those crosses, and blood always dripped from his hands, feet and side. To many OLG kids, based on what the nuns had taught them and how they had acted, there were only a few ways to punish people: by beating them with wooden pointers and rungs of chairs for minor offenses, and for major transgressions, crucifying them.

As Dennis and Jim saw it, Daniel's desire to befriend them was a major crime. If Jesus could be nailed to a cross, so could Daniel Bernas.

The boys stood their cross up and leaned it against the thick trunk of a cottonwood tree and admired their work. It was about five feet tall and sturdy enough to hold a kid. And like the crosses in church and school, it had a wooden foot pad to which they could nail Daniel's feet.

"Okay, we gotta dig a hole so we can stand this thing up in," Jim said. "And it's gotta be deep."

While Dennis was digging, he realized that they were missing something that was crucial to Daniel's punishment.

"We don't have a crown of thorns," he said.

"Shit. Where we gonna get one of those?" Jim asked while realizing the seriousness of their omission. "We gotta have a crown of thorns. It's required."

THEY WERE GOING TO CRUCIFY HIM

"I know. There's a rose bush in my yard," Dennis said with the enthusiasm of someone who has just solved a terrible problem. "The branches got thorns. We'll cut some of the branches and make them into a crown."

That too seemed logical, and the boys rushed to Dennis's basement four doors away, found his dad's rose clippers and set about destroying a perfectly trimmed rose bush.

Back at their cross, they tried to twist and braid the woody rose stems into a crown, but it wasn't working. The stems barely bent, the thorns repeatedly pierced their bare hands and they quickly gave up on the project.

Dejected, they sat down on the curb and talked about the setback.

"How we gonna crucify him without a crown of thorns?" Jim asked.

Dennis was glum and didn't answer. But after a moment or two he jumped to his feet and proclaimed: "We'll just tie some nails to a string and pound the nails into his head!"

"Yeah! Okay!"

They made another trip to Dennis's basement for string and more nails and soon had their strange, but acceptable, crown of thorns.

Their next step was to go to Daniel's house two doors away, call him out to play, lure him to the cross and nail him to it. Dennis was a little hesitant.

"Maybe we should just tie him to the thing instead of nailing him to it. Ain't the nails gonna hurt him?" he asked his partner.

"Naah. Don't you remember this stuff? The nuns said that the Romans didn't break any bones in Jesus's hands with the nails. From the pictures, it looks like they used pretty fat nails. Ours ain't half that fat. We won't break any bones in his hands."

"How about his feet?"

"I don't know. We can just tie his feet."

Cheered by the news that nailing Daniel to a cross wouldn't break the bones in his hands, Dennis led the race to Daniel's backyard. They rang the doorbell to his covered back porch. His mother peered out from behind a white curtain that covered the door's small window and asked what the boys wanted.

"Can Daniel come out and play?" they asked.

"Why do you want to play with him?" his mother asked.

"Because," they answered.

"'Because' is no answer. He can't come out. He has homework to do. Go away."

"Please let him come out. We want to play and we've got a big surprise for him," Jim said, not willing to give up.

"What kind of surprise?"

"A big one."

"No. Go away."

The boys shuffled dejectedly out Daniel's back yard, into the alley and onto Altgeld and their cross. They sat on the curb and tried to figure out what to do next.

"Let's just hide this thing between some garages, and next time we see him we'll get it out and nail him to it," Dennis offered.

"Good idea. I gotta get home anyway for supper. I'll meet you here after supper."

It wasn't to be.

It was Friday evening, shopping day for Dennis's family. This meant a drive to the A&P grocery store on Diversey near Milwaukee Avenue in the heart of Logan Square's shopping district. Dennis's dad and ma pulled up to the corner in their 1962 blue Chevy Impala four-door sedan.

George saw the cross, his hammer, saw, rose clippers and nails scattered around the lawn and was outraged. He cherished and loved his tools and kept them clean and rust-free and knew where every single tool was in his basement. He hated it when the kids used them because they usually ruined or lost them. Seeing his tools scattered on a lawn four doors down from his home simply enraged him and made him wonder to himself why he had bothered to have kids at all because all they did was ruin and lose things, cost money and cause trouble. He rolled down the car's front window and yelled:

"What the hell are youse doing? What goes on here?"

"We're just building a cross," Dennis answered.

"Why?"

The boys hadn't thought about how they would answer that question had any of the adults who walked past them on the sidewalk bothered to ask what they were doing and why they were building a cross.

Dennis was about to answer "Because," which would have gotten him hit, when his quick-witted pal stepped forward.

"Sir," Jim started as he stood stiff and in front of the car window, a sign that he was showing respect to a grownup, "it's because we want to practice the Stations of the Cross. We figured a real cross would make it holier. We're gonna carry it on our shoulders."

"Are you kids crazy?" George said as he buried his face in one of his hands and shook it in disbelief. He raised his head—reluctantly so, for he was aghast at seeing his precious tools scattered about, and because he didn't believe the kids and didn't even want to think about what crazy things they were up to—and shouted to Dennis:

"Get in the car and get those tools in here."

Dennis gathered up the tools, laid them on the car's back floor and slouched dejected and humiliated in the car's back, bench-like seat.

Two hours later, after having finished shopping, the blue Impala pulled into the alley at Altgeld. Out of the backseat window Dennis could see that the cross was still standing upright against the tree. He was thrilled that it was still there, that it could be saved and that one day soon he and Jim would be able to crucify Daniel Bernas.

Early the next morning Dennis raced out the door and down the alley to Altgeld. The cross was gone. He ran to Jim's house, called him out and they talked about their bad luck. They wouldn't be able to make a new cross any time soon because George had given strict orders that Dennis not use his tools ever again. Dennis knew that violating that order, at least for a couple of weeks, would get him whipped with a belt.

The boys found something else to occupy their active minds, and in an hour had long forgotten about wanting to nail Daniel Bernas to a cross.

CHAPTER 15

Parent-Teacher Conference
and Trouble

FTER THEY FINISHED talking about the great penalty ruse
and how Dennis had outsmarted Zita, Dennis and Jim split at the
alley on Altgeld and made plans to do something after supper. It was
September, it still stayed light for a while after supper, and as it was a Friday,
the kids didn't have much homework. That didn't really matter to them though,
as they rarely gave their homework the time and attention the nuns and their
parents demanded. To the boys, homework was an annoyance that interrupted
their lives and had to be completed quickly so they could go outside and play
and have adventures, and now that they were older, smoke cigarettes.

Dennis's homework habits, according to the nuns and lay teachers, were
those of someone who would never amount to anything in life. Because discipline and beatings didn't correct the problem, he would always be someone
to be pitied and prayed for. Whatever he learned in class he had forgotten
by the time it was homework time. Math confused him, except for simple
addition, multiplication and long division. Word problems scrambled his
brain, so did having to diagram sentences for English homework. He knew
what subjects and predicates were, and even verbs and adjectives, but when

it came to prepositional phrases, subordinate clauses, adverbs and metaphors and similes, he was hopelessly lost.

In fourth grade, his homework habits were put on full display to his parents by his teacher, Miss Florence Sturgis, during the school year's first parent-teacher conference.

Most OLG kids dreaded the parent-teacher conferences because they usually meant a beating when the parents returned home in angry moods after being told that their kids, depending on what grade levels they were in, were talkers, daydreamers, troublemakers, hoodlums, whores, Sunday mass dodgers, sneaks and sinners; individuals who, were they older, would deserve immediate excommunication.

During the first parent-teacher conference of seventh grade, the first words that Ruchinski's ma heard from Zita's mouth were, "What is the matter with your son?" The nun then went on to explain that Mrs. Ruchinski's son was a hopeless, degenerate hoodlum who belonged in reform school.

Dennis didn't think much about what Miss Sturgis would tell his parents that night. He was a daydreamer for whom reality was an insane and ridiculous world that he didn't understand and that everyone else but he lived in. He never understood the trouble he could get into, or usually was in. He had run out the back door that evening around seven and into the alley to find someone to play with when he saw his ma and dad walk into the alley from Altgeld on their way home from the meeting with Sturgis.

In his usual oblivious manner, Dennis walked up and said hello to his parents with his innocent smile. Neither of them was smiling, though, and the boy, knowing something had to have happened to put them in a foul mood, asked, "What's wrong? Have you guys been robbed or something?"

"Get in the house!" his dad barked, "and get in there now!"

Dennis obeyed and beat them into the house and into the living room and sat in front of the TV set. By then, he had figured that something had gone wrong at the parent-teacher meeting, but he had no idea what.

The kitchen door opened and Dennis waited nervously in front of the TV while his parents put their coats in the closet.

After a few moments his dad yelled, "Get in here!"

The boy shuffled down the home's narrow hallway, past the bathroom and past his parents' bedroom and into the kitchen where both parents sat at the kitchen table. Lying on the table was a gray cardboard folder emblazoned on the front with a picture of Our Lady of Grace School.

"Sit down!" his dad ordered.

Dennis pulled one of the vinyl covered kitchen chairs out from the table and sat down. His dad flipped open the folder, pulled a sheet of lined, loose-leaf paper out from one of its pockets and laid it on the table in front of the boy.

"What the hell is this?" his dad demanded, almost unable to speak.

Dennis's heart began pounding as he picked up the paper. It was his one of his homework assignments from a few weeks prior, English to be exact. There were six sentences scratched onto the paper. The sentences, it was clear, had been hastily and sloppily scrawled. Some took up two lines, others were on a slant, and some were so small as to be unreadable.

While that in itself was cause for fury on his dad's part, there was something else about them that enraged him. Every sentence was written in a different color ink—red, green, black, brown, blue and purple. Reality had intruded into Dennis's world.

The homework had been done quickly one night during the commercials of several TV shows. During those breaks, Dennis raced to his brown leather school bag, behind the dining room table in the dark, opened his loose-leaf notebook inside the bag, and scribbled the sentences secretly and quickly so as to be able to run back to the TV once the commercials ended.

There was a reason he had done his homework that way that night, and especially for the secrecy. That afternoon on the way home from school, he and Masciola had shoplifted packs of different colored pens from Saxon's. Dennis had been dying to use the pens, but he knew that if he had done his homework at the dining room table where he usually did it, and if he'd had that pack of stolen pens out, his parents would have demanded to know where he had gotten them. He had no job and no allowance, so he couldn't have said that he had bought them. Saying that he had gotten them from another kid at school might have prompted his parents to call the other kid's parents to corroborate the story. So Dennis had kept the pens hidden in his school bag and used a different colored one that night to write each sentence in secret.

"What is the meaning of this?" his dad demanded.

"It's my homework," the boy shrugged, still a bit oblivious to the situation, but in touch with reality enough to know that he couldn't dare say that he had stolen the pens.

"Why did you write them in different colored ink?" his dad shouted.

"I don't know. I just wanted to see what it would look like."

"Where did you get colored pens?"

"I don't know. Someone must have gave them to me."

"Who?"

"I don't know, a kid."

"Which kid?"

"I can't remember. There are a lot of them."

George Domrzalski knew that he would never get any information out of Dennis. Like the nuns, he thought his son was slow, or a bit crazy, and that further questioning would be useless and frustrate and anger him more.

"You're not going out to play for a week. You're gonna do your homework at the dining room table after supper every night where I can see you and I'm going to check it all. Now get out of here."

Dennis knew he had gotten off easy. Being unable to go outside and play for a week was a penalty that would be enforced for one day, he knew. It was the mothers in the neighborhood that raised the children and enforced most of the discipline. The fathers couldn't because they were at work during lunch and after school when the kids came home. Mothers, most all the kids knew, were more forgiving and not likely to keep kids in the house for days at a time. Dennis knew that his ma probably wouldn't even make him stay in for a day. She would let him out after school, but warn him to be home by four-forty-five in the afternoon when his dad got home from work.

CHAPTER 16

Paper Routes and Imagined Heroics

D ENNIS AND JIM made plans to meet after supper that day, and
not after school, because Dennis had a paper route that took up his
after-school play time. He'd had it since the start of fifth grade when
he was nine. He inherited it, delivering forty to fifty copies of the Chicago
Daily News and a few copies each of two Polish-language newspapers, to
homes, apartments and businesses from Fullerton to Diversey, and from
Springfield to both sides of Pulaski, from his brother Steve, who had quit it
to take a more lucrative morning route that had more than a hundred papers,
both the Chicago Tribune and the Chicago Sun-Times.

Dennis both hated and loved the paper route. He hated it because it took
away from his play time after school. While the other kids were goofing off
after school, he was pulling his ma's two-wheeled wire shopping cart around
and delivering newspapers to, as his dad repeatedly said, "make a buck."

He made only fifteen of those bucks a month, but the hour or so that it took
him to walk the route Monday through Saturday was pure joy. He was alone, no
one would bother him, and he could spend sixty minutes each day daydreaming.

His favorite spot on the route was on Parker Avenue on the west side of
Pulaski where he delivered one paper to a home down a block that fascinated
him. It was an industrial area with stamping, plating and paint factories. A

three-story red brick plating factory stood on one corner of Pulaski and Parker, and the Seven Brothers moving company on the other. To call the moving company, said an advertisement painted on its brick wall, all one had to do was "Dial 7, 7 times."

There were only five or six homes on the block, all but one of them on its south side. The home that he delivered to was the only one on the north side, and Dennis wondered why there weren't more houses there. He thought that maybe they had burned down—perhaps in the Great Chicago Fire of 1871—or had otherwise been destroyed. He knew that had to be the case because on the several, now-empty lots on that side of the street were old crumbling and buckling sidewalks that led to where the homes had once been. He imagined that those long-gone homes had housed pioneers or gangsters, or old people who had died in their sleep and who now haunted the empty lots, or scary old guys who chased kids and kept them prisoner in their basements.

He wondered how people could live on such a block, as it was mostly factories, and because it was surrounded by an industrial area and isolated from the residential neighborhoods east of Pulaski. He wondered who the kids on the block played with because there could not have been many of them in those five or six homes.

The house that Dennis delivered to was run down. It was a one-story wooden home that leaned to one side. The wooden front porch had long ago lost its gray paint and was separated from the home's front wall. The front windows were dirty and never open, not even on the hottest and most humid and sticky summer days, and in several places the asphalt shingles on the roof had blown away to reveal the roof's boards.

Dennis figured the place had to be at least a hundred years old. He imagined what the neighborhood had been like back then, before the factories, and what the people who lived there did. He saw them riding horses, building fires in their fireplaces for heat in the winter and to cook their food all year long, and shooting Indians with muskets, and maybe having a cow or two in the back yard. He thought the home was haunted, or at least inhabited by extremely old, ugly and scary people who would kidnap and torture him. He imagined being held captive in the dark, dank basement in a jail cell with steel bars, his old and ugly captors bringing him bowls of watery soup for breakfast, lunch and dinner, and that he would never see daylight again. He never stopped to think about why someone on the block would kidnap him or other kids, or if they did, how the cops never found out. Nor did it occur to him that no kids in the neighborhood had ever been reported missing. His mind raced, and to him, every old and decrepit building was haunted or filled with old people or kidnappers.

KIDNAPPERS LIVED THERE

Being kidnapped wasn't a mere fantasy dreamed up by kids with over-active imaginations or paranoid parents. It happened occasionally, and when it did it made the front pages of the city's newspapers so all could read about it and sputter in anger, sadness and disbelief.

Wally Domrzalski had almost been kidnapped in 1953. He was three years old and playing with a red fire truck on the sidewalk outside the family's attic apartment on Drake Avenue. He had been told to never talk to strangers, but three-year-olds don't always do what they're told.

It was in the late afternoon and a man in a dark trench coat and gray fedora approached Wally as he played. Before he knew it, Wally was following the man down the sidewalk toward Schubert Avenue to a corner store that sold groceries and candy. As they neared the store, the man asked the boy if he wanted money for candy. Wally said he did. The man said the money was in his car and that he'd have to open the door to the car, which was parked on the street near the store. The man opened one of the car doors and went to get money.

A few moments earlier, the boy's Aunt Sophie, who lived in the same building and who was coming home from work, had gotten off the bus at Diversey and Drake, more than a hundred yards from Schubert. Something told her to look down the street. When she saw her little nephew so far from his house with a man, she started running and screaming, "Walter! Walter! Walter!" The would-be abductor heard the wild shrieks and turned to look up the block. He saw Aunt Sophie running towards him and screaming, and he quickly put fifty cents in Wally's' hand, said, "Here's your money. Go buy some candy," jumped in his car and sped away. Wally always remembered the incident, and he rarely laughed when other kids joked about adults kidnapping kids. He knew it could happen.

Old people had scared Dennis since before kindergarten when he met his aunt Nana, a pale, shriveled, mean, gray-haired old lady who was his grandmother's sister and who lived in the apartment next to her on Drake near Diversey.

Nana smelled, of what Dennis didn't know, and she was strange. When the family visited the apartment, the kids often asked for milk, which Nana gave them only after heating it up in a pot on her kitchen stove. "You've got to take the chill out of it," the old lady would mumble to the horror of the kids who thought that drinking warm milk was the same as swallowing poison.

Whenever one of them was sick, no matter if it was a cold, headache, fever, cough, scratch or the mumps, Nana administered tablespoons of castor oil.

"You've got to coat that stomach," she would say while forcing a kid to swallow the remedy.

Once, when Wally had a cough, Nana gave him the hated castor oil treatment saying it would coat the boy's lungs. Even the kids knew that swallowing castor oil would coat the stomach, not the lungs, and they questioned the medical wisdom of coating lungs with oil.

The old lady never let the kids have soda, and she never let them watch TV. While in her apartment they were supposed to sit quietly on the couch. They might as well have been in school with the nuns.

Nana scared Dennis enough in life, but in death she scared him even more. At her wake, Dennis was made to kneel in front of her coffin and pray. He couldn't do it. The sight of a body lying stiff and not breathing or moving terrified him. He couldn't deal with it and walked away from the coffin. That angered his grandmother and others who demanded that he touch the corpse.

The boy resisted and said he didn't want to. How could he? She was dead, stiff and scary. They demanded again and he refused. Again the demand was repeated and again the boy refused. Finally, a family member grabbed one of his hands, dragged him to the coffin and placed it on the corpse's folded, cold, wrinkled hands. Dennis screamed, escaped the grasp and ran out of the funeral home. For weeks after that he had nightmares about dead people. No, he did not like oldsters.

Dennis never got too close to that run-down house on Parker for fear that someone would jump out from behind the front door and chase him. He threw the folded and rubber band-bound paper onto the porch from ten feet away, wheeled around and ran as fast as he could until he was halfway down the block, where he felt safe enough to walk again.

It was a gravel parking lot behind the plating factory that gave Dennis the most joy on the route. When he passed it on his way to and back from the haunted house, he entered a world of athletic stardom and beautiful girl-friends. To Dennis, that gravel lot became a baseball and football stadium with stands and seating for tens of thousands, and a field of lush, green grass where he was the greatest baseball and football player of all time.

In the summers on that field he pitched no-hitters and perfect games, hit grand slams by the hundreds, made impossible diving and leaping catches, threw out the speediest base runners with ease and led his team to victory in every game in which he played.

Many of his perfect games as a pitcher were truly perfect because every opposing batter he faced he struck out. No pitcher, he knew, had ever recorded twenty-seven strikeouts in a game, and he did it with regularity. He imagined the newspaper headlines after those truly perfect games, his picture splashed all over the front pages and the cheers, adoration and beautiful girlfriends that came with it.

HIS IMAGINED STADIUM

As a batter he hit line drives so hard that they ripped the mitts off the hands of players who tried to catch them and broke their bones. After a while, opposing players ducked or otherwise got out of the way of his fearsome line drives. His home runs were so powerful and long that they landed four or five blocks away. He started triple plays to save his team from defeat, and he routinely came up to bat in the bottom of the ninth inning of the seventh and deciding game of the World Series with his team down by three runs, the bases loaded and two outs. For fun in those situations, he let himself get two strikes, and then, when the opposing pitcher fired a fastball, he smashed it out of the park for a grand slam and victory. The crowds cheered deliriously and chanted his name as Dennis was paraded around the field on the shoulders of his grateful teammates. And always in those stands of wildly cheering and adoring fans was a beautiful girl who loved him.

In the fall and winter the grass was chalked into a football gridiron where Dennis made the greatest plays that football had ever seen. On defense he intercepted passes, most of them in the end zone, and ran them back for touchdowns, evading all eleven opposing players with a speed, grace and fluidity of movement that left all in the stands gasping in wonder and delight. He tackled opposing players so hard that their helmets flew off and they fumbled the ball, which Dennis always picked up and ran in for touchdowns.

In every game, any player who Dennis tackled was so hurt and traumatized by the hit that they left the game immediately and never returned.

On offense, Dennis was a halfback whose moves were so astounding that opposing players often stopped trying to tackle him because they were so awed by his grace, speed and moves that they just wanted to watch the greatest halfback who had ever played the game.

On many of those open field running plays, Dennis faced two opposing tacklers who were about to hit him from different directions. Just as they launched themselves at him, though, he cut and changed directions, essentially vanishing, and the two tacklers collided and knocked themselves out while Dennis scampered downfield to another of his thousands of touchdowns.

There were times, though, when even Dennis's amazing talents couldn't keep his team from being down by five points in the last two seconds of a game and at their own one-yard-line of the hundred-yard field. Some of those other teams were pretty good, and in his mind, Dennis acknowledged it, knowing that last-minute, game-winning heroics always made the fans crazy with joy.

Dennis had run the play a hundred times in his mind. With two seconds left and ninety-nine yards to go for the six-point, game-winning touchdown, he took the handoff from the quarterback, ran to his right to get around the end, only to find that several defensive players had strung the play out and closed off the corner. Two massive defenders blocked his way up the middle, but that was no big deal to the world's greatest halfback. If he couldn't go around the defenders, he'd go through them, sort of. He made two seemingly simultaneous head fakes, one to the left and one to the right, and the two defenders who blocked his way both fell for them at once, meaning they launched themselves in opposite directions, one to the left and the other to the right, leaving a giant hole for Dennis to glide through and start his run up field and toward the end zone ninety-nine yards away. The crowd and sports announcers gasped at the move, as it was like the parting of the Red Sea. No one had ever seen anything like it. It was the greatest move in football history. The crowd screamed as one, hoping their combined energy and thirst for victory would help propel the halfback forward and into the end zone.

Dennis was now beyond the line of scrimmage and into the open field, where it was much more difficult to bring him down. Other tacklers readied to smash the gazelle-like back and pound him into the turf with the game-winning tackle. Each time they were about to throw their bodies, head and shoulders first, at Dennis's legs—a sure way to tackle a runner in the open field—he delivered yet another astonishing fake at precisely the right moment. The defenders flung themselves through the air, their arms outstretched and ready to lock around Dennis's legs. And when they reached the point where his legs should have been, there was nothing! He was long gone. It was as if they had hurled themselves at an apparition! The defenders crashed to the turf and pounded their fists in desperate agony into the grass, knowing they had once again been humiliated in broad daylight and in front of the world by the greatest halfback ever.

Dennis glided down and zigged and zagged across the field. He imagined the radio announcer screaming himself hoarse while describing his run:

"Oh my God! What a move! What a move! He deked right and left and split two tacklers like Moses parted the Red Sea! Only this is better! There's no time left on the clock! He's at the thirty, the thirty-five, forty, forty-five. Gronkowski has an angle on him from behind. He's about to get Domrzalski from behind. Oh my! Domrzalski reverses direction and leaves him tackling air! He's got eyes in the back of his head, I tell you! He's at the fifty, across midfield. Defenders are throwing themselves at him left and right. Domrzalski stiff-arms Brunatelli and sends him to the turf. Abrams launches himself at Domrzalski and bounces off his thighs. This man is made of steel! He's got two people to beat. Gaskow's got an angle on him on the far sideline. He rolls into him. Oh my God! Oh my God! Domrzalski hurdles over him! He leaped seven feet into the air! Domrzalski cuts back to midfield. He's at the forty, the thirty-five. There's only one man left! The fans are going crazy, absolutely crazy! The noise is deafening. I can't hear myself talk and this stadium is shaking. The rafters are starting to vibrate and twist because of all this noise! It just might collapse!"

There was always only one man left on those plays, and he was always as great a tackler as Dennis was a runner. He had to be, for fairness and for the drama of it all. It would not have been as exciting or as glorious if Dennis scampered those last thirty-five yards into the end zone untouched. No, drama and even more unbelievable heroics were called for, and Dennis had them. He imagined the announcer going absolutely insane for the final few yards of his run:

"There's only one man left, one man to beat for this to be the greatest run in football history and to bring the championship once again to Chicago! Can he do it? Will he do it? The entire city, four million people, is counting on Domrzalski! He's at the thirty-five with only Gorgonski, the greatest tackler in the world, to beat. He dekes left, he dekes right, he dekes again, but Gorgonski isn't fooled! He's got Domrzalski's left ankle. He can't escape. It's like he's caught in a bear trap. Domrzalski starts dragging Gorgonski. He's at the thirty. Phillips has come from behind to try to bring Domrzalski down. He jumps on Domrzalski's shoulders. Domrzalski keeps running! He's dragging Gorgonski and carrying Phillips! No! No! Three more defenders are now on top of him! They're trying to push him backward to stop his forward progress and end this game. There are eleven men trying to bring him down! He's at the twenty and he won't go down! The pile keeps moving forward! The pile is at the fifteen! Now Domrzalski's teammates have caught up and are trying to tear the defenders off him. Some are trying to push him from behind! Can he make another fifteen yards with eleven men trying to stop him and another ten piled on top of him?

"People are fainting in the stands. I can't see Domrzalski, but he's in there because the pile keeps moving forward. He's at the thirteen, the twelve, eleven, ten, nine, eight, seven. How can he be carrying and dragging twenty-one men? Domrzalski must be Superman! The pile is at the five. It's at the four and almost not moving. Oh, to come so far and to be so magnificent, only to be stopped so close to the goal. It appears to be at the three-and-a-half-yard line. It's up to the three and barely moving! If they stop his forward progress it's over. Over! If he can just move forward an inch at a time! A half inch at a time! A quarter inch at a time!

"I can't see what's going on inside the pile, but it must be hell for Domrzalski. They've got to be doing everything to bring him down—beating him, battering him, biting his arms, grabbing his legs, tripping and kicking him and trying to strip the ball lose! They might even be calling him names and criticizing him!

"The pile has moved to the two-and-a-half-yard line. Domrzalski keeps churning away. There's a rut in the grass behind the pile. It's six inches deep. It's from Domrzalski's cleats pounding that turf and pushing forward with the might of a god and pushing and grinding and churning. Now there's dirt and grass flying out from behind the pile of twenty-two men! Domrzalski's legs are churning away at the turf like a super-charged rototiller! Domrzalski won't quit!

"The pile has inched forward to the two-yard line! It's at the one-and-a-half-yard line and it, it, it appears to have stopped! Domrzalski's legs are churning like crazy. He's a madman in there. It's good that his legs are moving, but if he's just digging himself a hole and not making forward progress, the refs are going to have to blow this play dead!

"The ref has put the whistle to his mouth! He's gonna call the play dead at the one-and-a-half-yard line! What heartbreak! What heartbreak! He's about to blow that whistle—Oh my god!! Oh my god!!! Oh my god!!!!! Touchdoooooooooown!!! Touchdoooooooooown!!! Domrzalski squirted out from the front of the pile at the one-and-a-half-yard line and tumbled into the end zone! It's a touchdown! Chicago wins the championship! Chicago wins the championship! Chicago wins the championship!

"But wait! Oh my! Domrzalski has no clothes on! Everything's been torn off—his shoes, socks, pants, jersey, shoulder pads and helmet. What a battle it was! He's got nothing left on but his athletic supporter and protective cup! His nose is bleeding! There are gashes in his arms and legs, and clumps of his hair are missing! How brutal it must have been in there!

"The fans are going crazy, absolutely crazy. They're chanting 'Domrzalski! Domrzalski! Domrzalski!' They want him to take a bow and celebrate. But no. Domrzalski hands the ball to the referee and signals to his bench that he needs a robe or an overcoat! What modesty! Such humility! Such greatness! Domrzalski is the city of Chicago's greatest hero of all time!"

Dennis imagined the praising headlines in the next day's papers, the breathless descriptions of his heroic run and pictures of the ruts he had made with his cleats. And he imagined beautiful women all over the city thinking he was the greatest guy of all time.

Dennis would linger in front of that lot behind the plating factory and play out his fantasies, and when he was done, he'd walk, exhausted, back across Pulaski to where he had left his shopping cart full of newspapers on the sidewalk in front of a factory and continue his route, eventually coming to one of the favorite places for kids—at least boys—in the neighborhood: Charlie Fox's Shell gas station. On hot, muggy summer days the small gas station was an oasis for kids who had money because of its soda machine that kept the bottles ice-cold. But the station offered another attraction that caused the boys to detour to it whenever possible: a naked-lady calendar, in color, on a grimy, oily wall of Fox's small, messy, dirty office.

THE GREATEST HALFBACK EVER·

To the kids, it seemed that the full-busted, beautiful women with bright red lips in the photos were smiling directly at them and inviting them into the picture to do, well, most of them had no idea of what they would do if they were in the pictures with those women. Most kids knew the unwritten rule of Charlie Fox and his calendars: they were supposed to sneak quick glances at the calendar, and not stand and gape at it for long periods of time. Fox didn't mind that his calendars fueled kids' fantasies, after all, it was a normal part of growing up, but he had a rule: no gawking.

The paper route took Dennis forty-five minutes to an hour to walk, longer if he daydreamed too much about his athletic heroics. He had inherited the route from Steve, who'd had paper routes since third grade. All the male Domrzalskis had paper routes, including their dad, who had a morning route. George's job assembling airbrushes barely paid enough to keep a family afloat, and he was always taking part-time jobs to make extra money. Having grown up in the Great Depression when masses of people were out of work, George, who had dropped out of high school to support his divorced mother and younger sister, was obsessed with having jobs.

The routes didn't pay a fortune, maybe thirty-five dollars a month for a large morning route, and fifteen to twenty dollars a month for an afternoon route, but it was money, and that's all that mattered.

Steve's first afternoon route had been delivering the Chicago Daily News about a mile east of their house. He walked, pushing a three-wheeled wooden yellow newspaper cart full of papers. The cart was about four feet high and three feet wide. Sometimes he rode his bike loaded with papers up and down the streets to deliver thirty or forty papers. Steve was a curious kid, and he often left his bike or cart full of papers on the sidewalk or in an alley for an hour or two while he would go into stores and read comic books. After losing himself in the comics he'd return to his papers and resume his route. No one ever touched or stole the papers or his bike.

Dennis had learned one lesson from his older brother about the route, and that was to never go into the apartment of an old lady who lived in a yellow-brick six-flat at the corner of Springfield and Schubert across from Koz Park.

She was, from what Dennis had gathered from Steve's stories, a nice lady in her seventies or eighties—a widow—who was lonely and merely wanted company. She often peered out the front window of her first-floor apartment that faced Springfield when she saw Steve walk up to the building's hallway to deliver papers, knocked on the window and motioned for the boy to come up to her apartment.

Often Steve would oblige, walk up the carpeted wooden hallway staircase to her apartment and keep her company. She fed him soup, pot roast, sandwiches and cake and cookies and milk and talked about her life, late husband, children and things that Steve, at such a young age, didn't understand.

Keeping the old lady company usually cost Steve forty-five minutes to an hour, and as her apartment was halfway through his route, he would race through the rest of it. But as fast as he ran or rode his bike, he never made up the time, and often got home just before supper at five o'clock or after it had started.

Steve liked the old lady. He knew that keeping her company cost him time, but he was a kind and compassionate kid, and while he often dreaded her face at the window, he told himself that she was lonely and that he couldn't just ignore her. But he also knew that visiting with her every day and getting home late wasn't right, so he developed a routine to avoid her. He'd park his bike or yellow, wooden, three-wheeled newspaper cart a few doors down from the apartment building and nudge himself close to the building's wall underneath her front windows so she wouldn't see him. He'd open the hallway door, throw the paper in and then slide against the building's front wall underneath her windows and back to his bike or cart. Then he'd run or ride past her house as fast as he could.

Dennis was determined to not have to visit with the oldster. On his first day of deliveries, Dennis parked his shopping cart on the sidewalk across from the lady's building. As he walked across the street to deliver her paper, he saw her staring out the window. She knocked on the glass and motioned for him to come up. Scared, he opened the hallway door, threw the paper in, ran back across the street to his shopping cart, turned the corner onto Schubert and ran west as fast as he could. During the next few weeks the old lady appeared at her window several times and tried to summon Dennis upstairs, but he never went, and eventually she stopped trying.

The kids with paper routes picked up their papers at a store front distribution point on Fullerton that was operated by Elmer, the guy who owned the paper distribution company in the area. The kids rarely saw Elmer, a man in his forties who had a big belly and who yelled a lot. The kids called the storefront "The Barn," and they had a little jingle about it that they sang it with a mixture of glee and contempt whenever Elmer wasn't around:

Hi-ho, hi-ho, to Elmer's Barn we go,
with razor blades and hand grenades, hi-ho, hi-ho!

For Steve, the morning route was a nightmare. He had more than a hundred papers to deliver and had to get up at four o'clock to get the job done. The nuns never knew that he was getting up so early to work before school. He often fell asleep in class, and when he did, they berated him for being lazy. When he failed to do his homework at night because he was too tired, which happened often, the nuns berated him again the following day when he had no homework to turn in.

Getting up at four o'clock was insane and bad enough, Steve thought. Being yelled at by the nuns for being tired because he had a job was worse. What made it all unbearable, though, was that most of the thirty dollars a month he was paid was confiscated by his dad, who justified taking the kid's earnings by always saying, "The family needs money." Steve put in all that work and got almost nothing for it.

Morning routes were fine in the summer when the streets and sidewalks were clear and the kids could push their four-foot-tall, heavy wooden carts with ease. The winters were hellish. Snow drifts and ice covered the streets and sidewalks, often making it impossible for the kids to get the carts through. Many times the carts tipped over, spilling the papers all over. A route that took an hour to do in the summer usually took twice as long in the winter when there was snow.

Then there was the bitter cold in January and February when the temperature often dropped to well below zero. The kids wore rubber boots over their shoes to protect them from the snow. But the boots weren't insulated, and within a half hour of being outside, the kids' toes went numb. They continued the routes, plodding along on frozen feet, swearing to themselves and wondering why they had morning routes in the winter, and wishing for the warmth of home.

Once, when Dennis and Steve set out to do Steve's morning route one cold, blizzarding winter Sunday morning, they basically said, "The hell with it" and threw more than a hundred thick, heavy Sunday papers in garbage cans near the newspaper barn. The wind-driven snow was stinging their faces, there was already more than a foot of snow on the ground, and it was deeper than the cart's three small solid rubber wheels. The wheels sunk into the snow, as did the cart's bottom and front end. When they tried to push the cart, it plowed the snow into a big mound in front of itself, went a few feet and stopped. No matter how hard and how often they pushed and pulled and yanked that cart, it barely moved. They realized that even with the most heroic of efforts it would take hours to complete the route, so they decided to dump the papers and go home. They figured—correctly—that hardly any of their customers would call to complain about not getting their papers. After all, it was a lot of snow, and most adults didn't expect kids to be delivering newspapers in such awful weather.

When kids got home on those frozen mornings, their mothers would have the kitchen ovens on and the kids would kick off their boots, untie their shoes, take off their socks and look at their toes, which were numb and white. They'd put their frozen feet near the open oven doors, and within ten minutes the sharp stinging pain of their toes thawing—like their toes were being jabbed with a hundred needles at once—would hit. That would last for another ten minutes, after which the kids would wash their hands and faces in their bathroom sinks, change into school clothes, eat breakfast, usually cornflakes or some other cereal, and then head off to school.

CHAPTER 17

The Game of Pinner

DENNIS FINISHED HIS paper route, ate supper—leftover baked chicken with melted margarine as gravy, mashed potatoes and green beans—and raced out the back door of the first-floor apartment to meet Masciola at the corner of Altgeld and Harding.

"Anything go on on the route?" Jim asked.

"Naah. Was over two papers. Threw 'em in the garbage in the alley by Fullerton. If you want a paper, we can get one."

"Naah. If I came home with one my dad would think I stole it from someone's porch. Besides, we get the paper. You deliver it to us. Let's play some pinner."

Pinner was simple game—a variant of baseball—that was played by almost every young boy in Chicago. Where it came from or how it got its name, no one knew. They couldn't even remember when they started playing it or who taught them how. It was just something they did, as if it were in their genes. It required only a rubber or tennis ball—no bats or mitts—and a concrete ledge with a sharp edge to it, like a concrete windowsill or decorative concrete ledges at the bases of apartment buildings.

The batter, or kid up at the plate, stood close to the windowsill and threw the ball at it, hoping to hit it perfectly on an edge so the ball would fly into the air. The kids had rules, depending on where they played, as to what counted as a home run and other hits. Jim and Dennis played in the alley on the concrete windowsill of an apartment building between Harding and Springfield. Opposite the sill and only sixteen feet away was the vast red brick wall of a facing apartment building. That wall had a window about fifteen feet up. Any ball that hit above that window was a home run. Just below it was a triple, and further down was a double. A base hit was anything below a double or that the "outfielder" didn't catch. Anything the outfielder caught was an out. The kids played nine innings, three outs each.

The game required some preparation. Most kids had favorite ledges and favorite spots on those ledges at which to throw the ball. Before a game they'd squat in front of the ledge and gently bounce the ball off it, looking for the perfect spot that would give the ball maximum velocity and height. Once they found that spot they memorized it and tried all during the game to hit it. There were surprises, though. Sometimes they'd miss their spot and the ball would fly off the ledge with speed and power and they'd have a home run. After those accidental homers, the batter would exclaim that he had found a new spot, the game would stop, and both players would inspect the spot and marvel about how they hadn't known of it before. They'd both squat in front of the ledge and take turns bouncing the ball against it to reassure themselves that it was no fluke.

Although it was a simple game, pinner required extraordinary coordination, more so than regular baseball, especially when played in an alley. The alleys were only sixteen feet wide, and the outfielder usually stood five or six feet away from the batter. When the ball flew off the ledge, especially as a line drive, the outfielder had to react instantly to make a play.

There were many times when kids, seeing the ball streak off the ledge, reacted instantly and stuck their hands out and caught balls. They were always amazed and proud when that happened and couldn't believe they had such great reflexes.

While the kids enjoyed playing pinner, adults usually couldn't stand it because it was noisy. The sound of rubber balls thudding off the concrete ledges could resound for hours at a time, as the kids, especially in the summers and on weekends, held pinner tournaments that involved several teams. This drove the adults crazy. Too often the games or tournaments were interrupted by parents or neighbors who screamed out their front windows that they were going to call the cops on the kids for making noise and that they didn't appreciate hours-long games of pinner being played directly below their front windows.

Jim and Dennis started their game. The windowsill on which they played had a tin sheet in place of the window. When the ball hit the ledge the wrong way, it would fly back and bounce against the tin, making a dull, but loud noise. They tried always to throw the ball true so it would hit the concrete edge perfectly, but they often failed, and the result was the sound of a rubber ball slamming against the tin.

The sill on which the two played was directly below a pantry window, so people from the apartment building rarely complained. But noise travels, and across Altgeld and three doors down from another apartment building lived an old, heavy, white-haired man who the kids called Mr. Don't-Make-it-the-Noise. He was Polish or German—the kids didn't know which his accent was, except that it was foreign—and he hated noise.

When the kids played pinner or softball in the alley, no matter how far away they were from the guy's back yard, he would appear in the alley, shake a hammy fist and shout, "Don't make it the noise! You make it the noise!"

DON'T MAKE IT THE NOISE!

When they were in first, second and third grades, the kids feared Don't-Make-it-the-Noise. He always threatened to call the cops on them, and they feared the cops. By fourth grade they realized that the guy had either never called the police, or if he had, they never showed up. The cops, the kids had figured out, had more important things to do than to shut down juvenile softball and pinner games.

Jim and Dennis were in the third inning of their game with the score tied at three when down the alley Don't-Make-it-the-Noise came out and shouted that they were making noise and that he would call the cops. By that age, the kids had developed a routine where when the guy shouted at them they would shake their fists and yell back, "You make it the noise! Don't make it the noise!"

The two yelled at the oldster and laughed. After he saw that they weren't scared or intimidated, he quietly slipped into his back yard and bothered them no more. They finished the game, which Jim won, and thought about what to do next.

CHAPTER 18

Girls, Stealing Tomatoes and Other Capers

"**L**ET'S SEE IF anyone else is around," Jim said.

"Yeah, maybe Frankie or Dave or Bob," Dennis replied, referring to Frankie Biedron, a short, sarcastic troublemaker who would have been an official Disturber had he been in Room 204, and fellow Disturbers Dave Ruchinski and Bob Kurkowski. Dennis and Jim headed to Ridgeway and Fullerton to a place they called The Corner, which was where kids met and hung out.

Halfway up the block and walking toward them were Frankie, Dave and Bob. They were carrying brown paper shopping bags and were laughing.

"What you guys doing with shopping bags?" Jim asked when they met up. "Going to buy diapers at Jewel?"

"Sheeeit, we're on a roll. We've already got fifteen bulbs," Frankie laughed. "We'll empty this entire neighborhood of light bulbs!"

They were stealing light bulbs, a prank that the neighborhood boys had gotten involved in a few weeks earlier. Every apartment building foyer and hallway was lighted, and the light bulbs were usually bare, meaning they weren't encased by a lens. So the kids, with nothing better to do, decided one day that they would steal all the hallway light bulbs they could. It was easy during the days and early evenings when the bulbs weren't lit and weren't hot. The kids would walk into the hallways, one would get on the other's shoulders, unscrew the bulb and then they'd run away. The apartment building owners usually replaced the bulbs, and the kids, on their rounds, would steal them again. They prided themselves on the fact that at night, at least half of the neighborhood's apartment building hallways were dark.

"Let's blow 'em up. You've already got a mess of these things," Dennis said. "What do we need more for?"

The boys didn't need to verbally acknowledge that the plan was a good one. They made their way to the nearest alley where they each took a handful of bulbs and threw them one-by-one at garage doors and garbage cans and reveled in the pops, or the explosions, as the boys called them, the bulbs made when they hit something.

Dennis pretended that his were hand grenades and that he was blowing up Russian soldiers with each bulb toss. "Just got another twenty Rooskies!" he shouted with joy as each bulb he threw exploded. "They'll never invade anyone again!"

In less than five minutes the bulbs were gone and the five needed something else to do. They weren't in the mood to steal more bulbs as it was getting dark and the hallways would be lit and the bulbs too hot to unscrew with their bare hands.

"Sheeeit. Let's go get Kolba," Ruchinski said. "He'll have some ideas."

The five headed onto Fullerton toward Monticello where Kolba lived. When they got to Ridgeway they saw in the distance a tall, skinny kid walking toward them. Dennis immediately recognized Kolba's shuffling gait.

"Kolbs! Kolbs!" he screamed. "It's Kolba! Kolllllbs!"

The five ran toward Kolba and he ran toward them, and they met halfway.

"Kolbs! What the hell?" Dennis shouted. "We just blew up some light bulbs. Damn, it was cool. What you doing, man?"

"Nothing. Just looking for you guys. Any more bulbs left?"

"Naah. Used 'em all."

"Shit, man, you should have saved me a few."

"How we supposed to know we'd see you?"

"I don't know. Ahh hell, no big deal."

The six headed down Fullerton, talking and trying to figure out what to do next. They were in their hanging out clothes, greaser garb that they wore with pride: baggy blue, gray or green work pants, short-sleeved, pullover Ban-Lon shirts, over-the-calf black socks and black combat boots or black, Stacy Adams dress shoes. In the winters they wore waist-length black or gray leather jackets with nylon-shelled blue or black quilted insulator jackets underneath, and black or blue stocking caps. They were older now and influenced by their older brothers and sisters in how they dressed, acted and who they hung around with. Those whose older siblings were greasers became greasers, and those whose siblings were dupers became dupers.

Greasers were cool and tough. They swore, smoked, drank, listened to soul music, caused trouble, ditched Sunday masses, hung out on street corners, stayed out late, shared irreverent humor, laughed loudly, weren't afraid to fight and laughed at authority.

Dupers were wimps. They wore jeans or other tight pants, white socks, penny loafers with pennies in the slots on the front, didn't smoke, drink, or fight, listened to folk music, shared wholesome humor, chuckled when they heard something funny, went home early, slavishly obeyed authority, went to Sunday mass and sang hymns and caused no trouble.

At least that's what greasers thought of dupers. The dupers thought they were the cool ones and that greasers were obnoxious jerks.

While all the neighborhood kids had played with each other in their earlier years, by seventh grade they were dividing into greaser and duper camps. Kids who were childhood friends were now growing apart, although the final break wouldn't come until the summer after they had graduated from eighth grade.

The guys bought their pants, or baggies, as they called them, at a small clothing store on Milwaukee Avenue that everyone called The Jew Shack. The store was run by a Jewish couple in their fifties and sold work clothes at reasonable prices.

Men in the neighborhood shook their heads in amusement and bewilderment when they saw greasers in their baggy work pants. Most of the men worked in factories, and most wished they could have been doing something other than manual labor in hot, dirty factories for a living. They couldn't fathom why anyone would purposely dress in factory clothes. Those men lived for the days, usually Sundays, when they could put on suits and ties, and take their minds off their work.

Kurkowski and Ruchinski considered themselves ladies' men, and they talked constantly about girls they had the hots for.

"I'm telling youse, April's got it for me. I mean, she wants me. I mean, reeeeeally wants me," Ruchinski boasted, referring to April Wallace, a budding brown-haired beauty with a great smile who all OLG boys had the hots for.

"Sheeeit. She's got it for me, man. I mean, maaaan, why wouldn't she?" Kurkowski butted in. "She looked at me the other day, and I mean, man, you shoulda seen it. She is hot and I think she's been passing notes about me, man."

The other guys weren't as girl crazy as Ruchinski and Kurkowski, but each had girls they liked.

"Ah, man, I just wish Linda would look at me," Jim said, referring to Linda Benedyk, a blond beauty who also had the attention of most every boy in the school.

"Nancy Istvanek," Kurkowski blurted out. "She's hot. I just know she wants to kiss me."

Nancy had dark hair and was truly beautiful, even in seventh grade. She had moved to the neighborhood in third grade. She lived in an apartment building on Harding just north of Wrightwood. In fifth and sixth grades she held pajama parties on the weekends for several of the girls, and the guys, led by Ruchinski, Kurkowski and Biedron, crashed the parties. Or at least they thought they did. Their crashing amounted to them hanging around in the alley outside of Nancy's first-floor apartment and making loud, spooky noises in an attempt to impress the girls. Then they'd climb on each other's shoulders, rap on the windows with their knuckles, shine flashlights and try to peek in. At some point, the boys would shout, "Does everybody have their clothes on?" They thought the line was the height of wit. They also ran up and down the alley outside Nancy's apartment and screamed as loud as they could.

When they first heard the noises the girls were scared, but after they realized it was the goofball boys from school they relaxed and laughed. They were flattered by the attention and played along and teased the boys, shouting things like, "Lillian, put your clothes on!" "I can't find my bra!" and "Where is my underwear?"

The boys, thinking the remarks were genuine, swooned with excitement, tried harder to peek in the windows, made louder noises, rang the apartment's doorbell and then ran away.

On Monday at school, stories of the crashing became great and exciting tales of how the boys scared the girls silly and caught glimpses of them half naked. The boys who hadn't been in on the crashing were sick with envy and prayed like crazy that Nancy would soon hold another party so they too could see the girls without most of their clothes on.

"Nancy's got the hots for me too," Ruchinski bragged. "She has ever since we crashed her pajama party. Remember that? Man was that cool! It was unreal. I mean, I saw them getting undressed. I'm the only one who did. And I'll tell youse, Nancy is hot. I mean, I saw. And I'll tell youse something else, no one screamed louder than I did. That got her attention. And I'll tell youse something else, I'm gonna feel her up in the cloakroom next week. Man, she's hot!"

Ruchinski was bragging, and no one knew if there was any truth to his boasts. It was true that the boys, from fifth grade on, tried to feel the girls up in the cloakrooms when they got their coats and jackets for lunch or at the end of the school day. The feels usually amounted to nothing more than the boys bumping into the girls and pushing themselves away with their groping hands. Sometimes, especially after school and on Saturdays, the boys would spend time on some girl's front or back porches, and if the parents weren't home, they would truly feel them up. Not all the girls let themselves be groped, but there were some who did.

In class, many of the boys would drop their pens or books next to a girl's desk and ask them nicely to pick them up. When the girls bent over—they wore dresses—the boys often caught glimpses of their underwear, which sent the boys into ecstasy.

As they walked down Fullerton, the boys talked about other girls— Susan Christensen, a stunningly beautiful blonde, Juanita Banez, Kathleen Anselmo, Lynn Charnota, Lois Gagliardetto, Debra Rizzo, Karen Schimanski, Cynthia Wierzbowski, Nancy Prewoznik, Kathleen Fagiano,

Chris Fulara and more. To them, any girl who was developing breasts, and they all were, was beautiful.

The talk quickly turned from the girls to what the boys could do for fun, or as Frankie called it, "pull off a caper." It didn't take long for them to develop a plan. Ruchinski, Kurkowski and Biedron still had their shopping bags, it was now dark, and they needed to fill the bags with something. That something was obvious to all of them: tomatoes.

Many of the neighborhood adults had vegetable gardens in their small back yards, and what they grew most were tomatoes. It was late September and the tomatoes had been ripening for a month. The weather was getting cooler, and by the end of the month most of the gardeners would pull the plants up as the first frost usually came in early-to-mid-October. The boys weren't interested in the ripe tomatoes; they wanted the hard green ones to throw at streetlights.

It was easy to steal tomatoes. All the boys had to do was walk down the alleys, open the unlocked gates to the back yards, and quietly pick through the tomato plants.

They headed down an alley and split up, with Kolba, Dennis and Masciola taking the yards on one side, and Ruchinski, Kurkowski and Biedron taking the other side.

The caper didn't come off as smoothly as the boys would have liked. Some of the homes had dogs that barked when strangers entered the yard, and sometimes the men were still on their back porches enjoying a final beer before going to bed.

Their first round of tomato stealing produced about a dozen hard green tomatoes which they dumped into the shopping bags. A few more trips to more back yards got even more, and the boys headed out to a street where they started throwing the tomatoes at streetlights, which arched over the streets about twenty feet from the ground. They had a contest to see who could break a streetlight with their missiles. They wound up and threw, flinging the tomatoes, most of which missed their marks.

Frankie had a strong and accurate arm and managed to knock one light out. He was cheered by the others who were determined to hit some themselves. That required more tomatoes, so the boys made more trips to the back yards. This time, they weren't so lucky. Some of the neighborhood men had heard the noise and figured something was up, and one guy raced out his back yard and chased them. They ran, but the guy recognized Frankie, caught him and demanded to know why he was stealing tomatoes.

Frankie shrugged and had nothing to say. He knew that if he told the truth the guy would take him home to his parents. After all, stealing and wasting food were sins. The guy, feeling somewhat sorry for the kid, told him, "If you are hungry and needed food you should have just asked me. I would have given you tomatoes. Don't be embarrassed to ask for help."

Frankie was crushed. In his mind he was pulling off a great caper, and here this guy was thinking that he was a pitiful, malnourished waif instead of a bold adventurer and fearless troublemaker. He mumbled to the guy that in the future he would ask for food if he was hungry and his parents couldn't afford to feed him.

The guy let Frankie go with the admonishment to always ask for food if he was hungry, and the kid walked, and then ran, down the alley to find the others.

They met up at The Corner outside the Studio Snack Shop, a place run by Andy, a former Chicago cop, and his wife Vera. The Studio was the place parishioners went for breakfast after Sunday morning masses. On weekdays, it was a place for the high school kids to hang out at after school.

Frankie related his story and the others laughed. They felt his embarrassment and talked about going back to the guy's back yard to steal more tomatoes to show him that they weren't starving misfits.

"We'll rip out all the plants. That'll show him," Jim said. "We won't let him get away with this."

Jim and Dennis were experts at ripping out plants. In fourth grade they ripped out all the flowers along the side of the Dronski house, five doors down from Dennis's house. They had convinced themselves that the flowers had to go because they needed more room to play hide-and-seek. The adventure ended badly for them as they proceeded with their destruction in the middle of the day on a Saturday. Mister Dronski saw them yanking out his flowers, knew who they were, and went right to their parents. When Dennis arrived home a little later, Mister Dronski was in his back yard talking to his dad.

When the two men angrily asked Dennis why he had ripped out the flowers, he shrugged and offered the truth: "Because we wanted more space for when we play hide-and-seek, and the flowers were in the way." The men were stunned by the complete lack of logic the answer showed, and they started arguing with the boy and trying to help him think more clearly.

"If you're playing hide-and-seek, you'd want more places to hide, not fewer places," Mr. Dronski explained to Dennis. "Right? You get that, right?"

"Tearing out flowers," Dennis's father began, "makes fewer places to hide. Do you understand that?"

Dennis answered that he understood.

"Then why, if you wanted more space for hide-and-seek, did you pull out my flowers?" Mr. Dronski asked. "That doesn't make any sense. Why?"

"Because that's what we thought," Dennis answered.

"That's just dumb," his father said. "Get in the house and stay there."

The two men talked to each other afterward. While they didn't come out and say that they thought Dennis was real, real slow, they both knew it to be the case and they felt sorry for the kid.

"Sheeeit," Frankie replied. "The guy already knows it was me stealing his tomatoes. If we rip up the plants he'll go straight to my parents."

"Yeah. Forget it," Jim said.

The boys headed west on Fullerton, not knowing where they would wind up. They passed Bill's Hobby Shop, the place where they all bought their model cars, planes and ships; The Little Nut Hut, a small store that sold nuts and loose candy; the Florsheim shoe store that had an X-ray machine for feet that the kids used almost every time they passed by; the Jewel food store; a couple of taverns; a real estate office; Becker's shoe store; Saxon's, the large store where men bought hardware, the kids shoplifted pens and bought records; Cramer's, a candy store where they stole potato chips and read comic books; Phil's, a hot dog and Italian beef stand that, according to all in the neighborhood, had the best hot dogs, beefs and French fries in Chicago; the Spotlight grocery, a small food store where Dennis's ma bought her lunch meat; a dentist's office; barber shop; lamp factory; a doctor's office; Harding Drugs; the Embassy Ballroom, a converted movie theater; a small record store; and, at the corner of Pulaski and Fullerton, Andes Candies, a place where they got malts, nuts, ice cream and phosphates, which were fizzy, flavored drinks.

Fullerton was the neighborhood's commercial center. It was one of the city's main streets, laid out on a grid system that placed main streets every mile, or eight blocks, from the starting point at Madison and State streets downtown. In a ten-block-long stretch from two blocks west of Pulaski east to Central Park, there was pretty much everything anyone would ever need: at least nine taverns or liquor stores; three grocery stores and a deli; a butcher shop; bakery; six restaurants, hot dog stands and pizza joints; a hobby shop and dime store; shoe stores; a doctor's and dentist's office; two barber shops; a real estate office; YMCA; three drug stores; a funeral home; candy and ice cream shops; two hardware stores; a department store; hotel; two bowling alleys; a dance hall; TV repair shop, beauty shops; a flower store and more. East of Central Park to Kedzie, the street had more taverns, restaurants, and stores and shops of all kinds. Whatever a person or family needed, they could find it on Fullerton, and they could walk to it.

The guys crossed Pulaski, where they passed a couple more taverns and restaurants before coming to the Maple Lanes bowling alley. The bowling alley was one of their hangouts because they could loiter there without having to spend much money, and because they could smoke there. They'd sit in the seats behind the lanes, watch people bowl and talk about whatever was on their minds. When they had money they'd put dimes in the pinball games and jerk and tilt the heavy machines as best they could to win free games. Frankie was particularly skilled and could easily spend thirty minutes at a machine getting free game after free game.

Kolba, Kurkowski, Ruchinski and Masciola went to the coffee and snack shop that was part of the place to sit down and smoke and drink coffee, which because it tasted so bad, they loaded up with spoonfuls of sugar. Dennis and Frankie stayed on the floor and began playing a rifle-shooting game where they aimed the plastic rifle at various things, including ducks and bad guys. They won a few free games and then lost several in a row. Frankie was bored, and not having anything better to do, he grabbed the rifle butt with his hands, yanked down on it and lifted his legs off the floor so the butt was supporting his entire weight. The two laughed, and then suddenly the butt cracked off and Frankie fell to the floor with the end of the plastic rifle butt in his hands.

The two howled with laughter. They couldn't believe the gun had broken, and they thought it was one of the funniest things they had ever done. But they also knew they'd be in huge trouble if they were caught. They had no idea how much those games cost, but figured they had to be expensive, more than they could ever afford to repair. If the bowling alley owner or manager saw the damage they had done, they would have been, as they often said, up Shit's Creek.

"Shit!" Frankie sputtered while laughing and picking himself off the floor. "We gotta do something."

Frankie stood up and tried to attach the cracked part of the gun butt to the place it had cracked off. He squeezed the broken parts together. When he let it go to see if it would stay in place, the butt fell off.

Dennis was nearly paralyzed with laughter but did manage a short but insightful sentence: "We gotta get out of here!"

"We can't just leave it like this. They'll know it was us," Frankie said.

They laughed a few moments longer, and then Frankie was struck with brilliance.

"Go get some gum," he said. "We'll stick it together with gum."

While Frankie stayed at the gun pretending to play it and hiding the damage, Dennis raced to the sales counter on the other side of the bowling alley, pulled a nickel out of his pocket and bought a pack of Juicy Fruit gum. He tore the gum open, put two sticks in his mouth and began chewing furiously. The counterman who sold him the gum was amazed.

"Jesus, you really like gum, huh kid?" the guy said.

Thinking quickly, Dennis replied:

"Not really. We been smoking and got to get home soon."

The counterman understood. As a kid he had probably loaded up on chewing gum before going home to hide the smell of smoke on his breath from his parents.

The guy shrugged and smiled, and Dennis raced back to Frankie, who stuck two sticks in his mouth and chewed like a madman. After a minute or so the boys took the big wads of gum from their mouths. Frankie fashioned a giant blob out of the two, stretched it out, put it in the piece of the gun that was still on the machine and pushed the other part in place. When he let go, it held!

The two were thrilled and proud and wanted to hang around and admire their genius. But they knew better and walked quickly to the snack shop where the others were sipping their sugar-laden coffees. They walked up to the booth where the others were sitting, jerked their heads as if to say something was up and mumbled to the others:

"We gotta get out of here. Let's go!"

The others asked no questions, instantly left their seats and their steaming cups of coffee and headed for the door. Almost before they were out the door, the others began asking, "What's up, man? What the fuck?"

They headed to the nearby Bressler's Ice Cream factory and the railroad tracks and went to one of their favorite places, one of the factory's concrete loading docks and sat down. Dennis and Frankie told the story and they all laughed themselves crazy.

"Man, was that ever a caper," Frankie laughed. "It was boss!" The guys used that last word often. It meant that whatever or whomever they used it to describe was cool, great and satisfying. If they used it to describe a meal, it meant the food was tasty and filling. For a car it meant the car was stylish, fast, comfortable, or in some other way cool. For an adult, and they rarely used for adults, it meant the person understood them and would probably make a beer run for them. If someone or something was truly extraordinary and really, really cool, the guys would exclaim "Bossanova!"

They imagined how funny it would be when the next person to play the game would have the rifle butt crack off. They laughed even harder when they pictured the person's shock at seeing the giant wad of chewing gum that held the pieces together. They admired Frankie's quick thinking but realized there was a downside to the caper. They'd probably have to stay out of the bowling alley for a couple of weeks, and that was not boss.

It was nine o'clock and the boys were still full of energy, and they talked about what to do next.

"Let's go to Gossage and bulk," Kolba said, referring to the Gossage Grill, with the word "bulk" meaning "eat." "Man, I'm hungry."

The others agreed and they started walking the half block to the hamburger joint. There were two Gossages in the neighborhood, one on Fullerton and the other on Diversey and Pulaski four blocks away. The places were loved by everyone because they offered cheap and tasty food. At one time they sold seven hamburgers for two dollars, a deal which fed many of the area's cash-strapped families.

On Wednesdays, beginning in fifth grade, OLG kids got off school at twelve forty-five in the afternoon so the nuns could teach religion, or CCD classes as they were called, to public school kids who would come to OLG. The early dismissal gave kids two-and-a-half extra hours to play or goof off. The nuns had strict rules about the early dismissal, which were that the kids had to go directly home, do homework and stay inside until three fifteen, the normal dismissal time.

The good kids obeyed those rules, but no one else did. The minute they got home they ate lunch, changed into play clothes and raced out their doors to play in the alleys and roam the streets.

Wednesdays were heaven for Dennis because his mother always seemed to have an extra couple of dollars to give to Steve, who would race out the back door, head north on Harding and run all three blocks to the Gossage Grill on Diversey to buy seven hamburgers. He'd run all the way back with the burgers still hot in their paper wrappers and grease-soaked brown paper bags.

The second Steve walked in the door with the food the kitchen filled with the wonderful aroma of grilled meat, grease and onions. He, Dennis, their sister Barbara and Florence devoured the burgers and washed them down with glasses of cold milk.

Even though Dennis and Steve fought a lot, and even though Steve's was the only name on Dennis's enemies list, Dennis liked and admired his older brother. Not only was he a first-class troublemaker, he was also kind of the rock of the family.

Steve was the one who raced to Gossage for burgers, and to the bakery on Fullerton on cold winter mornings for doughnuts, muffins and other biscuits. When he got home with those treats, they were still warm, steamy and beyond delicious. At sixteen cents a biscuit, two bucks could buy a bagful of them. In fifth and sixth grades Steve had jobs in addition to his paper route. He was always doing something that no one else dared do, something beyond what most grade-school kids were supposed to do.

But most importantly, Steve didn't take crap from anyone, including the nuns and his parents. He wasn't a mean kid; he just didn't like being yelled at and punished for what he thought were idiotic reasons. Many times when he was in first grade, Steve broke some rule or rules, and was sent to the kindergarten classroom as punishment. The move was supposed to shame and humiliate him, but it never did. Instead, the younger kids, including Dennis, saw him as a big guy and were in awe of him for being brave enough to break the rules. Steve often talked back to the nuns and to his parents, acts of rebellion and independence that usually got his mouth washed out with a bar of soap.

Steve and his pals were always in the middle of fun and trouble. In fifth grade, he and two of his buddies got in a big mess. They had studied for a couple of months to become altar boys. They had no real desire to be altar boys or to walk around acting pious and mumbling prayers, it was just that many of the other guys were doing it, and they thought they'd do what everyone else did. They learned the Latin phrases and prayers, the hardest being the Apostles' Creed, and they were accepted as altar boys. Their first assignment was to kneel in front of the church's altar during the Easter Vigil, a time a few days before Easter when parishioners would sit in the church and meditate, say rosaries or pray the Stations of the Cross.

The church was large, the altar was big, and the three boys were spaced about twenty feet apart with their backs to the pews and the people in them who had come to pray. When the boys were in the sacristy donning their red and white altar boy vestments before going into the church, one of them spotted a plastic bag full of hundreds of communion wafers, or hosts. They each took a couple of handfuls of the round discs, put them in their pants pockets and walked out, hands folded and heads bowed in holy reverence, to the positions at which they were supposed to kneel and pray for the next three hours. One of the guys took a host from his pocket, held it in one hand between his thumb and index finger, and then snapped it with his other index finger so that it flew across the altar.

The hosts were aerodynamically sound, and they easily flew the twenty feet that separated the guys. Soon, a war was on, and the guys were flicking hosts at each other and laughing like crazy. They didn't laugh long, though. Monsignor Flavin walked into the church and was horrified when he saw the three desecrating the hosts. He sternly ordered the guys into the sacristy where he yelled and yelled and yelled, telling them they would burn in Hell and how disappointed he was in them. Then he fired them. They had been altar boys for three weeks.

THE HOSTS FLEW

Dennis and his pals plopped themselves down on stools along the Gossage Grill's counter and ordered burgers and sodas. The grill and counterman, as did all Gossage employees, wore a uniform: black-and-white checkered pants—Gossage Grill Pants the kids called them, as whenever they saw anyone dressed in black-and-white checkered pants they'd immediately exclaim, "Gossage Grill Pants!"—and white long-sleeve shirts with the sleeves rolled up to the elbow. Most of the grill men were in their twenties, and the kids thought they were old and worldly, especially when they were able to manage more than two or three burgers on the grill at once.

The routine for preparing burgers was the same in every Gossage Grill. The counterman would take the order with a pen or pencil on a light-green paper order pad, walk to the grill and plop the meat patties on it. Then he'd take a knife to an onion, cut as many slices as he needed, throw them on the grill and then fill the drink orders.

While the guys were waiting for their drinks and laughing about the broken gun, the counterman, a guy in his twenties with short black hair, exclaimed, "Shit! I cut myself."

He had sliced a gash into one of his fingers while cutting the onion. He immediately grabbed for his white apron and wrapped a portion of it around the wound. After a few moments he pulled the finger out of the apron to check the wound, which was still bleeding.

"Damn, this thing won't stop bleeding," he said as he picked up the sliced onions with both hands and threw them on the grill. Then he started filling the drink orders and brought the guys their cups of soda.

They were disgusted. The sides of the plastic cups were smeared with blood.

IT'S ONLY BLOOD·

"Ain't you got a band-aid?" Frankie asked. "This is disgusting. These are blood glasses."

"Stop bitching," the guy said as he walked over and wiped the cups clean with his bloody apron. "You want to eat or don't you?"

"Yeah, but we don't want blood burgers," Kurkowski said. "Bet you the health department wouldn't be happy about this."

"Screw the health department. Do you want to eat or not? Those burgers are raw meat, all they got is blood in 'em."

"Just try not to squirt too much blood on our food," Ruchinski laughed. "And no blood on the buns."

"You're gonna get whatever I give you, you little punks."

The guy went to the back of the store, found a small rag, wrapped it around his cut finger and continued preparing the burgers.

The finger continued to bleed, and soon there was a big red blotch on the rag. It didn't deter the guy and he went about preparing the burgers.

"Actually, we changed our minds. We want a big shot of blood on 'em," Frankie shouted.

"Smart asses, ain't youse?" the guy replied as he started bringing them the burgers in small, green plastic boat-shaped baskets. "No more bitchin', otherwise I'll charge you double for these."

They inspected the buns and burgers to make sure they contained no obvious signs of human blood, loaded them up with ketchup and mustard and devoured them.

While they ate, the counterman tried unsuccessfully to stem the flow of blood from his finger. At one point he seemed amazed that it wouldn't stop bleeding.

"Never been cut like this before. This thing just won't stop bleeding," he said as he walked to the guys and held up the finger for them to inspect. "Look at it. It won't stop."

"You ain't got no band-aids in this place?" Frankie asked.

"Naah, the owners are cheap," the guy replied. "I just wish it would stop bleeding. I don't know if I'll be able to make it through the rest of the shift."

"How's that?"

"I can't stay here and serve people food with a bloody finger."

"But you just served us!"

"Yeah, but it just happened. I wasn't gonna let those burgers go to waste. I'd be charged for 'em. And if they found out that I cut my finger, they'd probably fire me."

"Why don't you suck the blood out of your finger? That might work," Kolba offered.

"You crazy? I ain't gonna eat blood."

"You just tried feeding us blood."

"Look guys, youse are funny, but I ain't in the mood for jokes right now. Just pay up and I'm gonna close up early and go home."

The guys got dollar bills out of their wallets and walked to the cash register to pay. When the counterman punched the keys on the manual cash register, his finger started bleeding profusely. He took the bills and gave the guys change that was covered with blood.

"It's blood money!" Frankie declared. "Blood money!"

They left the restaurant and walked down Fullerton shouting, "Blood money! Blood money!" while laughing hysterically. They were both disgusted and thrilled at the strange adventure.

It was nearing ten o'clock, and for seventh graders a little late to be out. The guys knew they should get home, and that if they got home after ten their parents would throw fits and yell. But they never wanted the fun of any day or night to end. They laughed and joshed with each other, which never happened at home with their brothers, sisters or parents, and to part company and end the fun, even if only for the time it took them to sleep, was, to them, the worst thing that could ever happen.

"I think I gotta be getting home. My dad'll kill me if I'm in after ten," Kolba said.

"Really, he's gonna kill you?" Dennis asked in a tone he used when he just wanted to be a smart-ass. "Kill you? Even if he doesn't like you he ain't gonna kill you. The cops would get him and he'd go to jail."

Kolba laughed the challenge off. He knew that if he got into wordplay with Dennis it would never end and he would never win.

They walked silently for a few minutes until Frankie had an idea that would keep them out and together just a little longer.

"Let's do some garage jumping. We ain't got nothin' better to do."

The guys headed to an alley to find a garage they could climb and then jump from it to the next garage, and then onto the next until they had jumped all the garages on a block.

It was an easy adventure that held the potential of danger. They would shimmy up a rain gutter on a garage at the beginning of a block—an easy task because the garages were only ten feet tall—walk to the other side and jump to the next garage. While it seemed dangerous because they could fall off a garage and break their bones on the concrete alleys, it really wasn't. The gangways between most buildings in Chicago were three feet wide, and that was an easy jump for twelve-and-thirteen-year-old kids. Garage jumping was done only at night when no one could see the kids, and never in the winter when jumping on ice and snow on the roofs would have meant slips, falls and certain injury.

Sometimes a group of kids would divvy up the garages. One group would take one side of an alley and another group the other side and they'd race each other to see who could get to the other end of the alley first. The punishment for losing those races was laughter and ridicule.

They found an alley, climbed to the top of the first garage and spent the next twenty minutes jumping from garage to garage. They jumped off the last garage on the block—a ten-foot leap onto the concrete alley was nothing for them—and laughed and congratulated themselves for being so fearless.

It was nearing ten-thirty and they knew they had to get home, so they made plans to meet on Saturday.

CHAPTER 19

Tormenting a Druggist, and Harry Scary

DENNIS RACED THROUGH his paper route on Saturdays so he could spend the rest of the day with his pals, and on this Saturday he finished it in forty-five minutes. After completing the route he washed up, had a sandwich, and went to Masciola's house to see if he was home. Jim's mother said he had already left, so Dennis raced out the gangway and sprinted to The Corner.

Most of the boys ran when they had to get somewhere. It was quicker and more fun than walking. There was something about running full-out that thrilled and filled them with a sense of power and accomplishment. They also ran because they were scared that someone might be following them. The nuns reinforced this, preaching constantly that children should never talk to strangers and that they should scream and run if one ever approached them.

In fifth grade, Kolba, in an attempt to be funny and cause the nuns grief, took that advice too far. One day when he was walking home from school past the convent, a nun who was new to the parish approached him to say hello. Since he had never met her before, Kolba figured it was legitimate to treat her as a stranger. When she approached he screamed and ran like hell.

The next day he was summoned to Vitaclaire's office for an interrogation.

"What was the meaning of the incident yesterday afternoon, Mister Kolba, when you screamed at and ran away from Sister Mary Christopher?"

"Who is Sister Mary Christopher?" he replied, feigning innocence.

"The sister you screamed at yesterday, Mister Kolba! Why did you scream at her and run from her?"

"Because, Sister, you always tell us to run away from strangers. I never saw her before. She was a stranger. I was just doing what you told us to do, Sister."

"Sister Mary Christopher is a servant of God! She is a representative of God here on Earth. You ran away from God?" the nun said, waiting for a response to her question. When none came, she demanded:

"Answer me!"

"I forgot the question."

Boom! The nun slapped the boy across the face. "Did you scream at and run away from God?"

"No."

The one-word answer infuriated the nun, and she could barely control her rage.

"Would you scream at and run away from God, Mister Kolba?"

"Not if he had identification, Sister."

Sister Vitaclaire's dam broke and she raged at the boy for blaspheming and being "in concert with the Devil."

Kolba saw an opening and knew he could torment her further.

"I am not in concert with the Devil," he replied while bracing for a beating.

"And why not?"

"Because, Sister, I don't play an instrument. I don't think you can be in a concert if you don't play an instrument."

The nun beat the boy until she could swing her arms no longer.

When Dennis arrived at the corner out of breath, he was horrified. No one was there! There was no worse thing for a kid than going out to meet pals and being unable to find them. It often meant that a kid would be on his or her own for the rest of the day, and being stuck alone on a Saturday was pure torture. The neighborhood was big, and those pals could have been anywhere. They might even have walked to another neighborhood! Walking was their preferred mode of transportation because it allowed them to daydream and talk, and they walked everywhere. Dennis even feared that his pals might have taken the subway to downtown.

Dennis's mind went to work and he started thinking about all the places the guys could have been and mapping out the route he'd take to run to each one. Koz Park, Milwaukee Avenue, the railroad tracks by Fullerton, the back of the lumber yard, a construction site near Pulaski and Fullerton, the empty lot off Wrightwood, Salt Mountain, or any alley, were among the places he figured they could have been.

If they were still in the neighborhood there was a good chance he could find them. It was just a matter of running from place to place and looking in store and restaurant windows. If they had left the vicinity, though, it was, as the kids said, history, and he'd have to entertain himself.

He plotted the routes, knowing that if the guys were still in the neighborhood he'd find them. Before he started running all over, Dennis headed to The Lot, a parking lot between an apartment building and a mattress factory on Fullerton that served as the playground for OLG's seventh and eighth graders. The Lot had basketball hoops and was a place the kids played softball, basketball and fast-pitch baseball against the factory's wall after school and on weekends. When he got there, Dennis was filled with joy. The guys were there playing basketball. He opened the three-foot-wide, six-foot-tall chain-link gate and walked to where they were playing.

"You're late. Get in. You're on our side," Masciola shouted.

Dennis was the fourth member of the team that included Maciola, Kolba and Michael Vanko, a classmate who at, less than five feet tall, could barely shoot a basketball. On the other team were Ruchinski, Kurkowski, Biedron— all good basketball players—and Rich Bozeman.

They played half-court ball, which, because the lot was small and the asphalt surface had no markings, was really quarter-court. The first team to score twenty-one points won.

The kids slipped and slid on their leather-soled shoes. None had gym shoes because most of the parents in the neighborhood refused to let the kids have them. The common refrain the kids heard when they asked for gym shoes was that they had no arch supports and if they wore them for any length of time they would get fallen arches and would be unable to walk. Their play shoes were their worn-out school shoes that had been re-soled and re-heeled.

His team was down twelve to four when Dennis entered the game, and he didn't do much to improve its chances except play aggressive and tenacious defense and foul the opponents by slapping their hands, wrists, necks and faces in attempts to steal the ball or block shots.

The kids called their own fouls. If they thought they had been fouled, they'd stop, cradle the ball to their bodies with both arms and shout, "Foul!" The guilty player would respond by shouting, "Bullshit!" and then a conference would ensue for both sides to argue the call's legitimacy. Truly obvious fouls weren't contested, but those were rare because each kid had a different definition of what constituted a foul. Those with a decent knowledge of the game considered the slightest tap, slap or bump a violation. None of the kids were that steeped in the intricacies of basketball, however, and those minor infractions, which occurred constantly, rarely led to foul shots.

To most of the guys, whether those bumps, slaps, holds, and occasional trips, charges and knockdowns amounted to a foul depended on the degree of pain the offender had inflicted.

When a kid called a foul, the offender would say, "Aw come on, that didn't hurt. You wimp." Or, "I didn't mean to trip you, you got in the way of my leg."

The arguments would escalate on both sides, often taking several minutes, and the determination of whether a true foul had occurred often depended on the physical evidence. If a kid's wrists were red or bruised, his arms scratched, or the palms of his hands scraped because of a fall, it was an agreed-upon foul. The offender was never happy with such a call, and after one was called would play even more aggressively, especially towards the kid who had called the foul, which resulted in more fouls being called.

Sometimes the arguments were so intense, and both sides so adamant in their positions, that no agreement could be reached and the game was called, or canceled. Any animosity between the players vanished because the solution to a called game was to pick new sides and start a new game. Sometimes the fouler and foulee wound up on the same team in the next game.

To a basketball purist the games would have been horrifying because at times they degenerated into something that resembled tackle football. To the kids, the games were physically demanding, but they reveled in the action.

The game ended quickly with Dennis's team losing twenty-one to ten. They picked new teams and played two more games before deciding to play softball. Dennis's and Kurkowski's oldest brothers and their friends had been playing pinner in the lot. Steve Domrzalski and some of his pals showed up and there were enough guys to form two teams.

They played sixteen-inch softball, a game that was invented in Chicago's working-class, blue-collar neighborhoods. It required only a bat and a sixteen-inch softball—no mitts—and players needed strong hands to catch the large ball. It was a slow-pitch game where the pitcher used an underhanded delivery to send the ball in a high arc toward the batter. Slamming a sixteen-inch ball that weighed at least a pound high into the air required strength and skill, which all the guys had developed because they had been playing the game in the alleys and streets since whenever they were strong enough to pick up a wooden baseball bat and swing it.

The games played in the alleys taught them how to hit the ball straight, as the alleys were only sixteen feet wide and a ball that was not hit down the middle wound up in back yards. Some of the adults got angry when a ball flew into their yards, and they'd yell at the kids to go play at Koz Park, with their usual comment being, "There's a park two blocks down. Why don't you go play there?"

The admonitions always mystified the kids. To them, the alleys and streets and back yards were their playground and their park. Why would they walk a couple of blocks away to do something they could right there in the alley or street?

THE ALLEYS WERE THEIR PLAYGROUNDS·

Games played in the streets also required the kids to hit the ball straight because an errant ball could wind up going through someone's front window. The street games were frustrating because they were always interrupted by cars, which caused the kids to yell at the passing drivers, "What do you think this is, a street or something?"

When they'd been younger, The Lot seemed as big as a stadium to the kids. Now, at fifty feet wide and a hundred-twenty-five-feet long, it was puny. The older kids hit the ball out over its back chain-link fence for a homer almost every time at bat. They played a couple of games, decided there were too many homers—an inconvenience because the ball usually wound up in the back yards of the homes that bordered The Lot and it always took time for someone to retrieve it—so they decided to play at Koz Park.

The group, including some older guys who were in high school, stopped at Voss's drug store at the corner of Fullerton and Avers to buy sodas. Normally they would have continued a little further to one of the neighborhood taverns and plopped down their seventeen cents for a sixteen-ounce bottle of RC Cola or Pepsi, but one of the older guys suggested they have some fun by tormenting the old man who ran the drug store, Mr. Sam Voss.

Voss's had always been there—it was one of three drug stores within a five-block stretch of Fullerton—and it had always been a creepy place, even for adults.

No one knew how old Voss, who ran the place with his wife, was, but that didn't matter because no matter what his age, he acted and looked old and strange. With white, pale skin and a balding head that was framed by thin white hair on his temples, Voss looked to everyone what they thought an undertaker looked like. His skin was pale because he never left the dark, musty interior of the store to go outside and get some sun. He didn't have to because he owned the three-story brick building that housed the store, and he and his wife, Mrs. Voss, lived in one of the apartments above the store. They merely walked up or down the back porch steps to get to or from work.

There were windows in the store, but they were always closed and covered with roll-down shades that had once been white but had turned yellow and dirty with age and dust. Even in the summer the store was cool—cool like death, everyone thought—because Voss never let any sun in. It had the shut-in odor of a place that never got any outside air. That, combined with a faint smell of medicine and a musty dampness, made it seem like a cave inside a building.

Voss and his wife were a cheerless couple who never smiled, were perpetually crabby and who seemed annoyed when a customer walked through the front door. It was a mystery to many why they ran a retail store.

The younger kids were afraid of Voss and his mortician-like appearance. The fear was stoked by the older kids who scared the young ones with stories of how Voss had coffins in the basement and would stuff kids into one if they went into the store by themselves. Even the adults warned the young kids to never go into Voss's alone. None of them ever did; they always went in packs of four or five, which annoyed Voss and his wife because they couldn't stand the chatter and laughter that came with the kids.

Despite their fears, the kids always visited the store. It was partly out of fear that they went. They were thrilled by fear, and many secretly wanted to know if Voss really did have coffins in the basement. To have actually been grabbed by Voss and dragged down the stairs to the basement and put into a coffin would have been an incredible story to tell and would have made a kid an instant hero. And every trip to the store left them with a story about Voss's crabbiness and strange behavior, which they always embellished, and which further fueled speculation that he was a child-killing maniac.

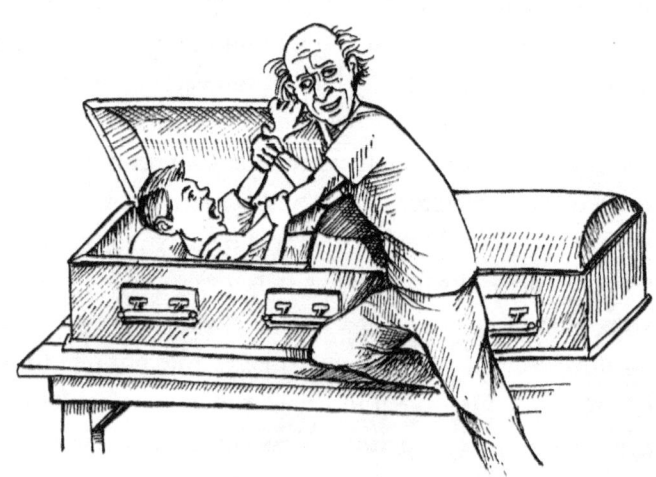

THE DRUGGIST WAS SCARY.

If Voss was grouchy, the story afterward was always that he had his eye on a particular kid. If he was even mildly pleasant, which was extremely rare, it also meant that he was after a kid. If Voss touched a kid's hand when giving him change from the cash register, it came out in the story that Voss had lunged at the kid and tried to grab him. Every kid who managed to touch Voss's hand when getting change breathlessly exclaimed afterwards that it was as cold and stiff as a dead person's, although few had ever touched a corpse.

They also went to Voss's because it had a sit-down soda fountain and because of the candy he sold, especially malted milk tablets that came in a tin box and whose malty sweetness sent the kids into ecstasy. The brown malt tablets were a delicacy. They were so different than straight sugar or chocolate candy bars; sweet without being too sweet, and a little grainy. No one ever chewed a malt tablet; that would have been sacrilege to the tongue and taste buds. They were left in the mouth to melt over as long a time as possible. Malt tablets were savored, and if a kid was disciplined, a tin could last two days.

Because of his dislike of people, crankiness and paranoia—he thought everyone who entered the store would try to steal something—Voss was an easy target. There were more than a dozen kids in the group, and when they filed one-by-one into the small store in a seemingly endless line, Voss was horrified and terrified.

Even though they were mostly grade-school kids, Voss thought he was going to be held up.

"What, what, what do you want?" Voss stammered as the kids milled around the store looking at various items and picking them up.

Dave Wilson, a friend of Wally Domrzalski, calmly, but loudly, replied, "Kotex. You got any Kotex?"

He was referring to the bulky sanitary napkins that women used. The name itself, Kotex, was almost a dirty word in the neighborhood, and one that was spoken only in hushed tones. No one, not even adults, ever used the word "menstruation," which was considered obscene and unmentionable. When on the rare occasions they referred to a woman's monthly period, it was said to be a "female condition," or a "female problem." If a woman sent her husband to the store and he asked what she needed, if a box of Kotex was one of the items, the word was whispered if kids were present.

Mothers often sent kids to the grocery and drug stores with notes for food, cigarettes and Kotex. Kids read the notes and knew what every item was except Kotex. They knew only that it was a mysterious item that came in a big blue box that was immediately hidden away when brought home. If they asked their moms what Kotex was, the moms would reply, "Oh, just something I need. Now go along."

By high school, kids knew what Kotex was and what it was for, and they gleefully passed the information on to their younger brothers and sisters, who, not understanding the human body, were immediately horrified.

Thanks to their older brothers, the Disturbers and their buddies knew what Kotex was, and when Wilson blurted out that word in the middle of Voss's store, they busted out laughing.

Voss didn't laugh. He was horrified that the word was uttered casually, loudly, in public and in his store. He was stunned by Wilson's brazenness and embarrassed and angered by the laughter.

"What do you need it for?" Voss asked as he tried to regain his composure.

"I don't need it. I mean, my god, I hope I don't," Wilson shot back to the laughter of the group. "My girlfriends need them. They're having their—"

Wilson paused, readying the hammer blow he was about to deliver to Voss, who was trembling. Wilson looked to the guys, laughed to himself and shouted as loud as he could:

"Periods! They're having their periods!"

Voss reeled as if had he been hit in the head with a pipe. He was shocked, angered and disgusted. He was so white to begin with that he couldn't have turned whiter. If he had, he would have been translucent. His first instinct was to rush to the telephone and call the cops, but he knew that they would never show up for a complaint of teenagers trying to buy sanitary napkins.

The guys laughed even harder, which made Voss angrier.

"Get out of my store," he ordered. "Go away now."

"I can't. My girlfriends are having their periods and they sent me here to buy Kotex," Wilson replied. "It's not illegal to buy this stuff. Here's the note. Look."

Wilson dug into his pocket and pulled out a crumpled note that he had written a few days earlier when he and his buddies were thinking of ways to anger Voss.

Voss read the note, which said, "Hello, Mr. Voss. We're Dave Wilson's girlfriends. Please sell him Kotex for us. We can't leave the house because of our monthly 'female problem.' Thank you."

Voss was beaten. He had an official note in his hands that referenced the monthly "female problem" in dignified terms, and he knew he had to comply with the request.

"Well, just this once. No more after this," Voss sputtered as he walked to behind the counter where he kept Kotex hidden as if it was pornography. He put a box on the counter and told Wilson the price.

"I need more than one box," Wilson said, his tone showing feigned respect for the druggist.

Voss was angered all over again and lost his patience. He again wanted to order the kids out of the store, but Wilson had a note, a sale was a sale, and Voss made a large profit on every box of Kotex as he always put a big markup on the product that women needed every month.

"How many do you want?" Voss asked with disgust.

Wilson paused and pretended to be counting in his head. The delay infuriated the druggist. Wilson waited to let Voss's anger build. Just when the oldster was about to scream at him, Wilson calmly replied:

"Seventeen. I need seventeen boxes of Kotex."

Voss lost it and screamed, "Seventeen! Seventeen! Seventeen! Why? Are you crazy?"

"No. I'm not crazy. I just need seventeen boxes of Kotex."

"Seventeen! Why? Why seventeen?"

"Because I got seventeen girlfriends and they all got their periods."

The guys laughed and Voss raged. He ordered the guys out of the store, saying he'd call the cops if they didn't leave immediately, and without the coveted Kotex.

The guys had succeeded in driving Voss crazy, and they left the store howling at Wilson's brilliance.

They walked to the tavern to get their sodas. This place was special because of one customer, a guy in his fifties or sixties who had a growth the size of an orange on his nose.

It was a tumor or something, the kids figured, and it was orange and fleshy and it dangled from and bounced around the guy's nose like it was attached to it with a rubber band. The guys felt sorry for the man, as did everyone in the neighborhood, and they all wondered why he had never gone to a doctor to have it sliced off. The kids tried not to stare when they saw the guy on the street, or sitting at the bar in the tavern, but they could never stop themselves from staring because it was the strangest thing they had ever seen.

The guys bought their sodas. The guy with the tumor was at the bar, and they all stared at him, never thinking of what it must have felt like to have a dozen teenagers stare at a deformity on your face. They walked outside, sat against the building's front wall, drank their sodas and watched people walk by on their Saturday afternoon errands.

Everyone in the neighborhood walked or took the bus to wherever they needed to go. Many families still didn't have cars, and those that did had only one, which was used by the father to drive to work. They walked because they didn't need to drive. Everything they needed was sold in stores on Fullerton or other streets like Diversey and Armitage and was within easy walking distance. Driving a couple of blocks, or even a mile or two, was a foreign concept to people.

The guys were all greasers, and as they sat drinking their sodas, someone pulled a black, plastic and brushed-metal transistor radio out of his pocket and turned the plastic dial on one of its sides until it clicked on. He turned the tuning dial on the other side to a station that played soul music and they listened and sang along as the radio blared out songs by The Supremes, Percy Sledge, The Temptations and The Righteous Brothers.

Every kid had their favorite song, and they argued with each other about the merits and the coolness of their favorite versus the other kid's. Most agreed that *When a Man Loves a Woman* had to be one of the greatest songs ever written and sung.

They could buy albums and forty-fives at Saxon and the small record store next to the Embassy Ballroom, but those stores had limited selections. The kids who were serious about music and records walked to a record store at North Avenue and Pulaski, more than a mile away. The store had a small booth with a table-top record player and headset that kids could use to play and listen to records before buying them. Putting on the headset made kids feel powerful and proud, like adults, because they were sampling something before buying it.

Hand-held transistor radios were valuable. Those who had them were considered cool and popular, and those who didn't, wanted them. And sometimes, older guys would try to steal them from the younger kids.

A few weeks earlier, Kolba and his buddy Terry Pieniazek were walking down Pualski to the record store on North Avenue and listening to Gary's radio. A car full of older guys, who Kolba didn't know, pulled up and followed them. The front passenger side window rolled down and one of the guys inside started demanding the radio.

Kolba and Pieniazek walked faster, but there was nowhere they could go or hide, and they couldn't outrun a car. Faced with the possibility of losing his radio, Kolba took the only course of action a kid could take when threatened, and that was to act tough and crazy, so crazy that the aggressors would be afraid to mess with him. Kolba stopped, turned to the car, which had also stopped, glared the meanest glare he could muster, and sneered, "Fuuuuuk you," stretching the first word out for effect.

For a moment, Kolba thought of making a move like he was going to kick in the car's door, which would have been a mistake. One couldn't take acting crazy too far. Going overboard and pretending to be too tough was a clear sign that one was acting, and merely pretending, and it signaled to the aggressor that the victim really was scared. Getting caught pretending was a sure way to get beaten up or robbed.

Kolba worked it perfectly; he sneered the obscenity and tilted his head slightly, held his glare for three seconds, spit on the ground, glared another two seconds and then turned and calmly walked away, which signaled to the guys that their threats meant nothing to him.

It worked. The aggressors figured that one guy challenging a car full of guys so calmly was indeed crazy, and they drove off.

The guys finished their sodas, took the bottles back in for their two-cent deposit, and headed to Koz Park. They were on the twenty-four hundred block of Avers, which had been famous from ever since the kids knew because of one resident, Harry Scary, another imagined child kidnapper and killer.

Harry lived in a one-and-a-half story wooden frame house. The wooden clapboards on the front of the house had long lost much of their light blue paint, and unlike the other small front yards on the block that had neat, trimmed lawns, Harry's front yard was what the adults considered a jungle—tiny islands of grass surrounded by seas of bare dirt and loaded with the one weed that said to everyone that the person's whose lawn contained it was a lazy good-for-nothing, drunk, and most likely a child killer: the feared and hated dandelion.

No one with any honor and self-respect could have anything but a perfect and weed-free front and back lawn. A lawn was an extension of one's personality and attitude toward life and work. Many of the neighborhood's men were machinists who worked metal with precision and to specific tolerances. If a part or tool wasn't machined to the required tolerance, it wouldn't fit properly into a larger machine or tool, and the end product wouldn't work properly. A part that was outside of those tolerances was considered a reject and a failure, as was the guy who made it. In the thousands of machine shops across the city, there was no room for failures.

Weeds and bare spots in a lawn translated into failure and a lack of precision. Failure was the result of a lack of discipline, skill, pride and an excess of bad habits such as drinking too much, laziness and having only one job.

The theory was borne out, neighborhood people saw, on the front lawn of the apartment building at the corner of Altgeld and Springfield owned by Mr. and Mrs. Joot. It was mostly bare, but had dandelions and a thick, leafy plant that grew close to the ground. The Joots, everyone also knew, were alcoholics, and their lawn was a reflection of that, and a disgrace.

If a single weed showed up in a respectable family's lawn, the men would send their kids out with a wooden handled, forked, steel weed digger to dig it out by the root because even a single weed was a disgrace.

Harry Scary's house was a mess, and his front lawn was full of weeds, a sure sign that he was no good. When he was younger, Dennis ran as fast as he could whenever he had to go past Harry's house, and he still ran, even when he was a half block past the place. Harry was said to hate kids, and no one wanted to be caught by the evil man who lived in the house with peeling paint and weeds in his lawn.

Yet exactly what Harry did to kids and why he was scary was a mystery to everyone. Dennis had never even seen the man he was so scared of. Once, he and Masciola hung out in the alley behind Harry's back yard to try and get a glimpse of him, but Harry never appeared. His failure to walk out into his back yard so they could see him further convinced the two that he was even scarier than everybody had said, and they shuddered as they quit their stakeout.

Now there were more than a dozen of them, high school and grade school guys, and none of them, despite their safety in numbers, could shake the fact that they were about to walk—walk!—by Harry Scary's house.

"Hey, that's Harry Scary's house up there," someone in the group said. "Maybe we oughta cross the street. He's scary."

"Sheeeit, that old man don't scare me. Never did," Wally Domrzalski, who was a junior in high school, replied. "Nothing scares me!"

The bravado made the younger kids, including the Disturbers, feel more confident about walking by Harry's house instead of running. Yeah, the Disturbers were bold troublemakers, but even they couldn't shake a lifetime of talk about how mean and frightening Harry was and what he did to kids. Ever since they could remember, from about three or four years old, every kid in the neighborhood had been warned that Harry Scary was a madman who was to be avoided.

"If you're so bold, why don't you go ring his doorbell," Wilson, also a junior in high school, said to Wally. "You ain't no sissy, are you?"

"Sheeeit. He don't mean nothing to me, and I'd ring his doorbell even if I was by myself."

"Ever rang his doorbell before?" Kolba asked.

"Never needed to. He never snatched one of my brothers, so I always thought it was best for him for me to stay out of his way. I mean, man, I'd deck that son of a bitch if I saw him. Just deck him."

Had Harry actually been a child kidnapper, Wally would indeed have decked him, and more, because the incident on Drake when he was three and was almost kidnapped never left his mind.

"Well shit, just go ring his doorbell. He'll probably know it's you and won't answer," Wilson said. "He ain't gonna mess with you."

"You guys don't think I can do it, do you?"

"I don't know, maybe you're still afraid of Harry Scary," Wilson said as the guys laughed.

Dennis offered his assessment of the situation: "I was always scared of this guy. So was everybody else. Why don't we just throw some rocks through his window? That'll show him."

"Or," Kolba added, "let's get some dog shit from the alley, put it in a bag, put it on his porch and light it on fire and then ring the doorbell. When he comes out and sees the fire, he'll step on it and get shit all over his shoes."

They all laughed at that because it was said to be one of the neighborhood's favorite pranks. Everyone talked about it, but no one knew anyone who had actually done it. Dog shit was readily available in any alley. No one ever picked after their pets, and some alleys always had at least a dozen excrement piles, which in the summer were always covered with flies.

The piles fascinated the younger kids who could never figure out why flies would eat shit. They were also an annoyance when kids wanted to play softball or football or tag in an alley because they didn't want to be running around stepping in the stuff. If there weren't too many piles, they'd get sticks and flick them to the sides of the alleys and up against the garages, which always infuriated the homeowners, especially the ones who never picked up after their dogs.

There was one kid in the neighborhood who was more than just fascinated with the piles of dog excrement in the alleys. His name was Guy Allen Lodgers and he lived in the apartment building at the corner of Harding and Altgeld. When he was five or six, Guy came to believe that he really was a TV cartoon character and hero named Underdog, a caped dog who flew around foiling bad guys and constantly saving his girlfriend, Polly, from certain doom. Unfortunately for Guy, though, putting a red cape over his shoulders, jumping off his first-floor backyard landing, and attempting to fly, while, like his cartoon canine hero, shouting, "There's no need to fear, Underdog is here!" always resulted in a fall to the sidewalk and bruised and scraped arms and legs.

Guy wasn't alone in trying to fly—all the kids wanted to, thought they could and tried to—but Guy was the only one who didn't realize after the first try and failure that kids couldn't fly on their own, and certainly not with homemade capes and flying contraptions.

In kindergarten and first grade, Dennis daydreamed of building his own helicopter out of a small, wooden rocking chair he sat and played in. He imagined himself lifting slowly off the ground, clearing the telephone wires and trees and housetops, hoovering for a while high above the house and then flying anywhere and everywhere, never stopping for fuel, and landing back home only when it was time for supper or bed.

After realizing that his rocking chair would never be transformed into a real helicopter, Dennis thought of other ways to sort of fly. One day, in second grade, he decided that he would parachute off the third-story attic landing of his house. Not one to just rush into things, Dennis made little practice parachutes out of hankies, old rags, and stones for weight, and tossed them off the attic landing. Some of them floated gently to the ground, but most of the time their canopies failed to unfurl, and they fell quickly to the ground.

But Dennis wasn't deterred. He started sewing a bunch of rags together in an effort to make a parachute big enough for him, but most of the rags he used were filled with holes and he realized that even if he sewed rags together for the next couple of years he would never have a real and safe chute.

So Dennis figured on trying what he thought was the next best thing. The Saturday morning cartoons the kids watched on TV always showed characters using umbrellas as parachutes, and they always worked, and so he figured he'd use an umbrella to get him gently from the attic landing to the ground about thirty feet below.

But Dennis wasn't so dumb as to think that one umbrella would suffice, or even be safe. He knew he needed a backup system, and so, with safety his number one priority, he went through the closets, got three umbrellas and raced up the wooden back porch steps to the attic landing where he intended to open the umbrellas, jump off and float gently and safely to the ground. He opened the umbrellas but realized he couldn't hold three at once, and so he junked one and held the other two, one in each hand.

There was another problem. Dennis was short and needed both hands to grab the four-foot-tall wooden banister that enclosed the landing and looked out over the yard. He needed to get his legs over the top rail and sit on it before launching himself off it to the ground. But he was unable to grab the banister with the open umbrellas in his hands, and so he was stuck and unable to go through with his magnificent experiment.

He was stuck, that is, until Steve and Wally walked into the yard from the alley, saw him up by the attic and yelled to ask what he was doing.

"I'm gonna parachute off!" Dennis excitedly yelled back. "I've got two umbrellas! Come up here and help me get on the banister so I can jump off."

"You're crazy!" Wally yelled. "You're gonna kill yourself. Get down from there!"

Steve said quietly to Wally, "Aww, so what. Let him do it. He's an idiot anyway." Wally replied:

"You're just as crazy as he is. He's gonna break his legs."

"So?"

"So? Shit, we'll be blamed for it, and they won't let us out of the house for a couple of weeks."

"Yeah, but it would be fun to see him try. And who knows, maybe it'll work."

Wally had two crazies to deal with, and not wanting to be blamed for Dennis's death, he raced up to the attic and dragged his brother down the stairs while yelling at him to never again try to do anything so stupid.

That Guy Allen Lodgers honestly thought he was Underdog made the kids both laugh and feel uneasy. They sensed that Guy might have been a little off, especially when he ran around the alley wearing his cape while shouting, "When Polly's in trouble, I am not slow, it's up, up, up and away I go!" And they knew he was more than just a little off by the intense interest he took in the piles of dog crap in the alley, and the flies that covered them.

One hot summer day when the flies were really thick, Guy stooped down near a pile, inspected it, pulled a popsicle stick out of his pocket, stuck it in the crap, shouted, "There's no need to fear, Underdog is here!" and started to put the stick up to his mouth in an apparent attempt to eat the vile stuff. Someone kicked the stick out of Guy's hand and screamed that he was crazy. Guy was startled and ran home. Thereafter, Guy Allen Lodgers was known as the kid who ate dog shit, and no one dared play with him.

Masciola dismissed Dennis's idea of hurling rocks through Harry Scary's front windows. "Jesus, you can't just do that," he said. "You gotta have a reason to throw rocks through someone's windows. You can't just do it for fun when you're walking by."

"A reason! Shit. He's scared all of us. Sounds like a reason to me," Dennis said, his feelings hurt that his idea was being rejected.

"Yeah, but we ain't scared now, not unless you are?"

"Screw you. I ain't scared. But you know, I mean, there's probably skeletons in his basement."

"So what? They're probably old. We can't do anything about that. I mean, that's private property."

"OK. Then let's get a reason. If Wally rings his doorbell and he comes out and scares us, we can throw rocks."

The guys debated the situation as they stood on the sidewalk in front of Harry's house. The high school guys, who had grown out of the idea that Harry was scary—they had never seen him either—amused themselves with the idea of tossing rocks through someone's windows, and they laughed at Dennis's anti-social instincts.

"DeeDee (Wilson's nickname for Wally), you ring the doorbell. If he comes out with an axe or something, we'll bust his windows. Go ring his doorbell, and we'll get some rocks," Wilson said.

"Why do I gotta ring his doorbell?"

"Cuz you said you would."

"Yeah, well. What if he's gotta gun? Or an axe? Or a rope with a giant hook on it that he'll throw through the window and get me and drag me in with it?"

"That'll give us a reason to break his windows!" Dennis shouted to his brother. "You ain't scared of Harry Scary, are you?"

The guys laughed at Wally's sudden reluctance to walk up the steps of Harry's front porch and ring his doorbell. After all, ringing someone's doorbell—without the fiery bag of dog shit—and running away was a prank they all played. They thought it was the funniest thing in the world when someone would respond to the bell, come out and see no one there.

"Get your ass up there and ring his doorbell," Wilson ordered. "We can't stand here all day. And if he does come out, at least we'll finally know what he looks like."

DeeDee had no more excuses, and he looked back with apprehension as he approached the six wooden steps to Harry's front porch.

"Hey, if this guy throws poison at me, you guys better help me," he said as he put a foot on the first wooden step.

"And if he throws acid at you, we'll run home and call the cops," Wilson laughed. "Sheeeit."

The guys found some rocks and clumps of dried mud on Harry's lawn and in the street and they waited to see what would happen as DeeDee hesitantly put a foot on the second step.

"Keep going, man," Wilson shouted as a way of encouragement. "Just four more steps. We're ready!"

DeeDee hit third step and then the fourth and then one of the guys shouted: "There's someone at the window! Holy shit!"

Their eyes, including DeeDee's, fixed on the front window closest to the front door. They saw a hand poking through the white blinds and pushing them apart to see what was going on. Then the hand turned over with its palm up and motioned with a curled index finger for the guys to come forward.

The guys were paralyzed. The madman was taunting them and demanding they come forward! He'd kill them all and hide their skeletons in the basement, they thought.

The blinds separated even further and the curled finger again moved, inviting them forward. Then two eyes appeared through the slit in the blinds. Evil eyes! The eyes of a maniac! It was the first time that any in the group had even caught a glimpse of Harry Scary and they were terrified.

Then the blinds closed, a sure sign that Harry was coming out to get them.

"Holy shit! He's seen us! Let's get the hell out of here!" someone yelled.

With that, the guys dropped their rocks and took off and raced away. They ran and didn't stop until they were a block away, where they had to stop and wait to cross a busy street. The wait jangled their nerves even more as it allowed time for Harry to catch up if he was chasing them.

They looked back to see if Harry Scary was after them, and when they saw he wasn't hobbling down the street toward them, they relaxed and talked about the incident.

"My god, that hand looked like it belonged to a skeleton. I mean, there was almost no skin on it," Ruchinski offered in his usual way of exaggerating everything and trying to turn a minor incident into a full-blown adventure. "Did you guys see that?"

"Almost? Almost no skin? There was no skin! It was just a bone!" Bozeman exclaimed. "And it was covered with blood!"

"Naah, the skin was falling off the bone like it was diseased and rotting. It was yellow and ugly, and I'll betcha it stunk," Kolba said as the guys tried to outdo each other's fabricated goriness.

"And those eyes, I mean, man, one of 'em was squirting blood and the other was yellow and had a hole in it!" Vanko offered.

HARRY SCARY

"I saw the blood, too," Dennis said. "He was probably eating kids and we interrupted him! Maybe we should call the cops."

"He was pissed, I mean really pissed, and he would have killed us. Man, I wonder why?" Ruchinski added.

"I know why," Frankie, ever the wise guy, said. "He got a bad pizza from Mary's and that just pissed him off. He ordered extra cheese and they didn't give it to him."

The high school guys, even though they had been a little scared, laughed at the younger kids' imaginations. They had outgrown the habit of characterizing everything that happened to them as a glorious, life-threatening adventure, and they figured that Harry was a scared, old, lonely guy who had probably been looking for some company.

It didn't matter, though, because Harry Scary, a guy who up until then they had never seen, had, in less than ten minutes, evolved from a mere child kidnapper into a walking, rotting, stinking corpse with a hole in one eye and blood squirting out the other who tried to murder a group of kids because he had gotten a bad pizza, and that story was fated to become a neighborhood legend.

CHAPTER 20

Koz Park

K OZ PARK WAS alive with kids yelling, laughing and screaming;
playing baseball, pinner, football, hopscotch, jump rope, army, cops
and robbers, It, freeze tag, dodge ball, guns and war, riding their
bikes and doing anything else that came to their minds. Twelve hundred
kids went to OLG alone. About the same number went each to Monroe, a
nearby public school, and to St. Hyacinth, a Catholic school just north of
Diversey. The park was always loaded with kids and with adults who sat on
the nine-acre park's green wooden benches, smoking, reading newspapers,
watching the kids, escaping the confines of their small apartments and
enjoying the fresh air.

Koz was like Mozart Park, about a mile south on Armitage and Springfield:
each was a center of neighborhood activity. Both parks had borne that role
since 1914 when they were built. Summer adult and youth softball leagues kept
Koz's four baseball diamonds constantly occupied on weekend and weekday
afternoons and evenings. The roars of the spectators watching the games and
cheering the players reverberated throughout the neighborhood, and on a still
day could be heard all the way to Fullerton.

For kids, the park was a sea of grass, trees and playground equipment
that was magical because it was open and so different from the narrow

gangways and alleys, cramped apartments and houses-squeezed-next-to-houses and grimy factories that made up the rest of the neighborhood. Being there meant freedom, and the instant they arrived, minds and imaginations raced. To the kids, nine acres of open space seemed like a wilderness that could keep them occupied for hours with fun, and away from grouchy adults who complained about the noise they made when they played in the alleys and streets.

Not only was Koz their playground, it was also a place where they learned life lessons and skills such as getting along with each other, negotiating, compromising, organizing, leadership, fair play and so much more.

Koz was the kids' domain; it was for, and run by, kids. But the place had rules, and those rules were simple. The older guys, those in eighth grade or high school, got the pick of fields, or the basketball courts in the gym, or the tennis courts or the pinner ledges next to the tennis courts. They would "call" the areas for themselves, as in "Callin' dibs on this diamond." When that happened, younger kids who were there before had to vacate and wait for the older guys to finish their games or face the consequences.

The rule was unwritten, but it was enforced. If younger kids decided to stay on a field or court after older guys called it, they were picked up by the older guys and dumped head-first into wire trash cans around the park or put on top of water fountains so the water would squirt on the front of their pants, making it look as if they had pissed on themselves. One time a kid was dumped head-first into a trash can and couldn't get out. The solution was simple: the older guys kicked it over on its side and the kid was able to crawl out.

One year the older guys formed a summer league for league baseball games, with the games being played on just one diamond, and the schedule being that seventh and eighth graders would play at eight-thirty in the morning, followed by the fifth and sixth graders at eleven, and the third and fourth graders at twelve-thirty.

Wally Domrzalski and his buddies, who were in fifth grade at the time, decided one day to start their game at eight-thirty and they called the field. That was a mistake. The older guys, recognizing that Wally was the leader of the group, had three words for him: "Beat it, squirt." When he didn't obey, they picked him up and stuffed him head-first into a trash can.

HE BROKE THE PARK'S RULES

No one disputed enforcement of the rules, and those who, like Wally, had been punished for daring to challenge the older guys didn't cry or run home to complain to their parents. They accepted the punishment, knowing that they were wrong and that one day they'd be able to do the same to younger kids.

The park was indeed the kids' domain. They formed pinner, baseball, softball, football and hockey leagues and held tournaments, a process that included picking teams, naming them, setting schedules and making rules, and they did it on their own without a single adult involved.

Most of the rules were commonly agreed upon and done so because of necessity. For softball and baseball games, the number of players available dictated some of the rules, such as the "right field fly rule," in baseball, which, because there weren't enough players to man right field, meant that a ball hit there was an automatic out. Disputes over rules were resolved, sometimes by yelling and screaming, with those who yelled the loudest prevailing, or sometimes by fighting, which was rare.

When just two kids were around, a bat, league ball and two baseball mitts were enough for a game. Dennis and Masciola played every summer by themselves in an area called the cinders by the tennis courts. It was a small patch of open space bordered by sidewalks and the tennis courts, and one kid would stand near "home plate," bat in hand, toss the league ball up in the air and then swing at it with his bat. The kids decided what would constitute a base hit, double, triple and home run, and they played that way for hours at a time.

For football games not played on the regular field, which had yard lines, sidelines and end zones marked with white chalk lines, the kids had to set their own boundaries because there were no markings or regularly shaped areas in which to play. Trees, bushes, sidewalks and benches made for various markings and boundaries, and the kids decided among themselves what would be a first down on such irregular fields.

Plays on those makeshift-field football games went something like, "John, run straight to the tree, and when you get there, cut to the middle and I'll throw it to you."

Hockey games on the ice in the winters were the same. The older kids got prime ice areas while the younger kids were shunted off to the sides of the rink. The kids set boundaries, net sizes—the nets were three-sided, squared off small snowbanks formed with hockey sticks—and, because most of the kids had no hockey equipment, they instituted a "no lifting" rule, which meant they had to shoot the puck flat on the ice so as not to injure each other with flying hockey pucks.

The pinner tournaments in the summer and fall were almost as fun as football, as they required only a rubber or tennis ball, and anyone could play. Teams consisted of two guys each, and on a Saturday or summer weekday they would play from morning until early afternoon, banging the ball on the concrete ledge at the bottom of the park house wall next to the tennis courts. The park house wall was at least thirty feet wide at that point and two games could played at once.

Tournament winners, who were declared the World Series Champs, got nothing except bragging rights and the knowledge that they were the best pinner team for that day or weekend. They relished the title while it lasted because they knew that the next day or weekend could find another team on top.

After the baseball, pinner and football games, hell, after any day at the park, the kids would head to Injun' Joe's, a candy store that had everything a kid could want packed in, up to and on the ceilings: candy, kites, potato chips, itching powder, pea shooters, sling shots, quarter balls, dime balls, ice cream, and soda—absolutely everything. Outside was a glider swing for kids to sit in and enjoy.

Koz was a starting point for all-day adventures and explorations that would take kids everywhere. Telling their parents that they were going to Koz when they left their homes at eight in the morning was a kind of code that said they would go anywhere, whether it was taking the bus and L—a shorthand reference to the city's elevated train and subway system—downtown, walking or riding bikes to Riis Park three miles away, roaming the railroad tracks, playing in empty lots, heading to Milwaukee Avenue and beyond, and well, just anywhere.

Those all-day adventures usually started with a kid calling a friend out to play—not by calling on the telephone or knocking on their front or back doors. No, a kid would stand in a friend's back yard, or at his fence in the alley and shout, "Yooo-ooo Jooohhhn!" or "Yooo-ooo Steeeeeve!" until their friend opened a window or door and yelled back, "Whaddya want?" The response would be, "Can you come out and play?"

A kid could almost always go out and play, and then those two kids would go to another friend's house and shout from the alley, "Yooo-ooo so and so." The third would join them and they'd go to another house and yell, and pretty soon, there'd be four or five kids yelling for another kid to come out and play, and once there were five or six of them, they'd head to the park and the day would turn into one impulsive decision after another and they'd wind up wherever their imaginations, or kids with other ideas of what to do, took them.

The kids had freedom to roam the neighborhood by themselves at will. The parents always wanted them out of the house, so they'd yell, "Whatcha doin' inside? Go out and get some fresh air" on summer and weekend days. The only rule was that they must be home by supper time, usually five in the afternoon.

The kids reveled in pretty much total freedom to do what they wanted and to roam the neighborhood and the city at will, by themselves and without adults; to make their own mistakes and to be able to correct them; to have fights, and, win or lose, know that they had at least stood up for themselves; to form pinner and softball leagues by themselves and to make and enforce their own rules; to learn about competition and winning and losing—no matter how disappointing the losing was—and to learn that losing a softball or hockey game wasn't the end of the world, nor winning one the summit of human existence; to learn how to explore and daydream and imagine and invent and create, and to try and fail, and try again—to persevere—and then to succeed; to stretch and break rules—especially stupid ones and those born of superstition, arrogance and abusive authority—to learn that other kids had opinions and ideas that were different than theirs, and that those differences didn't make their playmates strange or dangerous, only more interesting; to learn that each had different skills and talents and that all—well, most—were valuable; to learn, by themselves, that they could argue and fight and bicker and disagree mightily, and then walk home at the end of the day together side-by-side laughing and daydreaming of the adventures and fun the next day would hold. They reveled in being kids.

What they were learning by sorting out so many things by themselves were lessons that were preparing them in the best way possible to one day be good and strong adults capable of forcefully expressing their own ideas and opinions, standing up for themselves, and accepting equally forceful and opposing ideas and opinions without being deeply offended and dissolving into tears. They were learning the way the world really was: a great mash of different people, ideas, talents and opinions and they were dealing with it. They were figuring things out and solving problems and stretching and growing by themselves, without adults. They were not delicate creatures who needed an adult's overbearing and protective hand every step of the way; they were durable, persistent and free, and that freedom was simply magnificent.

Even if parents did want to have more control over where their kids went and what they did, they didn't have the means or time to do so. Families had one car, which fathers drove to work, and the mothers, who were usually stay-at-home wives, were busy with housework—cooking, cleaning, doing the wash, ironing and so many other things—and didn't have the time or the desire to follow the kids all over or even take them anywhere.

Doing laundry was an all-morning affair. Most families had three or four kids, and that meant several loads of laundry every week, or each washing day. The dirty clothes would be put into a wash machine with a big metal or plastic agitator, and the machine had to be filled up manually with hot water from a hose in the basement sink. Then the machine would be turned on, and two massive sinks would be filled with water for the rinsing.

Loads were segregated into whites, which had to be bleached, and colors; heavier items like pants and towels were separated so that each laundry day involved a woman doing several loads of wash.

After the machine had stopped, the water was drained by gravity into a sewer in the basement through a hose from the machine, and then the real work of doing laundry began. The machines had rollers into which the wet clothes would be fed by hand with a round wooden stick. Each piece of laundry, and there would be dozens in a single load, had to be fed individually into the rollers, which would squeeze out the dirty water. From there the clothes went into the first sink for an initial rinse. Then they were put through the rollers again and into a sink of water for a second rinse. After that they'd go through the rollers again and then into a laundry basket. If there were several loads, merely washing and rinsing the clothes took all morning.

After the clothes were rinsed, they'd be hung out to dry on clotheslines in the back yard, or in the basement, which took another couple of hours. Each item of clothing had to be secured to the clothesline with clothespins. Then, after drying on the lines for a few hours, the clothes had to be taken off the line, folded, put into laundry baskets and put away in dressers and drawers. Shirts and pants had to be ironed, and a load of ironing could take an additional entire morning. Any clothes that were torn were sewn and patched by hand.

Floors were swept or vacuumed daily and washed weekly. Washing a floor was done by getting on one's hands and knees with one bucket of soapy water, and another with clean water, a brush for scrubbing and rags for rinsing and drying.

Cooking daily meals for supper took a couple of hours as pretty much everything was made from scratch. Potatoes had to be peeled and boiled, meat fried or baked, and vegetables cut up and boiled or steamed. Then the table had to be set and the food put out. After supper came dish washing, a chore that kids were made to do. Finally, the dishes had to be dried with a towel and put away, also by kids.

After supper, a father, who usually worked in a factory or at some other physically demanding job, might drive off to a second job, or plop down in a chair and read a newspaper. Mothers were simply exhausted.

In the fall, storm windows had to be put up over the regular windows, an all-day job done by fathers on weekends. In the spring the storm windows were taken down and washed, and every other window and screen in the house washed inside and out. Metal blinds and their cloth bindings were washed once a year in the spring, another all-day affair. Furniture and blinds and shades and knickknacks were dusted once a week.

The fathers did work around the house fixing things: rewiring lamps; scraping, sanding and varnishing wooden windowsills; replacing washers in faucets; reupholstering chairs; changing the oil and other work on cars; washing and painting walls; unclogging drains and on and on. Life, it seemed, was one never-ending job.

Their mothers usually made the kids lunches: American cheese or bologna sandwiches wrapped in wax paper and put in brown paper lunch bags that they'd eat long before noon because roaming—walking, running, bicycling, climbing fences and garages and getting onto roofs of grocery stores and apartment buildings—burned calories and made them hungry, and because no one wanted, or had room, to carry bags with lunches. They had no backpacks or other means to carry the sandwiches other than to stuff them into pants pockets or into the waistbands of their pants.

When they ate at Koz, or at any other Chicago park, they washed the sandwiches down with cold water that ran continuously from six-sided, four-foot-high concrete water fountains. Those fountains, with their thick, steel plates that formed a kind of roof over the waterspout were a marvel and joy to kids and adults because once they were turned on in the spring, they never shut off—they ran twenty-four hours a day—and the cold, clean Lake Michigan water that from flowed from them quenched the mightiest thirsts and cooled the hottest, sweatiest heads on steamy summer days.

All one needed for a drink was to hunch over a fountain, lower a head to within an inch or two of the spout and suck and slurp and sip and let the cold water run into the mouth and over the teeth and chin and rejoice in the most incredible liquid refreshment ever. On real hot days—those scorching, humid days when every pore sweated and when cotton underwear and T-shirts stuck to skin and never let go—kids would cup their hands, fill them with water and pour it over their sweaty heads and rejoice at the blessing of fountains that never stopped spewing cold water.

There were unspoken drinking fountain rules which said that one could slurp and take in water for twenty seconds at the maximum when there were lines. Even that was a long time and made those in line impatient and angry. Sticking one's mouth—which younger kids did—on the spout was considered sick, and the kids who did that were considered slobs.

The fountains and their never-ending streams of water offered other joys to the kids. Because they never shut off and didn't require one to turn a knob to get the water flowing, kids could quickly and efficiently fill water balloons because both hands were free to place and hold the lip of the balloon over the spout. A finger over, or a stick stuck into the spout produced a stream of water that could be aimed and shot at kids fifteen or twenty feet away. It was a favorite trick of the bigger kids to squirt the little ones who were waiting in line for a drink. The kids also thought it was a hoot to pick up their playmates and sit them on top of the fountains so their pants would get wet.

*

The guys got to Koz, and, as they always did, they headed immediately to one of the park's three fountains to get drinks. It was an unspoken and unwritten ritual for kids that whenever they got to any Chicago park the first thing they did was head to a fountain. They never knew why they did it, they just did. They couldn't compare the quality and taste of one park's water to another's because it all came from the same Great Lake, and yet, they did compare. And there were differences depending on the age of the neighborhood and its water lines buried five feet underneath the city's streets.

They took drinks from a fountain next to the park house. Koz's two-story, Tudor Revival Style park house was a landmark in the neighborhood because it seemed so out of place in an area of bulky red-brick factories and three-story wooden frame homes. That it was designed by prominent architect Albert A. Schwartz meant nothing to them. They had no idea who he was, or had been, and didn't care.

All that mattered was that the park house had two gyms, one for boys and the other for girls, and meeting and playrooms in the basement and second floor. It also mattered that in the winter, the building, which was heated with steel radiators, offered warmth that enveloped them like a thick quilt when they entered after being out in the cold for hours.

After they drank, the guys surveyed the park and saw that all the baseball diamonds were taken, so they walked to the park's northeast corner for another ritual they engaged in, no matter how old they were, and that was to goof around on Koz's playground.

With its dirt surface, swings, slides, monkey bars, seesaw, and big sandbox, the playground was a magnet for little kids, and for the older guys when they couldn't think of anything to do. The older kids thought it was the height of comedy to squeeze themselves into the wooden baby swings, which were high off the ground, and pull the protective wooden bar down though the two chains to keep them in place.

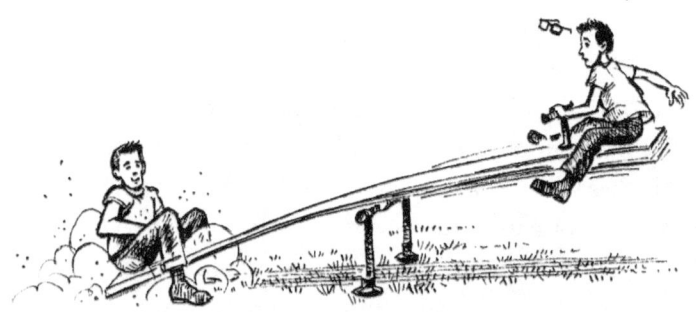

PLAYING AT KOZ

The regular swings with their wooden seats were only a couple of feet of the ground, and kids had contests to see who could swing the highest.

The bolder kids tried to swing so hard and high that they would fly over the horizontal metal pole that formed the top of the swing sets. Many would get to the point where just a few more swings and leg pumps would get them over and around the bar, but they usually chickened out, fearing they'd fall off when flying so high through the air.

No matter how old they were, none of the kids ever outgrew the fun of the seesaws, or teeter-totters, especially the heavier ones who could keep their pals in the air for as long as they wanted. The asphalt under each wooden seesaw seat had dual indentations from the thousands and thousands of times that the kids on the bottom suddenly jumped off, leaving the kid at the other end to crash to the ground.

The guys scattered around the playground, some going for the swings, some the monkey bars and others for the seesaws. Dennis and Masciola had used the seesaws since they were little, always with the same result of Dennis and his skinny body being stuck in the air while Jim contentedly sat with his seat on the ground amusing himself as his pal's skinny legs dangled in the air.

CHAPTER 21

Battling Conformity, and Booze from Bums

THE GUYS PLAYED for twenty minutes, checked out the ball fields, which were still taken, and decided to move on to Ken-Well Park, a three-acre patch of grass and not much else that always seemed to be empty. Ken-Well was four blocks west of Pulaski, past the giant Olson Rug factory, and a block north of Diversey, tucked away on a quiet side street and up against the railroad tracks. It had a small, one-story park house that also always seemed empty. Because no one ever went there, it was a good place for the older guys to drink beer on weekend nights, as not even the cops ever drove past.

They walked a block and came to the neighborhood's most beloved jewel: the waterfall and park at the Olson Rug factory.

Olson Rug was a monster, five-story, red brick and glass factory that stretched for nearly three blocks west of Pulaski and squeezed up against the Milwaukee Road railroad tracks.

The kids didn't know that the one-acre park with an 800-foot-long lawn had been built in 1935 by the factory's owner, Walter Olson, who wanted to replicate a Wisconsin north woods waterfall in the middle of Chicago. They didn't care; they just knew it was there and that it was the neatest place they had ever seen. The park's centerpiece was a 35-foot-tall stepped rock waterfall, complete with walking paths, flowers, trees, shrubs, thousands of rocks, benches and statues of Indians, Indian teepees and a duck pond.

The centerpiece of the waterfall was a flagstone footbridge near the top of the gushing rapids with no handrail. Mist from surging, rushing water covered the bridge, making it slippery and sometimes hard to cross. But the middle of that slippery bridge was pure heaven and solid refreshment to everyone in the neighborhood and to the thousands of people from around the city who visited the place every year.

THE OLSON RUG WATERFALL

Standing on the bridge got one sprayed with the fine, cool mist of the water crashing against the rocks, and on hot summer days it was the most magnificent feeling there was. Right there in the steamy, sooty city that was, in effect, a giant factory, was a waterfall with trees—spruces, pines and junipers that one never saw in the city—and one could stand there and get misted and cooled down without actually having to jump in the water. Kids and adults would linger on the bridge, savoring that fine, cooling mist and daydreaming about what it would be like to be in the woods of Wisconsin. Then they'd walk to the other side and down the path to a sign that pointed to a group of rocks and melted steel and other material that came from the Great Chicago Fire of October 8-10, 1871.

The Great Chicago Fire, every city resident knew, was the greatest, largest, most destructive fire in the history of the world, and there, right in front of them, were rocks from that mighty conflagration! They stared at and studied those rocks for what seemed like hours, imaging the miles-long sheets of flames that devoured the wooden city for three days and sent tens of thousands of residents fleeing into the filthy Chicago River and Lake Michigan for safety.

They had memorized the facts of the fire; that it started in the barn behind Mrs. Catherine O'Leary's wooden house at 137 West DeKoven Street southwest of downtown, that it destroyed 3.3 square miles of buildings, killed 300 people and left 100,000 homeless.

Their minds drifted and they imagined what it must have been like to try to outrun the mighty walls of fire and how those great Chicagoans carried on in the smoldering ruins and rebuilt their great city, the greatest city in the world!

Kids lingered in front of the Indian statues and teepees and daydreamed about roaming free in the woods, shooting deer and other animals with bows-and-arrows, cooking them over open fires and slaughtering pioneers whenever they felt like it. Families picnicked on the vast, green lawn and everybody bought hot dogs, lemonade and soda from a stand against the factory's wall.

In the fall, the park set up an Indian Summer display on the lawn that was a replica of the Injun Summer cartoon by John T. McCutcheon that the Chicago Tribune newspaper ran on its front page every October. The cartoon's top panel featured a white-bearded old man with a pipe, gray hat, blue jacket, red pants and wooden rake sitting on a log next to a tree. Standing next to him was a kid in a brown jacket, blue pants and boots. The two gaze across a log-rail fence into a field of stacked corn stalk shocks as smoke rises from a small pile of burning leaves next to them.

The man tells the boy that homesick Injuns come back to play when it's Injun Summer. In the bottom panel, day has turned into night, the moon is out, the smoke from the fire swirls into dancing Indians and the shocks of corn turn into teepees.

"See off yonder, see them teepees?" the old man says to the kid. "They kind o' look like corn shocks from here, but them's Injun tents, sure as you're a foot high. See 'em now? Sure. I knowed you could. Smell that smoky sort o' smell in the air? That's the campfires a-burnin' and their pipes a-goin'."

Olson's display included the corn shocks arranged on the lawn just as they were in the cartoon, and life-sized replicas of the old man and the boy.

For Halloween, Olson erected a giant moon over the waterfall that was lit up with floodlights. In the middle of that giant moon was a witch on a broomstick. Christmastime saw big Santas and fake reindeer on the lawn along with thousands of Christmas lights.

Olson had sold his factory in 1965 to Marshall Field & Company, which many years later destroyed and tore down that incredible spot of beauty to make an asphalt parking lot.

But in 1966 the park was still open, the waterfall was still flowing, and the guys stopped in to walk their favorite paths and linger on the bridge and enjoy its cooling mist.

As they walked the park's paths, the guys were unusually quiet. There was no horseplay and no threats of scalping each other as there usually were when they walked past the teepees, no feigned attempts at throwing each other into the waterfall, and no talk of how they should return at night, take off their shoes, roll up their pants legs, jump into the duck pond and steal all the nickels and pennies off the bottom.

They were lost in their own thoughts.

True to his status as an instigator and Disturber, Ruchinski hated OLG and the nuns. Yes, he laughed at the beatings he received and reveled in his role, but a kid could take only so much of being treated as a loser and a misfit and being told constantly, as he had been by the nuns since first grade, that he would never amount to anything. He longed for respect and real support, and he wondered how he would ever escape the hell that OLG was for him.

Steve Domrzalski was in eighth grade. He was tired of getting up at four in the morning to do his paper route and then getting yelled at for falling asleep in class. He was a bright kid and could excel at anything; he wanted to do well in school, but he was just too tired. He loved comic books, and he and a friend drew their own, which were good, and he dreamed of writing and drawing comic books. He also dreamed of the day not too far off, when, like his older brother Wally, he would tell his dad that he was quitting his paper route because he was in high school and needed to concentrate on school.

Other kids simply wondered why they had to go home. Some dads drank too much and beat their wives and kids. To some, going home was as bad as being in school with the crazy and abusive nuns.

The older kids like Dave Wilson and Wally Domrzalski wondered what they would do after high school. They were juniors and would soon be old enough to be on their own, a thought that was both exhilarating and terrifying. What would they do? How would they do it?

For the most part, their dads worked in factories, and while Wilson and Wally had held summer and after-school jobs in factories, they hated them. They knew they wanted lives and careers that were different from what their fathers had, and yet they weren't sure of how to go about getting them. The neighborhood's social structure and mentality said that kids should be just like their parents; that boys should work in factories and girls should get married and be stay-at-home moms or teachers or nurses. There were a few boys in the neighborhood who wanted to become priests, and they were considered strange by all the other kids. As far as anyone knew, there had never been a girl in the neighborhood who wanted to become a nun.

Previous generations of kids followed those rules, but this one was different; they knew they had talents—whether to be artists, architects, engineers, writers, musicians, actors, comedians, or whatever they were good at—and they wanted to bust loose and pursue those talents and dreams. The neighborhood's mentality, all the way from the nuns to the high schools, did everything it could to smother those dreams and talents by its insistence on conformity to rules and by rewarding those who did conform and punishing those who didn't.

Challenging the status quo and authority was considered a sin by the nuns, as was independent thinking, and those who did the challenging had to have those tendencies beaten out of them. It wasn't just a love of conformity, rules and doctrine that drove the nuns. Although they were well educated for the time, they were intellectual cripples who couldn't see beyond their own small world that demanded loyalty and unquestioning obedience to rules, no matter how oppressive, illogical and stupid.

A kid who cracked up a class with great jokes and silly routines was, to the nuns, a troublemaker, misfit and pathetic clown, not a budding comedian who might someday make the world laugh. A kid who asked why ancient Indians who had never been baptized were sent to Hell, even though they had never known about Catholicism and baptism, was considered a troublemaker and degenerate, not someone who actually thought about things and identified and challenged inconsistencies, flaws and an absence of logic. Kids who learned by doing things or seeing things done, and not by the rote memorization method taught by the nuns, were considered retarded and stupid. Anyone who dared question the Church's rules and doctrine, like why someone should go to Hell for eating meat on a Friday, or for missing a single Sunday mass, was considered a heretic, communist and colleague of the Devil.

The guys were smothered by rules. To live and breathe they had to challenge the mindless and often abusive authority they saw all around. It was their way of screaming, "We hate this shit!"

They challenged that authority with an unrelenting determination, zeal and brazenness that shocked the nuns and parents. For generations, conformity had been the norm, and those who obeyed, whether because they were too scared to challenge it, didn't know how to, or they simply thought it was the right thing to do, were horrified by the rebellious behavior.

Because of television and other modern innovations, the kids were aware of options their teachers and parents couldn't imagine. They weren't going to work in the factories; they were going to pursue their dreams, and they weren't going to buy into religious dogma they felt was stupid and the enemy of intellectual curiosity.

That rebellious behavior threatened those who made and enforced the rules, especially the nuns and priests who saw their authority and revered and privileged status in society slipping away. Without that upcoming generation obeying their rules and filling the collection baskets on Sundays, they would be nothing.

The parents of those rebellious kids reacted in different ways. Some were indifferent, while others were pleased that their kids were smart and had independent minds. Others were angry because it meant that their standing with the nuns was diminished, and they craved being liked by those in authority. A third group was resentful of that independence. They hadn't rebelled, although many of them wished they had, and they weren't going to let their kids have the freedom they never had. How dare those kids think they could be better than their parents?

The guys lingered for a while at Olson Rug before moving on. It was nearing three o'clock, and they junked the idea of going to Ken-Well for a game of softball because the older guys had something more important to do. They had to find a bum to make a beer run, and they had to do it soon in order to secure their supply of alcohol for the evening.

There was only one place for minors to get alcohol: from the bums who hung around "The Monument," as everybody in the neighborhood called it. The Monument was the center of Logan Square. It was a large park-like patch of grass at the intersection of Milwaukee Avenue and Kedzie and Logan Boulevards, complete with a 70-foot-tall marble column topped with a giant marble eagle. It had been built in 1918 to commemorate the 100th anniversary of Illinois's statehood and to honor John A. Logan, a Civil War general on the Union side.

Almost no one in the neighborhood knew The Monument's history or that of the Logan Square neighborhood. They just knew it as a neat thing and a place they could go to sit on benches and enjoy the outdoors on a Saturday or Sunday afternoon. For the guys, The Monument was the place to get their booze from the bums who hung around the place, and their favorite bum was Marty. The bums both fascinated and scared the guys. Their filth and ragged clothes made them look mean, and the fact that they rarely spoke, and when they did, never in complete sentences, made them seem even meaner.

But Marty and the other bums weren't mean. They were just tired and worn out from living outside, or in coal bins and from nourishment by alcohol, and they wouldn't have been able to hurt anyone if they had tried. Some of the more demented kids thought it was fun to taunt the bums and throw rocks and sticks at them, but those kids were rare and usually just a few weeks away from heading off to reform school.

The kids wondered where the bums got food, how they stayed dry during thunderstorms, where they got their clothes and how they managed to stay alive year after year. Since the bums never talked much, the kids never figured that out. It never mattered because all they needed from the bums was for them to make alcohol runs.

The process of getting booze was simple. The guys would determine how many six-packs of beer, pints of wine or half pints of whiskey, vodka or schnapps they wanted, figure out how much it would cost, and collect the money. Then they'd go to The Monument, approach a bum and ask him to make a run. The deals always included tips for the bums, usually enough for them to buy a couple of pints of wine for themselves.

MARTY ON A BEER RUN

The deals always went down as anticipated. The bums were good business-men. They knew that if they took off with the cash the kids would eventually find them and beat them up, and they also knew that if they did abscond with the cash, or if they took too long to deliver the order, they'd never get any repeat business. Repeat business was what they depended on from the kids. Walking—in Marty's case, shuffling—to a tavern or liquor store to buy booze for kids was a lot easier than shoveling coal or other manual labor, and it paid more, and immediately, in the cash the bums needed to buy their own alcohol.

The tavern and liquor store owners knew the bums were making runs for kids. After all, no bum could afford, let alone drink, all the stuff they would buy. But no one cared, and, in fact, they thought it was perfectly normal that high school kids would drink on the weekends and that the bums would get them their stuff. Everybody in the neighborhood drank, and they had to start some time.

The guys walked the mile to The Monument and found Marty, who immediately agreed to make a run for four six-packs, three pints of wine and three half pints of whiskey and schnapps. Only the high school guys ordered. Even though everyone in the neighborhood drank, there was an unwritten rule that the drinking didn't start until the summer after eighth grade. The younger kids had occasionally tasted beer from sips of half-empty glasses left on tables at family holiday gatherings, and it always made them sick, but they almost always waited until the summer after eighth grade to begin drinking in earnest.

Marty came back with the order and the older guys went off to stash their booze in an alley. Since it was late in the afternoon, they all split up and went home to eat before the evening's fun.

Dennis, Wally and Steve got home to the smell two Polish sausage links boiling in pot of water on the gas stove. Florence Domrzalski bought the sausage from a Polish deli on Milwaukee Avenue and usually put it on a slow simmer around two in the afternoon. After three hours of simmering, the links cracked in the water and spewed out their grease. Florence would pluck them out of the pot with a fork and put them on a large plate so everyone could cut their own slices and put them on rye bread, which always came from Weiss Bakery on Fullerton. The links were cut lengthwise with a knife, plopped on the bread and topped with mustard, sliced tomatoes and onion, and they were delicious.

After eating, washing up and watching some TV, the guys left the house to join their respective pals. The older guys would retrieve their stashed booze and drink it along the railroad tracks or in one of their basements. Then they'd head off to The Corner or a high school dance.

CHAPTER 22

Fire Missiles and Officer Jimero

DENNIS AND MASCIOLA met up on Altgeld and the alley, lit up a couple of smokes and headed to The Corner to share Jim's latest idea for fun.

"It's really cool. My brother showed me this," Jim said as he reached into a brown paper bag. He dug out a small, empty, wooden thread spool that had a rubber band wrapped around it so that a piece of the rubber band looped out by one of the spool's holes. Then he pulled a straw out of the bag and inserted it into the open hole of the spool.

"It's really neat. It's kind of like a slingshot. You stick a blue-tip match in the straw, put the straw in the spool, pull it through the other end, pull it back with the rubber band and then let it go and it shoots out, and when it lands on the sidewalk the match lights," Jim explained.

He demonstrated the device, and sure enough, the match-tipped straw shot out of the spool, flew through the air and lit when it hit the ground. The keys to the contraption were Ohio Blue Tip, strike-anywhere wooden matches and fat rubber bands with which to grab the straw and shoot it out the thread spool.

"This is really boss," Dennis said as he loaded a straw and match into the spool and shot it at the brick wall of an apartment building. "We'll have a blast with this stuff."

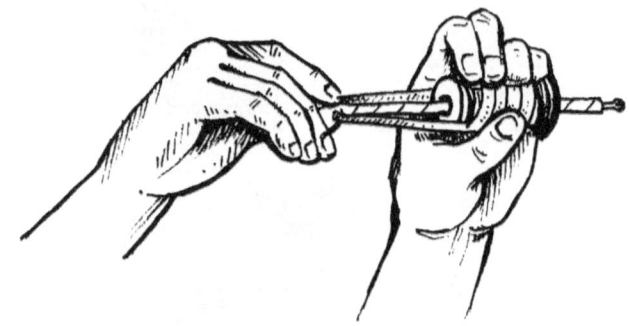

A SIMPLE, BUT INGENIOUS WEAPON

"Yeah, I've got like ten spools and the rubber bands. All we gotta do is buy some straws and matches and we can shoot these things all over the place."

They got to The Corner and found Kolba, Kurkowski, Ruchinski and Biedron and showed them their new toys and they all marched to the Jewel food store on Fullerton where they each bought a couple boxes of straws and blue-tip matches.

The guys sat against the wall of the Studio Snack Shop and loaded their straws with matches. Then they begged some string from the snack shop's owner and tied the boxes of loaded straws over their shoulders and pretended they were arrow quivers, and then they set out to have some fun with their fire missiles.

They spied Steve Domrzalski and his pals sitting on the OLG church steps down the block and hatched a plan to surprise them. They headed down the alley behind the school and church and came out across the street from the church. They crouched behind cars parked on the street, and when they were across from the church steps, they all loaded their thread spools and let their match-tipped straws fly. The effect was spectacular. When the six missiles hit the concrete church steps they burst into flames and Steve and his buddies jumped up and yelled and wondered what the hell was happening. The guys let another salvo fly, and when they hit, the older guys started getting pissed and began looking for the culprits.

The guys fired another round and were about to run, but they couldn't because they were laughing so hard. The older guys heard the laughs and ran across the street to where Dennis and his pals were laughing. Once everything was explained and the older guys saw the weapons, they were excited and wanted their own portable missile launchers.

Masciola had some extra thread spools, and one of Steve's pals lived nearby and raced home and got more spools and rubber bands. The older guys raced to the store to get matches and straws, and soon, more than a dozen guys were armed with a couple thousand straw-match missiles.

BLASTING AWAY!

They wasted no time in putting the weapons to good use, hiding behind parked cars and shooting at anyone they saw walking down the streets, which caused whatever they shot at—adults, kids, bums, cats, dogs—to scramble away in shock and fear at the matches suddenly bursting into flames at their feet. They roamed the alleys and shot into yards wherever they saw people. At one point they all stood across the street from an apartment building and fired at its brick wall as they imagined they were firing great artillery barrages at the structure.

That they might have caused a building to catch fire never crossed their minds; they never thought things through and were having too much fun to be worried about the consequences of their good times. Nor did it occur to them that some of those adults they fired at on the streets or in their back yards would be angry and scared enough to call the cops, which was what happened once some of the adults got home and to their telephones.

The guys figured some of those calls had been made when they saw a cop car drive slowly down a street. Everyone knew that when the cops drove slowly down a side street they were looking for something or someone.

The guys, especially the older ones, knew some of the area's cops because those cops had often confiscated their booze when they saw the kids walking down the streets carrying large brown paper bags full of six packs and half pints. The cops knew the kids were easy prey and that they could get free booze on Friday or Saturday nights just by cruising the side streets and suddenly stopping their squad cars and jumping out and confronting the kids with their bags of alcohol. Those cops, who liked to refer to themselves as "Chicago's Finest," rarely turned the alcohol in at the police station. They either drove home after a large haul and put the stuff in their refrigerators, or they got together in parking lots just before their shifts ended and divvied up between themselves a night's confiscation.

The guys recognized some of the cop cars by the numbers on the cars, and they sometimes knew the shifts the cops worked. As they were walking down an alley and saw a cop car drive by on a street, one of Steve's friends, Tommy Tamkin, shouted, "It's Jimero!", meaning officer Gil Jimero of the Shakespeare police district.

The kids hated Jimero because he was the only cop, it seemed, who would, when he caught them roaming the streets drunk, stuff them into the back seat of his squad car, take them home and lecture their parents about what bad kids they were raising.

Steve Domrzalski had been nabbed once by Jimero and taken home. The cop's routine was always the same when he caught a kid boozing. He would, upon pulling in front of the kid's house or apartment building, put on his police hat, exit the car, walk up the front stairs and ring the doorbell. When a parent emerged, Jimero would introduce himself as "Officer Gil Jimero of the Fourteenth District" and explain that he had caught their kid drinking. Then he'd launch into an explanation of the kid's behavior and how crazy he had been—usually an exaggeration the way the kids saw it—and end by saying, "If he gives you any more trouble, call me at the Fourteenth District, Officer Gil Jimero."

A ride home from Officer Jimero always got a kid a beating, not necessarily because the parents thought drinking was wrong—after all, they had done the same things as kids—but because the visits usually came late in the evening when they were drunk themselves or had been asleep, and were angry about having been awakened.

The guys knew that Jimero, not having seen any of them walking the side streets, would soon cruise the alleys, and so they hatched a plan to both evade him and have more fun.

They about-faced and raced down the alley to the back of the Jewel store, which fronted Fullerton. The store closed at six on Saturday nights and the guys climbed up the back stairs of the apartment building next to the one-story-tall store. At the point at which the stairs were at the same height as the store's roof, they jumped from the stairs onto the roof and prepared for an adventure.

They ran to the front of the roof and crouched behind the three-foot-tall brick facade that faced the street. The situation was perfect. It was early evening, Fullerton was busy with vehicular and foot traffic, and there was a bus stop on the corner right by the store. The bus stop was within easy reach of their match-missiles and the guys loaded their thread spools and occasionally peeked out over the facade to see if anyone had gathered at the bus stop.

After ten minutes or so, the bus stop had a crowd, maybe six or seven adults, and the guys raised their heads and arms above the facade and let loose with their missiles. The effect was all they had hoped for. The match-tipped straws popped and lit at the people's feet and those people jumped and screamed and wondered who or what was shooting fire sticks at them, and they scrambled away. The guys crouched back down behind the facade and laughed at their prank. They were confident that they hadn't been seen and that their scared and startled victims had no idea where the fire straws had come from. They reloaded, poked their heads back above the wall and fired, this time at cars and anyone walking on the sidewalk. The effect was even better. Cars braked and screeched to stops after they had been hit, and pedestrians ran when the matches lit at their feet. The guys reloaded one more time, let loose with a final barrage and then scrambled to the back of the roof and onto the apartment building porch and down the steps and into the alley. They knew that someone would have guessed that the missiles had come from the Jewel roof and they wanted to be away before Jimero and other cops showed up, cornered them and drove them home to a beating.

Knowing that Jimero was already in the neighborhood, the guys stashed their matches, straws and thread spools in a gangway between two garages and walked down the alley to The Corner.

When they got to the street, they saw Jimero's squad car driving slowly toward them. It stopped, the cop got out and quizzed the kids as to their activities. He looked them over to see if they had booze, which they didn't, and which left him disappointed.

"Been playing with matches, guys? Are you guys firebugs? Think it's fun to scare people with fire?" the cop asked. "Trying to burn some buildings down?"

"No sir, officer. We're just getting ready to go to confession," Kolba said. "We're good Catholic boys."

"If I catch you guys with matches or beer, you're going to the shithouse and you're gonna stay there until your parents come get you," Jimero said angrily. "Now get the hell out of here."

The cop drove off, and the guys, after waiting a half hour or so to make sure he had really left the neighborhood, retrieved their weapons and spent the rest of the night shooting their missiles at everything and anything.

CHAPTER 23

Invading Russia, a Wall of Doughnuts and Revenge

T HE SCHOOL YEAR was in full swing, and the Disturbers had settled into a routine and code of conduct in Zita's room. The unwritten code was simple. Every Disturber would do everything possible to enrage Zita, disrupt the class and torment the good kids.

The routine was simple. In the mornings during religion class, which was always the first lesson of the day, they would ignore the nun and occupy themselves by drawing pictures of cars, army tanks, bombers, navy ships, monsters and guns. They even started a newspaper called *Disturbers Row*, which they wrote by hand. If Zita called on any of them to answer questions about the day's lesson, which she did often to gauge their ignorance on a subject, the Disturber would bolt out of his chair, stand straight and bellow out a nonsensical answer, which always infuriated Zita and got the rest of the class laughing. Then the other Disturbers would stand up in support of their colleague and shout out goofy answers on their own.

Kolba was a master at the game and astounded his fellow Disturbers with his quick thinking and wit. Once when Zita asked him where Jesus was born, Kolba responded that he couldn't answer because he hadn't seen

Jesus's birth certificate. At that point, Kurkowski stood up and answered, "Away in the manger!" and the other Disturbers stood up and began singing the Christmas carol.

Zita harbored an intense dislike for Kolba, not only because he had caused a riot during the spelling bee in September, but because of the ease with which he tormented and embarrassed her. Unlike the other Disturbers, he didn't have to work at it; he was a natural and instinctively knew how to get to her.

A week after the spelling bee and the "WXYZ" riot, Kolba did it again. It was art class one afternoon, and the good kids were sucking up to Zita by showing her their crayons, paint brushes and other art supplies and slobbering on and on about where they bought them, how much they cost, what great quality they were and asking the nun if she approved of their stuff.

Zita slobbered back about the wonderful quality of those supplies and told the good kids who sought her approval that they would someday be great artists. It made the Disturbers want to puke and shout and scream about what frauds, losers and sissies those suck-up kids were.

Rather than shouting and screaming, Kolba played the good kids' game. He raised his hand, and when Zita asked what he wanted, Kolba, feigning sincerity, said, "Ster, my paint brush is real camel hair! And it's expensive! Come and look at it, Ster. I hope you like it."

Zita took the bait, and walking to Kolba's desk she said, "That's very nice, Gary. If it's such a good brush, you can paint a picture of Jesus for us with it."

"Sure can, Ster," Kolba replied. "But look at it, it's real camel hair!"

When Zita moved closer to get a better look at the brush, Kolba lifted his arm, shoved the brush under her nose and began tickle her by moving it back and forth while saying loudly, "Ster, I yanked the hairs out of the camel myself in Egypt! What do you think, Ster? Does it smell like camel hair, Ster?"

The class erupted in laughter, and Zita responded by beating Kolba about the head and shoulders.

Dennis wasn't as clever as Kolba, but he entertained his fellow Disturbers just as well with his blunt disrespect for the nun. Once, when she asked him to recite the Ten Commandments, he named only one, Thou shalt not steal, and reminded Zita that she would go to Hell for stealing their property.

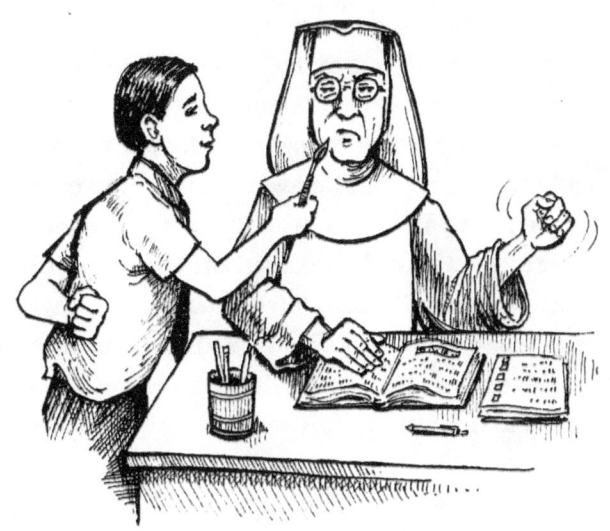

IT'S REAL CAMEL HAIR, STER

Zita called it confiscating the boys' things—rulers, pens, pencils, erasers, drafting compasses, notebooks and anything she could take from them—as punishment for their disturbing ways. Sometimes they were able to steal it back from the drawers in her desk, but for the past few weeks the nun had been locking those drawers so the guys couldn't reclaim their stuff.

Zita had a plan for the stolen goods, and it infuriated the Disturbers. Her idea was to have Bernard Heller and a few other good kids sell the stuff to kids in the lower grades and use the proceeds to buy pagan babies.

Zita had accumulated a decent amount of the Disturbers' property and had advertised to the nuns and kids in the lower grades that she would have the sale. That morning came and Heller and a few other kids took the stuff out of room 204 and went to the lower grades. About an hour later, Heller returned to 204 in an ecstatic mood.

"They're selling like hotcakes, Sister," Heller proclaimed as he burst into the room. "Like hotcakes, Sister! You've done so well with this sale!"

"That's wonderful, Bernerd. You're such a good student. You are certainly going to get an A for conduct on your next report card," Zita said. "And in another month we'll take more things from those hoodlums in the back row and have another sale."

The Disturbers were disgusted, not so much by the fact that their property had been confiscated and sold, but by Heller's sickening sucking up to the nun. In their minds, brown-nosing to the nuns, or to anyone in authority, was the ultimate crime and they vowed to make Heller pay for it.

Heller was a kid who loved and craved conformity and rules. His dad fought in the German army in World War II and had made it to the United States after the war. The father had passed on to his son his ideas about German superiority, and little Bernard felt blessed to be in charge of the sale.

By eleven that morning, all the Disturbers' things had been sold, and the boys plotted their revenge as they sat in the back row. But there were cars, battleships and guns to draw, and other ways to have fun before they would hatch a plan.

The Disturbers hated the good kids for lots of things, but they especially hated the ones who—it seemed like every year—would bring to class a letter they had gotten from President Johnson and the White House telling them what good kids they were. They were form letters sent in reply to letters the kids had sent to the President telling him what good kids they were, where they went to school, how they admired and listened to their teachers and how they admired the President.

The kids who received the form letters in reply never failed to bring their treasurers to school so the nuns could gushingly read them to the entire class.

Dennis, always being different and odd, decided one day to bring his own letter so Zita could read it to the class. By seventh grade he had begun reading national news magazines, books about World War II, particularly the German invasion of Russia, and anything that had to do with the Cold War and weapons systems. Like any red-blooded American he disliked Russia, specifically, the Soviet Union, and wanted to destroy it. As a result, he spent many of his spare hours daydreaming and drawing crude plans for the invasion of Russia by the United States. Those plans included tens of millions of soldiers, tens of thousands of tanks, bombers, aircraft carriers, submarines and other ships. Dennis had also gotten some of the Disturbers and Masciola to join in on his plan to build a submarine in which they would sail the oceans and tail and torpedo Russian warships.

The war plans were ridiculous, the work of a budding madman, and anyone who saw them either laughed or expressed deep concern about the boy's mental stability. But Dennis was committed and he kept revising and perfecting his invasion plans to the point where he felt confident enough to send them to Robert S. McNamara, the nation's secretary of defense.

Dennis never received a reply letter from the defense secretary, so, with the help of his brother Steve, he made up his own and bought it to class to have Zita read it aloud. The boy raised his hand and was reluctantly acknowledged by the nun.

"What is it you want, mister troublemaker?" Zita asked.

"Ster, I sent some stuff to Robert S. McNamara, the secretary of defense, and he sent me a letter back. Can you read it to the class? I'm real proud of it, Ster."

The nun was shocked and couldn't imagine that the boy could have written a legible letter to the nation's defense secretary. She was leery of the boy and figured that once again she was being had.

"Bring the letter up here and let's see if it is really from Mister McNamara. I can't imagine the secretary of defense sending *you* a letter unless it's to recommend you to reform school," Zita huffed.

Dennis walked the letter, which was still in its "official" Defense Department envelope, to Zita. Dennis and Steve had painstakingly created their own version of Defense Department stationary with art supplies stolen from Saxon's, and to anyone who didn't know better it looked official and real. Zita examined the envelope, and to her shock, it looked legitimate. She took the letter out, unfolded it and read it to the class as Dennis stood proudly by:

Dear Mr. Domrzalski:

I am in receipt of your document labeled: CLASSIFIED TOP SECRET; INVASION PLANS OF RUSSIA. The United States Post Office delivered this classified information in a timely and secure manner, despite the lack of any postage.

I thank you for your comprehensive, two-page, hand-written invasion plan, as well as your hand-drawn maps on lined loose-leaf paper. It is extremely helpful that you used a dull pencil with which to draw the maps, as it makes the Soviet borders quite legible.

The pencil drawings of your fifteen-foot-long wooden submarine are interesting as well, and your idea of armoring its hull by pounding tens of thousands of nails into it is something that will be talked about in the Pentagon for a long, long time, I assure you.

I must tell you that the United States Navy is doing an excellent job of tracking Soviet warships, and so at this time I must decline your offer to use your wooden submarine to, as you say, "tail Russian ships in the Black Sea and blow them out of the water."

I also thank you for your efforts in combating Soviet expansionism and global communism. Regrettably, I must inform you that we have rejected your plan, as it is the current policy of the United States of America to contain the Soviet Union, not annihilate it.

I will keep your invasion plan on file in the event that the policy of the United States of America towards the Soviet Union changes and the President and Congress deem it necessary to, as your plan calls for, "turn Russia into a giant, smoldering ash heap in three short weeks."

With Deepest Regrets,

Robert S. McNamara
Secretary
United States Department of Defense
United States of America

cc: Lyndon B. Johnson, President

Zita was aghast, and after finishing the letter could only stammer out:

"What, what is the meaning of this? What is wrong with you? Sister Vitaclaire will be told of this immediately!"

Not only was Zita stunned, but all the other kids, with the exception of the Disturbers, were shocked as well. Their classmate had proposed the destruction of the Soviet Union, which in itself was insane and mad, and he had sent his proposal to one of the nation's highest and most important officials. They didn't know whether to admire Dennis or to be afraid of him.

Zita sent one of the good kids down to Vitaclaire's office to summon the principal up to her room to deal with the deranged child. Not happy at being interrupted in whatever she was doing, Vitaclaire burst through 204's front door with a determination to beat the hell out of some kids.

"What is the meaning of this?" Vitaclaire demanded upon entering the room.

Zita shoved the letter into the principal's hand while saying, "Sister, there is something wrong with him."

"That is not news. There's something wrong with that entire family," Vitaclaire snapped as she began silently reading the letter. The nun's face turned white, and then red, as she read. When she finished, Vitaclaire too was stunned and could barely speak. Finally, she managed to blurt out to Dennis:

"What is wrong with you?"

"Nothing that I know of Sister. Why?"

"Why? I'll give you why! What makes you think you can go around planning to destroy entire nations?"

"You do, Sister."

"What?!"

"You do, Sister. You're always telling us about how bad communists are and how they tortured Father Fu because they don't like Catholics, and so I figured we should invade them as soon as possible so they don't ever again hurt another Catholic."

Vitaclaire ached to hit Dennis and strike him the mightiest blow she had ever delivered to a kid, but she knew that his demented logic had prevented that. After all, the nuns and the Catholic Church had always preached hatred of communism and of the Union of Soviet Socialist Republics. The kids and adults were constantly told to pray for the conversion of Russia, as well as of the Jews, and the priests and nuns never stopped talking about how the Chinese communists had tortured Father Fu and how evil the communists were.

"It is not for us to go around destroying other countries, that's God's job," Vitaclaire huffed as she handed Dennis back his letter. "Now get back to your seat and keep your invasion plans to yourself."

It was an exhilarating slow and triumphant walk to the back row for Dennis. He was immensely satisfied for having it known that he had developed his own plans to invade Russia and destroy that hated country, and he was thrilled that most of the kids were horrified to think that he was a twelve-year-old war monger and somewhat deranged. Very few people, he knew, would mess with a crazy kid, and he had just established himself as the craziest of the crazy. He was intent on destroying, not single individuals, buildings, neighborhoods, or even cities, but entire empires! No one could out-crazy that.

The beauty of the situation for Dennis, though, was that he hadn't tried to be crazy. He truly hated the Russians and wanted them destroyed, and his invasion plans weren't the work of someone who was working at being goofy, it was just who he was; he was a natural.

The other kids stared at Dennis as he walked to the back of the room, and their heads swiveled around to follow him as he passed their rows. They were mystified, scared and in awe of the kid who had worked up a plan to invade and destroy the world's largest country and who was building his own submarine.

The other Disturbers were proud of their colleague and his letter. Even they believed that the secretary of defense had read his invasion plans and had taken the time to personally respond, and to the guys, that was boss with a capital B.

Dennis passed the letter around and the guys marveled at it. But as cool as it was, the guys had more important things to do, and that was to figure out how to get even with Zita's pet, Bernard Heller.

The obvious and immediate thing was to shoot spitballs at the suck-up. The Disturbers coordinated their attack, all loading their empty plastic Bic pen tubes with little wads of spit-moistened paper and firing barrage after barrage at their despised target. To the Disturbers the broadsides were impressive, but the attack was problematic because Heller sat in the second row and was too far away for most of the missiles to hit, no matter how forcefully blown. That didn't matter, though, because the spitballs hit others, and to the Disturbers, hitting anyone was a victory.

They had other ideas, like getting to Heller's desk and dumping out his books and supplies on to the floor, or stealing his pens and compasses and getting them to Zita so she could unload them on the younger kids at her next stolen-goods sale. Dennis suggested they could crucify him, just like he and Masciola had tried on Daniel Bernas three years earlier, but the guys settled on something that they figured would permanently destroy Heller's standing with all the nuns and lay teachers. They needed to wait until the lunch break to pull it off.

Meanwhile, there was more fun to be had as that was the day that a truck pulled in front of the school to deliver boxes of doughnuts the kids had ordered three weeks earlier. The doughnut sale was a fundraiser for the school and the kids had been told to go door-to-door taking orders and money for boxes of doughnuts which were to be delivered at a later date.

That morning the truck pulled up and the kids got their boxes of doughnuts, which they were to put in paper shopping bags and take home and deliver to their customers. The Disturbers had been good salesmen and collectively they had nearly a hundred boxes of doughnuts, a dozen doughnuts to the box, coming. When the doughnuts were distributed the Disturbers put them to good use by stacking the white, shoebox-sized boxes on top of their flat wooden desks, moving their desks together, and thereby creating a solid wall of doughnut boxes six-or-seven-boxes high across the back row.

THE GREAT WALL OF DOUGHNUTS·

They called it The Great Wall of Doughnuts and they hid behind it and laughed themselves crazy at their prank, and they laughed even harder when Zita looked up and realized she couldn't see them hiding behind their wall of cardboard and deep-fried dough. The nun demanded that the barrier be dismantled immediately, but the Disturbers ignored her, and when the other kids looked back and saw The Great Wall of Doughnuts, another class-wide riot began. Some other kids stacked their doughnut boxes on top of their desks so they too could hide from the nun, but none could, as the Disturbers had done through their united effort, build a wall across an entire row.

Enraged, Zita, leaned her butt on the edge of her desk and huffed, "Mister Kolba, what is the meaning of this? You *will* get the back of my hand!"

Rather than standing as he normally did when called on by Zita, Kolba peeked his head just above the wall and answered:

"Ster, I've been studying architecture and The Great Wall of China, and this is my project. It's a pretty sturdy wall, but if we had cement, it would be even stronger. What do you think?"

"The Chinese are communists, and if you are emulating them, then you are a communist, too! A communist, Mister Kolba! Take those boxes down now!"

Before Kolba could respond, Ruchinski poked his head over the wall and shouted:

"Ster, we can't take it down. I heard this morning that public school kids are going to invade us today and this wall will protect us! They're going to invade us, Ster!"

"And why, pretty boy, why would they invade us?" Zita demanded.

"To steal our catechism books and turn us into pagans!"

The room dissolved into laughter and Zita threatened to call Vitaclaire up again to handle the matter, but the Disturbers knew she wouldn't because she didn't dare expose to the principal such a blatant disturbance and her total inability to control her classroom.

Zita gave up, the wall stayed put and the Disturbers went back to disturbing. They loved the wall and the invisibility it offered from Zita's eyes. They crouched and raced undetected across the back row to talk and punch each other and generally have fun. They crumpled dozens of sheets of papers into balls and lobbed barrage after barrage over their wall at the other kids, not caring where they landed. Broadsides of spitballs flew when the Disturbers poked their heads over the wall and fired in unison. They crept unseen to the sides of the room and launched surprise spitball and other attacks on kids, and then scurried back behind the wall before any kid or Zita could see which of them had launched the assault. That was irrelevant because it was a fact that every Disturber was guilty of something.

The games and assaults went on until the wall came down at noon when the kids loaded their doughnuts into their shopping bags and took them home during the lunch hour.

It was when they returned to the classroom after lunch that the Disturbers got their revenge on Heller. About fifteen minutes after class started, Ruchinski raised his hand.

"What is now, sweetie? Is the threat of invasion over?" Zita asked with disgust.

"No, Ster. They're coming, but I figure we can spray them with holy water and that will do them in and burn them up or melt them. But Ster, there's something else and it's really, really important."

"What?"

"Cigarettes, Ster! Someone, and I don't know who, but someone in this class has cigarettes in their jacket because I smelled them in the cloakroom! Cigarettes, Ster! I think you should check all the jackets, Ster. I know I would!"

Zita had no choice but to take Ruchinski up on the issue. She figured he was lying and trying once again to waste her time, but catching a student with cigarettes would be a coup that would make her look good in the eyes of the other nuns, and she needed that.

So she walked into the cloakroom and knew immediately that Ruchinski had been right because she smelled the stench of ashes. The odor sent her on a pocket-searching frenzy, and in a few minutes she had found her treasure: a boy's jacket with a crumpled pack of Marlboros and four smoked butts. The jacket stunk of ashes and Zita triumphantly yanked the garment off its hook and walked back into the room waving it while demanding:

"Whose jacket is this? Whose?"

Most of the kids were shocked because they didn't think anyone was dumb enough to bring smokes to school where they would surely be caught, and they cringed because they knew someone was going to get a hell of a beating from Vitaclaire, Yvonne, DeLasalle, Miss Donatello and from their parents. This was a big-deal crime.

"Whose jacket is this?" Zita demanded again.

Heller cringed and got sick. The jacket was his. He had always gotten in early from the playground, and knowing that, Bozeman also came in early that day and sneaked the smokes into the jacket's pocket after Heller had gone to his seat. To make things worse, Bozeman had picked some butts he found in a curb near the school and smeared their ashes over the jacket to stink it up and leave no doubt the cigarettes would be discovered.

It was a devious and terrible thing to do, but the Disturbers wouldn't brook Heller's sickening alliance with Zita to sell their stuff, and this was one way of getting total and permanent revenge.

Heller did the only reasonable thing possible for a kid in such a hopeless and terrifying situation; he kept his mouth shut and refused to acknowledge ownership of the jacket, hoping that by some miracle Zita wouldn't realize it was his.

Again, Zita demanded, "Who owns this jacket?"

Crazy, scared and sick, Heller's mind raced, and he thought he had an out because his parents had bought him the jacket and, technically, they owned it. That logic would never stand, but it was the only thing the terrified kid could cling to.

Except for the Disturbers, the kids sat in shocked silence and fear. Heller buried his face in his arms on his desk knowing that this was probably his last couple of hours of life. When Zita again demanded that the jacket's owner identify himself, Ruchinski jumped out of his chair and shouted:

"Ster, maybe, just maybe there's a name tag on it. I'd look if I were you."

A lot of the kids' moms sewed name tags onto their kids' jackets and sweaters, especially when they were young, and Ruchinski figured that Heller's mother was still babying him, and he was right.

Zita took the boy's advice and saw on the jacket's inside top collar a name tag. She read it silently to herself and went white when the truth hit her. She trembled to think that her pet was smoking, and at first didn't want to believe it. How could good little Bernard commit such a terrible sin, she thought? It just wasn't possible, he had to have been set up, she said to herself. But no matter how desperately she didn't want to believe that Heller had been smoking, and how she really knew that such a good kid could not possibly have smoked, Zita saw she had the opportunity of a lifetime, and she wasn't going to waste it by admitting the obvious truth that Heller had been framed.

After resigning herself to the fact that she was going to have to beat her pet, and that the other nuns would pulverize him as well, Zita played the situation for a little effect. She held the jacket in one hand and raised the other, which held the crumpled pack of cigarettes, to the class and said:

"Cigarettes are the work of the Devil, and this smoking hoodlum will be punished appropriately and immediately!"

She tossed the pack onto her desk and then pulled the butts out of the jacket's pocket and showed them to the class. "These are proof positive that there is a smoker in this class. Proof positive!" she exclaimed.

Then she paused for a moment, read the name tag again to herself, raised the jacket into the air and bellowed: "Mister Heller, you are going to burn eternally in Hell!"

Most of the class shuddered, not at the pronouncement that Heller would burn forever in Hell, but at the fact that he was the smoker. They couldn't believe it and they knew he would be handled with extra and extreme brutality because the nuns felt that betrayal by a pet was the worst sin of all.

Zita was pleased with herself, and she let Heller squirm and sweat and tremble for another moment before bellowing again: "Mister Heller, do you own this jacket?"

The boy was beyond terrified and couldn't think or stand or swallow or even see. He was a slumped and quivering mess. Zita picked up her pointer and wobbled to Heller's desk. She threw the jacket at him and demanded again: "Mister Heller, do you own this jacket?"

The boy mumbled the only thing that came to his spinning, dizzy mind: "No. My parents own it. They bought it."

Zita expected such evasive and contemptuous nonsense from the Disturbers, but not from her pet salesman. She exploded and hammered the boy with the pointer until she was out of breath. Heller was so emotionally and physically stricken that he couldn't even summon the mental agility, courage or instinct to deny that he had been smoking and protest that he had been wrongly accused.

After catching her breath, Zita played for another effect. She said somewhat indifferently: "I wonder what Sister Yvonne and Sister DeLasalle will have to say about your lying, Mister Heller? We'll just see about that." She then ordered two girls to summon Yvonne and DeLasalle to the room.

The two nuns burst into the room almost simultaneously, and when they did, Zita proclaimed triumphantly:

"I found a smoker, Sisters! A smoker!"

Yvonne and DeLasalle were pleasantly stunned. They didn't believe that Zita had any investigative abilities, but they were ecstatic at the pronouncement.

"Who?" demanded a cross-armed Yvonne. "Who has soiled this school by bringing Satan and his cigarettes into this classroom?"

"Is it one of them?" DeLasalle asked while glaring at the row of Disturbers and hoping with a depraved intensity for the opportunity to administer to all of them the most savage beating in OLG's history, and perhaps the greatest beating that any nun had ever given to any kid in all of history. She would beat them all by reasoning that if one smoked, the others had as well.

Zita couldn't contain herself, and before Yvonne and DeLasalle had the chance to angrily strut around the front of the room, she blurted out:

"The smoker is Mister Bernard Heller! I found the cigarettes in his jacket, Sisters. It's proof positive, Sisters! Proof positive!"

The two nuns were aghast at the revelation, for they couldn't believe that Bernard Heller had been smoking, and they didn't want to believe that such a nice boy could commit such an evil crime.

But Zita showed them the evidence, making sure to hold the jacket up to their noses so they could smell the smoke and ashes, and she turned the offending pocket inside out to reveal the ashes from the burnt butts.

Heller remained paralyzed and couldn't think, and neither could Yvonne or DeLasalle. They were so enraged and filled with the joyful anticipation of beating another kid that they failed to ask Zita the simple question of how she had discovered that Heller had been up to no good. Had they asked, and she answered that Ruchinski had instigated her investigation, their suspicions that Heller had been set up would have been confirmed. But they never asked, and Zita never offered an explanation, and so Bernard Heller was on his way to the worst day of his life.

"Sister Vitaclaire will want to hear of this, and so will your parents," Yvonne said. "Now let's go down to Sister Vitaclaire's office."

With that, Yvonne walked to Heller's desk and jerked him out of his chair by one of his ears. Then she and DeLasalle marched him out of the room and down to the principal's office where he was interrogated, tormented and beaten.

Heller never returned to class that afternoon. Instead, he was kept in Vitaclaire's office, and then, after school, marched to the convent from where the principal called his father at around six in the evening. The beating he got at home was worse than what the nuns had given, and Bernard had trouble sitting for a week because of the welts on his butt inflicted by his dad's belt.

The Disturbers knew they had done Heller a very bad deed, and they sometimes, especially the next day when Heller came to school with a pillow on which to sit, felt a little remorse. But each time the guilt crept in they reminded each other that he had helped Zita sell the stuff she had stolen from them, and their guilt vanished.

CHAPTER 24

The Nuttiest Penalty Ever

T HE NEXT DAY was Wednesday, which meant a shortened day because public school kids came to take religion classes. Wednesdays were fun because the kids didn't change classes and the Disturbers had nearly five hours of disturbing and driving Zita crazy. That fun came with a price. On Wednesdays, school was dismissed at twelve forty-five in the afternoon, that is, for everyone but the Disturbers. Since mid-September, Zita had been punishing them by refusing to let them go home early on Wednesdays.

While they hated that they didn't get to go home early, the Disturbers took advantage of the situation by using the time to dream up new ways to antagonize Zita. They brought their lunches on Wednesdays, and one day they decided to make the nun feel as guilty as possible. Kurkowski had a bottle of soda with his lunch, and before opening it he shook it vigorously, knowing that when he popped it open it would spray all over the room. He waited until he got Zita's attention and then opened the bottle, and the soda did exactly what the kids wanted and sprayed everywhere, including on Zita's desk.

An enraged Zita, pointer in hand, shuffled to the Disturbers, who were sitting in the second row. Instead of scampering away as they usually did, the guys stayed put, and when Zita whaled away at Kurkowski, he let her, for a few moments, anyway. After taking a few whacks, Kurkowski fell to the floor and lay there motionless pretending to be dead. Zita used the opportunity to kick him with her black nun shoes, but he refused to move. Zita demanded that he get up, but he didn't. After she backed off a bit, the other Disturbers ran to Kurkowski and pretended to examine him. They took his pulse, felt his forehead, and Ruchinski put his ear to his chest as if listening for a heartbeat.

After feigning deep worry and concern, the Disturbers started screaming frantically and crying. After a few minutes of pretending to try to resuscitate their buddy and failing, Kolba got up, ran to Zita and yelled, "You killed him! You killed him! You're a murderer! Call an ambulance. He needs to get to the hospital!"

"If he's dead, a hospital won't do him any good," Zita shot back. "Maybe we should just call the funeral home."

That took most of the fun out of the game, but the kids persisted and continued to insist that Zita had killed their friend. At one point, Zita kicked the fallen Disturber several times again, after which Kolba yelled, "Leave him alone! He's already dead!"

Zita kept kicking until she saw Kolba race to the cloakroom and walk out with his jacket and try to leave the room through the front door.

YOU KILLED HIM!

"Going somewhere, Gary?" the nun asked.
"Yes, Ster!"

"Where?"

"To the police station to report this murder!"

"You're forbidden to leave this room until I say you can."

"Then just say it. I really need to report this murder."

"Sit down before I show you what murder really is!"

"Well, since I can't get to the police station to report you, I will make a citizen's arrest! Ster, you are under arrest! Now get to your desk and sit there quietly while I fill out an arrest report."

Zita charged after Kolba, but he ran and easily avoided her. When she was winded, she sat down at her desk and said loudly so Kurkowski could hear:

"If Mister Kookowski wants to continue playing dead, I'm sure he'll continue the fun at home after I tell his father about this. Mister Kookowski, get up off that floor now or I will call your father tonight and we'll see what he thinks of your shenanigans. Now get up or else!"

Kurkowski knew the nun would call his father, and he wanted none of that, so he got up, but not without making a scene and pretending that he had been miraculously revived.

Zita relished Wednesday afternoons, not just because she kept the Disturbers in school when they wanted to be at home and out like the other kids, but because she could drive them crazy with senseless and totally impossible tasks. This Wednesday was no different. Angered by the fact that the boys had torn up newspapers the previous day and scattered the pieces on the room's floor, Zita devised a task that she knew they wouldn't be able to complete in a million years.

After the boys had eaten their lunches, and after Kurkowski had recovered from being dead and had cleaned up the mess from his soda, Zita told them what they had to do. She had stacks of old school and other papers—at least a couple of hundred pages—on her desk and she showed them to the boys.

"You are going to take each and every one of these sheets of paper, tear them into the size of a pinhead, throw them on the floor and then pick them up one at a time and count each and every one," she ordered. "And you will not go home until each and every pinhead-sized piece of paper is counted. Now get to work and no back talking."

That was the nuttiest punishment she had given them yet, and the guys knew that they would never be able to get the job done. They were horrified, that is, until they realized how totally insane it was and how much fun they could have. After all, how many kids got to throw tiny pieces of paper on their classroom floor on purpose?

Before they started ripping up the paper, though, the guys protested and made faces to show their displeasure. Dennis scrunched up his nose and pouted his lips, Kolba pulled the skin under his eyes down to reveal the blood vessels, which made him look scary, Bozeman widened his eyes to make it look like he was in shock, and Ruchinski scrunched his nose and mouth sideways.

Zita went berserk.

"If you make faces like that your faces will freeze into that position forever!" she screamed. "That's how God punishes people for making faces! Stop it!"

All the kids had heard that line before from their parents and aunts and uncles, and pretty much every adult. They were also warned repeatedly not to sit in front of fans because if they sat in front of one for too long they would freeze into whatever position they were in at the time.

The warnings seemed ridiculous since the kids always made goofy faces and none of them had ever suffered a permanently, or even a temporarily frozen face. None of them had ever been paralyzed by sitting in front of a fan, and no one knew anyone who had.

"You're right, Ster," Kolba said, faking hysteria. "My face ain't moving! It's stuck! Help!"

The other Disturbers swung into action and began examining each other and proclaiming that all their faces were grotesquely frozen in place, and they pleaded with the nun to let them out of detention so they could go to the hospital.

YOUR FACES WILL FREEZE LIKE THAT!

"I'll never be in the movies except as a monster," Kolba exclaimed. "None of us will be except as monsters!"

"Well, that's exactly what you are and so it's appropriate," Zita responded. "Now get to work."

The guys tore into the papers and made piles of little pieces, although not a single piece was as small as a pinhead. After fifteen minutes, Zita, realizing the boys were having too much fun, inspected their piles.

"These are not small enough. They must be the size of a pinhead. If they are not the size of a pinhead I will get more paper and you will have to start all over."

The guys went back to their piles and tore the papers again, but no matter how hard they tried, they couldn't get a single piece as small as Zita demanded, and so they stopped trying and tore them into any size they pleased. After they had made a decent sized mountain of torn paper, the guys scooped up handfuls, pranced around the front of the room like they were fairies and tossed the paper into the air. Ruchinski danced and skipped and hopped around Zita's desk, where she was seated, and threw paper in the air around her so it landed on her head and arms and on her desk. She was furious but had no energy with which to go after the boys.

"Aren't you funny, Mister Sweetie Pie? I hope you will still be laughing at ten this evening because that's how long you will stay here. You will stay here until this job is done the way I say it has to be done," Zita said. "Laugh all you want, but I will be laughing at ten this evening when you hoodlums are still here."

"But Ster, that would be past your bedtime, and if you get to bed too late you'll miss your six o'clock mass tomorrow morning, and that would be a sin," Kolba said. "And I'd hate to see you burn in Hell for missing mass."

Zita made no reply other than to get out of her chair and proclaim that she was going to get some lunch, and that if when she returned all the papers hadn't been torn up, strewn on the floor, picked up and counted, the boys would get the back of her hand.

"Don't lock the door," Kolba shouted to her as she was leaving. "Remember what happened to those children at Our Lady of the Angels."

It was a nasty, but accurate and necessary comment. On December 1, 1958, a fire had swept through the school on Chicago's West Side, killing ninety-two students and three nuns. The fire shocked the world, not just because the school had been a fire trap, but because many of the kids were kept in their seats by the nuns and told to pray the Rosary while the fire raged and smoke filled the hallways. Most of the kids had no way to escape other than jumping from windows on the second floor. The fire led to new building codes for schools, and everyone in the Catholic Diocese was hyper-sensitive about the potential for a school fire and more children's deaths.

And while Zita never would have locked the door, she could do crazy things, especially when she had to deal with the Disturbers, and she appreciated the boy's admonition. Sometimes those little brats had something intelligent and useful to say.

Zita left and the boys' immediate instinct was to leave the room, roam the halls and look for trouble and fun. But they figured—correctly—that Zita was lurking outside the door for the first few minutes and would have clobbered them and then called Vitaclaire had she caught them trying to leave. They confirmed their suspicion by ever so slightly opening the room's back door and peeking out, and sure enough, there was Zita and Yvonne hovering near the front door just hoping they would try to escape.

The guys decided to make the best of the situation by having some fun with the nuns. Ruchinski gathered them near the front door and announced loudly so the nuns would hear:

"Hey guys, let's pray the Rosary! It's my favorite prayer."

The others shouted in unison that the world's longest prayer was their favorite as well, and they started shouting Our Fathers, Hail Marys and Glory Bes. They sped through the prayers almost as fast as the nuns did when they said Rosaries as a group in church, or when they led the kids in the prayer. OLG kids were always amazed at how the nuns could speed-talk and rip through six Rosaries, never putting any space or time between the words, never slowing to properly enunciate them, and spewing them out like a long train speeding by in a blur. They never seemed to put any emotion into the prayer, or even stopped to ponder what the words they were firing out meant; they just spat them out as fast as possible. It always seemed to the kids that the nuns were trying to get through the things as quickly as possible because it was chore they had to do before they could move on to something they wanted to do.

Yvonne wasn't fooled, impressed or amused. She burst through the door and enjoyed the sight of the boys standing around saying the prayers.

"You must kneel when you say the Rosary!" Yvonne shouted. "And where are your Rosary beads? And, and why are you racing through this prayer like there was no tomorrow?"

The boys didn't bring their rosaries to school—only the good kids did, and usually just to show them off to the nuns—and they had been reciting the prayer from memory.

"You cannot say the Rosary without beads that have been blessed by a priest or the bishop or the cardinal," Yvonne stormed. "This is pure blasphemy and sacrilege. You are making a mockery of the Rosary and of all the Church's prayers. Whose idea was this?"

"It was mine, Sister. I figured we could say prayers in detention and help cleanse our souls," Kolba said in taking the heat off Ruchinski.

"Nothing can cleanse your souls. What makes you think God will hear your prayers?"

"Because," Kolba started, which, of course was the wrong way to answer a nun's question, and almost before he had the word out, Yvonne had launched her arm to slap him across the face. The angry, infuriated force of the blow shook Kolba's head from side to side.

"And why, mister, why were you racing, racing through this most beautiful of the Church's prayers? Have you no respect for this prayer?"

"Because that's how you sisters say it in church. We were just—"

Kolba had meant to end the sentence with "trying to be like you," but he never got there because Yvonne's cold hand slapped him again and slapped him repeatedly, while she yelled, "You will not talk back to me!"

Her fury unspent, Yvonne asked the other Disturbers to produce their rosaries, and when they couldn't, she smashed each of them as well.

"Since you boys are so intent on saying the Rosary, you will have to learn to say it correctly, and that means kneeling," Yvonne said. "And you *will* kneel."

And they did. Yvonne put one Disturber in each corner of the room and had each kneel facing the walls. She put the other, Kolba, in the middle of the room with orders that he bow his head and stare at the floor.

"I will check in on you, and if, when I do, all of you are not kneeling, even God won't be able to save you," Yvonne said as she walked out of the room and slammed its door behind her.

The Disturbers kept their kneeling positions for a minute or two before getting up. They doubted that Yvonne would check back in on them, and even if she did, a few slaps across the face were easier to take than kneeling on a wooden floor for two hours.

They went back to tearing paper, although not much. They shredded only a couple dozen sheets before Bozeman said:

"I bet youse Zita didn't lock her drawers. Let's see if there's anything in them."

The desk drawers weren't locked, and the guys rummaged through them, with one Disturber always keeping lookout near the front door should Zita or Yvonne return.

It was a treasure trove. One drawer contained some of the weapons Zita used against them and the other kids: a metal ruler, the rung of a chair, a box of rubber bands, a wooden paddle, a rubber ball that she occasionally threw at kids, and metal clasps that she often attached to kids' ears and noses. They decided to hide the stuff and crammed it behind a couple of boxes on a shelf in the cloakroom.

There were other treasures. One large drawer contained some of their school supplies that Zita had confiscated and apparently had forgotten to sell. They recognized their things, reclaimed them and put them back in their own desks.

"Hey. If we don't put stuff back in here, she's gonna know we took it," Kurkowski said.

That was obvious and the boys had a solution. They went through Heller's desk, and the desks of other kids who had annoyed them or had sucked up to Zita, took their rulers, pens, crayons compasses and erasers and stuffed them in the drawer.

Another drawer had the best thing of all: the homework assignments that had been due that morning and that Zita would take back to the convent that night to grade. The thing to do was obvious. They removed Heller's homework from the stack of papers, as well as those of some of the other kids, and tore them up into the smallest pieces they could manage and threw them on the floor.

Pleased with themselves and with what they had accomplished, the boys swept the classroom floor clean of all papers and hid them with the remaining papers they were supposed to tear, in a box in the cloakroom. Then they went back to drawing cars, guns and bombers.

Zita returned an hour later and couldn't decide whether to be pleased or angry. She was happy that they had swept the floor because a clean classroom floor was a sign of having control, but annoyed that they had once again disobeyed her by not completing the punishment as ordered. She had hoped to—dreamed that she would—see the entire floor sprinkled with hundreds of thousands, if not millions, of tiny pieces of paper and the boys on their hands and knees picking them up and counting them and worrying that they would never go home again. But that wasn't the case because even if she had wanted and tried to keep the kids in detention until ten in the evening—a hollow threat on her part—she couldn't because the kids' parents would have been outraged. Even good Catholic parents had limits to what they would put up with from the nuns, and the kids and nuns knew it.

"I thought I told you to tear up every sheet of paper into the size of a pinhead, throw them on the floor and count them," Zita huffed.

"We did, Ster," Kolba offered. "We tore up every single sheet. Some were smaller than a pinhead, and some were so small that we couldn't even see them, at least mine were, and we threw them on the floor and picked them up and counted them—every single one—even the ones we couldn't see."

"How many were there?"

"Four trillion, three hundred fifty-three billion, six hundred twenty-one million, one hundred twenty-two thousand and three!"

"No, Gary," Kurkowski yelled. "It was four trillion, three hundred fifty-three billion, six hundred and twenty-one million, one hundred twenty-two thousand and four! Don't give Ster a wrong answer."

"Uh-uh!" Dennis shouted. "It was four trillion, three hundred and—"

"Oh stop it," Zita spat out. "How did you count that quickly? No one can count that fast! You're all lying!"

"No we're not," Kolba answered. "I counted them myself."

"I think you are lying, Gary," Ruchinski started. "I mean, Ster, I counted them five times over, just to make sure. I mean, you've got to be really careful when you count that many things. And I counted them, and I counted four trillion, three hundred fifty-three billion, six hundred and twenty-one million, one hundred and twenty-two thousand and, and, and three and a half! That's the exact count, Ster."

"You're all full of it," Bozeman said. "I counted 'em and there was exactly four hundred zillion trillion and two. And that's it."

"How did you count that fast, boys?" Zita asked.

"Well, we counted by twos and threes, and sometimes by fives, tens and billions, and that made it go pretty fast," Kolba said.

"That's impressive, Gary. Since all of you can count that fast it won't take long to count them all over again, one-by-one, so we get an accurate count. I hate discrepancies," Zita ordered.

"Can't do that, Ster."

"Why not?"

"Because Mister Letart came and took them away. He said they were a fire hazard, and I think he's already taken them to the incinerator and burned them."

Zita had no more desire to deal with the Disturbers that day. Even though it was only two in the afternoon, she sent them home.

CHAPTER 25

Disturbers Win a Class Election

THE NUNS AND lay teachers were all aflutter the next day as it was one of the most important days of the school year, and even in OLG's history. The sixth, seventh and eighth grade classes were to hold the school's first-ever class elections to choose officers who would guide their classmates through the remainder of the school year.

The idea was to teach, in a practical way, good citizenship, civic responsibility, the joys and wonders of freedom and free elections, and constitutional law to the students by having them participate in their own electoral process.

Vitaclaire and the other nuns and teachers had made the announcement two weeks earlier in order to give the students time to determine whether they wanted to run for office, and if they did, to campaign and try to convince their classmates to vote for them.

"We are blessed to live in a free country, free of communism and free to practice our religion without interference from the government," Vitaclaire had said in announcing the upcoming elections to the kids in room 204.

"Freedom comes with responsibility; the responsibility to vote and to participate in this freedom, and the responsibility to run for and hold public office. We need leaders who will give of themselves to help protect the freedoms we have, especially those of religious freedom and the freedom to vote.

Remember why the pilgrims came here, and that was for religious freedom. When you leave this school and become adults you will be good and responsible citizens and you will participate in this process so we will always have religious freedom in this great country. There is nothing more sacred in a free society than religious freedom and the right to vote. This is a serious endeavor, and we expect each and every one of you to take this process seriously and elect responsible people as your class officers as they will be representing Our Lady of Grace School to this neighborhood and to the world. If you are going to enjoy the blessings of liberty, then you must participate in its process."

The goal of the elections for the nuns, however nobly put in Vitaclaire's announcement, was really to get their pets and good students elected so they could spread the message of Catholicism through the neighborhood. Class officers were expected to mobilize and direct the other students to do good deeds such as visiting shut-ins in the old people's home, making them Christmas cards, going over to sing to them, praying for non-Catholics and poor people, saying as many rosaries as possible and helping clean the class-rooms at the day's end.

After Vitaclaire left, Zita spoke to the class and began her effort to get her favorites swept into office.

"Roger (Krask) and Karen (Drokowski) and John (Klosk), I think you would make excellent officers and would be wonderful representatives of our school. We can start after school today in drafting a slate of fellow candidates and a campaign platform that will show what great leaders and dedicated students and Catholics you are."

The three eagerly stayed after school that day, and over the course of the next week they selected two more slate members and worked up a campaign platform that made the Disturbers sick. The platform had more than fifty items and included things like boosting donations to buy the most pagan babies of any Catholic school in the city, an after-school catechism club, contests to see who could write down the names of the most saints in five minutes, daily morning mass attendance, an end to spitball shooting and a plan to buy and give rosaries and prayer books to the neighborhood's non-Catholics.

The platform planks that angered the Disturbers most were a requirement to stop referring to Zita as "Ster," and to always address her as "Sister Mary Zita," and to break up Disturbers Row and distribute the troublemakers throughout the class so as to give them the benefit of interacting with "the most holy and pious among us."

The plank addressing Disturbers Row, which Zita helped write, was the longest in the good kids' platform. It read in full:

"Satan is wicked, but clever. His disguises are many, including those of communists, protestants, murderers, cigarette smokers, Jews and Disturbers. We pray for the conversion of Russia and the Jews, but prayer will not help Satan personified, which are the Disturbers in Room 204 at Our Lady of Grace School at 2446 N. Ridgeway Ave. in Chicago, Illinois.

"When the Disturbers, or communist hoodlums, disrupt Sister Mary Zita's class, we students are deprived of the loving, Catholic learning environment that God has envisioned and prepared for us with the Sisters of the Dominican Order.

"The Disturbers make fun of Jesus and the sacrifice of his life to save sinners. They disrupt Sister Mary Zita's class so that those of us who want to learn to become good Catholic citizens are prevented from doing so and are prevented from getting and enjoying the full benefit of a Catholic education. Satan's goal of denying Catholic school children the full benefit of a Catholic education, which is pure evil, is directly manifested through the Disturbers of Room 204.

"Satan can and shall be destroyed by the Loving Grace of God, and it is our duty to destroy the Disturbers of Room 204. While prayer will not save the Disturbers, destroying their, and thus, Satan's, ability to disrupt Sister Mary Zita's classroom each and every day of the school year is our sacred responsibility to the Catholic Church; to our Holy Father in Rome, Pope Paul VI; to the Archdiocese of Chicago and Archbishop John Patrick Cody; to the Dominican Order of Sisters; to God; and to Sister Mary Zita, the Most Holy and Pious Nun in the Dominican Order of Sisters.

"As does Our Lord and Savior Jesus Christ believe in redemption, so do we, the pupils of Our Lady of Grace School. The Disturbers can and will be redeemed and turned into productive Catholic students when Disturbers Row is eliminated and the disturbing sinners made to sit next to the most holy and pious among us.

"We hereby proclaim that Disturbers Row will be eliminated and that its Sinners will be distributed throughout the classroom so that the Sinners will have the benefit and enjoyment of sitting next to the most holy and pious among us, and that through such interchange become holy and pious themselves and respectful of Sister Mary Zita themselves. This is God's will."

The last plank was ridiculous because Zita could have eliminated Disturbers Row any time she wanted by reassigning the Disturbers to seats throughout the room. But she knew that rather than the Disturbers being inspired into good behavior by proximity to "the most holy and pious among us," those holy kids would be transformed into troublemakers within five minutes of sitting next to a Disturber, and she dared not risk the sure exponential increase in new Disturbers that would occur should she do such a reckless thing.

Election Day morning found Zita in high spirits at the prospect of holding a free election and having it turn out exactly the way she had planned and manipulated it.

After standing at their desks and saying their morning prayer and Pledge of Allegiance, the kids sat down and Zita announced that the election would commence, throwing in the admonition that it was serious business.

"Are there any nominations?" Zita asked with a smug smile and a nod to some of the good kids. "Remember, you cannot nominate yourself."

Several hands sprang into the air and Zita chose Mary Glonski, one of her favorites, who immediately stood up and, nearly shouting, said, "I nominate the slate of Roger Krask for president, Karen Drokowski for vice president, John Klosk for secretary, William Berckmeyer for treasurer and John Letart for clerk! They will make fine officers, Sister Mary Zita, and will represent our school and you and the rest of the sisters very well. We can be proud of them."

Zita nodded approvingly and asked if there was a second to the nominating motion. Gerald Mayer nearly jumped out of his chair and gushed that he was seconding the nomination and that he couldn't wait until the slate was elected so he could start going to mass every morning and starting up the catechism club.

"Wonderful, Gerald. You will make a fine president of the catechism club. Thank you," Zita replied. "Are there any other nominations?"

To Zita, the question was a required formality and one she figured would go unanswered, and she waited a few moments while anticipating a victory of her slate by acclamation.

"There being no other nominations, I think we can—"

"Wait, Ster. I have a nomination!" a voice shouted.

It was Kenneth Gordy, one of the Disturbers' pals.

"Yes, Mister Gordy, whom would you like to nominate?" Zita asked, greatly annoyed.

"I nominate Dave Ruchinski for president, Bob Kurkowski for vice president, Gary Kolba for secretary, Dennis Domrzalski for treasurer and Richard Bozeman for clerk. The Disturbers will make excellent officers."

Zita was stunned and angry. She had planned on there being no competing slate to her hand-picked choices. That there now was one upset her enough, but that it was the Disturbers made her want to slap Gordy silly.

"This is serious business, Mister Gordy. If you are just trying to cause trouble and aren't serious about this you should sit down before I give you the back of my hand. And if I were you I would sit down now!" Zita replied.

"I am serious, Ster. I nominate the slate of Disturbers."

"That's fine, Kenneth, but I don't think there will be any seconds to your silly and disrespectful nomination. And there had better not be."

Zita was wrong. Several hands shot up and she called on Michael Kwazigroph, another of the Disturbers' allies.

"I second the nomination of the Disturbers," he said. "And I urge everyone to vote for them!"

The turn of events staggered Zita, but not most of the other kids because it had all been planned and set into motion by the Disturbers two weeks earlier. Disgusted by the idea of having other kids try to give them orders and make them do way too many good deeds, the Disturbers hatched their own plan, which was that they would run as a slate for all five offices. They quickly settled on the slate's order, but the titles and positions were meaningless to them because they all figured they were presidential material and they just wanted to be in office and confound Zita and the other nuns.

The campaigning began on the playground the afternoon after Vitaclaire's announcement, and it amounted to not much more than the Disturbers telling kids they had to vote for them. The kids who balked were punched and told that the rest of the year would go hard for them if the Disturbers lost.

HE WAS SATAN'S CANDIDATE

It really wasn't that hard a sell. Except for the few hyper do-gooders, most of the kids were normal, meaning they weren't over-the-top Catholics. They too goofed off, didn't like authority and weren't about to be forced to go to mass every morning or catechism club after school. And they hated it that when they put money in the coffee cans for pagan babies they were yelled at for contributing only pennies, and not dimes, quarters and half dollars. They also hated it that when they went to the public library after school and goofed off or talked too loud, that the nuns knew about it the next day, or that if they took the money from their Sunday donation envelopes to buy soda or candy or potato chips, the nuns telephoned their parents. In short, they hated it that the nuns and priests controlled almost every aspect of their lives and that the nuns had a network of informants who watched and snitched on them. Many wished they had the guts to be as bold and as outrageous as the Disturbers, and they viewed the Disturbers as heroes for challenging the nuns at every turn, and in the process, providing tons of laughs.

The Disturbers campaigned on the walks to and from school in the mornings and afternoons, on the playground, in the school's halls and in the cloakrooms. Several kids did have to be warned and strong-armed, including Kwazigroph, who when he said one day in the cloakroom that he wasn't sure he would vote for the Disturbers, got a compass point to the thigh from Dennis.

"You're gonna vote for us now, ain't you Kwaz?" Dennis said as he pulled the sharp metal shaft from the kid's thigh. "And I think you should second our nomination when it comes up."

"I'm bleeding!" Kwazigroph shouted after the compass point was pulled from his thigh. "I'm bleeding!"

"It's just a little blood. Stop being a sissy," Dennis replied as he cocked his arm in preparation for another compass thrust into Kwaz's thigh. "You're going to second our nomination and vote for us, right?"

"Yes! Yes! Leave me alone!"

"And you ain't gonna tell anybody? Right?"

"No!"

That promise of secrecy was key to the Disturbers' campaign. They elicited the pledge from every kid they convinced to vote for them. It was important that the nuns not get word of their plan, for if they did, they would have canceled the election or otherwise found a way to thwart the Disturbers and their quest for office.

SHE DIDN'T WANT A FAIR ELECTION.

The guys knew what they were doing and approached only those they knew secretly despised the nuns and who wouldn't snitch, which was most of the class. They didn't have a written platform, but everyone who agreed to vote for them knew they would continue drive the nuns crazy, and that was good enough for them.

Although she was outraged by the situation, Zita knew she had no choice but to go forward with the vote, which was supposed to be by secret ballot. But she had a last-minute scheme and said she would poll each kid individually and publicly in the hope that they would be too scared to publicly vote for the Disturbers and risk the consequences of going against a nun's wishes and challenging her authority.

The voice vote was held, and when it was over Zita was sick with rage. The Disturbers had won twenty-seven to fifteen. Those twenty-seven kids, the Disturbers included, were joyous because they had publicly and overwhelmingly defeated a nun, and that sense of freedom and courage felt so sweet. They had won!

Laughter boomed from those twenty-seven throats and the Disturbers marched around the room stomping their feet, shaking the hands of their supporters and pledging all kinds of goofy things, including an end to having to buy pagan babies.

For Dennis the victory was especially sweet because he had experienced the thrill of elected office once before and he relished the idea of having power again. It was in third grade that he had been elected King Courtesy by his classmates, a position that came with a cardboard crown and the responsibility of passing out paper messengers, which were four-page propaganda sheets published by the Church and distributed to the schools every Friday afternoon. Nearly every week the messengers had stories of how the communists tortured priests, nuns and all Catholics, and they advocated prayer against the hated commies.

The position of King Courtesy was a revolving one that changed each week with a new election on Friday afternoons. After the one-week reign, the current King was to remind the teacher, Miss Edith Scalzitti, a short woman who limped, to hold a new vote. Not wanting to surrender his title and power to pass out messengers, Dennis refused to inform Miss Scalzitti that his time as King was up and to have a new election.

So the teacher was surprised the next Friday when Dennis again put on his crown and passed out the messengers. A few kids, figuring they should have been King, complained to Scalzitti that Dennis was still in office.

The teacher, a kind and gentle soul who never hit or verbally abused a kid, called Dennis to her desk and asked him quietly:

"Why didn't you remind me last week about the new election?"

"I don't know. I just forgot," Dennis lied.

"Well, you can continue passing the messengers out today, but we'll have to have another election. Remember, everybody gets to be King or Queen Courtesy."

After passing out the messengers, Dennis sat down and pouted. He loved being King Courtesy, not because he was courteous and wanted to spread kindness, good manners and respect for others, but because it had been the only time in his life when he had been afforded some respect. His brothers and cousins teased him and picked on him incessantly, and he hated to part with the feeling that, at least for a little while, his classmates thought he was a worthwhile human being.

Scalzitti took nominations for a new King, and when Matthew Bork was nominated, Dennis was disgusted and said loud enough for Bork to hear:

"Bork's too fat to be King Courtesy."

Bork heard it, raised his hand and said when Scalzitti called on him:

"Miss Scalzitti, Dennis made an insult. He said I'm too fat to be King Courtesy."

Had Scalzitti been as embittered and abusive as the nuns and some other lay teachers, she would have walked to Dennis's desk and clobbered him. But she wasn't and she didn't.

"I'm sure he didn't mean it that way. I'll talk to him after class," she said.

After class, Scalzitti called Dennis to her desk and said:

"You're a good boy. I know you respect your classmates, and I know it is difficult to not be King Courtesy. But how would you feel if someone insulted you like that?"

"I don't know. Probably not much because I'm not fat."

"Well, I think your feelings would be hurt. I want you to think about this. There will be other elections for King Courtesy, and if you continue like this, your classmates won't vote for you again. Would you want that?"

"No."

"Then go home and think about this, and remember, you're a very good and smart boy."

That was the nicest thing that anyone had ever said to him, and from then on, Dennis thought that Miss Edith Scalzitti was the nicest and greatest teacher ever.

CHAPTER 26

The Intoxication of Victory!

THE DISTURBERS CONTINUED their march around the room and the celebration continued, except, of course, for Zita and her slate of defeated and humiliated candidates.

Berckmeyer was sobbing, and through his tears and convulsions he stammered out:

"Sister, how could this have happened? This can't be God's will, can it?"

"Of course not, William, it's the work of Satan and of those hoodlums."

"But how could have everybody have voted for them and not us? That's not fair."

"It's not fair, William, and we'll see what Sister Vitaclaire has to say about this."

For the time being, though, Zita had to acknowledge the results and the will of the majority of her students. The election rules called for speeches by the winners, and Ruchinski and the other Disturbers demanded to be heard.

"Ster, we'd like to give our acceptance speeches," Kolba said. "I think our classmates want to hear our ideas."

"We don't have time for such nonsense. Sit down."

"But Ster, the rules say that we get to give acceptance speeches."

"I don't care, and the rules have changed."

Neither the Disturbers nor their supporters were about to accept such an arbitrary rule change, and many of the kids began shouting, "Speeches! Speeches!"

The Disturbers obliged and walked to the front of the room to strut about and show off and act silly, all to the delight of their classmates.

"Thank you, you have made a wise decision, a decision directed by God," Kolba said. "We promise to bring democracy and free speech to this classroom, and we will even do something nice for the old people at Christmas."

"And," Ruchinski offered, "from now on, none of us have to clean the blackboards or classrooms after school. That's slave labor and we refuse to be slaves. If they want us to clean the rooms, they'll have to pay us, and pay us big money!"

The room went wild with cheers as kids began chanting, "Pay us! Pay us!"

Bozeman was next: "We ain't gonna do anything we don't want to because I said so!"

Kurkowski followed, saying, "No more hymns! We ain't gonna sing anymore hymns!"

Then Dennis roused everybody with this:

"We're gonna get the money Zita made from selling our stuff, go to those kids who bought the stuff and get our things back. That includes all the stuff she has stolen from all of you! We're going to report Zita to the cops for stealing!"

Dennis added a final flurry that sent the kids into a frenzy: "Under the Disturbers, we will all have airier air, wetter water and saltier salt! We're gonna season our pizzas with salt from Lott's wife! And I guarantee you that under our rule, cotton candy will finally be made out of cotton, and rock candy out of rocks. No more of this false advertising. Finally, we will invade and conquer that filthy, stinking country Russia and take all of its resources for ourselves."

All was bedlam and joy in the room for the next few hours, as the kids didn't have to change classes that morning. The Disturbers held court in Disturbers Row as kid after kid came back to congratulate them, ask about their plans for governing and if there was any room in the Disturbers cabinet for them. The guys made more promises than they should have, but like all winning politicians, they were intoxicated by victory. They would soon forget all they had promised.

CHAPTER 27

An Election Overturned

THE GUYS REVELED in their victory on the walks home for lunch and they daydreamed about all the things they would accomplish, many of them good and wholesome, such as arranging outings for shut-ins throughout the neighborhood and helping old people rake their leaves.

The walks back to the playground were just as heady. On the playground the guys met and started to develop plans, which they intended to submit to Zita.

When the bell rang to end the lunch hour the guys filed into Zita's room and then the class was off to Miss Donatello's room as the regular class-changing schedule had resumed.

It was a little after one o'clock when they settled into their seats in Donatello's room and the front door burst open to reveal a very angry Sister Vitaclaire. It was rare for the principal to visit a class when they were in another teacher's room, and the kids figured something important and scary was up. Donatello appeared to know exactly the purpose of the visit and she stepped aside and let Vitaclaire have the floor.

Her arms folded, the principal wasted no time in getting to the point of her visit.

"This election will not stand," she said in an angry, measured tone that left no doubt as to her utter outrage. "This is a sham. We will not have hoodlums representing Our Lady of Grace School. As of this moment, this morning's election is void. I am installing the first slate of candidates nominated, as class officers. Are there any questions?"

The room was silent, as most of the kids were scared to ask a question, even though they knew that Vitaclaire's pronouncement and unilateral removal of fairly elected officers was the real sham and the work of a true dictator. They knew that any question they asked challenging the decision would be met with a beating.

"Since there are no questions, that is it. I will—"

THIS ELECTION IS OVERTURNED

At once, in unison, the five Disturbers raised their hands. Vitaclaire shot them looks filled with so much hatred that some kids feared she would actually explode or spontaneously self-combust. She preferred to not take any questions, but knew that her extraordinary, dictatorial action had to somehow be explained.

"Mister Ruchinski, since you appear to be the ringleader of this mockery, I will take your question. What is it you want to know?"

Ruchinski had a statement, not a question, and he was risking his physical well-being, and probably permanent expulsion, by making it. He had had it with all the abuse he had suffered over the years, and something in him made him stand up and give the most serious talk of his life.

"Sister, you've taught us that this is a free country, that we have a Constitution and that we have freedom of speech, free will and free elections. This was a fair election. By doing what you're doing you're being a communist and a dictator. We won. All these kids voted for us, and now you're saying that just because you don't like the results you will change it. How is that being a good citizen? How is that teaching us good values? You hate the communists, but now you're being one yourself. Why should we ever believe anything you tell us again?"

Vitaclaire was rendered momentarily speechless by the sincerity and the clarity of the argument. Apparently the little hoodlum had actually learned something. The other Disturbers kept their hands raised and Vitaclaire knew that if she didn't let them express their views and vent, they would make life even more hellish for Sister Zita. She also knew that she was wrong and that if the kids told their parents about this abuse, she would catch hell from some of them. Singlehandedly overturning an election, especially a lesson in democracy for seventh graders, might not be tolerated by many of the parents. Kolba was next:

"Sister, who or what else will you overthrow, and when? This ain't freedom, and I—"

"'Ain't,' Mister Kolba, is not a word. When you make an argument, you will make it in English. Am I understood?"

"Yes, Sister. This isn't freedom, and you have made a mockery out of all the things we have learned. How is this freedom?"

Kurkowski and Bozeman had similar statements and questions, and then it was Dennis's turn. He was the most infuriated of the Disturbers by the abuse of power. He too had had enough.

"Sister Mary Vitaclaire, you are a hypocrite," he said while his eyes focused on the nun and shot even more hatred at her than she had at them.

It was a remarkably courageous statement—suicidal, many of the kids thought—to make for a seventh grader and for a Catholic boy to make to a nun. It signaled an end of any lingering fear of the nuns and their alleged holy authority, and of any lingering respect for them.

"Sister," he continued, "I declare that you are no longer principal of this school. You are overturned."

No one, not even the other Disturbers, could believe what they had just heard. It was at once terrifying and exhilarating. Many feared Dennis would be killed right then and there, but they sensed—they now actually knew—that through her blatant and cowardly overreach, Vitaclaire and the nuns and lay teachers had been exposed as cowardly and hypocritical abusers, and in reality, had been defeated.

Vitaclaire knew it too, and she knew that arguing with the Disturbers, or beating them, would be wasted time and energy.

The principal shot one more glare at the Disturbers, but the sense of absolute authority and terror-invoking intensity it once conveyed was gone, and she stormed out of the room to the giggles of most of the kids.

In their defeat, the Disturbers had gained victory.

CHAPTER 28

A Secret Signal?

THE NEXT MORNING, Zita installed her chosen ones as class officers, but it was meaningless. No one, not even the kids who had voted for them, recognized their titles, offices or authority. After the installment ceremony, complete with sappy speeches, was finished, Kolba stood up in the back of the room and announced:

"The only legitimate officers of this class are those who have been lawfully elected by the people. We do not recognize these people or this sham installation. We the Disturbers announce that we are the only officers lawfully elected in a free election and that we have set up a Government in Exile right here in Disturbers Row."

Every kid but the five Zita had installed cheered and laughed. The Disturbers were the real class officers and power, and everyone knew it.

The guys spent the next hour, which was religion class, conferring among themselves, working up policy statements and drafting plans, and just before the bell rang for them to change classes, Zita, thinking she would embarrass the Disturbers by exposing their ineptitude at governing and inability to make any kind of plan, asked contemptuously:

"Mister Kolba, why don't you tell the class what your Government in Exile has chosen as its first priority."

"Yes, Ster!" Kolba said as he shot out of his chair. "This is serious business, Ster, because not everyone can run a Government in Exile, and we take our jobs seriously, and I can tell you that just seventeen seconds ago we declared war on Room 203!"

The room erupted with laughter and most of the kids were happy that the Disturbers were in charge. It was a lot more fun than having to listen to pious speeches from do-gooders and going to catechism club.

Their next class was with Donatello, a stout, dark-haired woman whose mustache, the kids joked, was thicker than the ones their dads grew. She too was a stern, humorless disciplinarian who brooked no nonsense in her room and who met each disturbance with an open-handed right cross that was second in power only to DeLasalle's. The kids didn't know exactly why most of their lay teachers were so angry, but their instincts said it most likely had something to do with the fact that they were all named Miss, and not Mrs.

Donatello's math and science classes weren't any fun because she was humorless and passionless, except when it came to disciplining kids, giving homework and getting angry when kids didn't immediately grasp the simplest scientific or mathematical concepts, or when they answered questions incorrectly.

Donatello was still emotionally ablaze—as were all the other nuns and teachers—over Room 204's election, and she began the class by berating the kids for having voted for the Disturbers.

"You disgraced yourselves and you disgraced Our Lady of Grace School, and you made God angry by joining with these, these reprobates," she started.

It was a good touch because none of the kids knew what "reprobate" meant. They understood monsters and hoodlums and delinquents and sinners, but reprobate was something new to them, and although they figured it meant the same thing, they were amused, especially the Disturbers.

"Those reprobates will never amount to anything in life, and neither will anyone who goes along with them. They are not funny, they are not smart, they are not cool, and they have already proved themselves total failures in life. If you want to know what failure looks like, just look at them! They will not get into high school, and they will live their lives as bums!

"When you make a mockery out of elections, out of Our Lady of Grace School and out of us teachers who are here to educate you so you can be successes in life, you make a mockery of God and of the Catholic Church. I, for one, will not tolerate their monkey business in this classroom. If they want to throw away their futures, they can do so, but I will not abide anyone else following their pitiful examples and walking the road to ruin. We, and their parents, are embarrassed and ashamed of them. They are beyond redemption. Lest anyone of you think I am not serious about this, I suggest you put me to the test."

The Disturbers had never been prouder of themselves. Never had they been so reviled. They were thrilled to have been called reprobates and pitiful, and they were proud to have made so many people ashamed of them. The berating also meant that they had gotten to Donatello and the other teachers in a big way, and that's what they were the happiest about.

Donatello's dare was one that none of the Disturbers wanted to pass up, but they were tired of getting hit. They decided not to wage a direct assault on this angry woman who was itching for a confrontation.

"Are there any questions about what I have just said?"

Although he knew better, Kolba couldn't resist. He raised his hand.

"What is it, Mister Kolba?" Donatello asked in instantly acknowledging his raised arm. "Surely you have something productive and respectful to add to the conversation?"

"I do."

"I do, to whom?" Donatello spat out, angered that he hadn't said, "I do, Miss Donatello."

Kolba knew better than to not address her as "Miss Donatello," but he also knew that refusing to would drive her crazy, and so he decided to drive her crazy.

"Shouldn't you call bums hobos? It's disrespectful to call them bums. That's what Sister Mary Zita has taught us," he said.

Like pretty much every other teacher at OLG, Donatello couldn't take it that a student would not just talk back to her, but would challenge her authority in a way that made her look like a hypocrite. Kids weren't supposed to do that. Donatello had been a perfect Catholic schoolgirl who obeyed every rule and regulation and conformed and conformed and conformed. She had buried her imagination, creativity and independence under a mountain of conformity, and she was going to do her best to make damn sure that every Catholic kid she taught suffered the same humiliation and self-loathing. No one was going to do what she had been too scared, but had desperately wanted, to do, which was to question stupid rules, challenge oppressive and abusive authority, stand up for herself and be an independent human being. She was going to impose her own cowardice and limitations on every kid she came across.

What Kolba said was true. The nuns had repeatedly admonished the kids to never refer to bums as bums, but to call them hobos because hobo was more respectful.

"Isn't it just big of you to quote Sister Mary Zita when it suits your opportunistic purposes?" Donatello said. "It's too bad for you, mister, that you ignore Sister Mary Zita ninety-nine-point-nine percent of the time. Now get to the front of this room and get here now!"

Kolba obeyed and began walking very slowly. Actually, he was shuffling and walking as slowly as he could to the room's front end. It was an easy way to torment Donatello and she was not amused.

"I said get here now, and if you continue to purposely prolong this, I will come and drag you by your ears, mister. Now move!"

Kolba continued his slow walk, which caused the hefty teacher to loudly and angrily ask:

"Why aren't you walking faster? What is wrong with you?"

Kolba paused, and from the side of the room said:

"Well, Miss Donatello, this is how slow hobos walk. I wanted to show you so you don't ever call them bums again."

Enraged, Donatello launched herself toward the side of the room and met Kolba halfway. He stood still as she whaled on him with her meaty fists and beefy arms, and after throwing the boy into the classroom's wall, she made good on her earlier promise and grabbed one of his ears and pulled him to the front of the room where she beat him again.

That the boy seemed unfazed by the beating, and unhurt, made Donatello angrier, and she whacked him a few more times before ordering him to stand motionless in front of the room for the remainder of the period.

"If I so much as catch you breathing, you *will* get the back of my hand and more," she stammered before ordering the rest of the class to open their math books and start the day's lesson.

The kids were anxious to see whether Kolba would comply with the order and drop dead for a lack of oxygen, or if Donatello would beat him for the mere act of breathing and trying to stay alive. They figured she would beat him for inhaling and exhaling just so she could prove who was boss, but she was so determined to make the other kids suffer through another painful math lesson that she ignored Kolba.

The boy stood as motionless as possible and held his breath until he got dizzy and fell to the floor. The kids were beyond entertained. It was pure ecstasy, for most of them, anyway, to see a kid disturb the class by *obeying* a teacher's orders.

Donatello was furious. She knew she had brought on the incident herself with her idiotic warning that Kolba would regret it if he breathed, and so she boiled and raged inside, knowing that once again she had been had by a seventh grader and by her own stupid order and idiotic overreaching in trying to impose discipline and authority.

As Kolba got to his feet he started to speak, wanting to get in another dig at the teacher who couldn't figure out what the kids instinctively knew. And that was for a threat to be effective it had to be credible, and they all knew that no one could punish a kid for breathing, not even the craziest nun. Kolba wanted to say, "Sorry, Miss Donatello, for breaking your rule and trying to stay alive. I promise it won't happen again. Next time I'll die."

Donatello knew what he was up to, and she could stand no more embarrassments, and she stopped him before the first word left his mouth.

"Not a word, mister, otherwise your parents will hear about this, and we'll see who gets the last laugh."

So Kolba relaxed and stood in front of the room and breathed normally, and while he thought about breathing deeply and making a lot of noise and another scene, he knew he had already won the admiration of his fellow Disturbers and most of the other kids, and that another disturbance would have been overkill. But there was to be no peace that afternoon in Donatello's room.

While Kolba stood in the front of the room, Dennis, who was in the back row, made eye contact with him and made a gesture that the Disturbers and many of the other kids had started using. He stroked his chin several times with his thumb and index finger. The kids called it "Yom Gypsy," and it had many meanings, but it mostly meant "Yeah sure," or "This is ridiculous," or "Bullshit," or "This is bullshit," or whatever the situation needed it to mean. It was flexible, and sometimes was simply a way to communicate when they couldn't talk to each other. But its universal meaning was one of disrespect.

Kolba acknowledged the gesture and he replied to Dennis with his own "Yom Gypsy," and the two amused each other by stroking their chins. Donatello glanced at Kolba, and then at Dennis. She and the nuns had seen the gesture before from students in their own classes, but they didn't know exactly what it was or meant, and while they suspected it might be devious, they hoped it was benign. But now that two Disturbers were using it, well, Donatello figured it had to be something horrible and designed to incite total rebellion, and she was not going to put up with two kids sending secret messages to each other in her classroom.

CHAPTER 29

They've Planned an Orgy!

DONATELLO CALLED DENNIS to the room's front, and when he arrived, she yanked him and Kolba out into the hallway where she loudly asked them:

"What does that mean? What secret signals have you been sending to each other? What?"

Donatello's loud inquisition was designed to get the attention of DeLasalle, Yvonne and Zita, and the three quickly arrived on the scene.

"They have been sending coded messages to each other," Donatello told the nuns. "In my classroom!"

"How?" DeLasalle growled.

"Show the sisters!" Donatello said. "Show them exactly what you were doing! Mister Kolba, now!"

The boy stroked his chin once, and as he was about to start on a second run, DeLasalle's open hand crashed into the side of his face.

"What is the meaning of that?" she demanded. "What?"

While DeLasalle was questioning Kolba, Yvonne started in on Dennis and ordered him to perform the gesture. When he did, she whacked him across the face.

By the rage the four showed, one would have thought that they believed "Yom Gypsy" was a signal from Satan that would lead to the immediate destruction of the entire Catholic Church, and not just a way for smart aleck twelve-year-olds to communicate with each other and have some fun.

"It must be code from the communists," Zita bellowed as she wagged a crooked and scaly finger at her two students. "They're in league with the communists! There are communists in this school. Call the monsignor!"

The nuns continued shouting at and beating the boys, and the commotion caused Vitaclaire to leave her office on the floor below and climb the stairs to see what was going on. Donatello and DeLasalle briefed her on the situation and ordered the boys to repeat the gesture for the principal. When they did, she instantly clobbered them with her open hand while demanding to know what the chin-stroking meant.

A SECRET SIGNAL?

"From where did this come and who taught it to you?" Vitaclaire demanded. "Who? What does it mean? You will be forthcoming with an immediate answer otherwise we will take this, not only to your parents, but to the bishop and to the police and other authorities. We will not brook communist, or other depraved signals in a Catholic school in the United States of America!"

"Maybe, Sister, they're signaling each other as to which girls they've got their filthy eyes on," Donatello raged. "They're planning an orgy!"

"Pagans!" Zita stammered, stunned by the use of the word orgy. Mentioning sex in a Catholic school was sinful and disgusting enough, but an orgy, oh, she nearly fainted at the word. "They're planning pagan rituals!"

Dennis saw his opening and decided to have some fun, although he knew it was fun that would cost him a severe beating.

"I'm not exactly sure what it means, but it could mean an orgy. What's an orgy? Could you explain that?" Dennis asked.

The boy was being somewhat honest. He and the other kids had heard that word a few times, and although they had an idea of what an orgy was, they weren't totally clear on its exact meaning. Dennis thought it meant groups of people getting together, stuffing their faces with food and then throwing up. "Maybe we can have an orgy in the class this afternoon," he continued.

The five women attacked the boy at once, shoving each other to get at him. Dennis covered his head and face with his hands and arms and withstood their combined fury. When they had finished beating him, Vitaclaire demanded:

"Where did you learn that word, and from whom?"

"From you, Sister, just now, and from our Catechism books. They say the pagans used to have orgies and worship golden calves. I don't have any gold to make a calf, but I know we can have an orgy—just to see what sinners the pagans really were."

The nuns were speechless with rage and disbelief. Their minds, which lost all sense of logic when they got angry, now spun wildly out of control. They imagined more than a hundred seventh graders indulging themselves in the most sinful and disgusting of ways, and they actually believed that OLG's seventh graders were planning a real orgy.

"Mister Kolba," Vitaclaire shouted. "When and where will this orgy be held, and who is the ringleader?"

Like Dennis, Kolba didn't really know what an orgy was, but he knew the word sent the nuns into fits and he played along with Dennis's instigation.

"We were thinking of having the orgy in the school hall, and I don't know who the ringleader is," Kolba answered. "Could be anybody."

The nuns and Donatello were apoplectic, and well, consumed and dizzy with rage. They couldn't stop themselves to consider the insanity of seventh graders planning an orgy, and scheduling it for the school hall, and they couldn't see that they were once again being had.

"Are girls going to be involved in this?" Yvonne demanded.

"Do they have to be?" Dennis asked. "Can't we do it with just the boys?"

That none of the women had a stroke was a miracle. OLG's halls had never before heard screams and shrieks like they heard that afternoon from the nuns and Donatello.

Yvonne and DeLasalle raced to their rooms to interrogate and terrorize their kids. They had one goal: to determine which girls would be participating in the upcoming orgy and beat them senseless.

Vitaclaire took Dennis and Kolba, stormed down to her office and telephoned Monsignor Flavin at the parish rectory. Flavin could hardly believe what he heard. Not only were Catholic school kids planning an unholy group sex party, but at least one boy didn't think girls should be involved. This was the emergency of all time, and God's immediate intercession, as well as that of officers from the Chicago Police Department, was needed.

AN ORGY OF FISTS

Flavin raced the half block to Vitaclaire's office where she briefed him more fully on the situation. Within ten minutes, two Chicago police officers arrived.

Upstairs in the seventh-grade classrooms, Yvonne and DeLasalle had already identified several girls they figured would be part of the orgy and were beating them. Zita was stumbling around her room, pointer in hand, clobbering kids for no reason.

In Donatello's room, the other Disturbers were wondering what had happened to their colleagues and what the commotion was all about. They knew something huge was up by the fury and speed with which Donatello was conducting her inquisition of the girls and beating them. Donatello called the girls individually to the front of the room and then quizzed them separately in the cloakroom on the room's right-hand side. Each girl entered the cloakroom scared and clueless about the situation, and they exited crying and with faces made red by the barrage of slaps from the crazed teacher.

April Noble was another frequent target of the nuns and teachers. She had received her beating from Donatello along with the threat that her parents would be called that night and told she was a floozie. The nuns had disliked April since second grade when she regularly committed the crime of talking in class. She paid for the sin by having to write thousands of times over the next few years, "I will be silent!"

The nuns thought that making the girl write those words over and over would stop her from sinning. It didn't work. April kept talking and the nuns gave her more and more penalties. The only good that came of the punishment was that the girl developed excellent penmanship when writing, "I will be silent!" April knew that she had often been wrongly accused and penalized, but she also knew that it was useless to protest the unfair treatment to the angry women in uniform.

April returned to her seat in the fifth row. Defiant and unbowed, she started whispering to others the reason for the inquisition.

"They said we're having an orgy in the school hall," she turned and told Kurkowski in the back row. "Everybody's involved and they've called the cops."

The news spread quickly and soon the entire class knew that this was the biggest and most serious thing to ever hit the school. Many were scared. Most weren't quite sure what an orgy was, but they knew this was pure scandal that would probably ruin their lives forever. Many of the kids got out their dictionaries to look up the word. The three remaining Disturbers also sensed how gigantic it was and knew they didn't want to be left out on the biggest disturbance in the school's history.

When Donatello came out of the cloakroom to call another girl forward, Bozeman raised his hand. Donatello did not want to acknowledge the boy. She was having too much fun beating the girls and she wanted no interruption. But Bozeman began jumping out of his chair, as did Ruchinski and Kurkowski, and so Donatello called on him.

"What is it, Mister Bozeman? I am busy."

"Miss Donatello," Bozeman said as he stood by his desk, "will you be at the orgy?"

Ruchinski wasted no time in getting in a comment of his own. "I think we should invite Monsignor Flavin," he said.

Then it was Kurkowski's turn. "I know who planned the orgy, Miss Donatello. I know!"

Within minutes the three were in Vitaclaire's office with Dennis, Kolba, Flavin and the cops. The principal and monsignor trembled when briefed by Donatello on their comments. They would have administered the greatest and most punishing beating of all time had the cops not been present. They restrained themselves and gave the officers a complete rundown of the situation.

The cops knew instantly that the holy people had been taken, and they asked to speak to the Disturbers alone in the hallway outside of Vitaclaire's office.

"Okay, you little shits, who started this?" one cop asked. "I don't appreciate my time being wasted by dumb little punks. And if you think this is funny, just try us and you'll end up in reform school or in Dunning, and I'll take you there myself right now. Now who started this?"

It took a few moments for Dennis to get the nerve to speak, but when he did, he stammered out:

"They did. I mean, Donatello did. She's the one who used the word."

After about fifteen minutes with the boys, the cops knew it was an idiotic mistake, and that once it had gotten going the boys took advantage of things. Satisfied that the school's seventh graders weren't going to have group sex in the school hall, the cops turned to report to Vitaclaire and the others. Before they entered the office, one cop turned to Dennis and asked:

"Do you even know what an orgy is?"

The boy shrugged his shoulders and said, "I think so. I mean, it's where people take their clothes off and eat a lot and throw up, right?"

The cops shook their heads, laughed to themselves and walked into Vitaclaire's office to deliver their report. The school officials were a bit embarrassed that they, actually Donatello, had sparked the disturbance, but they were unrepentant and determined more than ever to punish as many kids as possible. That night, calls went out from all five to parents who were told that school authorities had smashed an attempt by seventh graders to have an orgy.

CHAPTER 30

Fabricated Sins and an Overreaction

A FEW OF THE parents were aghast at the allegations of a class-wide orgy, but most recognized it as a repeat of a situation that had occurred a few years earlier in 1961 when Dennis and his classmates were making their first confession in second grade.

Confession was a big deal to the Church as it made seven-year-olds begin to think about sin and guilt, and it made it likely that they would spend the rest of their lives feeling guilty about pretty much everything and keep them beholden to the Church and its priests for forgiveness and eternal salvation.

The second graders studied hard for the big day when they would go into a confessional and tell their sins to a priest. The kids memorized prayers and Catholic doctrine, and they were tested on their knowledge of that doctrine.

They were also drilled about the horror of sin; how they were born with original sin, which was cleansed when they were baptized; how their souls became pure white after baptism; how those pure white souls got black spots every time they committed a sin; how a mortal sin made the soul entirely black; and how an honest and sincere confession could turn those souls pure white again.

Most kids blindly accepted it that they were born with sin, even though they hadn't done anything wrong. Some questioned the concept, arguing that if original sin were real, then birth itself was a sin. That usually got them beatings. Others questioned the church's teachings and said it was unfair that Indians or tribes in Africa who had never heard of the Catholic Church or of confession, would be doomed to an eternity in Hell simply because they had never seen a priest or gone to confession. How could they be punished for that, some wondered? And if they could, then the Church and its so-called loving God were anything but compassionate and loving.

The problem for the second graders as confession time approached—and for most of the older kids who had already received the sacrament—was to have enough sins to confess before entering the confessional. Older kids were required to go to confession once a month, and for those who weren't troublemakers or smart alecks, it was tough to come up with sins. No one dared enter the confessional without having sins to admit for fear that they would be called liars and beaten. Not having sins to confess was a sin itself, and even though the confessional was supposed to be secret, the kids figured the priests recognized their voices and knew who they were, and so they were always ready with an ample number of transgressions, most of which were made up.

The trick to a good confession was to have enough sins to avoid being called a liar who refused to confess, and to have sins that were mild enough to not draw huge penances—prayers that had to be mumbled in church after leaving the confessional. The kids went to confession on Friday afternoons with their classes, and the nuns eyed the church pews where the students sat and knelt after confession and timed them in their prayers to see who was getting light or heavy penances. Kids who fell into those two categories could expect to be spoken to by the nuns when they returned to class. The kids with heavy penances would be berated for being sinners, communists and partners with Satan, while those with light penances would be harangued for being liars.

The ideal penance was four or five Our Fathers and Hail Marys followed by a few Act of Contritions, which took five to ten minutes to recite. Anything longer than that could lead to an inquisition by the nuns as to what a kid had done wrong. Getting stuck with an entire Rosary for penance was one of the worst things because it meant a definite talking to and perhaps a call to one's parents.

A typical confession for a second or third grader was vague and went something like:

"Bless me Father for I have sinned. It has been three weeks since my last confession. In that time, I disobeyed my parents five times, thought bad things six times, did wrong things three times and was lazy twice. I lied three times, talked back to my parents and didn't take out the garbage or do the dishes."

The kids never got into detail about their sins because they were fabricating most of them, and the priests generally never asked for details because they didn't want to be bombarded with the inane details of hundreds of second graders' lives. Kids who knew the system always exaggerated the number of lies they confessed to so as to cover themselves for lying right then and there in the confessional. No kid was ever going to confess to shoplifting because if they did, the nuns would learn of it and trouble would ensue. So a kid would fail to confess to shoplifting, which was a lie. But by adding that lie to the number other generic lies he had told during the month, as in, "I lied fifteen times," he was in the clear and came out of the confessional with a pure white soul.

There was one sin that none of the kids made up, that none could avoid and that all dreaded confessing to: that of touching oneself.

The nuns preached constantly about the dangers and the sinfulness of touching oneself and they hammered it home every couple of days that that was to be avoided no matter what. They were, of course, afraid that the kids would masturbate, but they dared not use that term because it scared the hell out of them and would have frightened the kids into hysteria. Masturbation! Good god it was awful.

Rather than addressing the sin directly, the nuns called it "touching one-self," and they never specified which parts of one's body one wasn't supposed to touch. As a result, they turned many of the kids into neurotics. Up until the fourth or fifth grade, kids weren't ready to pleasure themselves, and they had no understanding of what the nuns were attempting to convey in their admonitions. Since they didn't know which parts they weren't supposed to touch, some kids feared touching any part of themselves, even their big toes, and they became worried sick when they dressed themselves or went to the bathroom or took a bath because they had actually touched themselves. They knew they couldn't help but touch themselves, and they couldn't understand how wiping themselves after going to the bathroom could get them a one-way ticket to Hell.

FATHER, I'VE TOUCHED MYSELF

While the kids knew they were supposed to confess to touching themselves, even if it meant combing their hair, they all pretty much refused to do so. It wasn't something they discussed with each other; it was just kids realizing individually and independently that the nuns were insane.

Both Dennis and Kolba were unsure of what sins to offer up during their first confession, and so they studied Catholic doctrine and the Ten Commandments and were prepared when the day came.

"Bless me Father, for I have sinned, this is my first holy confession," Kolba said during his first trip into the confessional. "I've committed seven venial sins and two mortal sins."

That a second grader making his first confession had a mortal sin got the priest's attention and he said:

"Well, let's get to the mortal sins first."

"Yes, Father. I have sinned. Yesterday I committed adultery, and before that I coveted my neighbor's wife."

"You what?"

"I committed adultery and coveted my neighbor's wife."

"Are you sure?"

"Yes."

"How is it you committed adultery, my child?"

"Well, Father, I saw her walking down the alley yesterday, and when she said hi to me I told her she was a nice lady and that she made good cookies."

"I see. Is this the same woman you coveted?"

"Yes, Father."

"And how is it you coveted her?"

"I looked at her hair, which is really shiny."

"I see. Well, let's get on to your venial sins."

"Yes, Father. I forgot to take out the garbage three times. Two times I didn't wash my hands before supper, and twice I looked at myself in the mirror."

"Tell me about that and why you think it's a sin."

"Because, Father, I was combing my hair and I think that's wrong."

"Very well. I absolve you of your sins, and for your penance you will say six Hail Marys, six Our Fathers and six Act of Contritions. Go in peace."

That was a hefty first-time penance, but Kolba figured he had it coming for committing adultery and coveting his neighbor's wife.

Dennis's first confession was a bit more dramatic. He loaded up on mortal sins, thinking that was what he was supposed to do and that the priest would be impressed by his willingness to confess to so many horrible things. He too had committed adultery and coveted his neighbor's wife, and he failed to keep holy the Sabbath, took the Lord's name in vain, bore false witness several people, worshiped false gods and made golden calves.

The priest didn't believe most of it, but nonetheless issued a severe penance of two Rosaries, thinking it would prevent future fabrications.

Kids traded information about sins and penances and which sins got what, and soon, most every kid was rattling off the exact same sins in confession. Sins gained and faded in popularity depending on kids' imaginations and the advice they got from their older brothers and sisters.

One that became the rage that year was a violation of the Fifth Commandment to honor thy father and mother. Kurkowski got it from one of his older brothers who advised that it was a good idea to always have a relatively harmless mortal sin handy.

"You just tell the guy that you failed to honor you mother and father," Kurkowski's brother told him. "He'll ask you how, and all you do is make some stuff up like you yell at them every day, refuse to obey their orders, like when they tell you to brush your teeth or do your homework or take out the garbage, and that you won't clean the house or yard or do the dishes, and that you don't like them because you got no respect for them. It's a big enough sin that they'll know you're not lying, but it ain't like you killed somebody or stole something. They hate stealing."

Kurkowski used it one day, making sure to embellish just enough to make it sound believable. He got off with a relatively light penance of five Our Fathers and five Hail Marys, and he had the satisfaction of knowing that he had confessed to a mortal sin.

Kurkowski spread the word around about the sin's versatility and the many ways in which it could be made more or less severe by embellishment or lack thereof, and it soon became a favorite of most of the kids. After a few weeks, the priests in the confessionals were being bombarded with stories of how kids were screaming at their parents, disobeying their every order or request, lying, and generally refusing to show them even an ounce of honor or respect.

Bozeman took ownership of the sin and found new ways every month to escalate its severity.

"When they tell me to eat my supper I throw the plate on the floor and run out of the room because I hate 'em," he said one day in answering the priest's request that he explain how he had failed to honor his parents.

The priests knew all about copycat sins, but this trend they were hearing about in the confessionals seemed real and alarming. It appeared as if the parish's social fabric was disintegrating before their ears. Even the good kids were confessing to disliking their parents and acting on that dislike.

While the confessional was secret, that didn't stop the priests from talking among themselves about sins in general and trends in the area, and after a while it had become clear that the parish was facing a crisis. If not stopped it could ruin the neighborhood and the Church.

Kids weren't eating, taking out the garbage, doing their homework, washing the dishes, cutting the grass, pulling the weeds, making their beds, taking baths, saying their prayers, going to mass, giving money for pagan babies or brushing their teeth; they were in open rebellion and contemptuous of all parental authority, and if something weren't done the neighborhood would in no time be a rat-infested, garbage-strewn slum and the world's center of tooth decay, never mind how much fluoride the city pumped into its drinking water.

That was bad enough, but even worse was the effect it could all have on the Church. After all, it was the parents who made the kids members of the church, enrolled them in Catholic schools and started them on a life of Catholicism and financial support of the Church. The kids had no say in whether they wanted to join the club. If those parents were losing respect and authority, and if kids—even in the second grade—were questioning their decisions and authority, well, those kids just might question the Church's authority, and that was unacceptable.

The priests went to Monsignor Flavin with their concerns about the rampant disdain for parental authority and the neighborhood's impending collapse. He agreed that action was needed. The parents, he said, had to be told of the ongoing and mushrooming subversion in their living rooms, kitchens, gangways and basements.

Flavin and the priests marched to the convent and discussed the matter with Vitaclaire and the other nuns. The nuns agreed that what the priests were hearing in the confessionals was directly related to what was occurring in the classrooms, and that an emergency meeting with the parents was necessary. The future of the parish, its families and children were at stake, and no time could be wasted.

The meeting date was set for two weeks later in the church. Most parish-wide meetings were held in the school hall in OLG's basement, but everyone knew that the hall was too small for all the parents. There were more than twelve hundred kids at OLG, and the hundreds of parents, aunts, uncles, grandparents and concerned neighbors would fit only in the church, which could seat more than eight hundred.

The priests got the word out from the pulpit on Sunday and weekday masses, saying things like: "My brothers and sisters in Christ, there is sin, terrible sin, amongst us. Monsignor Flavin and Sister Mary Vitaclaire have discovered some shockingly disturbing trends amongst our parish's young people, and they have called a special meeting to discuss this troubling development. It is imperative for the good of this parish and of Holy Mother Church that every parent attends. In the name of our Lord Jesus Christ, we expect every parent to be there. Those who fail to attend will have failed this parish, their children and God. I remind you all of your parental responsibility to raise and discipline your children properly and to instill in them respect for your word and authority and for the authority of the Church."

The nuns sent home mimeographed letters in sealed envelopes with each kid.

"It is with deep and abiding sadness that Monsignor Flavin and I must report that there is great sin amongst the children of our parish—your children. If this sin is not immediately eradicated there will surely be dire and shameful consequences," the letter, signed by Vitaclaire, said. "Satan is afoot with his work and attempting to influence your children and it must stop. As parents, you are our primary defense against Satan and his sinful ways, and it is your responsibility to raise your children with the proper respect for Holy Mother Church and its rules, and for your authority as parents.

"Monsignor Flavin and I have scheduled a meeting to discuss this evil that threatens your children and this parish. We expect every parent to attend, and we have asked members of the Chicago Police Department to be in attendance as well. Failure on your part to combat Satan's evil is a mortal sin and punishable by an eternity in Hell.

"Yours in a Loving God."

The announcements and letters staggered the parish's adults. They hinted at great sin and evil amongst the kids, but offered no details, a small matter to the nuns and priests, but one which sent the adults into wild and panicked speculation about what was occurring. The announcements and letters also laid the blame for the great wave of sin crashing over the parish directly on the parents. Many were frightened.

Telephones began ringing across the parish as parents tried to get some details about the problem. Neighbors rang each other's doorbells and stopped each other on the street and in the grocery stores, bakeries, butcher shops and taverns in an effort to determine exactly what Flavin and Vitaclaire meant. With no official details forthcoming, the speculation was crazy.

Maybe communists really had infiltrated the parish and were grooming the kids to be godless zombies who would soon be burning crucifixes, ripping out priests' fingernails and making golden calves. Were the kids forming criminal rings and burglarizing homes? Were they drinking alcohol and smoking cigarettes beyond what they normally did? Were they having sex and wild orgies? Were they torturing old people? Stealing communion wafers? Drinking wine in the sacristy? Burning prayer books? Holding seances? Sacrificing pets? Converting to Judaism?

No one knew, and the speculation grew wilder and crazier.

Parents began beating and interrogating their kids to get information. There was a run on holy water by parents who brought jars of it home to sprinkle on their kids in attempts to cleanse them of sin and purge them of communist and Satanic influences. Kids were locked in their rooms until they gave answers. But because they had no idea what was behind the letters, they had no answers and remained in their rooms. Some kids were sent away to stay temporarily with relatives in other neighborhoods. Adults in neighboring parishes got word and refused to let their kids cross OLG's boundaries lest they fall under Satan's wicked power.

For a few days, neighborhood streets were devoid of kids, who were locked in rooms. The candy stores and hobby shop on Fullerton saw a dramatic decrease in business.

Fathers were so troubled by the allegations of sin that they couldn't concentrate at their jobs, and as a result, their work suffered. Husbands and wives, stung by the vague accusation that they had failed their kids, argued with and blamed each other for letting their kids plunge into sin. Mothers were scared and couldn't do laundry, clean house or cook. Aunts, uncles and grandparents confronted their siblings and children demanding to know how and why they had sent their nieces, nephews and grandchildren straight into Satan's arms. Parents roamed Fullerton and asked shopkeepers if their kids had been shoplifting or acting strangely. No one had any answers, and most secretly didn't want too many answers because they so feared how awful the truth would be.

By the day of the meeting the neighborhood was dysfunctional, at a near standstill and in crisis. That evening, nearly every parent donned their best clothes and walked to the church for the six-thirty meeting. As they neared the church they were shocked to see three police cars. Three cop cars! Good god almighty! What was going on?

The parents hung their heads as they shuffled up the church steps, fearing eye contact with their neighbors would result in silent accusations that they were the ones who had started the kids and the parish on the road to sin and shame. Inside the church the parents silently found pews, sat down, stared straight ahead and said nothing to those next to them.

Six cops, Flavin, Vitaclaire and all the parish's other nuns, lay teachers and priests occupied pews at the front of the church, and at precisely six-thirty, Flavin arose and walked to the pulpit, which was elevated above the altar and congregation, and climbed its seven marble steps. His stern, pale and unflinching face told the crowd that they were in for trouble and a lecture, and Flavin, after addressing the parishioners as "My brothers and sisters in Christ," gave them what they were expecting.

"What in God's name is wrong with you?" he started. "Your children are God's children, and you are failing them, and failing them mightily. In doing so you are failing God, Holy Mother Church, this parish and the nuns and priests who have sacrificed so much to provide your children with a Catholic education. I will not stand by and let their sacrifices on your children's behalf be wasted because you cannot control your children, because you refuse to instill in them a respect for the Church's and your authority. That is sin, and unless you repent and change your ways, your children will go to Hell, and you will be right there with them in eternal damnation and everlasting fire."

The crowd had expected strong words, but for some, especially the women, it was too much, and many began to quiver, cry and take their cotton handkerchiefs out of their purses to wipe their eyes and noses. Flavin continued:

"We have a problem in this parish, and it is your fault, and it is up to you to rectify it. If you cannot control your children, they will be expelled from Our Lady of Grace School and will be forced to attend public school."

Those last five words hit the parishioners hard, and a collective gasp rose from the crowd. Having their kids kicked out of Catholic school meant total disgrace for the rest of their lives, and of course, a permanent resting place in Hell.

Flavin went on to explain that the cops were there to help any parent who was having trouble with their kids.

"These officers are from the Fourteenth District, and they have offered their services to any parent who is having a problem. I would accept their offer, as failing to do so could mean your child will wind up in reform school."

The crowd gasped again, and many women were now openly weeping.

Flavin continued, growing angrier and issuing more threats.

"This type of behavior on the part of your children, and on your parts for allowing it to grow and fester, is just what the communists want," he bellowed. "It is what leads to the breakdown of a Catholic society and the expulsion of God from our lives. We will not tolerate it. Now I ask each and every one of you, are you with God, or are you with the communists and Satan?"

No one was with Satan or the communists, but no one knew whether they should answer the question out loud or what, and many shook their heads and began mumbling to themselves and each other.

More than twenty minutes and numerous harangues into the meeting, none of the parents knew yet exactly what the problem was. After Vitaclaire ascended the pulpit and continued on Flavin's track, a brave guy in the middle of the church stood up and asked loudly:

"Monsignor, what on earth are you talking about? You have called this meeting, stationed police officers inside the church and told us we're going to Hell, but you haven't said why. If we're going to Hell we should at least know why."

Others in the pews nodded their heads in agreement, and mumbling broke out as everyone was thinking the same thing. Flavin shot the guy a glare that he wished could have sent him straight to Hell, and he would have continued glaring at the guy, but he recognized that the crowd was beginning to get a bit unruly.

"Yes, yes," the monsignor said. "That is my failing, as I was so distraught over the situation. What is going on is that your children have lost all respect for you, and they are failing to obey you at every turn. They are failing to honor their mothers and their fathers. It is rampant, it is a crisis, and I can only say that is your fault for letting them get to this unholy point."

The mumbling in the crowd intensified and many began shaking their heads in disbelief and asking each other what they thought Flavin meant. After a bit, a woman in the church's rear rose.

"Monsignor, my kids are behaving as they always have. They obey my husband and me. Where are you getting this?" she asked.

"It has come to my attention that your children are going into the confessional and confessing to the sin of failing to honor their mothers and fathers. It is rampant, and in the past month or so, nearly every child from the second grade on has confessed to it. They're not taking out the garbage, they're shouting at you, they're refusing to eat their meals, take baths, do their homework or say their prayers. You have collectively lost your parental control. It must and will stop!"

Most in the crowd were astounded and in disbelief because what they had just heard was mostly fiction to them. Oh, sometimes the kids got goofy and disobeyed minor orders, but from their experience, mass and blatant disobedience on the part of their kids wasn't occurring.

"Monsignor, I thought the confessional was sacred and secret. How do you know this?" another man asked.

"Yes, the confessional is secret, and priests are not allowed to divulge particulars of any individual," Flavin said. "But we do occasionally discuss trends in sins and how to deal with them, and based on our informal discussions and observations, it became clear that this mass sinning, this mass disobedience was occurring, and we felt we had to act in order to save the children and the parish. It was something we could not ignore. As God's representatives on Earth, we are duty-bound to battle Satan and sin."

The parishioners began talking amongst themselves even more and comparing notes about their kids. It soon became very clear that Flavin and Vitaclaire had no idea what they were talking about. Some of the more experienced parents, those who knew how kids operate, figured out what had occurred.

"Monsignor, you're saying that almost every kid in this school from second to eighth grade has confessed this sin in the past month or so?" another guy asked.

"Yes."

"Almost every kid?"

"Yes!"

"Did you ever stop to think that maybe some of them got it into their heads that this would be a good sin to confess and that they told their friends about it and that's how this whole thing got started? I mean, that's what we did when we were kids. We traded sins and figured out which ones would get the least amount of penance and we told each other about it, and pretty soon we were all confessing to the same thing. We thought it was funny. I think that's what's going on here."

Just about everyone in the pews recognized the behavior from their own days in Catholic school. They knew the guy was right and they began laughing, first to themselves, and then out loud, and soon the church was engulfed with the happy sound hundreds of adults laughing heartily. The parents were relieved to learn that there was no mass rebellion on the part of the kids and that they wouldn't be going to Hell, a least not for the sin of failing to control their kids.

Flavin, Vitaclaire and some of the other nuns, especially Zita, DeLasalle and Yvonne, weren't so amused. They wanted to quiz the parents as to specific behavior on the part of their kids, but the parents would have none of it. The meeting adjourned abruptly when the guy who had explained the situation to Flavin stood up with his wife and proclaimed loudly, "We're going home," and the other parents followed them out the church.

That night every kid in the parish who was old enough to go to confession got a lecture and a warning to never again confess to dishonoring their parents.

At confession the following month, the sin of refusing to honor one's mother and father had completely disappeared.

The nuns and priests were thrilled. They prayed, gave thanks to God and congratulated themselves for having restored order and holiness to the parish and for having saved it from certain and absolute ruin.

CHAPTER 31

Montezuma Budweiser

WORD HAD SPREAD after school and the next morning about the Yom Gypsy affair, and Dennis, Kolba and the other Disturbers reveled in the glory of it all and of how they had once again driven school authorities crazy. Kolba's and Dennis's faces were a bit bruised, reddened and scratched from all the beatings, but they wore those injuries proudly. They and the other Disturbers were the talk of the school the next day—even second graders knew of their antics and of the alleged orgies—and they dreamed of new ways to needle the nuns and cause more trouble.

The nuns, priests and lay teachers never stopped to think that it was their insane overreactions to relatively mild antics by the kids that caused situations to escalate into riots that might potentially undermine their authority and slow the educational process. Their fanatical insistence on control and authority was too often the very thing that eroded and destroyed that authority.

The kids considered it a victory every time the nuns and teachers lost their tempers, and they were always looking for opportunities to push them beyond their limits. Almost every day offered that opportunity, and the day after the Yom Gypsy affair was no different. The Disturbers spread the word about how the teachers hated the Yom Gypsy gesture, and that morning, pretty much every seventh grader was using it. To say that it enraged the authorities was an understatement, but the teachers knew they couldn't beat one hundred and thirty kids. They had no choice but to ignore the general instigation. While the kids were disappointed that their provocations had no visible effect, they were thrilled to have broken the rules.

That morning brought more fun for the Disturbers. Zita had prepared a lesson on life skills, which all the teachers occasionally did. The idea was to make kids balance check books, plan household budgets, calculate compound interest and other things that would be needed once they got jobs and started families. Those budgets had to include weekly donations to the Church and Catholic school tuition for kids. The most important aspect was to be able to get a job, so Zita had the kids fill out mock job applications.

After collecting the applications, Zita read some of them to the class. The ones from most of the kids were normal, listing names, skills and salary requirements and such. Then Zita read another one. The name on the application was Montezuma Budweiser, and Mr. Budweiser listed his salary requirements as three gold bars a month. Mr. Budweiser's skills included beer drinking, fighting and talking on the telephone.

THREE GOLD BARS A MONTH

Zita's hands trembled after she finished reading, and her face turned white. "What is the meaning of this?" she demanded. "Whose, whose application is this?"

"It isn't mine, Ster," Ruchinski stood up and said. "I'm not sure who would write such a disrespectful thing, but I think Dennis would. I don't think it's funny, Ster."

Zita eyed Dennis and demanded that he stand up and confess to submitting such a ridiculous application.

"It ain't mine, Ster."

"How can I be sure of that?"

"Because I don't drink Budweiser, I drink Schlitz!"

The class roared with laughter and Zia fumed. "Who is Mister Budweiser?" she demanded.

Kolba raised his hand and Zita told him to stand.

"Did you submit this fraudulent application, Mister Kolba?"

"Yes, Ster, I did," Kolba confessed.

"Why? Why have you made a mockery of this exercise?"

"I haven't, Ster. I have an uncle who's named that, and I thought I'd use it."

"No one is going to pay you three gold bars a month, mister. That is the truth."

"Then I won't work for them because I'm worth more than that."

Zita took the matter no further as she didn't want another disruption. But after school that day she read more of the applications and found four other suspicious ones. They were from Misters Dick Head, A. Hole, Sonny B. Itch and Sig R. Ett.

Misters Budweiser, Head, Hole, Itch and Ett each received an F on the assignment.

CHAPTER 32

Fall, Burning Leaves, and the Rags Man

I T WAS LATE October now and one of the favorite times of the year for all the neighborhood kids. The stifling heat, humidity and haziness of the summer had passed, the days were getting shorter, the air was crisp, football season was on, and Halloween, one of the most joyous days of the year, was right around the corner.

Most of the leaves had fallen from the trees and kids and adults raked them into huge piles for the kids to dive and play in, no matter how young or old they were. They made forts and mountains out of the massive piles, and battleships and caves, and magic carpets and mines, and tunnels and trains, and army tanks and anything they could think of, and they played in those mountains and forts and caves for hours and hours.

One group of kids a couple of blocks from the school were led by a serious fifth grader named Dorothy who had read a book, *Escape From Warsaw*, which she had ordered from the Scholastic Book catalogs the kids got every month in school. It was about Polish kids escaping Nazis in World War Two. Dorothy and her friends took the book very seriously, pretending the pile of leaves on Dorothy's front lawn was a fort and that they were protecting themselves from Nazis. To them, every car that drove down the street past their fort was filled with armed Nazis who were hunting for them. The kids ducked and held their breaths and kept perfectly still when those carloads of evil Nazis drove by. After the immediate danger had passed, they lifted their heads up over the fort's walls, looked around, decided it was safe and played like normal kids until the next carload of Nazis approached.

On weekends, adults would rake the massive leaf piles onto the streets and burn them. The fires blazed on every street in every neighborhood in the city. The glorious and magical smell of leaves burning on crisp and clear autumn days thrilled and energized and filled everyone with hope, joy and confidence in a way that nothing else could or ever did. The smell of those burning leaves acted as a kind of time-and-dream machine that triggered an instinctive and ancient memory in people's minds that took them back to a time when the massive city was nothing but swamps and prairies where Indians, pioneers and animals roamed freely, a time when there were no fences, factories, sidewalks or roads, nothing but open wilderness and pure freedom, a time when people answered to no one but themselves.

For the guys, burning leaves meant football season, and football season was a joy. It was the one game in which one was allowed to get dirty—filthy and covered with grass stains and mud and blood—and not get in trouble for it. You could tackle and crunch and slam another kid with all your might and it was okay.

Most of the guys had helmets and shoulder pads, and so they played tackle football, and on those fall afternoons after school or on Saturdays at Koz and Mozart parks, they played until it got dark and they could no longer see, or until they got tired. They played in the rain and drizzle, and the dirtier they got the better they felt. A perfect game was one where the grass had turned to mud which they could slip and slide around on until they were coated in it.

Dennis and his pals played by a giant sycamore tree on the south side of Koz. It was to the side of the four baseball diamonds that served as the official football field in the fall for the older guys. They would have loved to play on the main field, but the rules of Koz forbade it until they were old enough to claim the field for themselves.

Dennis, Masciola, John Klosk and his younger brother Chuck, David Pateras, David Podraski, Steve Domrzalski and a few others walked up

Harding one Saturday afternoon on their way to Koz to play football. As they walked, they passed The Grey House, a two-flat greystone building seven doors north of Dennis's house. It was a favorite place for the kids to play when they were younger, as it had a concrete front porch from which they could jump into the grass of the yard next door, or in the winters, into snowbanks in that yard. It was an imposing building, which to the kids seemed like a castle or a fort, and they used it as such, manning its walls and porch while pretending to fight off armies, navies, Indians and whatever else threatened them.

The kids were able to play uninterrupted at The Grey House. No one ever bothered them or came out of the hallway to tell them to leave. They often wondered if anyone actually lived there, and after a while, they figured it was either haunted or had a dungeon in the basement where people were tortured. Proof of the dungeon was found on the house's side wall off the gangway. Three or four bricks, spaced about an inch apart and placed vertically in the wall, gave the appearance of prison cell bars, and even though the bars were bricks, the kids figured there had to be a dungeon in the basement.

Many a day the kids pressed their eyes to the slits to see if they could see inside and who was being tortured, but there was a layer of bricks behind their brick bars and nothing to see. Nonetheless, they listened for screams coming from the basement, and occasionally they left notes in the bricks for those imaginary prisoners.

"If you are being tortured, let us know. We can help," the notes usually said, while always devoid of any information about who the prisoners should contact or how they should reach their would-be rescuers.

As he always did when he passed The Grey House, Dennis stopped to see if a couple of his dreams had ever come true. In first grade, Dennis played with Dennis Andrews, and one day the two figured out how they would get rich. They put a dime in a vise in Dennis's basement, used a hand drill to drill a hole through its center and then took an oil can and headed for The Grey House.

They dug two holes in the dirt off to the side of the home's front porch, squirted oil into one and covered it up with dirt. In the hole in the dime, they placed a tree seed, put the dime in the ground and covered it with dirt. They believed they had planted an oil well and a money tree, and they couldn't wait for a gusher and a tree loaded with dimes to magically appear.

They waited two or three days and returned to the site and were disappointed because there was no oil well or money tree. "I think we gotta wait longer," Andrews told Dennis, and they agreed to return in a few more days, which they did. But they were disappointed again.

The boys checked the site every week or so for a couple of months, and they were always disappointed. At one point they dug up the spot where they had planted the oil well, which had been marked by a stick, to see if maybe oil was growing underground. There was no such growth, and so they dug around looking for the dime, but never found it. After a while, Andrews moved away, and Dennis stopped checking the site. But Dennis always remembered the adventure, and when he got older, he would amuse his pals with the story of how he had planted an oil well and money tree.

As they passed the house, Dennis told the story again. The guys laughed at the ridiculousness of such a scheme, but they did join him in digging a little to see if the oil well had ever taken root.

The fall held other pleasures for Dennis and his brothers. Their street was loaded with maple trees that not only had big leaves that burned well, but that dropped seeds in the fall in pods that the kids called "whirlybirds." The whirlybirds, technically known as samaras, fell off the trees in pairs. They included the seeds, or nutlets, that were attached to what resembled flattened, paper-like wings. When they floated and twirled slowly and gracefully to the ground, the kids thought they looked like helicopter blades.

One year, Dennis and his brothers decided that the whirlybirds, when rolled up in cottonwood, or maple leaves that had fallen, but were still pliable, and then dipped in cough syrup, made for really good cigars. So one Saturday the three gathered up piles of leaves and whirlybirds, rolled them into cigars, and dipped them in cough syrup they had taken from the house, and sold them to the other kids for two cents each.

The cigars were meant to be sucked for the flavor of the cough syrup and for the thrill of looking cool while pretending to smoke and acting like an adult. But some kids did light them, and when they inhaled the blueish smoke, they got sick and ran home to their moms to complain and cry. While some of those moms demanded to know where their kids had gotten matches—the brothers had supplied matches to their customers—and that the Domrzalskis refund their child's money, hardly anyone complained, and the guys made seventy-five cents that day. They didn't refund any of the money because Wally Domrzalski berated the three moms who had demanded refunds.

One of those who wanted her money back was Sophie, a short, fat, jovial, red-headed lady who owned and operated what everyone called "The Corner Store" at Harding and Altgeld. Everyone called Sophie "Fat Sophie," and her small, crowded store on the first floor of a two-story brick building carried the basics—bread, milk, eggs, soap, canned goods, ice cream, soda and candy—that got neighborhood residents through in a pinch. No one did their regular, weekly shopping at Sophie's because it was too small and had only a limited variety of goods, but when they needed a gallon of milk or a dozen eggs in a hurry, it was the place to go.

Sophie wasn't really a mom, but an aunt whose nephew had plunked down six cents for three cigars. She found the brothers that Saturday afternoon and demanded a refund for her nephew.

"No," Wally said. "Ain't gonna do it."

"Why not?" Sophie demanded.

"Because a sale is a sale. You say that all the time when we're in your store."

"But your cigars weren't cigars; they were leaves and seeds."

"Would you rather we sold him real cigars? Huh? I mean, what kind of aunt are you, wanting your nephew to smoke real cigars? I got some in the basement, and I'll go get 'em if you want."

"Where did you get real cigars, young man?"

"None of your business. If you want, I'll go get 'em, but that's another dime. So, do you want real cigars for your nephew? Exactly how old is he? Seven?"

Sophie laughed at Wally's boldness and cleverness and knew the kid had beaten her. "Next time any of you three come into my store for soda or ice cream, I'm gonna double charge you," Sophie told the kids.

"Well, we'll just take our business to Cramer's on Fullerton," Wally replied. "And we'll tell every other kid to not shop at your place anymore. How do you like that?"

"You're just a little gangster, aren't you?" Sophie laughed.

"No, just a good businessman."

Sophie laughed some more and walked away.

Fall brought another wonder to the kids on Harding: a coal delivery to the six-flat apartment building across the street from Dennis's house. The building was one of the few that still burned coal for heat in the winter—most of the other buildings had switched to natural gas—and in the fall, a dump truck full of coal would pull up and unload its cargo onto the street in front of the building. Once the coal was dumped into a mountain on the street, a man would climb out of the cab, unhitch a wheelbarrow, large shovel and broom off the truck's side and begin the day-long job of getting that mountain of coal, shovel-by-shovel and wheelbarrow-by-wheelbarrow, into the building's coal bin through a basement window in the gangway.

The truck arrived around seven in the morning, before the kids were off to school, and they'd get on their front porches, or stare out their front windows and marvel as the truck's bed slowly lifted into the air and emptied its contents onto the street. The result was a mountain of black, dusty coal, and none of the kids could imagine how just one man could shovel all that stuff.

After the truck drove away, the man, who to the kids looked old and worn out, would scrape his shovel onto the street and into the coal mountain, pull it out, lift it and dump it into the wheelbarrow. When the wheelbarrow was full, he'd roll it ten or fifteen feet up the gangway to the coal chute window, lift it by its handles and let its contents spill down the wooden chute into the building's basement.

The kids never counted how many shovels of coal it took to fill the wheelbarrow, or how many wheelbarrows it took to get all that coal into the basement. No one ever talked to the guy who did all that shoveling, and no one knew his name or anything about him—whether he had a wife and kids, or what. The kids always wanted to help him because they felt bad for anyone who had to do that much backbreaking work. But they never could help because the coal deliveries always came on a weekday when they had school.

HE SHOVELED A MOUNTAIN OF COAL EVERY DAY

The kids, and even the adults, watched before they went to school and work as the guy filled and rolled those first few wheelbarrows to the coal bin. As they went off to school and work they always figured that the mountain of coal was just too much for any one person to handle.

When the kids came home from school for lunch, they'd race to their front windows to check on the coal man, and they'd see at least half the mountain still there, and they'd feel bad for the guy all over again.

Then, when they got home from school in the afternoon, the kids would race to their front windows and see that a miracle really had occurred. Most of the coal was gone! They'd watch, when, at around four in the afternoon, the guy would shovel the last pieces of coal into the wheelbarrow, roll it to the chute, return and sweep up the coal dust on the street. The man was indeed a superman! Then the dump truck would return and drive the man away.

The kids never really understood that the coal man shoveled a mountain of coal every weekday, but the adults did, and they always quietly gave thanks that they didn't have to do such hard work.

The summer and fall brought other regulars to the neighborhood: the knife-sharpening man, the rags man and the junk man. Whenever they showed up, the kids were in heaven.

The knife guy was old and pushed a wooden cart, with giant, wooden-spoked wheels up and down the neighborhood sidewalks and made his presence known by shouting so all could hear, "Knifes sharpened! Knifes sharpened!"

Women came out their front doors, kitchen knives and scissors in hand, when they heard the knife man's shouts and lined up at his wooden cart and watched and gabbed with each other as he used a foot pedal to spin his large sharpening stone to give their utensils a sharp edge.

Once, when the knife man wasn't very busy, Dennis and Masciola found him and started asking him questions.

"Do you sharpen axes, or butcher knives?" Jim asked.

"Yeah, but why are you asking?" the guy asked suspiciously.

"Any of the things you've sharpened ever been used in murders?" Jim asked breathlessly.

"Yeah," Dennis blurted out, "like to chop people's heads and arms and legs off and throw them in sewers?"

The old man had heard a lot of silly questions from kids over his more than forty years of sharpening knives on city streets, but those were two of the nuttiest he had ever gotten. He didn't know whether to yell at the two or to humor them. He decided on the latter.

"Well, yeah," the guy answered. "I'd say forty or fifty knives and axes that I've sharpened have been used to chop people up. Scissors, too."

"Really?" the boys shouted together.

"Yeah. All kinds of murders. Entire families cut to pieces—men, women, children, and even pets. There was one time when an older fella came to me with an axe he wanted sharpened. I did it, and got it really, really sharp. Ain't no one can sharpen like I can. He walked away and came back a half hour later with the thing full of blood and asked for it to be sharpened again because he had worked it so hard that it had gotten dull in just that short time."

"Wow!" the boys exclaimed. "What did you say to him?"

"I asked him what the blood was from—I didn't want to be involved in no wrongdoing—and he stared at me with the meanest, coldest, darkest eyes I ever saw and said it was none of my business. So I wiped the blood off and sharpened the thing again and got it real sharp, just like before. Then he walked away again, and you'll never believe, but he came back forty minutes later with the thing full of blood again and asked me to sharpen it again."

"Were you scared?"

"Well, of course. By this time I was getting a little suspicious, you know, and fearing that the fella was up to no good."

"Did you try to call the cops?"

"For what? I didn't have proof of nothing."

"But what about all the blood?"

"I just figured he might have been butchering cows, or a deer or something."

"Cows? In Chicago?"

"Well, you never know, and I do try to give people the benefit of the doubt."

"Then what happened?"

"Well, he came back a third time, and everything was just like before and I sharpened it for him again. And then he came back a fourth time laughing like the Devil himself and screaming and shrieking and carrying on. Then he said he was done with the axe and that I could keep it, and so I took the axe."

"What happened?"

"Well, the next morning I opened up the newspaper and read that the police had found seventy-three people hacked to pieces in a basement on that very same block I was on when I sharpened that axe. Seventy-three! The cops never found the guy, but on one of the hacked-up bodies they found a note that said, 'Someday I will get my axe back, and whoever has it will die just like these people.'"

"What happened to the axe?"

"Well, I kept it, and I got it in this here drawer on my cart. It's still got blood on it. I'll give it to you boys because I don't want that madman coming after me to kill me. You boys want it?"

"Noooo!" the boys screamed as they whirled and ran for their lives.

The old man laughed. He felt bad for telling such a gory story, but he figured the kids had it coming. From that day on, whenever the knife sharpener was on their block, or anywhere in the neighborhood, Jim and Dennis stayed several blocks away.

No matter what kids were doing and how much fun they were having doing it, they immediately stopped and ran for the alleys whenever they heard the deep male voices shout, "Raaaags man! Any old rags! Any old rags!" or "Junk man! Pots, pans, any junk! Junk man!" They raced to the alleys because they wanted a sight of something that was so rare that they almost didn't believe it was real: an old, worn, tired-looking man collecting junk and riding through the alleys on a wooden wagon pulled by a horse!

A horse! Dogs, crows, pigeons and squirrels were the largest animals anyone ever saw in the city, so to gaze at a six-foot-tall animal that weighed more than a thousand pounds, and to be just a few feet away from it while it snorted and swished its tail and shook its head and neck was a thrill that really couldn't be described. Horses were what Indians on the Great Plains rode when they hunted buffalo, deer and antelope, and when they attacked wagon trains and carried off settlers as their prisoners. Cowboys, outlaws and Pony Express riders rode horses, and so did cavalry soldiers when they charged Indian camps. Bold, rugged and fearless explorers who scaled the great Rocky Mountains and then pushed on to the Pacific Ocean rode horses. Horses pulled stagecoaches, buggies and farm machinery, got people from town to town and across the continent, and helped build the country before there were cars and trucks and buses and trains. Horses were a part of history; they represented something magnificent, raw, wild and pure, and they were a living, breathing link to a time that had passed and no longer existed. And there a horse was, right there in the alley in front of them!

The kids thought every horse was special and magnificent, even the old, tired and skinny ones that pulled the junk and rags wagons. Just like the smell of burning leaves, the sight of a horse in an alley triggered something in kids' minds that sent them off into a dream world of Indians and buffalo, wide-open spaces, oceans of grass as tall as a man, and hunks of buffalo and deer meat roasting over an open campfire.

The rags man and the junk man would stop their horses while they collected stuff and threw it in the back of their open wagons, and when they did the kids would stand behind their backyard gates and stare silently at the horses and daydream about long ago times. They also wondered what the old men did with all the junk and rags they collected and where the horses stayed when they weren't pulling the wagons. After all, none of the kids had ever seen a barn or a stable in the city, and no kid really understood how someone could make a living by roaming the alleys and picking up junk.

THEY WOULD SOON BE GONE·

Some of the older guys boasted that in years past they had used pea shooters and slingshots to shoot peas and small rocks at the horses, but the younger guys never believed them. No one, they figured, was creepy enough to shoot a horse. They were right, the boasts were just that.

When they looked at the horses and their minds drifted to long-gone eras, the kids never suspected that an era was coming to an end before their young eyes. In a couple of years, the rags man, the junk man, the knife sharpener, fruit peddlers and other individuals who worked for themselves and roamed the city while shouting for people to come out and do business with them would be gone, and no one would ever again see men driving horse-drawn junk wagons or pushing carts with big grinding stones through the city of Chicago's alleys and streets.

CHAPTER 33

Halloween and a Secret Weapon

THE GUYS FOUND pals at the park, they picked sides and played a few football games. While they had shoulder pads and helmets, not everyone had jerseys or sweatshirts to put over the pads so they played with the bare pads on their shoulders. No one had football pants or spikes, so they ran around in their play clothes and old shoes.

It was a perfect day for football: cloudy, drizzling, about fifty degrees and windy. The guys tackled and crunched each other, although they never tackled hard enough to really hurt anyone; they slid around in the grass and mud and got as dirty as they could. Playing in the cold, wind and rain made them feel like he-men, and they imagined themselves fierce linebackers, mighty fullbacks and graceful halfbacks.

They never timed the games. Instead, the team that scored a certain number of points first was the winner. After the games, the guys decided to take even more advantage of the mud and rain and they played slow-motion football, where they ran plays in slow motion, which allowed them to fall into the mud slowly and stay there a long time and absorb even more dirt.

After the games they walked to Injun' Joe's for sodas and potato chips, and they made sure to walk where other kids could see them in all their muddy glory. Some of the younger kids, especially those whose parents didn't allow them to get dirty, were in awe of these guys, and they yearned for the day when they would be free to play football in the mud.

As they walked to Injun' Joe's, the guys talked about their plans for one of the biggest days of the year, Halloween, which was two days away. Halloween was pure oxygen to the kids. From the time when they could first walk, they trick-or-treated—first with their older brothers and sisters—climbing the stairs of porches and apartment building hallways to get their candy. They walked the neighborhood at will, with no parents around, and because the neighborhood was so dense and crowded, they would get a shopping bag full of candy in a few hours. When their bags were filled, they ran home and emptied them on the floor and went out for more.

By second grade they were trick-or-treating with their own friends, meaning they no longer needed older sibling supervision. Most of the costumes were homemade and simple, as most parents had no money to buy costumes, and as most thought it the height of stupidity and laziness to buy one. With a little time and effort, anyone, parents figured, could make a better costume than any that could be found in a store.

Dennis and his brothers usually dressed as hobos, using their dad's old work clothes. Their ma would burn a piece of cork over the stove and smear the charcoal on their faces, put a black plastic hat on their heads, tie a bunch of old rags in a bundle, attach it to the end of a stick or tree branch and send them out the door. One year, Masciola dressed himself as a package of Chesterfield cigarettes. He painted a cardboard box to look like a pack of Chesterfields, cut it in half and tied the two halves around his body. Unfortunately, it rained that day, and within a couple of hours the cardboard had turned to mush and Jim lost his costume.

Almost everyone gave candy, and on Halloween the sidewalks were full of groups of kids racing around, screaming, singing, laughing and giving tips to each other about which houses gave what kind of candy.

The apartment buildings were their favorite stops because they could hit six different households in a matter of minutes, and the narrow hallway stairways in those buildings were always packed with kids hurrying up and down the stairs and bumping into each other. The Therriaults—Danny, his brother Tim, sister Diane and their parents—lived in the apartment building at Altgeld and Harding, and Mr. Therriault always put on a show for Halloween. He dressed as a monster or mummy and stood outside his apartment door and made scary faces and noises when the kids reached his second-floor apartment. The kids loved it and him.

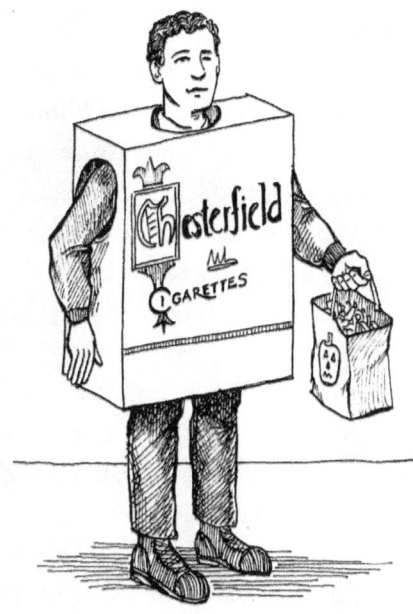

HE DRESSED AS A PACK OF SMOKES·

Some people hung fake skeletons from their porches, and one guy hauled out a homemade wooden coffin, filled it with a bloodied fake corpse and put a bowl of candy at its base, daring the kids to take from it. Although they knew the corpse was fake, the mere sight of a coffin scared them and they hurriedly reached into the bowl for a couple of candy bars, threw them in their bags and then raced down the stairs screaming that the corpse had moved.

Grouches, mostly old people who didn't like kids and who didn't give candy, lived in some homes, and when they didn't answer their doors, the kids got even. They'd stick toothpicks between the doorbell button and the outside ring, forcing the button to stay depressed and the bell to ring non-stop.

When Halloween fell on a weekday, the kids would run home from school as fast as they could, and usually they'd be out the door in twenty minutes because they didn't want to lose a precious second of candy-collecting time.

Saturday Halloweens were the most glorious of all. Hundreds of kids were on the sidewalks by ten in the morning, and they roamed all morning and afternoon and often got two full bags of candy. Saturdays were great because if kids got tired of walking, and they usually walked miles, they could go home and rest and then go out for more.

Koz Park even joined in the Halloween spirit. Park District employees would recruit high school kids to man a haunted house, which was nothing more than the room in the basement that was used as the hothouse in the winter for ice skaters, with its lights off, which made it perfectly dark. Park workers used sheets of plywood to make a maze in the room and the older kids would place themselves along the walls and in crevices in the maze. Because it was so dark, the younger kids had to walk with their hands on the walls and on the plywood in order to make their way through. When a younger kid's hand touched one of the haunters, the older kid would light a flashlight and hold it under his chin so that he looked like a monster and scream as loud as he could. It wasn't an elaborate haunted house, but it always scared the living crap out of the youngsters, and they loved it.

Weekend Halloweens brought another treat. When it fell on Fridays and Saturdays, Koz Park would turn one of its gyms into a movie theater into which hundreds of kids would cram and sit on the floors to watch cartoons and trade candy.

The day after Halloween was even better for Catholic school kids because it was All Saints Day, and they had the day off from school. They'd spill the candy from their bags onto the kitchen or living room floor and stare at the piles and cherish them and separate the candy out by type and size and trade with their brothers and sisters and calculate how long the stash would last.

By seventh and eighth grade it was considered corny and childish to trick-or-treat, and the kids had to find new ways to celebrate and entertain themselves. Some went to Halloween parties with their friends, and some just stayed home. But Dennis, his brothers and their pals roamed the streets and egged people.

As they walked to Injun' Joe's the guys talked about their Halloween plans, which amounted to nothing more than buying dozens of eggs and saving them for the big day when they would egg people, cars, buses, houses, store windows, and, well, anything.

HALLOWEEN

Ruchinski had already stockpiled at least fifteen dozen eggs in his base-ment, and most of the other kids had done the same. It was crazy because there really was nowhere to hide that many eggs and the parents always found them. Some parents wondered why their kids were buying so many eggs, but most knew the reason why and said nothing. Many of the neighborhood's men would laugh when they told stories of how, when they were kids in the thirties and forties, in the summers they would sprinkle tooth powder on the seats of parked cars with open windows. In the heat and humidity, the powder would foam up on the drivers and passengers and they would be covered in the stuff.

Some of the guys had specific people, houses and stores that they wanted to bombard with eggs, and others would just roam the streets and look for targets of opportunity, which meant anything or anyone that moved. The roof of the Jewel supermarket on Fullerton was a favorite place for the kids to hide out and lob eggs down at cars, buses and pedestrians. A favorite tactic was to hide in gangways or behind bushes and jump out when a target passed and smash eggs on their heads. The guys always looked for girls to egg, and they would do it at close range and smash the eggs on a girl's chest, ass or crotch, getting a cheap and sleazy feel-up for their efforts.

The girls knew that Halloween night was an excuse for guys to egg them and "cop a feel," as the saying went, but they didn't stay home. They roamed the streets as well, most of them hoping to get egged at least once. They made sure they always wore pants.

Dennis, Masciola and Kolba had already taken to calling themselves The Destructors, and they acted like it. On nights when they were bored and no one else was around, they'd roam the alleys, turning over garbage cans, unlocking backyard gates, opening garage doors and effecting whatever mayhem they could. One night they had turned over every garbage can in a stretch of alley, and when they got to the end of it and looked back on their work and saw the entire alley filled with garbage, they swelled with pride at their destructive abilities and congratulated themselves.

The three, though, had discovered a secret weapon for Halloween night that they believed would change the day forever and set new standards for assailing friends and enemies alike, and they were just itching to unveil it.

CHAPTER 34

The Greatest Halloween Ever

I T WAS MONDAY, October 31, and the kids ran home from school, the younger ones jumping into their costumes and racing out to trick-or-treat, and the older guys heading to their basements, eyeing their stashes of eggs and waiting until it got dark to go out. The older kids didn't have to wait that long. The sun set at five-forty-five in the afternoon, and by six-fifteen it was dark.

Kolba, Masciola and Dennis had headed out and met up long before that. They had to in order to make sure the night went right. The first and most important thing for them was to go to the Jewel store and walk off with a metal shopping cart. That wasn't easy because the store had no parking lot; it was sandwiched between other buildings and there was nowhere to find a stray cart. The guys figured they would enter the store, put eggs in a cart, pay for them and head out the door, but they knew it would have aroused suspicion if they rolled a shopping cart out the store with a few dozen eggs.

So they waited outside the store on Fullerton where some shoppers would park their cars and take the shopping carts out to put their groceries in the trunks. They hadn't waited long when an old man and his wife wheeled a cart out the door to their car, which was at the end of the block and about fifty feet away from the store's entrance. As they were loading the groceries in the trunk, Masciola approached and offered to return the shopping cart to the store so as to spare them the trouble.

"I ain't got no money and I ain't tipping you," the old man growled at Masciola. "I'll take it in myself."

"Sir, I don't want a tip. This is for a school project to do good deeds and contribute to the community."

"What school you go to?"

"Our Lady of Grace, sir."

"You're not looking for money?"

"No sir! That would be a sin."

"Looks like they've trained you well. Take the cart."

As he drove away, the old man eyed Masciola in his rear-view mirror to make sure he was returning the cart, and Jim was indeed walking toward the store.

"I think that young man was trying to pull something over on us," the guy's wife said.

"Well, he obviously needs a shopping cart for something," the guy replied. "I just hope it ain't for transporting stolen goods or dead bodies."

Masciola made a quick U-turn on the sidewalk just before the store's entrance and pushed the cart to Hamlin and then down to the alley where Dennis and Kolba were waiting. Then, under the cover of darkness, they headed off to get their secret weapon.

When they left their homes that afternoon, the guys had put their eggs in shopping bags and hid them in a couple of garage gangways. They picked up the eggs, about fifty dozen between them, on their way to the secret site, put them in the shopping cart and continued down the alleys to their destination, a several blocks long and wide industrial area off Wrightwood and two blocks past Pulaski.

Pulaski was a busy street, or main arterial, and just before they reached it, Dennis went ahead to scout for traffic and cops. When all was clear he waved to the others and they ran the cart out the alley, across Pulaski, then to Wrightwood. They continued past the railroad tracks to the back of the Newly Weds ice cream cake factory. Strewn among the junk behind the plant was their prize: a couple of wooden pallets full of broken, forty-pound bags of flour. To the factory workers, the broken bags were spoiled and couldn't be used, but to the kids they were as good as gold. They took the eggs out of the cart, threw bags of flour into it and put the eggs on top. They were going to egg people, places and things and then coat them with flour, and they thought it was the funniest thing ever.

"It's like we'll be making batter out of 'em," Masciola said. "This stuff will never come off!"

"We should get some butter and smear 'em with it. That'd be even funnier," Dennis laughed. "Once we coat 'em with this they'll be able to fry themselves up. Just like fried chicken!"

Now came the hard part. The guys had to get the cart full of flour and eggs back across Pulaski and into the alleys without being seen by cops. No cop would have passed up the opportunity to stop three kids any night who were pushing a shopping cart full of industrial-sized bags of flour and eggs.

They got the cart back onto Wrightwood and headed east, one kid pushing the cart, and the two others walking in front and to the side of it in an attempt to hide it. Dennis again went ahead to scout, and when he signaled to them, Kolba and Masciola pushed the cart as fast as they could across the street and into the alley. They were clear, sort of.

Harding was the first street east of Pulaski, and because Dennis and Jim lived on the street, they feared their parents or neighbors might see them. That would be the end of their adventure. They rolled the cart down the alley, and when they got past the next street, Springfield, they were really in the clear and they began to hunt for victims. First they had one more thing to do. They pulled the combination stocking hats and ski masks out of their coat pockets, put them on and pulled the masks over their faces so their victims wouldn't be able to identify them.

The first victim appeared quickly, a kid named Donald Kukinski, one of their classmates and one of the good kids who always did his homework and obeyed the nuns. The guys eyed him as he walked past the alley on Avers.

"He's probably coming home from the library or something," Kolba said. "Let's get him."

They yelled out Donald's name, and when he turned they rushed him. Kolba and Dennis had the eggs and Masciola had bag of flour on his shoulder. They grabbed Donald and smashed a half-dozen eggs on him. Dennis and Kolba held the kid while Masciola dumped flour on him. The poor kid wailed, and when they were through, he was as white as an undertaker and ready for the frying pan.

They let Donald go. He raced away and they ran back to the cart and headed down another alley to hunt for more victims. The problem with their close-range battering was that they got egg and flour on themselves, and they were coated in almost as much flour as Donald.

READY FOR THE FRYING PAN·

Their next target was a car that was parked in an alley. They had no idea who it belonged to and they didn't care. They smashed eggs on all the windows and then coated them with flour.

Proud of their work, they made their way to The Corner to find some pals and show off their new weapon. They rolled the cart to the back of the Studio Snack Shop and walked onto Ridgeway where Ruchinski, Bozeman, Kurkowski, Frankie Biedron and others were hanging out.

"What the hell, you guys look like snowmen," Biedron said. "What the hell?"

"What the hell is right. You guys gotta see what we got going," Masciola said. "Come here and look at this!"

The guys walked into the alley where Dennis, Masciola and Kolba proudly showed off their mobile assault weapon.

"Goddamn! This is cool! Where'd you get the flour?" Kurkowski asked.

"At the Newly Weds. There's pallets full of it," Dennis explained. "You just take it."

"Let's go get some. We'll dump flour on everything," Bozeman said. "Goddamn, this is cool."

"Yeah, but how you gonna carry it?" Kolba asked. "I mean, you ain't gonna carry 'em are you? I mean, that'd be too hard, and our cart's full."

"Naah. There are some shopping carts in that apartment building yard by the Jewel. We'll get them and go load 'em up with flour," Biedron replied.

"You sure?" Dennis asked.

"Yeah. The bums hide 'em there so they got something to put stuff in when they make large runs. And I know a couple of other places where they hide 'em. Exactly where is the flour?"

The guys explained where the flour was, and Biedron, Ruchinski and the others set off.

"You guys wait here 'till we get back. With all of us with flour, we'll just destroy everything," Bozeman said. "This is incredible!"

"Yeah, but you guys got eggs?" Masciola asked. "We ain't giving you our eggs."

"Yeah, we got eggs, and a lot more than you got," Ruchinski called back as he and the others ran down the alley toward the Jewel. "Just wait here."

Dennis, Masciola and Kolba lit smokes and sat against the snack shop's wall and reveled in the fact that they had come up with the greatest Halloween caper of all time. They imagined the destruction they'd soon be causing when the others returned.

"Man, this is cool. I mean, this whole neighborhood's gonna be coated with flour when we're done," Dennis said as he took a drag from his smoke.

"Fuckinaaay," Kolba said. "This is crazy. And we got all the flour we could ever want."

Suddenly, there was a crunch and a splat against the brick wall, and then another and another and the guys realized they were under an egg attack.

"What the fuck! Let's get 'em," Dennis shouted as an egg broke against his jacket. "Noooo prisoners!"

They bolted up and raced to the alley and their eggs and their attackers followed, assaulting them with barrage after barrage of eggs, many of which hit their mark.

They got to their eggs and fired back at the black silhouettes that stalked them. Soon they were fighting at close range and smashing eggs on each other. Masciola grabbed handfuls of flour and dumped it on the attackers. Then he took a bag and dumped part of it on one of the attackers who had fallen to the ground.

"What the fuck! Asshole!" the victim shouted. "Whachu doin'?"

"Fuck you! You got it comin'!" Masciola replied.

The fighting stopped, and the attackers, Steve Domrzalski and his pals, marveled at their comrade who was covered in flour.

"Where'd you get this shit?" Steve asked. "This is boss!"

The guys explained where they got the flour and said that Biedron and the others were on their way to get more.

"Jezus. We need some," Steve said.

"Yeah, but how you gonna haul it around?" Kolba asked. "Frankie said he knew where the bums hid some shopping carts. They went to get 'em. What are you guys gonna do?"

"We can get some wagons or something, and I got the keys to The Barn," Steve said, The Barn being where the guys got their newspapers for their paper routes. At The Barn were those yellow, three-wheeled paper carts, and he figured they could haul the flour around in them.

"It'll take us a while, but we'll run. When Frankie and the others get back, you guys wait for us. This is just too boss," Steve said.

So Steve and his pals raced off to The Barn to get carts and then to the Newly Weds, and Dennis, Kolba and Masciola waited.

Frankie and the others found three shopping carts by the apartment building, and they pushed them as fast as they could to the factory where they loaded them with bags of flour. As they headed back to the neighborhood they saw Steve and his pals pushing three yellow newspaper carts.

"Holy shit! You guys gonna get flour too?" Biedron asked as they stopped to talk.

"Fuckinaaay. Dennis and Masciola told us. This is boss!" one of Steve's pals said. "You guys wait for us when you get to The Corner and we'll do this shit together, and we can even attack the Apostles. This is boss!"

The Apostles were Wally Domrzalski and his pals who hung out on Wrightwood between Lawndale and Monticello. Although they were in high school and were egging people themselves, a little friendly war between everyone would be fun. Besides, The Apostles deserved a big and messy payback for what they had done to a city bus driver a few weeks earlier. Or at least what Wally boasted about what they had done.

According to Wally's story, he and five other Apostles had waited for a Fullerton bus on Lawndale. When the bus stopped and opened its doors, the six guys climbed single file up the three steps. When the first guy got to the driver, he said the guy behind him would pay the fare. The second guy said the third guy would pay and so on. By the time the sixth guy had reached the driver, the first guy to board was already at the back door where had pulled the emergency exit handle, or the cherry, as it was called, to open the back door. Then the last guy to board smashed a whipped cream pie in the driver's face and they all raced out the back door laughing like crazy.

At least that's the story that Wally told. No one believed him due to the fact that he made stuff up to make himself look tough and cool. Most of the younger guys figured that ninety percent of his stories were bullshit.

It didn't matter whether the story was true or not. What did matter was that The Apostles had thought about doing such a thing to a bus driver who had never done anything to them and who was merely taking people where they needed to go. Such an attitude, the guys thought, needed to be severely punished.

Biedron and the others returned about a half hour later, followed in fifteen minutes by Steve and his friends. Together they had well more than a hundred dozen eggs, three shopping carts and three newspaper carts full of flour.

"Sheeeit. Let's get Flavin's car," one guy said.

They all agreed, and the small army rolled their carts down the alley in back of the convent and school to behind the rectory where Flavin's car was parked. They worked quietly, smashing eggs all over the car and then covering it with handfuls of flour.

The gang moved to Wrightwood and Ridgeway where they ran across three eighth-grade girls who they egged, floured and felt up. They crossed into an alley to sneak up on the Apostles, who they found hanging on a corner. Some guys took bags of flour while the rest carried cartons of eggs, and they charged the Apostles shouting, "No prisoners!" and lobbing eggs. The Apostles stood their ground and close-quarter combat ensued and the Apostles were astounded when they were buried in flour.

The battle stopped and all laughed, and the Apostles inquired about the flour and then they too were off to the Newly Weds to get some themselves. They found a few shopping carts in an alley and returned a half hour later and the entire gang set off to do as much damage as possible.

Houses, garages, store windows, cars, people—everything was egged and floured. They headed back near OLG and climbed the Jewel store's roof, managing to get a couple bags of flour up with them. Then they waited until a group of trick-or-treaters passed underneath and they poured two bags of flour on them and fled.

NO PRISONERS!

They egged and floured the convent and the church. They went to the front yard of a girl they knew and dumped flower over it so that it looked like it had snowed. Around eleven, when the evening was nearing its end, they egged and floured each other in a massive war. They chose sides, formed opposing lines, and charged each other, eggs and flour flying in the street, front lawns and sidewalks. When it was over they were exhausted, laughing and coated with batter.

It was the wildest and most incredibly fun Halloween that anyone could remember, and they congratulated themselves for pulling off one of the greatest capers ever.

After the battle they returned the shopping and newspaper carts—after all, they were somewhat responsible—and headed home. When they arrived home, they all headed to their basements to try to clean themselves off. When this proved nearly impossible, they went to bed.

The next morning found at least a dozen cars coated with batter. Flour seemed to be everywhere, and adults were aghast at the destruction. Word spread quickly that the convent and church had been egged. Everyone wanted to know who the culprits were so they could be punished.

All the guys were smart enough to wake up early and head to their basements to wash their clothes and clean their shoes. It worked. The evidence was destroyed, and no one ever found out who had turned the neighborhood white with flour.

CHAPTER 35

A Field Trip

O N WEDNESDAY, THE school was abuzz with news of The Great Flour Caper. The nuns were furious, and they were on the hunt for the offenders. The guys who participated were itching to brag about their exploits, but they knew better and kept their mouths shut.

THE NEIGHBORHOOD WAS COVERED IN FLOUR

Donald Kukinski admitted to being assailed, but even under intense questioning from the nuns he couldn't identify his attackers. He didn't see their faces because of the masks, and he didn't recognize their voices.

Several girls had been egged, but none admitted to it. The nuns were stymied. They figured they knew who was behind the destruction, but lacking even a shred of evidence they gave up and went on with the business of trying to nail kids on other things. The Disturbers continued the business of doing everything possible to disturb Zita's class, and all was normal.

Well, not quite normal. This was a big day at OLG because the kids were going on a trip to the Field Museum of Natural History, Chicago's premier museum. It was a big day because it was the first field trip in OLG's history, and the nuns wanted no trouble.

The kids were thrilled because it meant getting out of the classrooms and to the museum that they had all heard about. It was the world's largest natural history museum, with more than twenty million pieces of stuff in its collection, and it had exhibits of dinosaur skeletons, mummies, meteorites, plants, animals and just about everything else to do with the natural world. All the kids could talk about was how badly they wanted to see the mummies and dinosaurs.

The kids and nuns boarded chartered city buses at eight-thirty in the morning and arrived at the museum about forty minutes later. They formed lines and marched into the gigantic, neoclassical building like good Catholic school children and then immediately scattered, although they were supposed to stay in one group.

The Disturbers and others headed for the dinosaurs and mummies, and they marveled at the size of the skeletons and the stillness of the mummies. Most had never been to the museum before and it was truly an educational event. Although the kids did scatter, they caused no real trouble because they were fascinated by the exhibits.

They left the museum around one-thirty and returned to the school an hour later, which meant they had forty-five minutes of class left. Zita used the time to ask the kids what they thought of the experience. The good kids gushed about everything they had learned and how they wanted to return, and they profusely thanked the nun for helping arrange the trip.

At one point a Disturber raised his hand to give input.

"Yes, Mister Kolba, what impressed you most about the Field Museum?" Zita asked.

"Well, Ster, I gotta say that the people who put those dinosaur models together didn't do a very good job because you could see the glue marks and the wires holding them together. I think it was very sloppy work. Those guys should be fired."

Bozeman was next: "Ster, those mummies looked dead to me, and the wrappings on them were filthy. They should be washing those things."

THE MUMMIES WERE FILTHY.

"I don't know, Ster. It was okay, I guess," Ruchinski said, "but those dinosaurs had rotten teeth. I don't think they ever brushed them."

"Ster! Ster!" said Dennis. "Those dinosaurs were nothing but bones. Don't they ever feed them? I think they're starving them, Ster. Someone should call the cops!"

They continued with their nonsense another few minutes until Zita shuffled to the back of the room and beat them with her pointer.

Not even a trip to one of the world's greatest museums could impress or reform the Disturbers.

CHAPTER 36

A Plywood Submarine

I T WAS A Sunday morning and all OLG kids were supposed to attend eight o'clock mass and put their little light-brown offertory envelopes in the collection baskets. By seventh grade they were ditching mass on a regular basis.

The nuns knew they weren't there because they could see that. While not attending Sunday mass was a sin, the bigger sin was not getting those offertory envelopes and their money into the collection baskets. School officials routinely sent letters home informing parents that their kids' envelopes, which were numbered and traceable, didn't appear. At first, most of the parents were angry, but after a while they didn't care. They had almost no extra money, and money that didn't go into those envelopes was money for gas or bus fare, clothes, food and other bills.

Dennis, Kolba, Masciola and Ruchinski met at the Gossage Grill on Fullerton to drink coffee and discuss their newest project: Dennis's wooden submarine. He had gotten the idea after reading a Popular Mechanics magazine that had a story about a one-man, plastic bubble submarine that could be made for a few thousand dollars. Not having that kind of money, and wanting a bigger submarine, Dennis went to daydreaming and planning. One day when the guys showed up at his basement, he was conducting experiments with round cookie tins in tubs of water. When they asked what he was doing, he explained he was doing ballast experiments and shared his idea of a submarine.

"We can build this thing and take it on the river or the lake and get out to the oceans and we can tail Russian submarines and ships in the Black Sea and torpedo 'em," Dennis said with enthusiasm. "I mean, man, we can destroy the whole Russian Navy! Eventually, I'm gonna build missiles—things that are a lot stronger than nukes—and we'll carry a bunch of 'em on the sub, and just when the Rooskies think they can scare everyone and control the world, we'll launch our missiles and destroy them.

"We can sail the Pacific and hit deserted islands and eat coconuts and pineapples and stuff. It'll be a blast! We get this thing into the river and into Lake Michigan, and we go through the St. Lawrence Seaway and out to the Atlantic. Or we can go down the Illinois River to the Mississippi and out to the Gulf of Mexico. This'll be so easy and so cool!"

The others were immediately hooked and they began working up plans for a four-man submarine made of plywood and powered by them pedaling bicycle sprockets linked together by bike chains and attached to a propeller.

They finished their coffee and decided to walk to Riis Park, three miles away. The park covered fifty-six acres and was one of the largest in Chicago, complete with a swimming pool, lagoon, ball fields, hills and room to roam and run. To the kids it was much more of an oasis that Koz, especially in the winter when they used torn up cardboard boxes as toboggans to sled down its hills.

They had already drawn plans for the fifteen-foot-long sub, which was going to be six feet wide and five feet tall. They figured that was big enough to comfortably house them, food, beer and torpedoes. The sub was basically a rectangle with an angled front that they believed would reduce water resistance and help them cruise easily through the world's oceans.

Dennis had really wanted to build a forty-foot-long steel submarine, but since they had no steel, didn't know where to get any, and figured steel would be too expensive anyway, they decided to reduce the size of their underwater boat and build it out of plywood.

"We're gonna need a frame and it's gonna have to be strong enough to withstand pressure under water," Ruchinski offered as they headed to Riis.

"So, what do we build the frame out of?" Kolba asked.

"There are a lot of two-by-fours underneath my porch, and my dad ain't using them for anything," Dennis said.

"Yeah. I got some too. If we ain't got enough, we can find some in the alleys," Masciola said.

"This thing's gonna have to be strong, so we'll have to put the two-by-fours every three feet or so," Ruchinski offered. "And we'll nail them together, and plus we'll use glue, which'll make it stronger."

THEY'D SAIL THE OCEANS IN THEIR PLYWOOD SUBMARINE

"How about the ballast tanks?" Kolba asked.

"We'll use old cylinders they use for welding gasses, and we can use compressed gas to blow them out, and as a backup, we'll have four bike tire pumps that we can use to blow them," Ruchinski answered.

"I'll be the safety engineer," Kolba said.

"Yeah, 'cause we're gonna need one," Dennis replied. "What are you thinking of doing?"

"I'll have packs of red dye, and if we're sinking or just can't surface, I'll open the hatch and dump out a pack of red dye."

"The hatch is gonna be on top, ain't it?" Masciola asked.

"Yeah. So?"

"If you open the hatch to throw out the dye, all the water's gonna come in and we'll drown."

"Yeah. Well, let's make a little compartment at the bottom that we can fill with water, and I can get the dye out that way."

"Yeah, that'll work," Dennis said.

"We'll run this thing with all of us pedaling in unison. With all four of us going, I'm sure we'd be able to make twenty miles an hour," Ruchinski added.

"Wow! This is gonna be so cool! What about the torpedoes? I mean, man, I don't think they're gonna let us buy dynamite," Kolba said.

"I know. I got some ideas for a new kind of explosive that I think will be more powerful than atom bombs. I don't think we'll have any problem making 'em," Dennis said. "They'll be so powerful! They're gonna be real compact and light, maybe just like a four-foot-long pipe, so we'll be able to carry ten of 'em at least. Maybe more if I can get 'em smaller. These things will blow holes in aircraft carriers, cruisers, destroyers, anything."

"Boss! Think we'll be able to follow Russian subs? You know, the one's with missiles in 'em?" Masciola asked.

"Hell yeah," Dennis replied. "And here's the thing, we're gonna be so small and quiet that the Rooskies won't be able to detect us. Radar ain't gonna see us. Sonar ain't gonna see us. Nothing will. So we'll be able to sneak up on Russian subs and blow 'em out of the water and no one will know who did it!"

"No shit!" Kolba exclaimed.

"Yeah shit!" Dennis replied. "And then after we're done sinking the Russians, we can go to the Pacific and find some of those deserted islands and just hang out there for a couple of months."

"Oh!" Ruchinski said. "Those lagoons are just beautiful. I mean, the water is crystal clear and they're loaded with fish and we'll just pig out on fish and just sit around and do nothing all day but fish. Then we could go to Hawaii and goof around there, and we ain't gonna need money because we'll just catch fish and eat whatever veggies grow on those islands."

"Then when we come home, if we ever do, everybody's gonna think we're so cool," Masciola said.

"Yeah, and the babes will be all over us. I mean, we won't be able to keep 'em away, at least they won't be able to stay away from me!" Ruchinski boasted.

"So, we're gonna have to cover the frame with plywood, right?" Kolba asked.

"Yeah. We'll use two layers of it for extra strength, and we'll use the water-proof kind that they use for boats," Ruchinski said. "That way it won't fall apart."

"Even under water?" Masciola asked.

"Yeah. I mean the stuff they make today is so strong and that glue is so water-proof."

"Why are we using plywood? Why don't we just layer boards on top of the frame?" Kolba asked.

"Cuz plywood is like ten times stronger than regular wood because they take thin sheets of wood and glue 'em together in opposite directions and that gives it more strength," Ruchinski explained.

"You know, I know we can't get steel, but it'd be nice if we could somehow armor this thing," Kolba offered. "Maybe we could cut and straighten out tin cans, you know, coffee cans, and nail them to it or something."

"Or," Dennis said, "we could pound nails real close together into it. That'd make it heaver, but I think it would work, and that'd give us extra protection."

"Good idea," Kolba said. "How many nails you think it'll take?"

"Probably not more than thirty, maybe forty thousand. Nails are pretty cheap, too, and my dad's got like a hundred boxes of nails in the basement."

"Mine too! He's got metal cutters that we can use to cut the ends off if they poke through the wood," Masciola said.

"And the bike sprockets won't be a big deal because we've all got extra bikes," Ruchinski added. "And what we do is take the master links out of the chains and fit 'em together into one long chain and we've got power."

"How we gonna know how deep we are?" Masciola asked.

"We can buy a depth gauge at a boat store, or something. They gotta make 'em," Kolba said. "If not, we can just make one out of a watch or something."

"How deep we gonna be able to go?"

"I don't know," Dennis replied. "We just dive, and when the thing starts creaking, that's when we stop. We won't go any deeper because we don't want to take any chances."

"That makes sense," Masciola said.

"How we gonna know where we're going?" Kolba wanted to know. "We're gonna be inside a submarine. There ain't gonna be any windows on it."

"You're right. We'll have to add a conning tower onto the top so we can see," Dennis said. "When we ain't tailing Russians, we'll run on the surface. We can get some nautical charts and a couple of compasses and we'll be okay. For under water, I'll work up some kind of radar and sonar thing. Shouldn't be that hard."

"That sounds good," Kolba replied. "We pretty much got the wood for the frame, but how much plywood we gonna need, and how much is it gonna cost?"

"We got the dimensions. If we use five-by-five sheets of plywood, and if we use a double layer, I don't think we'll need more than thirty or forty sheets. I mean, we're gonna want some extra for repairs and stuff. We're probably talking like a hundred bucks max or something," Ruchinski said.

"Where we gonna build it?" Kolba asked.

"Ah, we can make the thing in my garage. My dad will probably help us. He likes stuff like this," Ruchinski said.

"How we gonna get it to the river or the lake?"

"We'll just rent a trailer and have someone drive us. We can start on it in a couple of weeks, and by the summer we'll have it done, and man, we're gonna sail the seven seas!"

The guys went on and on about their submarine, the Russian ships they would sink and the tropical paradises and exotic foods they would soon experience.

CHAPTER 37

You'll Blind Him!
A Massive Beating

A T SCHOOL ON Monday, Dennis, Kolba and Ruchinski spent much of the morning in Zita's room refining their submarine drawings, calculating its cost and how much time they'd need to build it. They made plans to hook up with Masciola and head to the library after school to study encyclopedias and magazines to figure out where they'd go in the Pacific and where they'd have the best possibility of finding uninhabited islands. While they had previously paid no attention to Zita's geography lessons, they were now far more interested in the subject than anyone else in class. Now that they were going to be sailing the world's oceans, they were intensely devoted to discovering and learning about faraway places, and in a couple of weeks they would know more about geography than any of the other kids.

As the morning wore on, Dennis and Ruchinski, bored with the class, decided to start smashing each other's forearms with their fists. Actually, they didn't decide to do it, it just happened. At one point Dennis called Ruchinski a name and Dave retaliated by punching his fellow Disturber on the forearm. Dennis returned the blow, making sure his fisted knuckles landed squarely on his partner's forearm. Ruchinski fired back, Dennis did the same, and soon the two were punching each other furiously, trying to inflict as much pain and damage as possible. After twenty minutes of nonstop forearm bashing, the two were exhausted and back-and-blue, and just before lunch they called a truce.

They had hurt each other, and when they got home for lunch and took off their jackets, the bruises were visible as they wore short-sleeved white shirts.

"What's wrong with your arms?" Dennis's mother asked when he sat at the table for his salami sandwich and bowl of chicken noodle soup.

"Ah, nothing. Me and Dave were hitting each other. You know, just for fun."

"That doesn't sound like fun to me. Weren't you paying attention to the sister?"

"Yeah, I was. We just hit each other a few times."

"Just a few? Those are some big bruises. He must hit hard."

"You should see his arm. I got him real good. He's got even more marks than I do."

"Isn't that wonderful. So, what did you learn in class?"

"A lot. All kinds of stuff."

"Like what?"

"A whole lot. I can't even remember, it was so much."

"Why can't you remember?"

"We had geography and spelling and religion."

"What did you learn in geography?"

Dennis hadn't learned anything in geography that morning because of the preoccupation with the submarine and the fight with Ruchinski. But he did know that he and the others would soon be sailing their sub around the world and so he talked about islands in the Pacific Ocean, something his ma knew nothing about, and that got him off the hook.

"Well, you make sure to wear a long-sleeve shirt at supper otherwise your father will see those marks. Now eat."

Dennis gobbled down his lunch, and in twenty minutes he was out the door to meet Masciola and have a lunchtime smoke before getting to the playground.

When school resumed in the afternoon, Dennis's class switched to Miss Donatello's room for science class. But Donatello was sick that day and Mrs. Corbet was the substitute teacher.

Corbet had been substituting at the school for several years, and the kids thought she was crazy because, to them, she *was* crazy. She sipped all day long from a huge thermos of coffee, occasionally swallowed pills and was pretty much wired all day. She was in her forties and tall and skinny with stringy black hair, and it seemed that whenever she opened her mouth she screamed. She fidgeted constantly and talked fast and shouted even faster. There was nothing calm or serene about Mrs. Corbet.

At one point, Ruchinski, who was sitting across a row of desks from Dennis, decided to have some fun. When Corbet was at the blackboard and had her back to the kids, Ruchinski took out his red Swingline Tot 50 mini-stapler, opened it up and shot some staples at Dennis. Ruchinski laughed and Dennis was angry and ready to retaliate by launching a barrage of staples at Ruchinski from his own Swingline Tot 50.

Dennis waited to make sure Corbet wouldn't see, and then he got hit with more staples fired by Ruchinski and lost what little patience he had and immediately opened up on his pal. It was the worst timing possible because right then Corbet had turned around and saw Dennis firing staples.

She immediately screamed:

"You are going to poke his eyes out! You can blind him! What is wrong with you? You're going to blind him! My god, you're going blind him!"

Corbet screamed some more and sent Dennis to stand in the hall outside the room. Ruchinski laughed, but the other kids didn't because they knew that DeLasalle's room was next door, that she had heard Corbet and would investigate.

They were right. As Dennis stood in the hall, DeLasalle lumbered out of her room and confronted the boy.

"What is the meaning of this, mister?"

Dennis did the only thing possible: he told the truth.

"Dave shot some staples at me and so I shot him back. He started it."

To the nuns, no improper behavior or fight was ever justified by saying someone else had started it. In fact, saying that made it worse for anyone who used that excuse because the nuns preached constantly the idea of turning one's cheek.

"Is that right? We'll see," DeLasalle huffed. She opened the classroom door, stood inside and demanded loudly: "Mister Ruchinski, get out here."

YOU'RE GOING TO BLIND HIM!

In the hall, the nun asked Ruchinski what had occurred.

"Dennis shot staples at me, Sister."

"Did you shoot first?"

"No, Sister."

"Get back to your seat."

DeLasalle turned to Dennis and asked:

"Do you still insist that Mister Ruchinski shot you and shot first?"

"Yes."

KABOOM!

Dennis's head snapped back and forth from the mighty, open-handed blow DeLasalle had delivered while saying, "Liar!"

"But Sister, I—"

Boom! Another blow landed on his face.

"Don't you 'But Sister' me. You could have blinded him!"

DeLasalle then went crazy on the boy, throwing him up against the wall several times and beating him mercilessly. She yanked him off the wall, and as he covered his face with his arms and hands, she whaled on his back with the insides of her massive forearms.

Inside the classroom, the kids were horrified. The solid plaster wall of the room seemed to shake, or at least vibrate, from the force of Dennis's thin body being hurled into it time and time again. The sound of DeLasalle's blows reverberated through the hall and into the classroom in the form of dull, but sickening thuds that never seemed to stop. The beating seemed to go on forever. Those who had seen what had really occurred knew that Ruchinski had fired first, and they were disgusted that he had put the blame on someone else. But they also knew that they would have done the same. If by lying you could avoid a beating, then you lied.

After the beating was fully administered, Dennis could barely stand. His face was red from the repeated blows and his back and shoulders were aching.

"Now you get back to your desk, mister, and if I ever catch you doing something like this again, you'll get worse than this," DeLasalle said.

THE MOST SAVAGE BEATING EVER

Dennis opened the classroom door and walked in, trying not to wobble and give away that he had been hurt. The other kids were amazed that he was still standing, and they figured he was hurting real bad and that he'd probably cry a little, which would have been justified. But Dennis didn't cry. He put on a bold front, and as he walked to his desk he cracked a smile—although it was a struggle to do so—and made like it was no big deal and that he could have taken three or four such beatings every single day.

The next morning in Zita's class, Dennis discovered why the truth hadn't worked and why he had been beaten so furiously.

"She likes me," Ruchinski said of DeLasalle. "I used to go to her room when I was a kid to pick up my sister's homework when she was sick, and she would tell me how cute I was and what a good kid I was for picking up Joyce's homework. Man, you didn't have a chance. For a minute there, I almost felt sorry for you. I mean, she was killing you."

CHAPTER 38

Hockey, and Brains
Blown Out for Love

I
T WAS WINTER now, and one morning after finishing his paper route, Steve Domrzalski flew through the kitchen door shouting: "They froze Koz! There's ice! They froze Koz!"

They were the happiest words the kids could hear in the winter besides, "It's snowing out!"

Ice at Koz meant ice skating and playing hockey all day long while the kids were on their two-week Christmas vacation from school. It meant being out in the cold and snow and braving the elements and being tough. For the kids, there was nothing like winter. The snow and cold muffled the city's noises and hid its grime and made so many kids feel like they were Indians and hardy pioneers trudging through thick, pristine forests filled with waist-deep snow. For them, snow magically transformed one of the world's largest and grittiest cities into a soft, white wilderness.

Steve headed through the kitchen to the dining room and the family's black, rotary telephone on a shelf of their oak china cabinet and began dialing as fast as he could. He was calling his pals to let them know there was ice at Koz.

Every winter the words, "They froze Koz!" spread through the neighborhood as fast as kids could dial phones or race to their friends' homes to breathlessly shout the news. Within a couple of hours the news was everywhere and the skating rink at Koz was packed with ice skaters and hockey players.

THEY FROZE KOZ!

The ice rinks that sprang up in almost every one of the city's parks were simple. Park employees used small tractors to plow the snow on the baseball fields into banks and circular rinks. At night they'd use fire hoses to fill those rinks with water, and in the mornings, there was ice! Every couple of nights they'd put more water down, and as long as the temperature stayed below freezing the kids had the greatest winter wonderland they could imagine.

Everybody skated at Koz and the city's other parks: boys, girls, kids, teenagers, adults, figure skaters, hockey players and racers, just everyone. There was no admission charge, and the only thing all that fun and joy cost was the price of a pair of skates and hockey sticks and pucks.

The kids had waited for this day all year long and had pined intensely for it since a few days earlier when their Christmas vacation had begun. They had a half-day of school, and when the bell rang at noon to free them for two glorious weeks, the Disturbers, as did so many of OLG's kids, headed straight to Mary's Pizza on Fullerton for what was now a tradition for the start of Christmas vacation: ordering fifty-cent, six-inch pizzas before heading home to change into play clothes and running out the door to look for fun.

Mary's was heaven for anyone in the neighborhood who liked pizza, which was just about everyone. Its pizzas were thin, greasy, gooey, cheesy, delicious wonders that were sliced into squares. Everyone had their favorite pieces; some loved the crust pieces and others craved the middle pieces which were folded between one's fingers and eaten in all their cheesy glory, slice after greasy slice.

There weren't many places to eat on Fullerton, but the places that were there were considered to have the greatest food on the planet. Mary's had pizzas and other Italian food, and a green pepper sandwich—fried, sliced bell peppers on crusty Italian bread—that was stunningly delicious.

Down the street was Phil's, which had the world's greatest hot dogs and Italian beef and sausage sandwiches and the world's hottest and most golden-brown French fries that Phil cut by hand, deep fried, loaded into little brown paper bags and covered with a dash of salt. Phil's hot dogs contained almost every food group: starches, meats and vegetables, which came in the form of the hot dog on a steamed bun, which was loaded onions, cucumbers, relish, tomatoes and mustard. When ordered with a bag of fries, they constituted a complete meal. When customers were really hungry, they ordered a "combo," a combined Italian sausage and beef sandwich. Phil's menu was simple: hot dogs, beef and sausage sandwiches, combos, tamales, fries and soda.

On a cold winter's night there was nothing like walking outside with a steaming bag of Phil's fries and biting into that first piece. They were golden brown with a little crunch and a steamy, starchy center. That first bite burnt the tongue and warmed the body as it slid into the stomach.

Half a block away from Phil's was Villa Roma, an Italian restaurant owned by two women. Like Mary's, it was a sit-down place but was classier and more expensive than Mary's. While its Italian beef sandwiches were a bit tastier than Phil's, they were more expensive, and didn't have as much meat. Phil packed his beefs with mountains of thinly sliced meat. Villa Roma had great quality, but if you wanted a "good count," as the saying went, you had to go with Phil's.

Across Pulaski on Fullerton was the Dang Ho Chinese restaurant that was renowned throughout the city. Most of the neighborhood's families ordered take-out from Dang Ho, sending their kids to pick up the brown paper bags loaded with white cardboard boxes of the most delicious Chinese food.

For kids, though, Mary's was the place to celebrate the beginning of a vacation. The kids would pile into the place's green vinyl booths or sit at tables in the back. Behind most of the booths were the remains of fries that kids had tossed overboard in attempts at humor, and on the underside of the tables were what had to be pounds chewing gum that kids had stuck to them in more efforts to rebel and be funny.

The six-inch pizzas were the perfect size for kids, and at fifty cents, anyone could afford one. It seemed like half of OLG tromped to Mary's that day to celebrate the beginning of Christmas vacation and to make plans for fun during the two weeks. Talk around the tables and booths ranged from anticipated ice skating and hockey games to snowball fights and snow forts to making money by shoveling snow and to just doing anything and everything possible to enjoy the time off.

The Disturbers ordered their pizzas and talked about hockey and skating and snow forts, and when their pizzas arrived they dived into them, savoring each greasy, gooey bite. At one point, the guy who owned the place, Old Man Mary—no one knew his real name—walked by the Disturbers' booth, snatched a piece of pizza off Dennis's metal pizza plate, shoved it into his mouth and proclaimed, "That's a good piece of pizza!" It was normal behavior for the owner, and no customers complained when he sampled their food.

Steve kept making his phone calls, and pretty soon he announced that all the guys were going to Koz to play hockey.

Around the neighborhood the ritual was the same. Boys and girls put on long underwear, threw a pair of woolen sweat socks over their regular, thin cotton socks, put on their sweaters, jackets and coats, topped their heads with stocking hats, headed to their basements and garages to get their skates and hockey sticks, and began the walk to Koz.

At the park, the kids sat on the green wooden park benches outside and changed into their skates, leaving their shoes under the benches, or they walked down a dozen concrete steps to the hothouse, a small room in the park house basement.

The boys separated into older and younger groups and picked teams amongst themselves, with the older guys getting the best areas of the ice. Any snow on the rink was pushed away with snow shovels or hockey sticks. Boundaries were agreed upon, other rules were made and the games began.

Some of the kids were good skaters, but most were just okay, and everyone was self-taught. Dennis had learned to skate one Sunday in third grade when he walked to Koz with a new pair of skates he had gotten for his birthday. He sat on a snowbank and watched the skaters and tried to figure out what they were doing. When he thought he had it down, he laced up his skates and ventured onto the ice.

Anyone's first time in skates on ice was crazy and terrifying, and Dennis's was no exception. He could barely stand on the thin blades, and he fell, and were it not for the hockey stick that he used like a cane, he would have stayed down until a kind soul would have taken his hand and helped him up. He used the stick for balance, and after an hour or so he was skating pretty decently.

Lots of kids had what the adults called "weak ankles," which meant that their ankles caved inwards when they skated. Part of it might indeed have been weak ankles, but most cases of weak ankles were due to the fact that kids' skates were way too big. Parents and relatives always bought skates a couple sizes too big, knowing that the kids would grow into them. The thinking was that the kids were growing and that they'd need a new pair of skates every year if the correct size was purchased, and no family had money to be buying new skates that often.

The games began in the early mornings and went for as long as the kids could skate, or until they could no longer take the cold. Dennis played goalie, which meant long periods of inactivity and which led to his big toes always going numb. When kids got too cold they'd head down the hothouse, walking down its steps on the toes of their skate blades so as to not dull the rest of the blades. The hothouse was small, lined with benches and had a couple of metal radiators for heat. It wasn't well lit, and it always took a while for a kid's eyes to adjust to the dark after skating for hours outside.

The hothouse offered instant relief from the cold, and kids sat on its benches, untied their skates, peeled off their wet socks and put them on top of the metal radiators to dry. If their toes were numb and white, the stay in the hothouse took longer. When those toes began to thaw, they would hurt and burn and feel like someone was sticking hundreds of needles into them. Still, no one wanted to stay inside for too long because the fun was out on the ice. The kids walked around and massaged their toes and did everything they could to get them to thaw faster.

Sometimes the kids would change out of their skates and walk home for lunch, and those were also glorious times because mothers usually had hot soup and hot chocolate prepared. After lunch and some warmth, it was back to Koz for more skating, hockey and games.

Kids who didn't play hockey had other games, things like Crack the Whip, races, Tag, or It, and anything else they could think of to keep them moving. Boys tackled girls, who did their best to not be caught and dumped to the ice. The girls always had figure skates, and almost every boy had hockey skates. Boys and girls tried to impress each other with their skating skills, and being on the ice and skating and playing games offered chances—excuses, really—to hold hands and otherwise get close to each other. For shy kids who were terrified of the opposite sex, skating was the perfect opportunity to meet the boy or girl they liked by bumping into them, holding their hands or tackling them to the ice.

Hockey was pretty much played during the days, with the nights being reserved for games among the boys and the girls and those opportunities to bump into each other, hold hands and laugh and talk.

When Dennis and his pals were in the fourth and fifth grades, pretty much every boy was in love with Susan Christensen, a beautiful blonde who smelled nice because she wore perfume and bathed with perfumed soaps. The nights found those boys skating at Koz, which was lit by the banks of lights for the ball fields, doing everything they could to get Susan's attention and affection. Most failed.

Dennis thought Susan was the most beautiful creature ever and was in love with her. The problem, though, was that he was painfully shy and afraid of people he didn't know, especially girls, and he had no idea how to approach and talk to her other than purposely crashing into her when they were skating. He did that a few times in fifth grade, and Susan actually understood why, and she was a little impressed and curious to know more about him. She laughed when she fell to the ice after Dennis collided with her, and each time she held out her had so he could help her up, which he did.

That was a sign, of course, that she was willing to talk, but even though Dennis recognized it as such, he was just too scared to work up a conversation and so he always skated away without saying anything. The poor kid hated himself for being so scared and unable to do the thing he wanted most, which was to talk with Susan and get her to like him. He wasn't alone. Other kids were just as scared, and so those cold winter nights, although filled with laughter and shouts of joy, were also permeated with the misery and self-loathing those shy kids felt and had for themselves.

Dennis's misery became unbearable one night in fifth grade when, while skating at Koz by himself and waiting for his pals to show up, Susan skated up to him, took one of his hands, smiled and said, "Hi Dennis. How are you?" Dennis was trembling with joy. Susan Christensen had skated up to him—to him and not anyone else—and called him by his name! And she called him by his name in such a sweet and loving voice that it was clear that she was madly in love with him! She loved him as he loved her! He had daydreamed about and visualized this moment for a year. In his head he had gone over a hundred times what he would say to her and what her reaction would be, which was always to fall into his arms and say that she loved him and would love no one else but him forever and ever. Then they would kiss and skate around and hold hands and laugh and fall into a snowbank and kiss some more and the night would never end.

SUSAN SAYS HELLO

But even though he had so often rehearsed in his mind what he would say to Susan given the chance, Dennis was, at that moment, emotionally paralyzed. He shook uncontrollably as he tightened his grip on her hand,

and his mind raced faster and faster and out of control, kind of like a car on a highway with no driver. He was dizzy and sick. He knew what he wanted to say and how he wanted to say it, and he desperately wanted to say it—to shout that she was the most beautiful girl he had ever seen, or ever would see, and that he loved her and hoped that she loved him too. He knew that if he could just get those words out all would be perfect forever and that he would be loved by the most beautiful girl in the world.

"Are you cold? You're shaking," Susan asked.

"Naah. I'm okay," Dennis said with a phony bravado that was fueled by fear and meant to mask his terror and panic.

"Are you sure?"

"Yeah."

"We could go to the hothouse and sit for a while."

"Naah."

It was the most painful and saddest thing the boy had ever experienced. He was afraid to do the thing he wanted most to do, and he hated himself more than ever.

"Okay," Susan responded. "Have you seen John? I've been looking for him."

Oh! Talk about being sick, hurt and angry! The girl that Dennis loved had just asked about John Klosk. Dennis and John were friends, not rivals, but now John was stealing his girlfriend and ruining his life. The devastation caused by Dennis's inability to bare his soul to and profess his love for Susan was total, but her interest in John made it permanent and unbearable. The only girl he could ever love liked someone else, and for the rest of his life he would never know love and would live his days in complete loneliness and total misery.

When John showed up and he and Susan began skating with each other, Dennis's despair was beyond comprehension. He skated like a madman in giant circles around the rink, going faster and faster and plowing over anyone who got in his way and working up a rage that was so intense that the boy felt that his head and body were going to explode. That, he thought, would have been the greatest thing ever because it would have shown just how thoroughly he had loved Susan. He envisioned his blood and brains splattered all over the snow and ice and how impressed Susan would have been to have finally known the sincerity, depth and permanence of his love.

Having his brains blown out in the name of love was not a new idea for Dennis. Ever since President John Fitzgerald Kennedy had been assassinated on November 22, 1963, by a sniper in Dallas, Texas, the boy had fantasized about the same thing happening to him. It was all the attention and out-pouring of love for Kennedy that followed the killing that affected Dennis. He wanted the same.

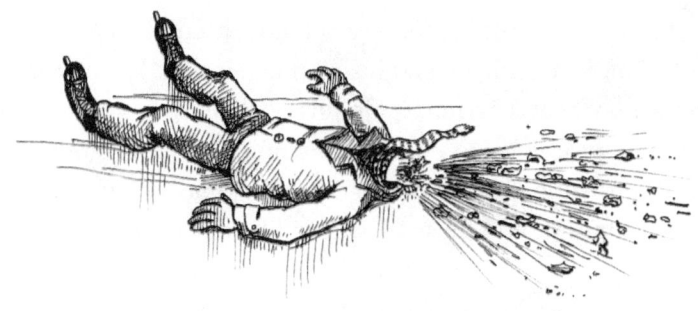

PROOF OF HIS LOVE!

So, he would play "motorcade," a game that involved the boy riding his bicycle down the alleys and streets while pretending to be part of a presidential motorcade. He, of course, was the President, and always, shots rang out and Dennis's head would be hit and he would slump over the bike's handlebars. Then he'd be rushed to a hospital where is wife—Susan—and scores of beautiful women would gather to pray for his recovery. He always did get well, and upon his release from the hospital he was always greeted by crowds of millions of people lovingly and adoringly screaming his name and demanding that he be president forever.

Dennis's grand vision of martyrdom in the name of love had one giant flaw, though. Since he had never told Susan how he felt about her, she would not have known that all that blood and brains on the ice represented his ferocious and eternal love for her.

There was only one thing Dennis could to do ease his tortured mind and correct the situation. He would get revenge on John and beat him up or otherwise embarrass him. That would show both John and Susan how much he loved her and would forever memorialize his love for Susan as the greatest love ever in the history of ever.

From that moment, Dennis daydreamed about how he would get revenge. His plans ranged from the elaborate to the simple. One idea was to sabotage John's skates by dulling their blades with a metal file so that he would slip and slide and fall all over when skating. Susan would be there to witness his incompetence and clumsiness and would laugh and dump him. Another was to just attack John without warning, throw him into some bushes and beat him silly.

The next day, still humiliated by his failed attempt to get Susan to fall in love with him, Dennis launched his plan to get John Klosk. On their way home from school that afternoon, Dennis walked up to John, and without saying anything, proceeded to pummel him on the head, shoulders, neck and back with his brown leather school bag. John had no idea why he was being attacked by his friend, and he screamed at Dennis asking him why he was being attacked.

"Admit it, you love her! Confess!" Dennis screamed.

"Love who?"

"Christensen! She's mine. I love her! She's mine. Admit it that you love her!"

"I do love her."

"I thought so, you jerk, you." Dennis beat John until his arms got tired of swinging the school bag, and after the beating stopped, the two calmed down, confessed their love of Susan and admitted to each other that she probably didn't like either of them.

CHAPTER 39

Playing Guns and War

WHEN THEY WEREN'T trying to woo girls at Koz, the boys engaged in one of their other favorite winter pastimes: making snow forts and having snowball fights.

Dennis's brothers had perfected the art of snow fort construction one winter out of necessity. They had built a fort on their front lawn, but a bully down the street, Ed Scully, came by, taunted them and wrecked it. So the two brothers got to work rebuilding it bigger, better and stronger. They formed bricks out of snow packed into cardboard shoe boxes. The bricks provided much greater strength than just piling snow up into walls, and when the brick fort was complete, they got buckets of water from the basement and spilled it on the fort so it would freeze and become even stronger.

It worked. Scully came by one morning and tried to tear the fort down with his hands, but he couldn't dent its walls, which had turned into solid ice.

Wally Domrzalski laughed as he watched out his front window at Scully trying to wreck the ice fort. Never one to ignore a threat or challenge, he made a plan to destroy Scully's fort, which was a few doors down. Trying to smash it during the day would not have done because someone would have seen and told the bully, who would have retaliated. So one cold morning Wally got up at four o'clock, dressed, sneaked into the basement, got his dad's long-handled pickaxe, walked to Scully's fort and hacked and beat it to smithereens. The bully never found out who destroyed his fort.

Snowball fights consisted of any two kids, or groups of kids, who were around and ready for action. The best fights were between large groups of kids from different streets, with one army invading or attacking another. They'd spend an hour making snowballs, which they'd load into wagons or onto sleds, and then they'd go off hunting down the enemy. Kids hid in gangways, behind garages and cars and trees, and when the attackers appeared, they'd ambush them and shout the alarm that the attack had begun. At that point, everyone would come out of their hiding spots and charge the invaders, and magnificent clashes between dozens of kids would commence. For protection, some kids used the lids from small metal garbage cans as shields, and kids so equipped charged their enemies with reckless abandon, knowing they couldn't be hurt. Those who didn't have shields relied on their legs and their ability to dodge incoming missiles to stay safe.

Hand-to-hand combat usually ensued, and when the supply of snowballs was exhausted, the kids scooped up handfuls of snow and tried to dump them on their foes' heads. That was the worst part of the fights. A kid on the receiving end of a handful of snow usually got the icy stuff down his neck and back, and that resulted in a painful, stinging sensation and a ton of discomfort.

The battles ended peacefully when everyone got tired, but some, especially when the groups of kids didn't like each other, continued into alleged fistfights. Those fights mostly ended harmlessly because the kids squaring off against each other were too scared to get close enough to each other to do any damage. Hundreds and thousands of punches were thrown, and almost none landed.

Dennis loved the snow and the cold, and on nights when snow was predicted, he would stare out his front window to the streetlight to see if, through the hazy glow of the light, the flakes were falling. If it wasn't snowing, he would pray like crazy for it to start. When it did snow, he was always the first up and out the door in the morning because he always wanted his to be the first footprints in the stuff. Being the first to make footprints in the virgin layer of snow made him feel like an explorer tramping through some untamed wilderness. He imagined himself an Indian tromping through forests of waist-deep snow looking for rabbits and squirrels to kill, take home and cook over an open fire. He daydreamed about walking into the door of a log cabin deep in the woods and being greeted with the soothing warmth of a roaring fire, a huge kettle of boiling stew and a beautiful, smiling wife dressed in buckskin clothes.

Cold fall and winter days—hell, any day—were perfect for the games of "War" and gunfights the kids played. They'd arm themselves with whatever toy pistols, rifles, bows and arrows and sticks and branches they could find, pick sides for the opposing armies and, with a dozen kids on each side, charge each other while shooting, shouting and screaming. They'd flop to the ground, bury themselves in the snow or under leaves and fire from long-range at their enemies. "Dowzh, dowzh!" they'd shout, with each "Dowzh" signifying a firing of their weapon. When they believed they had hit an opponent, which always took a couple of shots to do, they'd stand up and shout to the victim, "You're dead! You're dead!" That never kept the dead kid out of the fight because he would stand up and shout, "Ain't dead! You missed!" And then he'd aim his weapon at the kid who claimed to have shot him and shout, "Dowzh! Dowzh! You're dead! You're out! You're out!" That never ensured a death either because the other kid would give it right back to his opponent by shouting, "You missed! You can't hit nothin'! Ain't dead. You're dead! I got you first!"

EVEN STICKS WERE GUNS

Some kids enjoyed getting shot and the glory it offered. They'd charge the enemy lines, hear a broadside of "Dowzhes" being hurled at them, and then, upon being hit, leap and sprawl and contort themselves into grotesque positions and fall to the ground in the most dramatic and theatrical way possible while screaming in terrifying agony. Some would take dozens of bullets to the chest, arms and legs and contort and twist and shout and scream and, despite the terrible wounds, keep charging and charging until they fell dramatically dead right at the enemy's lines, their fingers on the triggers of their guns. They'd lob hand grenades—clumps of mud and snowballs—at each other and simulate explosions by shouting "Boom!" For effect, kids at the receiving end of the grenades would leap and shout and flop around, pretending they had been battered and bloodied by the explosions and shrapnel. Those kids never died. Although grievously injured, and with blood and guts gushing and oozing out of their bodies, they'd crawl and slime around in the snow and leaves and mud, shooting and mounting heroic, single-man defenses of their positions. If the enemy made it to their lines, they'd summon the strength to stand up and engage them in hand-to-hand combat, bayoneting and clubbing them, no matter how badly outnumbered. But even those brutal skirmishes never led to any deaths. No matter how many times they had been shot, stabbed and clubbed, the kids always summoned the strength to continue and carry the battle to their enemies with a terrible and unrelenting fury.

They loved reenacting famous battles—Gettysburg, Shiloh, Lexington and Concord, D-Day and the Battle of the Bulge. The Civil War battles were special because the kids found immense pleasure in taking time to load and shoot their "muskets" and charge each other with fixed bayonets. Lexington and Concord thrilled them because they used the guerrilla tactics of the colonial militias, hiding behind cars, bushes, trees and garbage cans, and in gangways, while popping out to fire occasional, but deadly, rounds against the British. Their favorite battle was Custer's Last Stand, and when they played it, they all wanted to be Indians so they could wipe out the Seventh Cavalry and shout and whoop and laugh at their total victory and scalp the dead soldiers. A few brave kids always volunteered to be Custer and his doomed troopers, and they always put on the most extraordinary show, continuing to shoot Indians while pierced with dozens of arrows and bullets. Playing Custer was the actually the best part because it offered an incredible opportunity or prolonged drama and a glorious and gory death. A good Custer would still be standing defiantly and fighting with more than two hundred arrows in his body, and even with all those wounds, he'd choke and club and shoot any Indian who dared to try to scalp him while shouting that all the savages would die. When death was finally near, Custer would yank a handful of arrows out of his body, fling them contemptuously at charging Indians, fall to his knees, fire a few more rounds at the savages, and then, after having his skull crushed with a stone club, fall face down on the ground, lift his head one last time and mutter, "Tell the President we licked 'em."

The wars and battles were fought at a moment's notice, whenever the kids were bored and wherever they happened to be at the time. Someone would say, "Hey, let's play war!" and the kids would run home for their guns, or find sticks and branches, and the fighting would commence. They'd battle in and on the lawns and streets and sidewalks and trees and bushes and alleys and gangways, and they'd shoot and scream and holler and charge no matter what, and when adults drove or walked through their battle zones, the oldsters smiled and wished desperately that they were kids again. On Saturdays, the battles would involve dozens of kids and range up and down and across entire blocks and would go on half the morning. They'd charge and counterattack and plan ambushes, rebuff charges and counterattack again, and no matter how terrible and gruesome the carnage, after the battles, every kid recovered instantly from his wounds and they'd spend the next half hour reliving every shot, glorious charge and gruesome death.

After reveling in their all-out wars, the kids would either go home or find something else to do. In the winters, the braver kids flung their weapons over their shoulders, or stuffed them in their waistbands, and slid their way home by grabbing on to the back bumper of a car. It was called "skitching," and it was only for the real daredevils. The streets were covered with ice—snow compacted by car tires—and a brave kid would crouch behind a parked car and wait for a car to come down the street. If the cars were going slow enough, and in the winter most of them were, the kid would jump out from behind the parked vehicle, grab onto the rear bumper of the moving car and catch a ride by being pulled along on the ice. They had to bend their knees and crouch down so as not to be seen by the driver out of his rear-view mirror, and it required balance and guts, because if the car suddenly stopped, the kid was likely to crash into its rear end, although that rarely happened. The more common occurrence was that the driver would see that a kid had latched onto his bumper and slowly bring the vehicle to a stop Then he'd charge out of the car, slip and slide to its rear, and scream at the kid for being a jerk and endangering himself. "You're going to get yourself killed!" the driver would usually shout. "My insurance is gonna go through the roof! Get the hell out of here before I tell your parents!"

Skitching was winter's version of "Trolley grabbing" in the summer, which was an incredibly dangerous maneuver where a kid would ride his bike up behind one of the CTA's electric trolley buses, grab onto the wire that extended out of the back of the bus up to the trolley that connected to overhead copper wires, and hang on for a ride as the bus drove on. It was one of the dumber things a kid could do because bus drivers would often have to slam on their brakes to avoid a crash, and it left open the very real possibility that a kid and his bike would slam up against the back of the bus.

SKITCHING

CHAPTER 40

A Blizzard, and Meat for the Nuns

MOST WINTERS, CHICAGO didn't get huge amounts of snow,
which disappointed the kids. But on Thursday, January 26, 1967,
that changed. A few days earlier the temperature had soared to
above fifty, and the city was wondering if spring was coming early.

But it suddenly cooled down, and at two minutes past five in the morning it
officially began snowing. Only about four inches was predicted, and that was no
big deal. By seven thirty when the kids began walking to school, it was snowing
furiously—blizzarding—and the kids were having a blast playing in the stuff
and making snowballs having snowball fights. Little balls of sleet stung the
kids' faces as they tromped through the snow while hoping it would never stop.

Not a single kid learned anything in school that morning because they
were staring out classroom windows and watching the snow pile up. By noon
there was much more than four inches on the ground, it was still blizzarding
and school was called for the day. The walks home were glorious as the kids
figured they'd get the next day off as well, and that was crazy because in all
their years at OLG they had never gotten a single day off because of snow
or cold or anything.

That afternoon and evening was pure joy as the snow continued to pour out
of the sky. Brick buildings were becoming encased in the wind-driven snow,

drifts were piling up high, and no one had seen that much snow before. Kids jumped off porches into the mighty snowdrifts. On Harding, they went to The Grey House and jumped off its porch and ledges into the drifts in the next-door yard. When they had to go home for supper it was still snowing, and when they went back out after supper it was still snowing. It was snowing and snowing and snowing, and cars parked along the streets were becoming buried in the stuff.

At eight or nine at night when they returned home it was still snowing, and when they woke up the next morning it was still snowing! Newspaper headlines the next morning shouted that it was the greatest snowstorm in the city's history. Radio and TV newscasters warned people to stay inside lest they get buried in snow. Oldsters fretted and checked their refrigerators, pantries and beer and liquor supplies, hoping and praying that they had enough to get them through the disaster.

By the time it finally stopped at little after ten on Friday morning, twenty-three inches of beautiful snow had fallen! Twenty-three inches of snow! It was the largest single snowfall in the city's history.

Snowdrifts in some places were ten feet high, and alleys and streets were impassable. Cars and trucks were buried in snow. More than fifty thousand cars and trucks, including eight hundred city buses, were stranded on the streets and expressways. No vehicle could move, and the only way to get around was to trudge through the mountains of snow. Thousands upon thousands of workers had been stranded at their jobs. The city's airports were closed, the nation's second largest city was paralyzed and in chaos, and every kid in the city was in heaven!

Kids were set to work by their parents shoveling sidewalks and trying to unbury cars. The alleys had to be shoveled, too, because the massive snow drifts had trapped cars in garages. Mountains of shoveled show piled up everywhere. On the lawns in front of Dennis's house and down the entire block, the snow mountains were more than eight feet high.

Adults pulled sleds to grocery stores and taverns and began hoarding food and booze. It wasn't long before store shelves were empty because delivery trucks couldn't get through the snowy streets and alleys to resupply them. No one dared get sick because fire trucks, ambulances and police cars couldn't get through the blocked streets. People turned to their TVs and radios to get news because the newspaper trucks were as stuck and as stranded as every other vehicle.

THE GREATEST BLIZZARD EVER·

Some adults were starting to panic, especially those whose cars had been buried in snow or abandoned in the streets. For kids it was pure joy and the greatest adventure they had ever had. Into those mountains of snow they began tunneling and digging mazes of rooms. Some hollowed the mountains out and turned them into the most massive snow forts and igloos ever. They tunneled down entire blocks, carving out rooms, pretending they were miners, and praying for cave-ins. They climbed to the tops of those snow mountains and skied down them, their rubber boots substituting for real skis. Snowball fights broke out everywhere and continued all day as there was no shortage of raw material. Kids hurled themselves into the massive drifts and laughed themselves silly with the fun they were having. Even the kids had limited mobility because it was so difficult and tiring to trudge through two feet of snow, so most of them stayed on their own blocks. It was the most incredible and wonderful thing they had ever seen. The mighty city of Chicago—the greatest city on Earth—was paralyzed and shut down. Most people secretly marveled at and stood in awe of nature's incredible power.

It was in the aftermath of that massive snowstorm that the nuns of OLG made one of their biggest hauls ever. Ray Pagentini's dad worked at the Jewel grocery store on Fullerton and just down the alley from the convent. Delivery trucks were stuck in the snow, people couldn't get to the stores and there was fear that the store's perishables—milk, meat, eggs and produce—would spoil.

Ray's dad got some kids together and took them to the store, where he had them haul hundreds of pounds of meat and milk down the alley, past the convent and to the homes of friends, relatives and neighbors. The kids filled the freezers of those relatives and built three large igloos in Ray's back yard for the meat.

As Ray was walking down the alley with another load of meat, DeLasalle came into the alley to throw out garbage. She saw Ray and his haul of meat and immediately accused him of stealing it. The kid pleaded innocence, but DeLasalle decided to investigate and made it through the snow to the Jewel's back door where she chatted with Ray's dad and asked if they had extra meat. On his next trip, Ray and his pals detoured into the convent and filled their walk-in freezer to the top with meat. It was good that they did, because for the next several months, DeLasalle refrained from beating Ray. When she did resume hitting him, Ray figured that the meat had run out.

Ray liked DeLasalle, and she liked him, but affection for a kid never prevented the nuns from doing them bodily harm. One day Ray was angry at the large nun and swore at her under his breath in Italian. DeLasalle called him to the front of the room and began an interrogation, asking what he had said. When he replied "nothing," DeLasalle calmly informed him that she had once taught deaf students and that she could read lips and that he had said something.

That rattled Ray, but he figured he was in the clear because he had sworn at her in Italian, and even if she could read lips, she didn't know Italian. As he congratulated himself, DeLasalle spoke softly to the boy, and he was horrified. She was speaking Italian! The kid was through. DeLasalle took Ray and her classroom's other Italian boys—Masciola, Jim Montessi and Mike DelGallo—together to the back row and beat them senseless.

That day after school, DeLasalle marched Ray across the street to his house and promptly informed his mother what he had said and the two women beat him, as he explained the next day, "like a rented mule."

CHAPTER 41

An Electric Chair for Mice

HEADING BACK TO school after their two-week Christmas vacation was misery for the kids. They faced more than five straight months of school with no major holidays to break things up. The holidays at the end of the year—Halloween, Thanksgiving, Christmas and New Year's—were joyous. Everyone looked forward to them. After that, the only holiday to come was Easter, which was always on a Sunday, which meant no time off from school. Hell, they didn't even get Good Friday off. The months after Christmas were a grind that included standardized tests. The tests were key in determining if one would be promoted to the next grade, which scared the hell out of most of the kids. They also included the nuns handing out Lenten Banks, little silver and blue cans that the kids were expected to fill to the brim with change, sex education classes, Friday afternoons of practicing hymns in church for the May Crowning celebration, and for what many kids was the most terrible and frightening thing of all: science projects.

After the Russians launched their Sputnik satellite in October 1957, everyone and every institution and profession in the U.S. panicked, especially educational institutions. Fearing there was a massive science gap between America and Russia, an unacceptable situation that would give the hated Russians the advantage in everything, and that American kids were brainless idiots when it came to science, U.S. leaders demanded a renewed emphasis on science in the nation's grammar schools, high schools and universities. Every school system bought into the panic, including the Catholic schools. The nuns at OLG were determined to turn every kid they taught into a scientific genius. So, beginning in fourth grade the kids had to do science projects, and most of them dreaded the yearly exercise because, well, they weren't very scientific minded and had no idea what to do. They understood the science that the nuns taught, and they liked it, but they weren't researchers. That they had to come up with projects, complete with hypotheses, experiments, records, posters and results to either prove or disprove any theory, and then get up and explain it all in front of the class, made many of them sick to their stomachs. For most of the good kids it was easy because their parents—usually their dads—designed the entire assignment for them. But for kids whose factory worker dads didn't have the time or knowledge to help them, it was awful.

As always, the nuns played favorites, lavishing praise on the stuff the good kids came up with even though there was no experimentation or actual science in what they did. The good kids always had elaborate models of nuclear reactors that their dads built, volcanoes that "erupted" by pouring baking soda and vinegar down the top, rocket ships and models of the solar system. Some worked up studies of photosynthesis, which were nothing more than copying entire pages from their science books or encyclopedias. Once, a truly smarmy, suck-up kid came in with a plaster model of Jesus's tomb, complete with blood stains and a Shroud of Turin drawn with a pencil on a handkerchief. Even though it involved not a single piece of experimentation or scientific examination, the nuns swooned over it and had the kid go to other classrooms to show it off. Other kids were stuck with bringing in rock or stamp collections, electromagnets, model planes and cars, and the all-time favorite and standby of every kid who didn't have a single scientific gene in his or her body: anything to do with growing lima beans.

Anyone could grow lima beans on their dining room table, windowsills or in their basements, and all they had to do was grow the beans under normal, or control conditions—dirt, water and light—and then come up with experimental conditions like excessive amounts of fertilizer, little or no light, no water, or growth-stimulating solutions. Doing up lima beans that way constituted true experimentation, which pretty, cut-away models of nuclear reactors didn't, but the nuns always scoffed at bean projects and gave them low grades.

While Dennis loved science and often did his own scientific experiments at home, he had absolutely no talent in the area. His idea of a big and ground-breaking experiment involved putting pieces of butter on the metal radiators that heated his home in the winter and then putting kernels of popcorn in the butter to see if they'd pop, which they never did. His fourth-grade electromagnet fiasco was proof of his lack of scientific aptitude, and so was his sixth-grade science project, which he truly believed would revolutionize agriculture, feed the masses and end hunger forever and all time. To him it was a breakthrough effort at discovery. The idea hit him one day when he was daydreaming in class, and so moved and excited was he by the bolt of scientific inspiration that he raced home after school and started growing lima beans in Styrofoam cups in his basement. He toiled over and watched and cared for the beans for a month and recorded their progress, or lack thereof, in detailed, handwritten notes that he intended to preserve for posterity. He figured his experiment would wind up in the Smithsonian Institution and that farmers around the world—and probably the Universe—would put his findings to use. Like a movie playing over and over in his head, he dreamed about being celebrated and honored as the world's greatest agrarian scientist ever. He imagined the cheers, the medals, the trophies and the gobs of money that would be showered on him, and mobs of beautiful girls that would want to marry him. It was the first time that he wasn't dreading having to stand before the class and present and explain his work. With past projects his classmates had laughed at his idiotic efforts at science, but this time would be different.

Two weeks before the day they had to bring their projects to school, Dennis began preparing his report and poster. He drew the poster with a ruler and sharp pencils, and it looked professional, brilliant and scientific compared to the freehand joke he had presented in fourth grade. He hadn't told anybody about his project out of fear that they would steal his idea, and now, as he walked to school on the morning he was to present, he couldn't wait to unleash his scientific genius on the world and reap the world's praise and everlasting gratitude.

There were some halfway decent projects that preceded his, and some stinkers, too. Walter Fong had something about germs, bacteria and disease that none of the kids understood, but which the teacher, Miss Laffey, hailed as brilliant and said would probably win a first-place medal at the city-wide science project fair that the nuns and teachers desperately wanted the school to be represented in. Russell Lambert, who had transferred that year from a public school, had a fossil collection that he figured was sure to impress. Everyone loved fossils because they represented the physical manifestation of the past. The kids didn't explain it that way, but they were thrilled to see and touch the stone outline of some strange creature that had lived millions of years before, and when they did touch an actual fossil, they imagined themselves wandering around back in ancient times clubbing dinosaurs to death and throwing spears at giant flying reptiles.

So, when Russell calmly announced that he had fossils that were millions of years old, the kids perked up and waited to be transported back in time. There were fossils of frogs and lizards and ants and petrified wood that interested the kids. But when Russell held up fossils of nails and pieces of glass, the kids got a little skeptical. They liked the show, though, and listened attentively as Russell grabbed bigger and bigger rocks out of the cardboard boxes that held his fossils. Saving the best for last, Russell breathlessly announced that he had a dinosaur fossil that was sixty million years old. The kids were stunned to hear that a kid from the neighborhood had a real dinosaur fossil—they figured that only the world's top scientists knew where to find them—and they watched intently as Russell lifted the thing out of its box.

"This is a dinosaur footprint," he proclaimed proudly as he held up what to the kids looked like a big chunk of concrete, "I think it's fifty to sixty million years old!"

That got everybody exclaiming and whispering to each other. No one had ever seen a sixty-million-year-old rock, and there was one right in front of them! While Russell proudly displayed his dinosaur footprint and waited for the kids to gasp in admiration and awe, Miss Laffey calmly asked, "Where did you get this fossil, Russell?"

"I found it in the alley by my house," he replied.

Before Laffey could ask another question, the kids busted out laughing. They might not have been scientific geniuses, but they knew that sixty-million-year-old fossilized dinosaur footprints weren't lying around in alleys. Russell wasn't fazed. He stood defiantly, sort of sneered, and looked at the kids and Laffey like they were crazy for thinking you couldn't find dinosaur fossils in an alley. It appeared that he really believed the chunk of concrete he was holding was a sixty-million-year-old fossil.

"Why do you think archaeologists from the Field Museum or other museums haven't found fossils in the alleys like you have?" Laffey asked, implying that he was either demented, an all-out liar or just a lazy punk who had slapped together a science project at the last minute in order to avoid a flunking grade.

"Because they don't know what they're doing," Russell answered. "They don't know where to look. These things are all over the place."

"Why don't you sit down," the teacher said, wanting to end the fiasco quickly. As Russell collected his fossils and shuffled back to his desk, the kids laughed louder and realized that they had been right all along about public school transfers: they were idiots.

HE FOUND A DINOSAUR FOOTPRINT IN THE ALLEY.

Finally, it was Dennis's turn to unveil his scientific masterpiece. He strode confidently to the front of the room and set up his poster, as well as an array of white Styrofoam cups he had used to grow lima beans. When all was ready, he stood before the class, and because he was so excited about his breakthrough and so determined to tell the world about it he forgot to explain what his experiment was, why he did it and what he had hoped to accomplish. Instead, he got right to the main point and excitedly blurted out the main result of his grand botanical experiment.

"What I found," he said, almost shouting because he was so excited, "is that you can't grow lima beans, or any other plant, in talcum powder!"

That was a stunner that neither the kids nor Laffey had ever heard of, and despite being shocked by the fact that someone thought you could grow lima beans in talcum powder, they gave Dennis their full attention.

"I grew lima beans in dirt, talcum powder mixed with dirt, and pure talcum powder," Dennis continued. "The lima beans grew in the dirt, but they didn't grow in the mixture of talcum powder and dirt, or the pure talcum powder. My conclusion is that no one should try to grow things in talcum powder; it doesn't work. And farmers should never put talcum powder on their fields! It'll kill the plants!"

No one could dispute those conclusions, or that Dennis had put solid effort into his project, but even the kids who were scientifically ignorant wondered to themselves why anyone would try to grow anything in talcum powder. Even the dumbest kids instinctively knew that no one in the history of Earth had ever thought of trying to grow plants in talcum powder, and that no one except Dennis ever would. It wasn't even an option for scientific inquiry. It was beyond ridiculous. They didn't think Dennis was crazy or was trying to scam them; they could see by his enthusiasm and passion that he truly believed he had made a brilliant scientific breakthrough. They felt sorry for him because they could see that he lacked an understanding of the basic principles of, well, just about everything.

Miss Laffey recognized the kid's effort, and was compassionate, but as the teacher she had the responsibility of teaching the kids about the rigors of science, so she asked Dennis:

"Why didn't the beans grow in talcum powder?"

"I don't know," was the response.

"Could it be that there are no nutrients and minerals in talcum powder that plants need?"

"I guess so."

"Is it that talcum powder is so fine that that it cakes up when wet and denies the plants' roots the ability to absorb water, oxygen and nutrients?"

"How would I know?"

"Is there a problem in that farmers are trying to grow plants in talcum powder?"

"I don't know."

"Why did you decide to try to grow plants in talcum powder?"

"Because."

"'Because' is not an answer! Why did you try to grow lima beans in talcum powder?"

"Because everyone has to know that you can't grow plants in talcum powder! Don't you understand? It's as clear as day, you can't grow plants in talcum powder! This is a huge deal!"

"Do you know of anyone besides yourself who has tried to grow plants in talcum powder?" the teacher asked.

Dennis, realizing that Laffey was doubting his scientific aptitude and world-saving breakthrough, and also questioning his judgment, and thus his entire existence, snapped. He screamed back with the anger, frustration and horror of someone who believes that those who question and doubt him are too intellectually deficient to recognize his genius and that the world will suffer dire and irreversible consequences because of that intellectual deficiency: "Everyone needs to know that you can't grow plants in talcum powder! If farmers try to grow crops in talcum powder, the crops will die, and humans will starve! They've got to know about this! This is huge! The Russians don't have this information yet. I—we—have beaten them to it! Don't you see? Don't you see?"

Laffey was stunned by the boy's passion and intensity. Never in her more than twenty years of teaching had someone acted that maniacal over a simple, and, in all honesty, worthless science project. She was trying to be compassionate by gently prodding the boy with questions and getting him to think, but his outburst, bulging eyes and reddened face scared her like nothing had before. She wanted to tell Dennis to sit down, but for a few moments she was so stunned that she couldn't speak. Dennis filled the vacuum of her silence by waving his arms, looking wildly around the classroom at his classmates and shouting:

"This is really important! You can't grow lima beans in talcum powder! Can't you see it? Can't you see it?"

Laffey regained her composure and told the boy:

"Of course we see it. What I don't understand is whether there is a problem that needs to be addressed here. Have farmers or gardeners or anyone anywhere tried to grow crops or flowers or grass, or anything in talcum powder? I don't think this is a problem. Do you?"

Dennis had to admit to the teacher that there was no evidence that anyone on the planet had ever tried to grow plants in talcum powder and that the idea for the project just popped into his head one day and that he considered it a sort of divine inspiration.

"Well," Laffey said, "God does work in mysterious ways. He appreciates your effort. You can sit down now. We've got a few other projects to get through."

Dennis gathered his poster and Styrofoam pots—none of which contained any live lima beans—and walked to his desk thinking that Laffey was insane for questioning why someone would try to grow plants in talcum powder.

The lima bean-in-talcum powder debacle didn't dampen Dennis's zeal for science or his attempts to come up with more scientific breakthroughs. The genius of the plywood submarine was his and his alone, and in seventh grade he was determined to produce another science project that would benefit all of humankind.

So in February, when they had to begin planning their projects, Dennis was ready with an experiment he had been thinking on for a couple of years and had finally refined. Before embarking on their science projects, the kids had to write up proposals, which they submitted to their teachers. It was a way for the teachers to stop really dumb ideas and focus the kids on real science. In sixth grade, Miss Laffey hadn't read Dennis's proposal to grow plants in talcum powder, and she was embarrassed when he presented his idiotic experiment to the class. That wasn't going to happen again because Laffey had notified Sister Zita and the other nuns of Dennis's strange ideas.

But Dennis didn't know that, and so he once again plunged into a project that he believed would make the world a better place forever and all time. He collected Popsicle sticks, bought a bottle of glue, copper wire, nails and six dry-cell batteries and worked away in his basement. Finally, he had the thing perfected and wrote his proposal, which was entitled: Electric Chair for Mice.

To Dennis, it was another brilliant idea. He built a tiny chair out of Popsicle sticks and glue and stuck nails into its arms and legs. The nails and the chair were wrapped with bare copper wires which were attached to the dry-cell batteries, which were wired in series to produce the maximum amount of voltage. The idea was to catch a mouse, sit it on the chair, wrap it in bare wires, connect them to the batteries and wait for the blast of electricity to kill the creature.

To Dennis it was pure science. He had learned about wiring batteries in series from the nuns, and he was eager to show how he had put that knowledge to use in a beneficial way. And what greater benefit was there than electrocuting mice? If the project worked, Dennis planned to build larger chairs in which he could electrocute rats.

Dennis turned in his written proposal, complete with sketches of his little electric chair, and waited to be told that he was a scientific genius. The next day he got the proposal back with the word "Rejected" written across the front page in red ink. A note from Zita went home to his parents that afternoon and Dennis figured he was in big trouble.

DENNIS'S CONTRIBUTION TO SCIENCE.

"Your son has proposed a dangerous and troubling science experiment," the note read, "and you must get him to see a priest immediately. This will not stand. As Catholic parents and members of Our Lady of Grace Parish, you have the responsibility to raise your children in strict adherence to Catholic values. Failing to do so will land you in Hell. You must control your son!"

Dennis's parents were alarmed and scared and they asked him about his science project. When he told them it was an electric chair for mice, they shrugged. It seemed like a good idea to them, and they threw the note in the garbage.

But Dennis had to come up with another science project, and so his mind went immediately to work. The next day he turned in his new proposal, which was called, "Calculating How Long It Took Jesus To Die On The Cross." The experiment, his proposal read, would require "nailing a kid to a homemade cross, and we've got a kid we don't like, and waiting to see how long it takes him to die."

That proposal was also rejected, and another note went home to Dennis's parents. This one detailed his proposed experiment and urged quick and severe punishment for the child. That night, Dennis's dad whipped him with a belt.

CHAPTER 42

Ingrown Toenails and Pistol-Whipping Soldiers

DESPITE THE LONG grind of five months of nearly uninterrupted school that was ahead of them, and the depression that brought to many kids, the Disturbers managed not to think of it. They had settled into their routine of disrupting Zita's class. While not every day disintegrated into a riot, they did disturb each day by stomping their feet on their way to the cloakroom. To them it was a minor but necessary act of defiance, and one that always got the other kids laughing. It always reminded the other kids that the Disturbers were a force and the kings of the classroom.

But to Zita it was pure hell. Sometimes all she wanted and prayed for was one day, just one day, with no disruptions or assaults on her authority. Just one day where she would get some respect from those troublemakers. Just one day of peace. That those hoodlums, as she called them, had not a single ounce of empathy for her saddened her, and she really did worry that they would turn out to be good-for-nothings. She and the other nuns had a mission, and that was to educate kids so they could function in life, and turn out good Catholics, steeped in faith—and fear—who would perpetuate the Church's teachings. That they could fail in those missions saddened and hurt them.

Some days the Disturbers were quiet and subdued. No one, really, could be "on" every moment of every day, and some days they didn't have the energy to start a riot. That didn't mean they weren't acting up. Many days when Zita was conducting her spelling, religion or geography classes, the Disturbers sat in the back row and ignored her. They didn't openly refuse to participate, they just didn't. They had better things to do. For the first week after Christmas vacation, the boys ignored Zita and worked on their special project: a newspaper.

It was called "Disturbers Row," and was hand-written and hand-drawn on lined loose-leaf paper. It contained headlines that screamed: Zitabug's Bad Breath Kills!; Miss Donatello's Mustache-Shaving Secrets For Girls!; DeLasalle Breaks Truck Scale!; Shrink: Zita's Pets Are Deranged Losers!; Pontius Pilate Got A Bad Rap!; The Pope Is Jewish!; Holy Water Doesn't Get Dishes Cleaner!; Sister Yvonne Is Really A Mummy, Museum Wants Her Back!; Nuns Have Bad Habits!; Arson Blamed On Holy Spirit's Tongues of Fire!; Holy Communion is Cannibalism!; J.C. Appears to Disturbers, Approves Of Their Boldness And Makes Them Wine!; Bozeman And His Dad Chop Out Ingrown Toenails With Bowie Knives!; and, Disturbers Defend Freedom Of Kids Everywhere, Hailed As Heroes!

READ ALL ABOUT IT!

The guys also published a jingle, or poem, that had been part of OLG's lore for years, especially among the kids who made trouble for Zita, and that was often sung loudly by many kids on their way home after school:

OLG's my prison, 204's my cell.
Zita is my warden, and she can go to hell!

Although the jingle had been sung for years by trouble-making kids who had Zita, its publication infuriated the nuns, and they launched an inquisition as to its origin and authorship. Of course, by any logical standard, the investigation was pure insanity because the jingle was basically a neighborhood folk song, and no one would ever be able to say exactly how it came about. Logic mostly always lost out when the nuns smelled an opportunity to beat kids, and this was another chance to clobber the Disturbers.

"Who wrote this sinful insult to Sister Mary Zita, God's Representative on Earth?" Vitaclaire demanded of the Disturbers in her office the day the song was published. "Who defiled Sister Zita's holy name, Our Lady of Grace school and Holy Mother Church? Which one of you, or is it all of you, who walk hand-in-hand with the Devil? Only a confession here and now will save you from an eternity in Hell! Confess or suffer the consequences!"

Even if the guys had wanted to, there was nothing to confess. They had heard the song from their older brothers and sisters who had heard it from their brothers and sisters who had heard it from, well, pretty much everyone in the neighborhood.

DeLasalle and Yvonne, who were also in the office, both demanded at once:

"If you think this school is a prison then it will be for you hoodlums." Then they both started slapping the guys across their faces. Vitaclaire pulled out a wooden chair rung from a drawer in her desk and held it menacingly in the air so the kids had no doubt as to the punishment their inquisitors would mete out.

"If you think we're wardens, then we will grant your every wish, and grant it promptly, and you *will* be sorry," Yvonne snarled. "Which one of you wrote it?"

"No one wrote it, we just heard it. It's something that's been around for a long time," Kurkowski offered.

"How long?" DeLasalle demanded.

"I don't know, a long time."

"You do know, and you will confess now," DeLasalle said to the boy. "If no one wrote it, how did it get written? By magic?"

"I don't know," Kurkowski answered.

"Yes you do know! Which one of you wrote it? If you know what's good for you, you will confess now!" DeLasalle shouted as she repeatedly clobbered Kurkowski across the side of his head with her forearm.

"God wrote it," Bozeman shouted out in a manically defiant voice. "God wrote it!"

That was beyond anything the nuns could take and they instantly attacked the five boys, beating them with their hands and arms.

When their fury had subsided, Yvonne asked sternly:

"And how, Mister Bozeman, exactly did Our Lord write this sickening and sinful slander?"

"Because we're all made in the image and likeness of God, and he inspires and controls all of us," Bozeman responded. "That's what you've taught us. Whoever wrote it was inspired by God."

To the nuns that was heresy and an unforgivable direct and Satan-inspired attack on God, and they beat the kids again. As the interrogation and beatings wore on, the Disturbers and the nuns were getting worn out. There was only so much beating a kid could take in one day, and there was only so much violence the nuns could administer in a day, even if it was administered to save and purify God's holy image.

"If you don't confess, we're going to call your fathers, and then we'll see who will be laughing after that," Vitaclaire said. "And we're going to expel you and you will all have to repeat seventh grade over again. What will your fathers say and do about that?"

It was a credible threat, so the guys decided to confess and have some fun doing it.

"My father wrote it," Dennis shouted. "He told it to my brother Wally, and he told it to me."

"A communist wrote it," Kolba offered. "The communist gave it to me."

"And where did you see this communist?" Vitaclaire demanded.

"Behind the rectory, Sister. I think communists have invaded the parish."

"Sister, it was a pagan who wrote it," Ruchinski said. "A pagan!"

"And how do *you* know pagans?" Yvonne asked. "Do you associate with them?"

"I think it was one of the pagans we bought as a baby. He grew up, and—"

KABOOM! Yvonne clobbered Ruchinski across the side of the head.

"And where, Mister Ruchinski, did you see this pagan?" Yvonne asked. "In your house?"

"No, Sister, in the church. There was a pagan in the confessional, and he was dressed like a priest. Those pagans are really, really sneaky. I threw holy water on him and he started smoking. I hope there aren't any pagans trying to invade the convent."

It went like that for another few minutes before the nuns realized that they had once again been beaten and that no amount of punishment or threats would break the Disturbers. The interrogation ended. As the Disturbers staggered together out of the school building that day they sang loudly in triumph:

> OLG's my prison, 204's my cell.
> Zita is my warden, and she can go to hell!

The Disturbers' favorite story from their paper was about Bozeman's toenails, which he had told them one day during Christmas vacation when they were at Kolba's house. Gary's dad had a tape recorder, and the kids taped their goofy pal and wrote up the story exactly as Rich told it. It read:

Fellow Disturber Rich Bozeman told us this goofy story about his ingrown toenails and what his dad did during the war. We don't believe him, but we laughed our asses off. Here's the story as Bozeman told it to us:

Kolba: Hey, Rich, you're limping. What happened?

Bozeman: Ahh, nothing.

Kolba: Nothing? Bull. You're limping.

Bozeman: Hey, I said nothing, you got it?

Ruchinski: Richie must have hurt himself! What happened, did you hit your little baby toe on a chair leg or something?

Bozeman: Shut up before I kick your ass.

Ruchinski: Bullshit. What happened? I mean, you're limping real bad. What, did a little pebble fall on your foot? Are you clumsy?

Bozeman: Shut the fuck up before I kick your ass.

Kolba: Jeez, Boz, we just wanna know what happened.

Bozeman: Ahh, all right. Had an ingrown toenail and I cut it out with a Bowie knife.

Dennis: A Bowie knife? What the hell you talking about? Are you crazy?

Bozeman: Bullshit. Me and my dad, when we get ingrown toenails, we sit on the couch, put leather straps in our mouths so we can chew down on 'em, and then we cut our toenails out with the Bowie knives.

Dennis: Bowie knives? Those are like butcher knives. Why are you cutting out ingrown toenails with butcher knives?

Bozeman: They ain't butcher knives; they're longer and sharper. Nine-and-a-half inch blades. They kick ass.

Kolba: Why don't you just go to the doctor?

Bozeman: 'Cause doctors are full of shit. They charge a ton of money, and they don't get all the nail out. My dad learned how to cut out his own ingrown toenails during the war.

Ruchinski: Does it hurt, Boz?

Bozeman: Shit, it hurts like hell. That's why we chew on the leather straps. Sometimes we chew on pieces of wood. I mean, you start digging around and it gets all full of blood and, damn, it hurts. And sometimes, when I ain't getting the nail out right, my dad uses his knife on my toes.

Ruchinski: Boz, that's insane! It's unsanitary. I mean, it's all full of his blood. That's crazy!

Bozeman: Say that again and I'll kick your ass!

Ruchinski: Boz, no one hacks out ingrown toenails with Bowie knives. You're crazy.

BOWIE KNIVES AND INGROWN TOENAILS

Bozeman: I ain't crazy. It's true!

Kurkowski: What else did your dad learn during the war?

Bozeman: How to clean out donkey's assholes and to pistol-whip people.

The other Disturbers at once: What? That's insane!

Bozeman: It's true, assholes. In the war they used donkeys to carry supplies up mountains, and if the donkeys' assholes weren't clean, they wouldn't move. So guys had to clean their assholes out.

Kolba: How?

Bozeman: With soap and water and sponges. They'd wet the sponges in buckets of soapy water and stick their arms up the donkeys' assholes and clean 'em out. And if a donkey's asshole wasn't clean, the sergeant would pistol-whip them.

Kurkowski: They stuck their arms up their assholes? Naah.

Bozeman: They did!

Kolba: How far?

Bozeman: Up to their elbows, at least. And farther if they had to.

Dennis: How could they tell if the assholes were clean?

Bozeman: The sergeant would inspect them. He'd wear white gloves and walk behind the rows of donkeys and stick his fingers up their asses, and if they came out brown, he'd pistol-whip the guy who was supposed to clean it.

Dennis: Pistol-whip them? Naah. Sergeants pistol-whipping their own guys? In the U.S. Army? You're crazy!

Bozeman: Bullshit. I ain't crazy. They'd pistol-whip the living shit out of them.

Ruchinski: Then what would happen? I mean, if the asshole wasn't clean?

Bozeman: They'd have to clean it again, and sometimes they had to stick their heads up the donkeys' assholes to make sure they were clean before the inspection because they didn't want to get pistol-whipped.

Kurkowski: That's insane! Where do you get this stuff?

Bozeman: From my dad. He was there. He was a sergeant, and it was his job to stick his fingers up donkeys' asses. He pistol-whipped a hundred guys. I'm telling youse, the donkeys' asses had to be clean or they wouldn't move. And if guys kept having bad inspections, they'd get court-martialed. My dad helped win the war, assholes.

Ruchinski: What evidence would they use at the court-martial?

Bozeman: The brown gloves, idiot.

The Disturbers often mimeographed their papers at the public library and gave them away to the other kids. The paper was always a huge hit, but the edition with Bozeman's ingrown toenails and his dad's white-gloving donkeys' asses was the most popular of all. It had crude drawings of Bozeman and his dad gouging out their toenails while biting down on two-by-fours, and more elaborate drawings of the donkeys and his dad's white gloves, and of soldiers being pistol-whipped by Bozeman's dad.

The nuns hated the newspaper, which they often got because some good kids gave them copies, and they fumed about stories that made fun of them, the Church and the sacraments. The profanity in the article about Bozeman's toenails appalled them, and the Disturbers were sent to Vitaclaire's office where they were beaten and sent home with notes to their parents. The story about Communion being cannibalism was beyond what they could handle. Vitaclaire berated the boys intensely for daring to say, or even think, such a monstrous thing. When they insisted that feasting on the body and blood of Christ was nothing more than eating a person, they were clobbered. When they demanded that the nuns explain how it wasn't cannibalism, they were nearly expelled.

CLEANING THE DONKEYS' ASSES

The story about how holy water didn't get dishes cleaner was another that nearly gave the nuns strokes. They demanded to know where the kids got the holy water and how much they used. They nearly fainted when told that after washing dishes in holy water, the kids sent the stuff down the drain and into the sewers. It never occurred to the nuns that the guys made the story up and didn't misuse or abuse holy water, but as usual they took everything way too seriously.

The joke, though, at least for a while, was on the Disturbers. The nuns ordered the workers at the public library to stop mimeographing anything from the five kids or anything that had anything to do with the Disturbers. For a few weeks there was no distribution of the paper. But that changed when Kolba's oldest brother, who was in high school, agreed to run off copies of it at his school's library. When the paper reappeared, the nuns stormed any neighborhood business they thought had mimeograph machines and demanded that they stop printing the paper. None of the businesses that had the machines had ever seen the Disturbers or run copies of their newspaper, so the nuns were stymied again.

CHAPTER 43

Sex Education

THE SECOND HALF of the year brought something that truly excited the kids: sex education classes. Easing grammar school kids into the strange world of sex through educational classes was gaining momentum in the 1960s, even in Catholic schools. The nuns and priests set to the task with a zeal for education that was muted by an equal and counterbalancing zeal for holiness and caution. The nuns and priests were uncomfortable teaching the kids about sex, but it had to be done. It seemed more than a little odd to the kids that adults who were never supposed to have sex—and who supposedly never did—were their instructors. What did they know, the kids wondered?

The classes were purposely held on Friday afternoons so as to not have the kids babbling throughout the week and giggling about what they had learned. The idea was that they'd be off for the weekends and thinking about anything but school, and that they'd quickly forget what they had been taught.

The boys and girls were sent to separate rooms where priests lectured the boys about things like intercourse and erections, and nuns told the girls about things like menstruation and pregnancy. At least for the boys, the classes often turned into laugh riots because many of the smart alecks and wise guys had already gotten their sex education from their older brothers and their friends, and they figured they knew more about the subject than did celibate priests who were holed up in the rectory reading prayer books all day. They had learned the sexual terminology of the street—and that pretty much everybody, even adults, used—as opposed to the clinical terms the priests relied upon.

Boys with older brothers knew pretty much from the first day they walked out the door to play in the alleys that they had dicks and would someday get boners. The older kids often brought up the subject by asking one another, "Hey, where'd you get your dick?" Another kid would pretend to think about it for a moment and reply, "Walgreens! They were on sale at Walgreens." The younger kids would laugh and get in on the game and exclaim that they had gotten their dicks at Woolworth's or the Corner Store or anywhere else their young minds could come up with.

The game would continue with the older kids asking each other how much they had paid for their dicks. The more expensive the dick the better. Then they'd ask:

"Did your dick come with a boner?"

"Are you crazy? All dicks come with boners," was a typical response. "And my boner is the biggest there is! Bigger than yours!"

"How long is your boner? Mine's three feet!" was another line that would get a response something like:

"Shit, mine's three-feet-two-inches."

They'd laugh and go back and forth with their questions and replies, always boasting that their dicks were the best, and boners the longest. Everyone would laugh, and usually, a younger kid who had never heard such talk before would ask, "What's a dick and what's a boner?" The older kids would explain, and the younger kids would be fascinated to know that they too had dicks and would one day get boners, and everybody was happy and satisfied. As the kids aged, the older guys would expand their talks to include details about whacking off and fucking, which sometimes horrified the younger kids. The older guys were proud that they had passed on knowledge to their younger brothers and friends, and the recipients were thrilled to know that they had learned something of incredible value, and they couldn't wait until they were older so they could pass the knowledge on to a younger generation.

Once during one of those talks about dicks and boners, a younger kid in Dennis's neighborhood excitedly said that he had gotten his first boner while taking a bath on a Saturday evening.

"What did you do with it?" an older guy asked.

"Grabbed it, and then I ran out of the bathroom into the kitchen and told my ma, 'Hey Ma, look! I've got a boner!'"

Everyone cringed as they instinctively knew that no one was ever supposed to show a boner to a parent, let alone a mother.

"You can't show boners to people," an older kid explained, "only to girls, and not 'till you're older."

"How old?"

"I don't know, maybe thirty-five or something."

The kids' curiosity about sex and their bodies couldn't be muted or killed by the nuns' constant warnings that they were never to touch, or even look at themselves lest they go to Hell. A ritual of growing up was the game of "Pull Pants Down," which usually involved two kids finding a secluded place—an empty basement or grove of trees along the railroad tracks—and pulling their pants down to see what they looked like underneath. Girls did it with girls and boys did it with boys, usually in first or second grade. By third grade, some of the more adventurous boys and girls were playing it with each other. Nothing ever happened during those encounters other than the kids giggled and felt incredibly liberated and exhilarated by taking their clothes off and staring at each other.

The highlight for the kids in Dennis's crowd came one fall day when his brother Steve's friend, Eddie Meister, rode up to a group of them on his twenty-inch banana-seat bicycle and breathlessly announced loudly that he had a rubber.

"You got a rubber?" the younger kids asked, "Holy cow! Let's see it!"

Eddie dug a brown leather wallet out of his back pants pocket, opened it and proudly displayed a thin foil package inside. "That's the rubber," he said. "I got it from my older brother. It's a Trojan!"

The kids stared with reverential awe at the thing, just like the nuns demanded that they treat prayer books, communion wafers, rosaries and bottles of holy water. That it was a Trojan, the biggest name in rubbers at the time, impressed the kids even more.

"Take it out! Can we see it?" a kid asked.

"What, are you nuts," Eddie replied. "This thing is too special. Don't want to lose or break it."

"Aww, come on, let's see it."

Eddie reluctantly and gently took the package out of the wallet and held it up as if it were truly a holy object. That he had secured a rubber—an item that only adults could buy from drug stores—made the kids think he was a super-human miracle worker, almost like Christ himself.

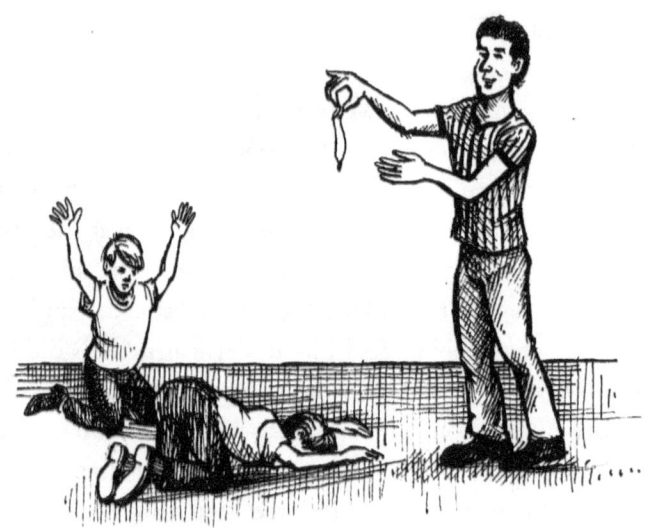

THE SACRED LATEX

"What you going to do with it?" someone asked.

"Gonna use it to screw Sue Bodowski."

"What?! When?"

"Tomorrow night on the tracks."

"Can we come and watch?"

"Are you crazy? No!"

"How you gonna screw her? What are you gonna do?"

"I don't know. Just gonna screw her."

Eddie allowed the rubber to be passed around, and when the kids touched it, they felt they had graduated to a new world. For the next week all they could do was boast to their pals and classmates that they had seen and held a rubber. No one ever followed up to see if Eddie and Sue had actually done the deed on the railroad tracks. They didn't, but no one cared because they had seen and touched a rubber.

CHAPTER 44

A Talented Artist
and an Angry Priest

T HE BOYS ALTERNATELY giggled, punched each other, laughed
loudly and tried to act cool, calm and knowledgeable as they walked
through the hallway to their sex education class. They speculated
about what the topics would be and tried to pretend that nothing the priest
would tell them was new.

"I already know what he's gonna say, and it ain't nothing that I ain't heard
before," Ruchinski boasted loudly. "This stuff is for, like, kids."

Others who didn't have older brothers to teach them about "life," as it
was often called, were thrilled that they might learn something about sex.

After they had taken their seats and the bell had sounded for class to
begin, Father Jack Dempsy walked into the room. The kids were surprised
and happy. Father Dempsy was young and cool, and not at all like the older,
deadly serious priests they hated. He told decent jokes—real jokes that weren't
religiously themed—laughed, played softball with them and seemed to understand what they were going through at the hands, forearms and fists of the
nuns. In fact, he was a new breed of priest, one of those post-Vatican II types
who were more in touch with normal human beings and not as maniacal

about making people feel guilty about minor infractions of Church rules. He had never threatened any of the kids with Hell, and if a kid or parent came to him with a problem, he listened, provided common-sense solutions and never berated anyone.

The class started off with the usual topic: masturbation. By seventh grade, every boy and girl had done it despite being warned to never touch themselves in a dirty and unclean manner. They couldn't help it; it was just nature. Some got around the warning against touching oneself in an unclean manner by first washing their hands. They figured they were at least clean.

None of the kids, though, could understand why, if they were made in the image and likeness of God, as they were constantly told they were, they were supposed to be ashamed or afraid of their bodies. How could it be a sin that they explored the feelings and bodies that God gave them?

One of the bolder kids put that question to Father Dempsy, and his response stunned them. "It isn't a sin that your bodies do these things and that you feel these things," he said. "It's natural, and everybody has these feelings. The sin is in not controlling yourselves. We're human beings and we have free will and we can't give in at every moment of every day to our urges. That would make us animals. We're better than that. Intercourse must be saved for the appropriate time, which is marriage."

Later in the class the priest told the kids that they would get erections during the night. He didn't explain why, but he advised them on what they should do when they got one.

"Don't touch yourself, just roll over on your stomach and go back to sleep," he advised. Everyone was quiet for a moment, and then a wise guy shouted:

"Father, if I do that, I'll be three feet off the mattress!"

Even the priest laughed. It was the most useful sex education class the boys had ever had.

The girls had it especially difficult because they were saddled with a double dose of responsibilities. They not only had to resist their own urges, but they also had to fight off the boys, who were nothing but animals who would use any sneaky trick to despoil their holiness. Chastity and purity equaled holiness and a ticket straight to Heaven, the girls were told, and it was their duty to God to maintain the holy purity of the temples that were their bodies from attacks by the boys. If they didn't, they were whores, and being a whore was the worst sin of all. It was stunningly unfair. While the boys were just crazed animals who were always on the prowl, any girl who got a mash note from a boy was suddenly a slithering temptress who lured the helpless, always-on-the-prowl-animal-boys into soul-blackening sin. It was always their fault, and not the fault of the boys who sent them the notes and who were always trying to overcome their defenses. The boys' uncontrolled aggressiveness was somehow normal, but a girl who even slightly entertained an advance was in league with the Devil.

THREE FEET OFF THE MATTRESS!

A few girls believed the nuns' warnings with every atom of their pure white souls and had nothing to do with boys. But most inherently knew that the nuns were crazy and ignored them. Human nature and biology were more powerful than Church doctrine and threats of Hell.

The greatest triumph of any kid in OLG's history regarding sex education occurred four years earlier when a kid's artistic skills showed just how talented some of them were and how much fun they had in challenging authority and messing with the nuns and priests. The eighth-grade boys were looking forward to yet another Friday afternoon sex talk. The priest, Father Ed Sedlecki, had brought a large drawing pad and easel to the room the day before in preparation for his talk. Sedlecki, who was in his forties, was a decent guy who everybody liked. He was balding, wore silver-and black-rimmed glasses and looked older than he was, but he had the zeal and energy of a young man.

His Sunday morning sermons were serious, but not maniacal, and usually inspiring. He spoke the language of blue-collar people and understood their problems and struggles. He wanted them to live good lives on Earth and to get to Heaven after they died. One of his most notable qualities was that he was an incredible, or at least a loud, singer. He'd end the masses with booming and inspiring renditions of two hymns: "Holy God We Praise Thy Name," and "Holy, Holy, Holy."

His rich, baritone voice boomed off the cavernous church's walls and ceilings, and at times it seemed as if the building's stained-glass windows shook, and the crucifixes and plaster statues of the saints rattled with joy at the power, vibrancy and passion of his voice. A Father Sedlecki Sunday morning mass was a powerful and moving religious experience that left some of the more impressionable kids vowing to become priests and nuns, and most of the adults in such a loving and forgiving mood that they said nice things to their neighbors in front of the church after mass and avoided reverting to their normal selves and sinful ways until later in the afternoon.

While not an arm-waving, screaming, sputtering, spitting grouch like Monsignor Flavin, who demanded total subservience to the Church's rules and to his and the nuns' authority, Sedlecki did demand adherence to the Church's rules. He got angry when he saw kids purposely break those rules because he did believe in authority, but mostly because he felt those kids were screwing up their lives, and it pained him to watch people hurt themselves. Even though Sedlecki was a decent guy, he was a priest, and someone in authority, and the bolder, more independent kids took great joy in challenging him.

It was harder for kids to mess with priests, though, because they were stronger than nuns and hit harder and could do a kid real damage, and because they made it seem like they were closer to, and more friendly with God than were the nuns. Priests were God's generals on Earth who had direct lines of communication with him. The nuns were like expendable foot soldiers who couldn't reach the Almighty directly or instantly. But the priests could, or at least they made it seem like they could, and that made it riskier to challenge them. Humiliate a nun and God might not notice for a couple of weeks, and by then his anger would have dissipated and not much would happen in the way of punishment. But dump on a priest, and the Creator of the Universe would know instantly and discharge immediate and awful punishment.

While the more independent kids didn't believe that God would immediately blind or cripple them, or burn down their houses if they disobeyed priests, that he might do it was always somewhere in the back of their minds. They had been told that for eight years, and no matter how much they resisted the brainwashing, the thought, however fleeting, was always there.

Sedlecki had brought the easel and artist's pad into the room so he could draw or write some of the things he thought would inform the kids—words such as "condom," "penis," "erection," "intercourse," and "masturbation." The pad was also a good way to hit the kids again with the Ten Commandments, the obligation to attend mass every Sunday and the need to go to confession as often as possible.

Sedlecki's easel and giant pad of paper were an invitation for great mischief, and a boy named Buzz sneaked back into the room after classes had ended for the day, got out a black pencil, flipped over five or six blank sheets and put his artistic skills to work. After a half hour of giggling and drawing, he flipped the pages back over, so the blank ones were in front, and left the room. Two other boys, including Wally Domrzalski, had stood guard while Buzz drew his masterpiece on the white sheet of paper, and they left the room hoping and praying that the next afternoon during Sedlecki's lecture their classmates would get the shock and laugh of their young lives.

Sedlecki began his talk in the usual way, reminding the kids about their obligations to control their urges and not give in to lust, impure thoughts and other degradations. For the boys, that meant prohibitions against wearing tight pants, combing their hair too often and looking at girls. He went on to the sanctity of marriage and how intercourse was appropriate only in a marital setting. He warned against the dangers of masturbation, or self-abuse, which was always a high point for the kids as they got to throw their street-corner knowledge at him.

"You mean, Father, that I can't whack off or beat my meat?" a kid asked to great laughter. Another asked, "So Father, I can't grab Julia Gostowski's knockers, huh?" Then another threw out a question that he thought was the ultimate in cleverness:

"Father, are Trojans the best rubbers? What brand do you use?"

Sedlecki smiled, which told the kids that he appreciated their wit, and the smart-ass questions continued for a while.

"Father, you mean I can't dream of Karen Silvio? What if I knock her up?" someone asked to more laughter.

"Father, what do I do if I get a hard-on and it rips through my pants?" another wise guy asked.

The questions continued until the kids had used up their wit and energy. Then Sedlecki took out a black felt marker and listed a few key Commandments on the first sheet of paper, emphasizing the ones about adultery and no false gods. He flipped the page over and scribbled something about the difference between animals and humans with their free will and ability to resist temptation. On the third page he drew stick figures of a man and woman at the altar getting married, and on the fourth he drew the result of blissful matrimony sanctioned by the Church and God: a baby being baptized.

Wally, Buzz and the other conspirator were insane with anticipation. Buzz's artwork was on the sixth page, and they couldn't wait for Sedlecki to flip over page five. Under their breaths they urged him to keep going. Instead, Sedlecki paused and walked around the front of the room, explaining more about marriage, and asking if anyone had questions. A few boys did and the conspirators silently berated them for delaying the biggest disturbance OLG would ever see.

"Father, what do two people do in marriage that makes them have a baby?" one kid asked, hoping for an explicit answer.

"They love each other, and they have intercourse," Sedlecki answered, his honesty destroying the trap the kid had tried to set.

Another kid asked, "So how did Mary get pregnant? Did she have intercourse?"

"Let's move on," Sedlecki said, refusing to answer the question.

More kids raised their hands with questions, and the three conspirators were ready to jump out of their chairs and scream at their classmates to stop asking questions. That wasn't necessary because Sedlecki returned to his easel and on page five wrote the dreaded phrase: "Self-abuse."

"Self-abuse is a sin, and it is to be avoided at all times," Sedlecki bellowed. "Who here has practiced self-abuse?"

Nearly every arm flew up to answer affirmatively, and one kid shouted from the back of the room, "Three times a day, Father! I'm practicing it until I get it right!" Sedlecki didn't quite know what to do with all those sinners and so he continued with the lesson.

There were only ten minutes left in the class, Sedlecki was still babbling on about the evils of self-abuse, and Wally, Buzz and the other kid were just plain bummed. Thirty minutes before, they were on the verge of their greatest triumph ever, and now all that potential glory was slipping away second by second and minute by minute. They watched the second-hand on the clock on the classroom's front wall slowly and inexorably tick away, and they wanted to shout to the priest to draw something else on the paper, but that would have given them away, and so they slumped in their seats resigned to defeat.

With eight minutes left a kid began to raise his hand to ask a question, but Wally and Buzz, who were sitting next to each other, instantly shot him with spitballs. When the kid turned around to confront his attackers, they silently but angrily motioned for him with their eyes, hands and facial expressions to shut up and keep his hand down.

Had Sedlecki seen the kid begin to raise his hand he would have called on him, which would have cost more precious time. But he didn't, and seeing no other hands raised, he looked at his wristwatch and said, "Well, time's about up. We've had a good lesson."

At that, the kids started talking to each other and laughing, as they always did when class was about to end. The conspirators were crushed and knew that God had conspired against them and wasn't going to answer their prayers. Their lives and their dreams of greatness and glory were over, at least for that day. The commotion and breakdown of discipline in the class worried Sedlecki and he moved to restore order. He looked at his watch again and proclaimed:

"We have a few precious minutes left, let's get to one more point. Now sit down, keep quiet and pay attention."

The talking and laughing stopped and the kids reluctantly stared at Sedlecki as he walked to the easel, turned to them and flipped the sheet of paper over without looking at it. There was an ever-so-brief moment of stunned silence and then a massive explosion of laughter, hoots, hollers and jeers. Buzz's artwork was revealed, and it was magnificent: a detailed and anatomically correct drawing of a naked Sedlecki screwing a naked Sister Mary Luciel, OLG's principal at the time. Sedlecki was on top of the nun and his head was turned to reveal a wicked and devilish smile, complete with a lit cigarette dangling from his lips.

Sedlecki was confused by the uproar and had no idea what the guys were laughing about. Then he turned to look at the drawing the eighth grader had done in pencil. His face instantly turned redder than red, and he stood stunned and speechless. That an eighth grader had drawn something so detailed, correct and good—such a damn good picture—was astounding to him. That he himself was the object and victim of that talent and ridicule was worse.

The nuns, priests and adults in the neighborhood never really knew or appreciated just how talented and smart some of their students and children were. They couldn't have because the educational system they used and put their kids in was rigid and didn't allow for talent and creativity to come out, and that was the sin of what they did. Before their very eyes, and in their classrooms and homes every day were budding artists, comedians, writers, architects, engineers and scientists, and they couldn't see all that talent waiting to bust out.

Yet the sin really wasn't a sin. The nuns and parents had the same mission: to ensure the kids learned to read, write, do arithmetic, be good Catholics and be prepared for the world as it was at the time: one of getting married, raising kids and working in factories. For that world, the nuns prepared the kids better than anyone else could or did.

While the system discouraged imagination, creativity and independence, it was there in the kids, and it found ways to show itself and develop. The price for discouraging that talent and creativity to flourish in an open and supportive setting was that it directed itself at the people who purposely, or unknowingly stifled it: the nuns and priests. Buzz's drawing was the proof.

THE PRIEST WAS EMBARRASSED

Sedlecki was embarrassed and angry, but he knew better than to make an issue of it and start demanding the name of the artist, which would have led to an outright insurrection, so he covered the offending piece of art by flipping sheets of paper back over it. Then he dismissed the class and took his easel and drawing pad to the rectory where he burned Buzz's masterpiece in the building's coal furnace.

CHAPTER 45

Slugs in Lenten Banks and the FBI

I T WAS LATE February, the days were getting warmer and the ice at
Koz was melting, a sad sight to the kids as their winter playground was
disappearing. Spring and summer were on their way, which was always
a good thing, but seeing another winter, and skating rink, pass—especially
the rink—hit the kids hard, much harder than watching summer slip into
fall and fall into winter. The rink was a friend that shouted for them to come
out and play no matter how cold, snowy or windy, and it was always thrilled
when they showed up. It always rewarded them with fun, and for those who
were just learning how to skate, a sense of accomplishment and confidence.
It was a friend that gave its all to the friendship because it seemed to know
that its time was very limited, and it wanted to wring all the joy out of that
time that it could.

Late February brought the beginning of another school ritual the kids
had to endure: Lenten banks to mark the beginning of the forty-day Lent
season where Jesus fasted in the desert and resisted Satan's temptations.
They were small metal cans with light blue labels and pictures of Christ, and
each kid got one with their names written on them, and each was expected
to fill their bank with money, preferably dimes, quarters and half-dollars,
and certainly not ever pennies. Where the money from all those banks was

supposed to go, or went, none of the kids knew, other than it had something to do with missionaries and pagans. They also knew it was their obligation to fill those banks with coins. As with the pagan baby coffee cans and their Sunday donation envelopes, failure to fill the banks with real money generated scorn, contempt and punishment from the nuns.

Kids didn't have their own money, except those who had paper routes, and their parents didn't have extra money either, so many of the kids shoved pennies down the slots of their banks, hoping that at least filling them up would win them some kind of credit and good will, and maybe a couple of hours off of their likely thousand years in Purgatory. The real fun for the more troublesome kids was to put slugs—blank, round pieces of metal that resembled coins—in their banks, a practice that infuriated the nuns. Slugs weren't readily available, but they could be found along railroad tracks, and sometimes in the alleys, and when found they were saved for the Lenten banks.

The Disturbers wanted to fill their banks entirely with slugs, but because they didn't have very many slugs that was impossible, and so they did the next best thing, which was to put pennies on railroad tracks and wait for trains to roar by and flatten them. They loaded their banks with deformed pennies, regular pennies, and some slugs, and when it came time for the banks to be collected and their contents counted just before Easter, the boys were in their usual trouble. All five of their banks contained nothing but slugs and deformed and regular pennies, and when the nuns, who counted the contents of all the school's Lenten banks in the convent after school was out, saw the blatant disobedience they were furious. Especially Vitaclaire, who supervised the money counting.

The way the nuns saw it, the Disturbers had conspired against God, missionaries, charity, goodness and pureness of heart, people in need, pagans, Holy Mother Church, and worst and most unforgiving of all, their authority. Their first instinct was to call the Disturbers' parents and berate them for having raised Godless and miserly kids, but they knew that wouldn't work because most of the parish's parents were lower-middle-class people who increasingly took offense to the fact that they were constantly being hit up by the nuns and priests for money they didn't have. Almost none of the parents—many of whom had three or four kids at OLG, and for whom having to fill that many Lenten banks was an impossibility—cared about Lenten banks being full, empty or filled with slugs. Some parents thought it was funny and clever that their kids filled the banks with pennies.

The nuns decided that their authority had to be maintained, and they figured that they would at least cause the Disturbers some emotional pain for failing to slavishly obey their orders. In other words, they would try to scare the living daylights out of the Disturbers the next day in class.

So, when the eight o'clock bell rang the next morning for the start of class, the nuns—Zita, Yvonne, DeLasalle and Vitaclaire—were already in room 204 and ready to destroy the Disturbers. Even while the bell to start the school day was still ringing, Vitaclaire, who stood cross-armed with the other nuns at the front of the room, snarled at the kids to get into their seats.

The kids had rarely seen such a concerted and preemptive action by the nuns, and most of them figured that something really terrible had happened, maybe someone smoking in the church, or failing to return public library books on time, or worse, turning in their Sunday donation envelopes empty.

Yvonne, who considered herself exceptionally clever and dramatic, went first.

"Can any of you tell me," she started in a calm, almost sweet voice that sounded like she was about to ask a reasonable and innocent question, "is it a ten-year, or is it a fifteen-year—no, I'm sorry. Is it a twenty-year, or is it a twenty-five-year prison sentence that one will receive for destroying and defacing the currency of the United States of America?"

Many kids gasped loudly at the question. They had heard about kids being sent to reform school, and crazy people to Dunning, the city's insane asylum, but never to prison, and never for twenty-five years. This was big and they were shocked and scared. When Vitaclaire spoke, their shock turned into terror.

"You don't have to answer the question," Vitaclaire said, "because agents from the Federal Bureau of Investigations are on their way here to answer it for you. And answer it they will!"

That was big stuff, and Yvonne cracked an ever-so-slight smile as she let the enormity of her and Vitaclaire's words sink in for a few moments. The FBI was coming to OLG to throw kids in prison for twenty-five years! She seemed even more pleased with herself when some of the good kids panicked and started crying and trembling. Then DeLasalle had her turn.

"Our Lady of Grace school will not tolerate hoodlums who break the laws of the United States of America, and it is our duty to turn the lawbreakers over to the federal authorities. You know who you are back there," DeLasalle said while pointing an index finger at Disturbers Row. "I suppose, Mister Ruchinski and Mister Kolba and the rest of you hoodlums—"

"They're communists, Sisters!" Zita stammered out. "Communists!"

DeLasalle continued: "Yes, Sister, they are communists, and they will pay for it. I suppose you hoodlums think it's funny to destroy United States currency and to fill your Lenten banks with pennies and slugs. Well, it's against the law to possess slugs, and you will burn in Hell for cheating our missionaries, and the pagans they are working to convert, out of the support they need and deserve. When you put pennies in your Lenten banks you mock Holy Mother Church and all her saints. Hell might be too good for you gangsters, but twenty-five years in prison won't be."

FEDERAL LENTEN BANK CRIME UNIT

The good kids settled down and regained their composure when they realized that once again it was the Disturbers that the nuns, and now, apparently, the FBI, were after. The Disturbers were a bit shocked and confused by the tactic. Never had the nuns threatened to send them away to federal prison for twenty-five years. The boys weren't scared because they knew that FBI agents weren't going to arrest seventh graders for smashing pennies on railroad tracks, that federal authorities didn't care if kids put pennies in Lenten banks, and that they didn't care about pagans being converted to Catholicism. They doubted that the nuns had actually called the FBI. They were confused because the nuns didn't seem interested in beating them, only in scaring them.

"Now, if those hoodlums back there pledge to bring their banks back tomorrow filled with dimes and quarters, we will call the FBI right now and tell them things have been settled," Vitaclaire said. "If not, may God have mercy on their blackened souls. We'll see how bold and disrespectful they are in the federal penitentiary. Now I want all five of you to walk immediately to the front of the room, apologize to your classmates and to God, promise that you will bring those banks back tomorrow filled with dimes and quarters, and confess that it was a sin to fill your Lenten banks with pennies and slugs."

The Disturbers knew extortion when they saw it, and they all stayed in their chairs, much to Vitaclaire's embarrassment. After a few moments the ever-defiant Bozeman raised his hand.

"Mister Bozeman," Vitaclaire snarled. "Are you ready to confess your mistake and sin, and apologize to your classmates?"

"No!" Rich shot back angrily.

"Then what is it, mister?"

"Ster, if I'm arrested, I want to go to Alcatraz. That's where they keep all the really dangerous criminals, and that's where I belong."

"Alcatraz, mister, closed in 1963. You are obviously flunking history. You will get your wish, though, what other federal prison would you like? And you will address me as 'Sister.'"

"Yes, Ster."

Rich's boldness snapped the other guys out of their confusion, and they collectively got back to their disturbing ways.

"Sters," Dennis shouted while still sitting in his chair, "Will the FBI arrest all the other kids who put pennies in their banks? I mean, that would be fair, wouldn't it?"

"You will stand up when addressing us, mister," Yvonne snapped.

"Yes, Ster," Dennis said as he arose from his chair. "Can we open all the banks to see who put pennies in them?"

"And why would you want to do that, mister? God can see what's in those banks. Are you challenging God?" Yvonne said in what she thought was supreme sarcasm and unassailable logic.

"Because!" Dennis replied while his partners laughed. "Because!"

"'Because' is not an answer!" Yvonne raged. "How many times have we told you that 'Because' is not an answer? You will not answer a question with the word 'Because.' Do you understand?"

Ruchinski was next. "Sters, why can't we answer a question with the word 'Because?'" he asked as he stood up from his chair.

Yvonne, the self-proclaimed expert grammarian, raged as she stammered out an answer: "Because—"

Before she could finish her thought, the Disturbers shouted in unison, "'Because' is not answer!"

The entire room howled—even Zita twitched a slight smile—and the nuns saw that their bluff had failed, and they prepared to charge Disturbers Row to start beating the boys with their customary fury.

"Sters," said Kurkowski as he waved his arms furiously, "why did the government make pennies if they can't be put into Lenten banks? Does the United States government know that pennies are illegal for Lenten banks?"

Then Kolba stood up and said he could explain why all the Disturbers' banks contained pennies and slugs.

"Speak, Mister Kolba," DeLasalle said as she started toward the back row with a wooden pointer in her hand.

"Well, Sters, we all filled our banks with quarters and half-dollars. I swear we did because I supervised it all. But either someone switched them out for pennies and slugs, which I don't think happened, or the money we put in the banks was transmorgified."

"What are you talking about?" DeLasalle demanded. "That is not a word! That is not in the dictionary!"

"Yes, Ster, it is a word. It's the Devil's work and it's kind of the opposite of transubstantiation, you know, where the host is changed into Christ's body. Satan used transmorgification to turn our money into pennies and slugs. He does it, Sters, in order to stop the missionaries from converting pagans. It's the Devil's work, Sters, and I'm scared. Maybe the Devil is in this classroom!"

With that, Kolba dropped to his knees on the classroom's floor, folded his hands as if in prayer, and said loudly, "We must all pray so that Satan doesn't transmorgify the rest of the money in all those banks into pennies."

The other Disturbers followed Kolba's lead and dropped to the floor as if in deep and solemn prayer. DeLasalle, Yvonne and Vitaclaire, realizing that they had once again been beaten, stomped out of the room. The FBI agents never showed up at OLG, and for the next week all the kids could talk about was how the nuns had tried to make a federal case out of kids stuffing Lenten banks with pennies.

CHAPTER 46

The L, Downtown and Shoplifting

L ATE MARCH AND early April brought the first signs of what all the kids were dying for and daydreaming about: warm weather and three glorious months of summer vacation.

Plans for summer vacation started after Christmas vacation and when the ice started melting at Koz. Dreaming about summer was one of the ways the kids got through the second half of the school year. Their plans and daydreams were about three months of total freedom: riding bikes and playing baseball and pinner at Koz, going downtown on the L and bus, riding bikes to the forest preserves and hunting rats and birds with BB guns, water fights in the alleys, blowing off fireworks on the Fourth of July, scouring vacant lots and exploring on the railroad tracks, and running and playing and laughing and roaming outside from morning until night with no adults around. Summer had no stench of the nuns' habits, no depressing, suffocating classrooms, no hated homework or penalties or science projects, and no glaring nuns to berate one for the slightest infraction of the rules, or for merely being a kid.

The first day of summer vacation in early June was the most anticipated day of the year, and when it came the feelings of joy and excitement from OLG's kids almost burst the walls and blew out the roof of the school buildings. There was still a bit of dread for that final, half-day of school. During the morning the kids got their final report cards and would learn if they had been promoted to the next grade or if they had flunked and had to repeat the grade over. On the bottom of the left side of the report card would be the decision: a hand-written note by the teacher saying either "Promoted to the (next) grade)," or one that said a kid had failed and needed to repeat the grade.

While it was a tense moment for the kids to learn whether they had been promoted, it really wasn't a secret. If a kid was to be "held back," as the adults and nuns put it, a kid's parents would have been informed long before that final day.

Once the kids learned around mid-morning that they had passed to the next grade, it was all happiness and talking and laughing until the noon bell rang and they were free for three months. When that bell rang the kids sprang from their seats and desks, raced out of the school and then sprinted home to change into their play clothes and begin the fun and games. No one wanted to waste a single minute of vacation and kids were into their play clothes and out their doors within minutes.

For Dennis and his brothers, and Masciola and John Klosk and the other kids who lived close to Koz Park, that was the first place they ran to after bolting out their doors. That first afternoon of playing baseball or pinner or football, or just running around, was pure joy and freedom.

For Wally Domrzalski and his pals, the summer meant days of sneaking into the L station at Logan Square, going downtown to shoplift yo-yos from the Walgreens store on State Street and spending endless hours playing on the escalators and elevators at the forty-one-story Prudential Building, then the tallest building in Chicago, or having escalator races at the Marshall Field's department store.

Wally and his pal Buzz were nine or ten when they started heading the six miles to downtown by themselves, either on their bicycles or on the L. Their grandest adventure came one Saturday when they were riding their bikes to downtown and were stopped by a cop.

"Where are you kids going?" the cop asked the two after he had gotten out of his squad car and approached them on the shoulder of the road.

"Downtown!" the boys gleefully shouted.

"No you're not," the cop told them.

"Yes we are," they replied.

"Not on this road you're not. You're gonna get killed."

The cop was right. The boys had managed to ride their bikes onto the Northwest Expressway, a massive, eighteen-mile-long, eight-to-ten-lane highway that cut through the city's Northwest Side to downtown. The cop directed the boys to the nearby Milwaukee Avenue, which at that point paralleled the expressway, and told them that that street would get them downtown. The cop stayed to ensure that the kids left the expressway, and Wally and Buzz took Milwaukee Avenue to their destination.

What a place downtown was for kids! Tall buildings, busy streets with huge amounts of traffic, pedestrians everywhere, giant department stores, candy and popcorn stores, book and dime stores with more comic books than a kid could dream of, the Walgreens on State Street and the Treasure Chest, a magic and toy store on Randolph Street.

The Walgreens and the Treasure Chest were favorite places for kids throughout the city to go and shoplift. For Wally, the Walgreens had one of his favorite toys: Duncan yo-yos.

Yo-yos are simple toys: two thick, grooved wooden or plastic disks held together by a center axle. A long string is wound around and attached to the axle. A kid could tie a slip knot on the free end of the string, put it around a middle finger and flip the toy downward out of a hand and make it rise and fall by unwinding and rewinding the string with upward and downward motions of a hand. There were all kinds of different models of yo-yos—Butterfly, Imperial and others, and every kid wanted every model to be able to do the various tricks with them: Walk the Dog, Around the World, the Cradle and others.

While parents were willing to put out the money to buy a kid one yo-yo, none had the resources to buy multiple models, and so at one point it seemed that no kid in the neighborhood had actually paid for a yo-yo; most of them were obtained through the "Five-Finger Discount" that the kids obtained for themselves at the downtown and neighborhood stores. Kids rarely paid for yo-yos because they were small and easy to steal—just stuff one in a pants pocket, or a couple down the front of the pants and run like hell out a store's front door.

Wally, while not exactly obsessed with yo-yos, wanted as many as he could get. He had a wooden Butterfly model that he had painted light blue with model car paint, and others that he had painted with various designs. In an apparent attempt to further his painting skills, he took his younger brother Steve and Jim Masciola downtown one summer Saturday morning to the Walgreens to steal yo-yos.

Steve was just out of fourth grade, Jim out of third grade, and Wally was three and five years older than his companions. They walked the mile to the Logan Square L station and, not wanting to pay for the subway ride downtown, decided to sneak into the station. There were a couple of ways to do that. One was to climb a seven-foot chain-link fence that surrounded the facility, and another was to wait for someone to come out of the six-foot-tall turnstiles that let people out of the place and squeeze their skinny bodies through and past the turnstile's metal bars. Sneaking through the turnstile was Wally's and Buzz's preferred way, and for the past several years the two hadn't paid a single fare at the Logan Square station.

Since it was a Saturday morning and there weren't many riders on the L, and thus no one to come out of the turnstiles, the three decided to climb the fence. It bordered an alley and was beyond the sight of the station's employees. It was easy enough for Wally as he was older, but for Steve and Masciola it was a difficult and dangerous climb. It was easy for them to get their fingers and tips of their shoes through the fence and climb to the top, but once at the top is where they had trouble. The challenge was how to get their bodies over the top horizontal metal pole of the fence and get their shoe tips and fingers into the links on the other side without falling to the ground. That was difficult because the twisted metal tips of the fence's links often protruded over the top horizontal pole, and if a kid tried to merely slide is body over the pole there was a good chance that his shirt and skin would get caught on those metal tips, and that would lead to ripped shirts and scratched and bloody chests and stomachs.

When Steve and Jim got to the top of the fence, Wally was already at the bottom on the other side yelling at them to hurry up lest they get caught. When eight-and-nine-year-old kids are seven feet in the air on a fence and trying to get over it without hurting themselves it's no time to yell at them to hurry up. They were scared, afraid of falling and afraid of getting caught. They gingerly maneuvered themselves over the top of the fence, secured toeholds on the opposite side and carefully climbed down.

They raced up the stairs to the train platform, and when the two-car train arrived and its doors opened they ran in, plopped themselves down on some seats, pressed their noses up against the windows and settled in for the ride. The L was an escape and adventure for city kids. Once they got on it they were mesmerized by the scenery as it wound on its steel and iron elevated structure through miles of the city's alleys and neighborhoods. They were at once awed and hypnotized by the clank and screeching of a train's steel wheels on the steel tracks, the screeching when the train rounded a curve, and the steady rhythm of the train as it slowed and stopped at a station and then sped up and then slowed again and stopped. Their eyes followed, and then looked back, as the train approached and then flew by the hundreds of small and large factories and the grimy two-flats and apartment buildings whose grey wooden back porches were the view of the city the L offered. As they stared out those train windows they were in a kind of trance. They didn't think about the people in those two-flats or apartments or factories, or what they did or who they were. Mostly their minds were blank and had not a thought about homework they should have done, or school, or the nuns, or problems at home, or anything. That was the beauty and the thrill of the escape that riding the L offered kids; they could spend hours riding the train, blanking out and thinking about nothing, all while seeing the city and having an adventure.

Steve and his pal Eddie Meister often spent entire Saturdays on the L riding the different lines from one end to the other and then back again, and then doing it all over after that. Downtown was their usual and eventual destination, but sometimes they'd forget to get off at the right stop, and sometimes they mistakenly got on lines they didn't really know which took them to the city's far South Side. When they made such a mistake, they never panicked. Instead, they chose to ride the train to the end of the line and then take it back in the opposite direction. When kids got home after a day of riding the L, and maybe doing some shoplifting downtown, their parents would ask what they had done all day, and the kids would answer with something like, "Not much. Just goofing around the alleys and the park and stuff." That answer was usually accepted, and unless kids were caught doing something illegal, stupid or dangerous, their parents never knew about it.

RIDING THE L

As the train rolled on and carried Wally, Steve and Masciola towards downtown, it came to the point that all kids loved and that broke their trances: the spot where the Logan Square line gradually descended into its subway tunnel that ran for several miles under the streets of Chicago and under the Chicago River. The train slowed as it descended, and the bright sunlight quickly turned into darkness that was broken by light bulbs in the tunnel. Shortly into the tunnel there was a curve, and the steel wheels of the train grinding against the steel tracks made the sound that the kids loved: a long, loud, sharp, tight and piercing screech that echoed off the tunnel's arched concrete walls. After the curve there was a straight section of track where the train picked up speed and the roar of the wind as the train rushed through thrilled the kids to no end.

About twenty minutes after they had boarded the train, the kids were at their destination, the Washington Street stop. They ran off the train, up the platform and up the stairs into the sunlight and magnificence of the heart of downtown Chicago. It was always beyond incredible when they walked up those stairs and onto the street because in that instant they were transported to a completely different world—from a neighborhood of two-flat brick and frame houses, small brick factories and tree-lined, narrow streets into a place of towering monsters; giant, massive steel and brick buildings that blocked the sun; wider streets, especially the magnificent State Street; more people and cars and buses and trucks and stores and offices than they had ever seen; more noise and the clamor of traffic and commerce than they had ever heard; and almost no trees or other vegetation. It was the ultimate concrete jungle and they reveled in its power, size and energy, and when they stepped onto the sidewalk and absorbed downtown's energy they felt like little supermen.

Those little supermen had a job to do, which was to steal yo-yos. With Wally in the lead, they headed to the scene of their soon-to-be crimes: the Walgreens store. There were preparations to be made before they could pull off this bold caper, and Wally knew exactly what they were. Once in the Walgreens they headed to the store's basement floor, which opened to a subway station under State Street and out the doors to a subway platform that had small lockers the public could use. The kids put a dime in one of the lockers, which allowed them to pull out the key, stuffed the key into one of Steve's pants pockets and headed back into the store to complete their mission.

They cased the store, looking for the yo-yos, and then bought some candy and comic books, which the cashier put into a paper bag. But instead of leaving the place they slowly circled back to the aisle that had the coveted yo-yos, and after lingering a while and pretending to be innocently looking for more stuff to buy, stuffed yo-yos into their pockets and hurried to the escalator which took them to the basement floor and the door to the subway station. Once out the door, they ran to the locker, and with a trembling hand, Steve tried to get the key into its lock, and he failed on the first and second tries—the pressure was immense. Wally yelled at him to hurry up, and on the third try he got the key in and opened the door. The kids stuffed four or five yo-yos into the locker, slammed the door shut and started walking back to the store to steal more stuff. But just then a male store employee who had spotted them stuffing the yo-yos into their pants appeared and demanded that they return the precious merchandise or he would call the police and their parents.

Steve and Masciola were terrified—what kid wouldn't be?—but not Wally. He had been shoplifting for several years and had become something of an expert at it, especially at denying things when caught and confronted. He had learned that an angry and aggressive denial, coupled with plausible and bombastic threats, no matter how contrary to the facts and evidence, could overpower the truth. He had also learned that even a kid, if he acted crazy enough, could bluff an adult.

Wally confronted the employee with a such a belligerent denial that the guy was momentarily stunned and thought he was battling a lawyer, not a thirteen-year-old kid.

"How dare you accuse my brother and his friend of stealing," Wally, glaring, said to the guy. "That's against the law, and we come from good families. If you think they stole something, then check their pockets. If you don't find anything, and you won't, my dad's lawyer is going to sue you and your company, and you'll be sorry for falsely accusing my brother and his friend of stealing. You're a slanderer!"

The employee recovered from Wally's verbal assault and insisted that the kids had stolen merchandise. Wally responded by shoving the paper bag that contained the candy they had bought, and the receipt for it, into the guy's hands while saying, "Look, we bought candy, and there's the receipt in the bag."

The guy saw that the candy had indeed been purchased, but he still insisted that the three had shoplifted. At that point, Wally, now pretending to be enraged, again threatened to have the guy sued. Then he turned to his two companions and said, "Steve, Jim, empty your pockets and show this man that he's a liar." Steve and Jim turned out their front pants pockets, which, of course contained no yo-yos, and they turned around to show there were no bulges in their back pockets. Wally then wagged an index finger at the guy and said, "If you ever accuse my brother and his friend of stealing again, my father's gonna sue you."

The guy was beaten, and he turned around and walked back to the store. The kids ran up the subway station stairs and roamed around downtown for a couple of hours. Then they went back to the locker, removed the yo-yos, put them in their pockets, got on the subway and took it back to Logan Square.

~

The massive Prudential Building was another destination for kids throughout the city. The forty-one-story glass and steel monster was completed in 1955 and basically defined the downtown area as it was the first skyscraper built in the city since the Great Depression and World War II. It was brand new, had a top-floor observation deck with escalators and, most importantly, automatic elevators that would zoom people from the first to the top floor in what seemed like mere seconds.

It was the building's fame as the city's tallest, and those automatic elevators, that attracted the kids. Many of downtown's older buildings had manually operated elevators that were run by men who manipulated a large dial-like wheel or lever that would start and stop the elevator car at the various floors. When someone got on a car they would tell the operator what floor they wanted, and the guy would stop it there and let them off. With a human being at the controls there was no way that kids could play in elevators and conduct their simple experiments into physics and gravity. Automatic elevators had no operator, so all one had to do was press the button of the floor they wanted, and the machine would whisk them to it.

Saturdays were the day for kids to head to the Prudential Building because the place was pretty much empty of its thousands of weekday workers, and they could ride its elevators and play for hours with no one caring or interrupting them or yelling at them to stop. Heading to the Prudential Building was an adventure that was planned a few days ahead of time with a discussion that went something like:

"Whadda we gonna do on Saturday?"

"I dunno. Got to the park and play baseball? Go to the tracks, uhh, look for junk in the alleys?"

The possibilities were endless. They could play guns and war, and cowboys and Indians, or Freeze Tag or It or Hide and Seek; climb garage roofs and apartment building walls; catch grasshoppers in vacant lots; blow up rolls of caps with baseball bats; burn ants and start fires with magnifying glasses; ride their bikes to who knows where; catch flies and ants and put them in spider webs; go to the movies; play baseball at the park; ride the L all day; have a pinner tournament; go swimming at Riis Park; hang out at a store and read comic books; make homemade slingshots and bows and arrows; light matches; blow up model cars with firecrackers; walk or take the bus to Wrigley Field and see a baseball game; and well, just anything.

At some point a kid would say, "Hey, we haven't been to the Prudential Building in a long time. Let's go there!" Then someone would answer, "Okay!" and the day was planned.

They'd spread the word, and by Saturday morning there'd be a group of six or seven kids heading off to the Logan Square L stop where they'd climb the fence to sneak in and take the train downtown. They'd get off downtown and head to the building where they'd bend their heads upward and gaze in awe at their destination, which announced itself with giant brownish-red letters at the very top of its 601-foot height for all to see: PRUDENTIAL.

Once inside, the kids wasted no time. They headed straight for the building's two express elevators, crammed themselves into a car, hit the button to the top floor and waited in great anticipation for the experiment they always did in that building and which never stopped being fun.

The elevator was fast, and when it neared the final floor, which the kids could see by the floor-button lights flicking on, they waited for the right moment, and when the car was about to stop, someone would shout "Now!" and they'd jump as high as they could. The idea was that when the car came to a stop they would see how close to the floor their feet would come. On the downward trip it was the opposite. As the fast-moving car neared the bottom and was about to stop, they'd shout and jump and see if their heads would hit the ceiling. It never occurred to them that had they been tall enough, or had they jumped high enough, their heads would have crashed through the car's roof and they probably would have broken their necks or otherwise been injured. After the car stopped and they fell to the floor they'd laugh and tell each other how close they had come to the ceiling, each one trying to claim bragging rights for having nearly crashed their heads through the car's roof.

The building's last two floors were linked by escalators, and the kids used them for races—running up and down the things to see who could climb or descend them the fastest. Then they'd go to the observation deck, and if they had money, a few would slide coins into the telescopes and try to find their neighborhood. One landmark they always found was Wrigley Field, the home of the Chicago Cubs, on the North Side.

A WAY TO MAKE MONEY

The Prudential Building was a source of income for some older kids, including Wally Domrzalski. One summer he wanted money of his own and didn't want his parents to know about it lest they confiscate it for family expenses, and so he bought a wooden shoe-shine box. Then on weekday summer mornings for a couple of weeks he'd head downtown on the L, park himself in front of the Prudential Building and make decent money—all cash—by shining shoes. No adults who saw him and other kids shining shoes or doing other things to make money thought it odd that ten-or-eleven-year-old kids were downtown by themselves and working to make a few bucks. It was normal.

After spending a few hours at the Prudential Building, Wally, Steve and Dennis and their pals usually headed to the Marshall Field's store on State Street where they also engaged in elevator races. But Field's, as it was known, was a stuffy, upscale place where energetic, adventure-seeking kids unaccompanied by adults weren't welcome, and so, after only a few elevator races, they were politely, but sternly asked to leave by store employees. That was no big deal because they had the rest of downtown's stores to wander in and out of. A couple of places sold cheap hot dogs, and they ate and wandered the streets, and by three in the afternoon they boarded the L and headed back home.

CHAPTER 47

The Great Water Fight

SUMMER, WITH ITS oppressive heat and humidity, brought the need for kids to cool off. Most homes at the time had no air conditioning, and the kids were always outside, anyway. It was universally understood that the way to cool off was with water. Koz Park had the eternal water fountains; kids would go there and squirt themselves from the fountains until they were drenched. There were some Park District swimming pools within a few miles, but there were always too many kids at those pools, and the lifeguards made sure that everyone behaved and didn't get too rowdy. While the pools were refreshing, they didn't offer the freedom and fun that the kids craved.

Water fights in the streets and alleys did. Groups of kids would fill up dozens of balloons with water from the faucets in their basements, along with squirt guns, and buckets and cans and sponges and rags, and anything else that could hold or absorb water, everything except glass jars. They'd put them into wagons and head to the alleys and streets and wage water fights against each other. The groups would face each other at a distance, each kid armed with a water balloon and squirt gun, their respective leaders would yell "Charge!" and they'd rush each other, flinging their balloons only when the distance was close enough, at four or five feet, to ensure a direct hit on the target.

After that initial coordinated rush of opposing lines, the battles descended into chaos and a free-for-all of kid-on-kid skirmishes. After tossing their balloons in that first mad charge, the kids would race back to their wagons, grab more balloons and cans of water and race back to the "front" to hunt down their foes. The goal was to get so close to an opponent to smash a balloon on his head or back or pour out a can directly onto his head. That, of course, meant leaving oneself open to getting hit and drenched. When a kid doused an opponent at close range, he'd pause to clench his fists, raise his arms in the air in triumph, shout, "Gotcha!" and then get drenched himself in return.

The battles were usually over in around ten minutes because the supply of balloons and buckets of water were used up. Once they were soaked the kids had no more need to get wet, at least for a couple of hours. The fights not only refreshed kids physically, but mentally as well because they were a safe outlet for aggression, just as playing guns and war was. There was nothing more satisfying than drenching a kid who just a couple of hours earlier had beaten you in a foot race or a game of pinner.

The greatest, grandest and most incredible water fight in the neighborhood's history had occurred a few years earlier one July day when the kids on Springfield and Harding faced down kids from the other end of the neighborhood on Lawndale and Monticello, five and six blocks away. It was orchestrated by Wally Domrzalski and his pals, and the Malcheks, a family of kids who used to live on Altgeld and Harding but who had moved to Lawndale, and their friends. Wally and his pals and the older Malcheks were just out of seventh grade, and the battle had been planned for a couple of weeks in order to settle some grudge that was known only to them.

For more than a week the kids on Springfield and Harding talked about and planned for the upcoming battle and dreamed and boasted about how they would pretty much drown the invaders when it came time to do battle. Both sides prepared by buying hundreds of balloons, filling them with water, tying them off and storing them in wagons. They also scrounged up dozens of buckets and pails and cans and plotted their strategies. The strategies weren't very complex: at the time and date set for the war, the Malcheks and their gang would invade the Springfield and Harding kids and the defenders would drown and humiliate them. The question for the Harding kids was where would the Malcheks attack? Would they come head-on straight down the alley between Springfield and Harding? Would they be sneaky and try to surprise and ambush their foes by taking a longer but more secretive route? Who knew, and that was all for later and the day of the war.

The Springfield and Harding kids had a couple of advantages in that they were on their own turf and could run into two basements and replenish their stocks of water and balloons. In other words, they had an unlimited supply of water. The Malcheks, though, had to carry all their water with them, and if they ran out—when they ran out—they'd be history. If the Malcheks did come down the alley, well, there would be kids with water buckets deployed on garage roofs and in back yards ready to race out and surround and drench them. The Springfield and Harding kids had another advantage. A few weeks earlier they had discovered in the overgrown yard of an abandoned house on Pulaski, right next to Charlie Fox's Shell gas station, hundreds of brass cans that held a couple of quarts of water each. They had no idea how the cans got there or what their true and intended use was, but they didn't care because they now had hundreds of cans which they could fill with water.

The day and night before the great battle was tense. Both sides finalized their strategies and recruited more warriors, and each side had at least a dozen kids ready and willing to fight. Wally Domrzalski was the leader of the Springfield and Harding kids, and, like a good general, he walked the alley and picked out a couple of flat garage roofs from which his troops could climb and dump water down on the invaders. He also had plans for what to do if the Malcheks took a different route; he wasn't going to be surprised. No, he assigned kids as scouts and sent them to different spots in the neighborhood so they could race back to the main army and report any sneaky and treacherous movements by the Malchek gang.

The next morning the kids in both armies were up and out early making final preparations: the Malcheks looking for extra wagons and buckets, and the Springfield and Harding kids rolling at least a dozen wagons filled with balloons, buckets and cans to strategic locations in the alley. The Harding kids had extra cans and buckets stored in nearby yards, but their biggest cache of ammo was in the wagons they had parked across the alley between two apartment buildings on Altgeld, and the dozens of cans they had set on the alley's concrete surface.

General Wally sent his scouts out and all waited nervously for their reports on the enemy's movements. The battle was set for ten in the morning, and now it was nine-thirty and still there was no sign of the Malcheks. Had they decided to detour and hit the kids from the rear? Who knew? The scouts were out there, and they just had to provide accurate intelligence. Finally, one scout who had been stationed two blocks away spotted the Malcheks crossing that street in the alley just south of Wrightwood. He raced back to the main army and reported to Wally.

"There's fifteen of 'em. Maybe twenty, I don't know," the kid breathlessly reported. It was clear from this report that the Malcheks were going to make a frontal attack straight down the alley. Wally ordered kids to signal—just shout—to the other scouts to come in as the battle was soon to commence. Based on the reported size of the Malchek gang, every man was going to be needed in this epic struggle.

The three other scouts came in and Wally sent kids onto two garage roofs where buckets, balloons and cans of water had been pre-positioned. He ordered others into yards where they could hide behind bushes and garbage cans and race out and ambush and surround the attackers once the full body of the advancing army had passed by. Everything was set. The Malcheks were going to march straight into a watery slaughter.

Then, at about five minutes to ten, one of the Springfield and Harding kids sent out a shout that gave them all goose bumps: "Here they come!"

The kids looked down the alley and saw the first units of the Malchek army turning the corner at the T in the alley. First there were a couple of kids pulling wagons, and then five or six, and then more, and then even more, some of them on bicycles! The scout had been right, there must have been fifteen or twenty of them! And each was pulling two wagons! This was indeed an army!

After a few moments the entire Malchek horde was in the alley along with their trains of ammo. They spotted the massed body of the Springfield and Harding kids and paused.

"They're scared! They won't dare come down here!" one of the Harding kids shouted.

"We're gonna drown 'em!" shouted another. And screamed a third: "They'll never make it out alive!"

The Malchek army wasn't scared. It had paused to regroup and to form its battle lines. The older and bigger kids, and those with the strongest arms—elite shock troops they considered themselves—were in front and armed with as many balloons as they could carry, and with two or three squirt guns each tucked into their pants. They even carried paper shopping bags that were filled with balloons. Behind them were the younger and weaker kids, some of whom were assigned to pull two ammo-laden wagons each, and they each had a shopping bag full of balloons.

With its battle lines formed, the Malchek army stayed put and sized up its opposition at the other end of the alley. That opposition was formidable, and while the Malchek kids knew it, they tried to convince themselves otherwise.

"The minute we start they're gonna run away and go crying to their moms," one kid said.

"Yeah," said another, "they're afraid of getting wet. Once we get through with 'em, they'll never get dry! Never!"

Then the invaders started slowly and deliberately down the alley, thinking that this confident show of what they thought was overwhelming force would be enough to scatter their opponents. To kids on both sides it was a grand spectacle, kind of like the massive and massed brigades of Civil War armies advancing shoulder-to-shoulder, line after line, flags flying, across open fields into the teeth of the enemy, both sides determined to annihilate each other.

When the Malchek army was half-way down the alley, and the two camps within shouting distance of each other, both sides let loose with what they thought were terribly offensive insults, things like, "Sissies!" and "Scaredy-cats!" and "Yellow-bellies!" And then came the threats, which flew wildly and uninterrupted from every mouth of every soldier on the field and which further infuriated all of them and hardened the determination of both sides to destroy each other.

The head of the invaders' line got to the Domrzalskis' yard, which was four doors and a little more than a hundred feet from where the Springfield and Harding kids had set up their battle line. They quickened their advance, and when they were about seventy feet from their opponents, they yelled "Charge!" and stormed, running in a single, massed wave toward their foes. When the entire army had passed the Domrzalski garage, three defenders sprang out from the yard, and three more from the yard on the other side of the alley to complete a pincer movement and surround the attackers. The six defenders had totally surprised the attackers and surged toward the rear of their lines, dousing whoever they could with buckets and cans of water.

The defenders had struck the first blow and the invaders were briefly stunned by the surprise maneuver. They took their causalities and surged forward. When they got to within fifty feet of their foes, the defenders sprung another surprise. Kids on garage roofs on both sides of the alley stood up and lobbed balloons and poured buckets and cans of water down on the attackers, who were now caught in a terrible crossfire.

Before they had even thrown a single balloon or fired a single squirt gun, at least half of the attackers had been hit. They could wait no longer, and, according to their battle plan, they halted, and every one of them lobbed a balloon in a massive and concentrated volley that scored direct hits on many of the defenders, who then fired back with their own massed fusillade of water balloons. After that, great shouts of "Charge!" and "Attack!" issued from every mouth and the two sides launched into each other and the battle turned into a frenzied, chaotic, man-on-man affair with kids smashing balloons and emptying cans on each other's heads, using their squirt guns to humiliate their opponents by shooting them in the face with weak streams of water that could fly a couple of feet at the most, and then racing back to their supply lines to get more ammo. Then they'd charge forth again to find another target, and that process was repeated again and again.

Both commanding generals had planned well and employed some of the younger kids to act as ammo runners who would race back to their respective supply lines in the rear and shuttle fresh balloons and cans and buckets to their front-line comrades.

The Malcheks had planned well, too, and knowing that their water supply would run out, they launched an attack on the defenders' line in an attempt to capture their water supply. It was a partial success; the attackers made off with several wagons full of balloons and buckets. This would have been a crippling blow to the defenders had they not planned for that very possibility. Several of the Springfield and Harding kids lived in one of the apartment buildings at the end of the alley where the battle raged. They had keys to the building's basement and laundry room, and they shuttled empty cans and buckets to the basement sinks, refilled them and hurried them back out to the battlefield.

The battle raged furiously, with the attackers capturing even more of the defenders' water wagons, and the advantage swinging back and forth with every can and balloon poured and smashed on an opponent's head and back. Just when it seemed that the attackers' furious charges and unrelenting aggression would carry the day, the battle turned. One of the Malchek brothers had knelt down to dip his squirt gun into a bucket of water to refill it when General Wally sneaked up from behind and dumped an entire bucket of water—two or three gallons—directly onto his head. The Springfield and Harding kids let out a deafening cheer and surged forth with renewed enthusiasm, vigor and determination and drove the attackers back. To add to the humiliation, two of the younger defenders—the ammo runners—also managed to douse the Malchek brother that General Wally had soaked from head to toe.

THE BATTLE RAGED·

The Malcheks tried to retreat, but the six defenders who initially attacked them from behind had regained their positions and continued to attack them. Then came the death blow. The defenders employed their two secret weapons: garden hoses attached to the faucets in the basement of the apartment building and in the Domrzalskis' back yard. At General Wally's signal—a simple screamed order to "Bring out the hoses!"—the kids dragged them out, turned them on and sprayed the helpless attackers from the front and the rear.

Shouts of "No fair! No fair!" immediately rose from the drenched and beaten attackers, and they were met with roars of "Is too fair! Is too fair!" and even stronger language from the Springfield and Harding kids. The defenders then demanded complete and unconditional surrender and said they'd turn off the hoses only when the Malcheks officially and loudly admitted that they had been beaten. The attackers, by now huddled together in a knot of soaking humanity in the middle of the alley by their wagons, loudly conceded defeat, and The Great Water Fight, which had lasted fifteen or twenty minutes, was over.

The hoses were turned off. The combatants, as they surveyed the giant puddles of water in the alley and the hundreds of pieces of broken balloons and dozens of empty cans and buckets, laughed themselves crazy over the carnage they imagined they had wrought. For the next twenty minutes they relived the battle with each other, saying things like, "And then, when you weren't looking, I got you right on the head with a balloon! It was a direct hit!" and, "Man, after I got you, I thought you were gonna float away," and, "I never seen anyone so wet in my life after I got you!"

The two sides vowed to have another water fight in a couple of days, and the soaked and beaten Malchek army slunk away back up the alley, pulling their empty wagons behind and leaving a lengthy trail of water on the concrete from their dripping clothes. There was only one benefit the Malchek army could glean from their defeat: they were so wet and clean that they wouldn't have to take baths for a couple of days.

After the invaders had left, the Springfield and Harding kids declared the battle a "slaughter," and for years afterwards The Great Water Fight was indeed remembered in the neighborhood as the most terrible and pitiless slaughter ever.

CHAPTER 48

Getting Out of Accordion Lessons

T HEY WERE THE words that every kid wants to hear from his older brother: "Let's go play catch in the alley after supper."

When Dennis heard those words from his brother Wally that summer Friday afternoon when he was in fourth grade and Wally in eighth grade, he was thrilled. They'd get their baseball mitts and a league ball from the basement, head out to the alley and play until they got bored.

Playing catch was always special. It didn't mean merely lobbing the ball gently into the air so it could easily be caught; it was great and exciting drama and theater. It meant kids pretending they were great pitchers with blazing fastballs or unbelievable curveballs that even the greatest hitters couldn't hit, or speedy outfielders making impossible catches and robbing hitters of home runs, or infielders easily handling the trickiest grounders. When they were pitchers they wound up and fired the ball as fast as they could at their pal. Those fastballs often hurt a kid's hand when caught, and in return, the catcher would hurl the ball back as hard as he could at his pal, and the game of throwing harder and harder at each other escalated until the pain in both kids' hands became unbearable.

Grounders were especially tricky because all the bumps and cracks and stones on an alley's concrete pavement sent the ball bouncing off in crazy directions, severely testing a kid's reflexes and fielding skills. When balls were thrown into the air, they were tossed as high as a kid could throw them, or thrown near garage roofs and walls so as to make them harder to catch.

During the games, kids often narrated the action as if they were sports announcers calling a real contest on TV or radio. They even let out roars of approval from the fans they imagined were breathlessly watching their every exploit and pitching or fielding gem. So many times during a game of catch a forty-or-fifty-foot length of an alley became a massive baseball stadium filled with thousands of adoring and cheering fans, and the two pals the greatest baseball players of all time.

After supper ended at five-forty-five that afternoon, Dennis got his mitt and went to the alley behind their house and waited for his brother. Wally got there a few minutes later, threw the hard league ball to his brother and told him to throw it back as hard as he could. Dennis caught the ball, wound up, and was set to fire the ball at this brother when he noticed that Wally didn't have his mitt.

"Hey, where's your mitt?" Dennis yelled at his brother. "You can't catch a league with your hands."

"I ain't got it. Just throw the ball, and throw it hard," Wally answered.

Dennis thought that was strange, but he did as was told and whipped the ball at his brother, who caught it with his bare hands. Wally fired the ball back to Dennis and again told him to throw it as hard as he could. Dennis obliged, and the game went on like that for a while. After having thrown a dozen pitches Dennis called out to his brother, "Hey, aren't your hands getting sore?"

"Not sore enough," Wally replied. "Throw it again, and this time harder."

Again, Dennis obliged, and after another dozen or so pitches Wally looked upset. "You're not throwing it hard enough," he said as he walked toward his brother. Dennis thought he had thrown blazing fastballs, and he saw Wally's hands as evidence of it; they were red and a little blue and were starting to swell up.

"What are you doing?" Dennis asked.

"I'm trying to break my hands," Wally replied. "C'mon, follow me."

Dennis followed as Wally walked to the red brick wall of the two-story apartment building that faced the alley. There, Wally tossed the ball into the air and began slamming it with his bare hands against the wall as if he was playing handball. Dennis was astonished and again asked Wally what he was doing.

"I'm trying to break my hands so I don't have to go to accordion practice," Wally replied. "Need to break 'em, or at least get 'em swelled up real bad. I ain't going to that lesson tonight. I hate accordion lessons."

Dennis always knew that Wally, who had been taking accordion lessons since first grade, disliked both the lessons and the instrument, but he had no idea until then just how deep and ferocious that dislike was. He watched in amazement as Wally continued to pound the baseball with his bare hands against the brick wall.

"Why don't you just hit your hands with a hammer, or a brick?" Dennis asked. "That'll probably break 'em, and it'll be a lot faster. I'll go get a hammer."

"Naah, gotta pretend that it's a real accident. The old man will kill me if he thinks I did this on purpose."

After fifteen minutes of abusing his hands, Wally deemed them to be sufficiently swollen and damaged to present them to their father and beg out of that night's accordion lesson. They were almost as red as a ripe tomato and swollen to at least twice their normal size.

It was an ugly scene when Wally went back into the house and showed his hands to his dad and said there was no way he could go to accordion practice. Their dad had forced Wally and Steve to take accordion lessons, and he had dreamed of his kids playing the Polish wedding circuit, banging out polkas on demand.

HE HATED ACCORDION LESONS

Wally and Steve hated the accordion, or squeezebox as it was called, and they dreaded the Friday night lessons at a music studio on Milwaukee Avenue with an instructor named Nick. Why, they wondered, did a kid have to take accordion lessons on Friday nights? They hated the hours they had to spend during the week practicing the bulky instrument when they should have been out playing. They also hated it that their dad would yell at them and exact punishment if they had a bad lesson or failed to practice.

What they hated most, though, was having to haul their accordions in the trunk of the family's 1962 blue Chevy Impala to relatives' houses at holidays, or when they went to their aunt's dairy farm in northwestern Wisconsin during the summers and basically give performances for the relatives and their neighbors. When the words, "Get out the squeezebox," came out of George's mouth the kids cringed and got sick. It was like they were trained animals being put on display for the benefit of everyone else but themselves, and it was total humiliation. When the kids played for those relatives, they were usually sick, nervous and resentful, and they usually didn't play well, and that made George mad and his anger at the kids made them even more resentful.

But having his kids play the accordion was one of George's dreams, and he put out scarce money for the lessons and the two accordions he bought for Wally and Steve, and he expected them to take his dream as seriously as he did. But they didn't. What was so horrible for the kids was that they couldn't quit because George wouldn't let them. No matter how desperately and how often they pleaded, and no matter how logical and passionate their arguments—like they should be doing homework instead of practicing the accordion—George refused to let them quit. They were going to become members of a polka band, play at Polish weddings and make money doing it. Even worse for Wally and Steve was that they had morning paper routes they had been forced into. The two wondered if they would ever have any freedom and be able to do anything on their own and have fun.

So, like other kids in the neighborhood who were forced to take music lessons they didn't want, Steve and Wally looked for ways to get out of them. They feigned illness, argued that their homework was more important and that the lessons were basically taking food out of the family's mouths because they cost so much. But no one in the neighborhood had ever tried to break their hands in order to avoid a music lesson.

At first, George insisted that Wally go to the lesson that night as scheduled, despite his massively swollen hands. He knew that his son had purposely injured himself, and he was furious about it. Wally refused to go. The two shouted and screamed at each other for a few minutes. George told his son that he was lucky to have the opportunity to play an instrument. It was an opportunity, George said, that he himself had never had. "Be grateful," he told his son.

Wally still refused, and in the end, won the battle because of sheer stubbornness. For the first time in years, he didn't attend a weekly accordion lesson. Within a few months he had quit the lessons altogether.

Word got around about Wally's triumph, and soon other kids who had been forced into music lessons by their parents were seeking his advice on how to get out of them. Wally gave the advice freely, and for about a month afterwards the music schools in the neighborhood had a big drop in business.

CHAPTER 49

BB Guns and Shooting Rats

THE CHICAGO TRANSIT Authority bus driver laughed to himself when the two boys climbed clumsily up the front steps of his green and yellow electric trolley bus that was headed north on Pulaski Road that summer Saturday afternoon. The boys tried to pretend like everything was normal as they plunked their twelve cents into the farebox, but there was nothing normal about two kids whose right legs were stiff and unable to bend at the knees and who were walking like they each had a full-length plaster cast on their legs.

As the boys gimped their way stiff-legged to the back of the bus, the driver asked, "Where you kids going?"

"Gompers Park!" they both shouted at once.

"You guys okay? Those limps look kind of bad. You haven't been hurt or anything, have you?" the driver asked.

"No. We banged them a little playing football," one of the kids replied nervously.

The driver laughed to himself again. During his years on that route he had often seen kids acting exactly like the two sixth graders who were now on his bus: nervous, evasive and excited. He knew exactly what the two—Steve Domrzalski and Eddie Meister—were up to. They had each stuffed a BB rifle down one of their pants legs and they were going to Gompers Park and the adjoining forest preserves about four miles away to shoot birds, rats, squirrels, mice, turtles, chipmunks and whatever else they could find along the North Branch of the Chicago River. They were going to have an afternoon of fun.

THE DRIVER WASN'T FOOLED

As Steve and his pal spread themselves across the bus's back seat so they could stretch out their right legs, they figured that the bus driver had believed their story and that they had gotten away with sneaking BB rifles onto a city bus. Actually, it was more than rifles. They each also had an air pistol stuffed into their pants—Steve a pellet gun revolver, and Meister a BB gun—along with boxes of BBs and pellets in their pockets.

The two had been on this adventure a few times before, starting in fifth grade when Meister's dad had bought Ed a BB rifle. The kids saved money from paper routes and soda bottle deposits, and with Mr. Meister's help (he took them to the sports store and pretended to be both boys' father), bought more weapons. Sometimes they stuffed their pistols into their pants and rode their bikes the four miles to the park and forest preserves, hiding the bikes in clumps of bushes before returning hours later to ride them back home. But today they wanted to use rifles, and they couldn't ride bikes on city streets with those slung over their shoulders.

Because there was nowhere to shoot BB guns in the neighborhood, or at regular city parks, they had to go to Gompers to shoot. The parks, with their baseball fields, playgrounds and basketball and tennis courts were too open and too crowded. If adults saw kids with guns, they were sure to call the cops or the kids' parents. Kids could shoot at birds in their back yards or in the alleys, but if they did, they usually wound up accidentally shooting a window of a garage, house or apartment, and that brought on a bunch of trouble. A lot of kids bought their guns in secret. Steve had ordered one of his through the mail and had it delivered to Meister's house. Few ever told their parents. If kids whose parents didn't know they had guns were caught, they'd get a huge beating and the guns would be confiscated, busted up and thrown in the garbage. They could shoot along the railroad tracks, but that was iffy because, while there were some trees and other vegetation along the embankments that concealed them, the tracks ran through residential neighborhoods, and some fun-hating adults were bound to see and report them.

So the best place for neighborhood kids to shoot without being seen, harassed and yelled at was the forty-two-acre Gompers Park and the adjoining forest preserve, LaBagh Woods, a giant patch of oak, maple and cottonwood forest that straddled the North Branch of the Chicago River on the city's far northwest side.

After they got off the bus at Foster Avenue, about three and a half miles from the neighborhood, Steve and Meister had to walk stiff-legged another mile through the park until they got to the shelter of the woods, where they could finally pull the rifles out. They ran to the bank of the river, which was really a slow-moving, muddy, shallow, junk-strewn stream, and in the euphoria of their freedom, and concealment from adult eyes, began shooting at just about everything: logs, rocks, cans, pieces of discarded furniture, trees, bushes, chunks of concrete, and the river's muddy banks. It was all joy as they imagined their targets to be enemy soldiers, Indians, robbers, foreign spies, kidnappers, murderers, gangsters, wolves, bears, elephants, eagles, kids they didn't like and stingy, grouchy old people who never gave out candy on Halloween.

After the initial excitement of being outside in a forest, and of having killed thousands of enemies, spies and grouchy old people wore off, the boys got to work doing what they had come for, which was to shoot any creature that moved, especially rats. Getting birds was easy as they were everywhere. The two didn't waste precious ammo on sparrows; they went after robins and pigeons and whatever else was larger than a sparrow. They'd spot a bird in a tree or on a rock, level and aim their pump-action rifles, and pull the triggers. Sometimes the birds fell over dead, but mostly they flew away because the kids had missed. Squirrels were tougher to hit because they were so agile and darted around so quickly. Because the rifles weren't very powerful, it seemed that when the BBs did hit, especially at long distances, they'd merely annoy the squirrels, which would then run away.

For the rats, though, the boys had more powerful weapons—pistols powered by CO_2 cartridges—which could easily kill the large and hated rodents. Rats were what they wanted. Rats were everywhere in the city because the kids always saw "Rat Poison" signs stapled by city crews to telephone poles in the alleys. But they rarely saw a rat in the alleys, so, spurred on by older guys who said there were rats as large as dogs at Gompers Park and LaBagh Woods, they went to the woods to hunt them.

The boys didn't consider that rats as large as dogs would be incredibly dangerous to sixth graders, or anyone else, and that if there were rats that big it would have been stupid for them to chase and hunt them. But instead of being cautious they were fascinated, excited and determined. If a dog-sized rat suddenly turned and attacked them, well, that would be an incredible adventure and something they could brag about for a long, long time.

Steve and Meister slung their rifles over their shoulders, pulled out their pistols and dared the giant rats to come and get them. The area along the river in LaBagh Woods was a target-rich environment. Huge turtles, some maybe twenty or thirty pounds, lumbered and plodded along the river's muddy banks. Squirrels were everywhere, and so were chipmunks, rabbits and ducks. The boys, feeling like they were on a safari, shot at all of them.

Even though they are nocturnal creatures, some rats were out during the days, scurrying around the river's banks and up and down rocks. As dusk approached, more rats came out and the kids blasted at them with their pistols, scoring many a hit.

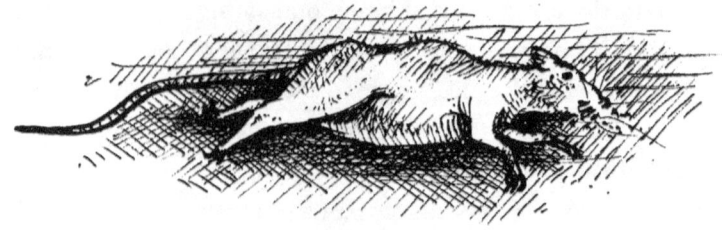

NO ONE LIKES A RAT

It was getting late that evening, around seven or eight, as Steve and Meister were stalking rats coming out of their holes along the riverbank. The boys crouched behind a clump of bushes and Steve whispered to Meister that he saw a big rat about twenty feet ahead. The boys raised their guns, aimed and were about to fire when Steve suddenly felt a sharp jab in his side and heard a man's voice shouting, "Drop it! Drop it!"

He immediately flung his gun "about a mile," he later said, trembling with fear. Meister was also ordered to drop his gun, and like Steve, he threw it as far as he could.

"Chicago Police," the voice shouted. "What are you guys doing?"

"Shooting rats. Those are BB guns," Steve said weakly.

The cop, who had sneaked up on the kids, withdrew his very real pistol out of Steve's side, backed up and shook his head in amazement.

"How old are you kids?" he asked.

"Eleven," they answered at once.

"Are you kids crazy?" the cop exclaimed. "You could have gotten yourselves killed."

The officer then went and picked up Steve's gun, which had been the real problem. It looked, not like a pellet gun, but like a real .38 caliber revolver. The cop, who had gotten a complaint of kids in the woods with guns, had thought they had real firearms.

After asking the boys where they lived, the cop asked how they had gotten there.

"The bus," Steve said.

The cop shook his head again, this time in frustration and disbelief. "You brought these rifles on the bus? Why?"

"We couldn't bring them on our bikes," Meister replied. "That would've gotten us in trouble."

After learning how the kids had sneaked the rifles onto the bus, the cop gave up. He kind of admired the kids, and they weren't causing any real trouble. "Here's the situation," he told the boys. "I'm not going to call your parents, but I want you two out of here now and to go home immediately. I don't ever want to see you here again. Do you understand that?"

They said they understood, put the rifles down their pants legs, put their pistols in their pants waists and walked like cripples for a mile to the bus stop. On the twenty-minute ride home they realized that they'd had a huge adventure and were really lucky that the cop didn't turn them in.

As they split up at the alley to get to their homes, Steve asked Meister what he wanted to do the next day.

"Let's go to Gompers and shoot rats!" he said.

They both laughed and ran home.

CHAPTER 50

Walking Everywhere

STEVE AND MEISTER didn't go back to Gompers Park the next day, or for the next couple of weeks; they found other things to do.

A day after their rat-shooting adventure, they and a group of neighborhood kids walked the five miles to Wrigley Field to see a Cubs game. The following day it was a three-mile trek to Riis Park to go swimming, and the day after that one they hiked three miles to Riverview, the city's great amusement park.

They walked because they wanted to save what precious little money they had. None of the kids got allowances from their parents, but most earned small amounts of cash by returning soda bottles for their two-cent deposits, mowing lawns with push mowers for fifty cents, delivering newspapers and whatever work they could get. They spent their precious money on candy, chips, soda and other stuff. Spending it on bus fares was a waste. Besides, their hikes were always an adventure, never boring or tiring, and often more fun than the destination itself. Wherever they went they wandered and explored. They never planned a route and always headed off in the general direction of their destination. They made their way up busy streets, side streets and alleys. If they stumbled upon a park, they took time out to play, drink from the water fountains and goof around. They stopped in candy stores, climbed trees and building walls, hopped fences and cut through yards and gangways. Sometimes in alleys they tipped over garbage cans. They were always tempted to steal clothes that were drying on clotheslines in back yards, but they never did, figuring they'd look suspicious carrying around partially dried sheets, towels and underwear. They held footraces between themselves, and jumping contests to see who could leap farthest on a sidewalk from a running start; played pinner when they found suitable spots; wrestled on front lawns; played catch; played war by ducking behind bushes, trees and front porches before charging, guns blazing, toward a tree or porch that represented an enemy stronghold; told each other wild stories and dumb jokes; bragged about anything and everything; and generally had so much fun that they had no concept of how far they had walked or how long the trip had taken. And they didn't care.

Cubs games started at one-thirty in the afternoon, so the kids would leave the neighborhood by nine in the morning so they could get to the park by noon. They'd gather the sandwiches their mothers had made and wrapped in wax paper and stuffed into brown paper lunch bags and head off in search of adventure and fun.

The experience at Wrigley Field when the kids walked up the steps from the stadium's concourse to get to the field and the grandstands after plopping down a dollar for their tickets never changed. It was beyond magic and beyond joy. When they got to that last step and the field spread out before them, they were blasted by the most intense color of green they had ever seen. The infield and outfield grass was green, the ivy on the outfield walls was green, and, as Sister Zita might have said, it was greener than green and even greener than that! Not only was it green, but it was open, and because it was close to Lake Michigan, cool when the rest of the city was sweltering. All that green and open space was the most wonderful and beautiful contrast to the crowded, grimy, smelly, smoky, noisy asphalt and concrete city. It made them feel free and excited.

The Cubs weren't a very good team. In fact, they stunk. That was good because the team never drew anything near sell-out crowds. Ticket prices were extremely affordable: $3.50 for box seats, $1.50 for adult grandstand seats, and a buck for kids. More than twenty-thousand unreserved grandstand and bleacher seats went on sale the day of every home game. That meant that anyone could show up at the park and get in as long as tickets were available, which was pretty much always.

That the Cubs stunk didn't prevent several thousand people from showing up at the ballpark on those summer days. They came to bask in the warm sunshine, fresh air and enjoy a few hours off work at the factory, office or home. It was those thousands of people, all talking and shouting and screaming and laughing and arguing and eating and drinking, combined with the aroma of the food—hot dogs, hamburgers, sausages, pizza and peanuts—all mingled with the wonderful aroma of cigar and cigarette smoke that made going to the ballpark such a treat, joy and adventure. It was a giant outdoor party, and everyone seemed happy to be there, no matter whether the team won or lost.

The players liked the kids as much as the kids admired them. During batting practice when the kids raced down the box seat area to the Cubs dugout, stretched themselves out over its roof and shouted and wildly waved their programs and scorecards for the players to autograph, the players always smiled and took the time to sign them. They were patient and answered the same questions from the kids day after day. Questions like:

"Hey, Ernie, you gonna hit one out today?" or, "Is the wind blowing out today?" or, "You gonna steal home today?"

After getting autographs, the kids would roam the stadium, which to them was a vast, magnificent, beautiful, almost palatial place where they could roam and hide and get lost and daydream about being big-league players making stunning and unbelievable plays and earning the hysterical and adoring cheers of the crowd.

But the place wasn't really that big. It held about forty thousand people, although there were never anywhere that many in attendance. If the upper deck was closed, which it was on most weekdays, that left less room to roam. The concourse below the grandstands was wide and open, with almost no place to hide or get lost in. That never stopped the kids from being in awe of the place and imagining that they were in a massive palace that was built by and for the gods.

The best part about Wrigley Field was the food and how affordable it was. If a kid left home with three bucks and walked to the park, he feasted. Hot dogs were thirty cents; sodas, fifteen cents; Oscar Mayer smokie links, thirty-five cents; peanuts, fifteen cents; hamburgers, forty-five cents. A kid with three bucks could spend a dollar on the admission ticket, buy three hot dogs, a soda, a frosty malt (twenty-five cents) and have fifty-five cents left over.

Subtract seventeen cents for the bus ride home, and a kid still had thirty-eight cents in his pocket, enough for several candy bars and a bag of chips.

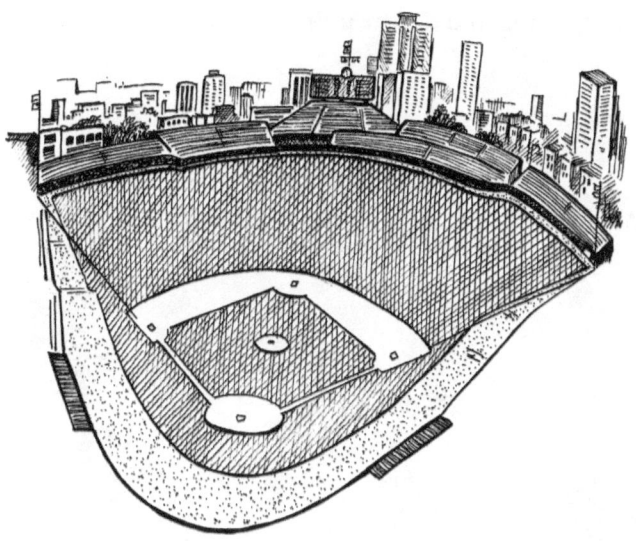

THEY WALKED TO WRIGLEY FIELD·

The kids kept still enough in their seats to always catch a few innings of a game, and while they kept track of the score, they didn't care who won. It was just too much fun to be outside and at the park. While some kids thought that catching a foul ball was the greatest thing anyone could ever accomplish at a ballpark, the OLG kids could care less if they snagged one. They certainly never brought their mitts to the park because that was something well-behaved kids did when they came to Wrigley with their fathers. Mitts at a ballpark, the kids thought, were for, well, sissies. If you were going to try to catch a league ball at a major league baseball game, you should do it with your bare hands.

The kids hardly ever stayed till the end of a game. After walking and running and playing all morning, and roaming the park for a couple of hours, they were exhausted, or as they would say, "pooped." They'd leave in the seventh inning or so and hop on a bus because they weren't going to walk five miles home. They'd get back to the neighborhood by suppertime, which for most of them was five or five-thirty in the afternoon.

No matter what their moms put on their plates for supper, the kids gobbled it down as if it was the most delicious thing ever served because that's how hungry they were after eight to nine hours of goofing around and playing and running and exploring and daydreaming and having fun.

CHAPTER 51

The Fourth of July

A FTER THE LAST day of school, the greatest, most magnificent and most looked-forward-to day of summer was the Fourth of July, a day when it seemed that every rule ever written could be broken without consequence, a day when kids and adults mingled and celebrated as equals, and a day when anyone who wanted to was free to experience the ultimate and absolute peak of human joy and existence: the thrill of blowing stuff up.

There was no more joyous, fun and free day than the Fourth. The anticipation started weeks, even months, in advance, and it started with the few kids in every neighborhood who knew how and where to get fireworks, and got them. And not just wussy things like sparklers and punks and tiny firecrackers that made hardly any noise. No, they got real and dangerous explosives: cherry bombs, M-80s, silver salutes, aerial bombs, firecrackers that could destroy stuff, bottle rockets, Roman candles, and all kinds of other things that made huge and glorious amounts of noise and that they weren't supposed to have. They obtained massive quantities of them that the other kids could buy from them: grosses of silver salutes and M-80s, countless bricks of firecrackers and boxes and bags of other stuff.

THE THRILL OF BLOWING STUFF UP

For the kids around Springfield and Harding it was Steve Domrzalski and Eddie Meister who had the connections to get real fireworks, and the other kids viewed their ability to procure explosives with awe. It was a mystery as to who their suppliers were, and that made their ability to get the stuff something special.

Every summer, though, it was a question of whether the guys would be able to get fireworks The people who sold them changed every year, so new suppliers had to be found. They always were found, and there was never any shortage of things to blow up or stuff to blow them up with.

The Fourth of the summer before had been one of the greatest the kids had ever had in terms of fireworks. It had begun a few weeks before the big day when Steve and Meister stopped their bikes near the alley on Altgeld between Harding and Springfield to show off some of the goods they had already bought. Out of brown paper shopping bags that hung on the handlebars of their twenty-inch Stingray bikes they gently, as if they were incredibly precious and fragile items, pulled out a couple of bricks of crackers and two white boxes, one with a gross of M-80s and the other with a gross of cherry bombs.

The other kids were nearly insane with excitement, wonder, awe and envy. A brick of crackers contained forty packs of fifty crackers, for a total of two thousand. A gross of M-80s was a dozen dozen or one hundred and twenty-four pieces. They had never seen so many fireworks, especially the powerful M-80s and cherry bombs. The kids nearly fainted when they listened as Steve and Meister said, almost in unison:

"We got a lot more stashed away. We're gonna get a lot more before the Fourth."

They were going to be able to blow up the entire city!

There was stuff that kids who didn't have suppliers, or the nerve to find any, could buy and stockpile. Boxes of rolls of red caps could be purchased or stolen from the dime store on Fullerton. So could blue-tip, strike-anywhere stick matches, and so could bags of cracker balls, the small, round paper balls that exploded when thrown onto the ground. So could things called snakes, which were black, charcoal-like pellets that burned and expanded into long, puffy strings of ash.

Kids also collected anything they thought could be blown up and destroyed: empty coffee cans; model planes, cars and ships they no longer wanted; stuffed animals; dolls; cardboard boxes; old books; rusty pails; old leather school bags; plastic pencil cases; worn-out shoes; telephone books; and, well, anything.

By the time the Fourth had come around Steve and Meister had bought enough fireworks to sell the kids in the neighborhood whatever they wanted, and they sold it at a nice profit for themselves. On the morning of the Fourth the kids gobbled down their breakfasts, got the stashes of fireworks that they had carefully hidden—usually in the basement or attic—so their parents wouldn't find them, and walked and ran with their paper shopping bags full of explosives, matches and things to destroy to the alley by Altgeld. There were eight of them, including Steve and Meister and Dennis and Masciola. Although it was only nine in the morning, they were excited and ready to start blowing stuff up and making noise.

They talked and compared their bags of explosives to each other's and tried to claim the biggest supply for themselves, but that title always went to Steve and Meister. Then they tried to make a plan, but that was useless because when roaming the alleys and streets on the Fourth with the intention of destroying things, there was no such thing as a plan, only opportunities that presented themselves at random. But they had to start somewhere, and Masciola got things going.

"Let's get Don't-Make-it-the-Noise's garbage cans, or maybe his doorbell or mailbox," Masciola proposed. Without even acknowledging the idea, the guys instantly turned and headed down the alley to Don't-Make-it-the-Noise's garage where his fifty-five-gallon-drum, city-supplied garbage cans were in the back yard by the alley fence. One of the guys lifted the metal lid off the can while another got out a silver salute and lit it with a stick match. When it seemed that the light had taken to the waxed green wick, the kid tossed the salute into the garbage can, the other kid plopped the metal lid back on and they all ran like hell. Then, KABOOM! The thing had gone off and had probably started a small fire in the garbage can and Don't-Make-it-the-Noise was sure to come out and threaten to call the cops on everyone.

The guys stopped in another alley and laughed like crazy knowing that they had made Don't-Make-it-the-Noise crazy. Steve got out a coffee can and a cherry bomb, put the can over the explosive in the middle of the alley and lit the wick. The kids ran and hid behind garbage cans and telephone poles, and when the thing exploded it sent the can so forcefully straight up that it lodged in a telephone wire! That, thought the kids, was damn good destruction. They figured they had disrupted phone service in the entire neighborhood and were proud of their accomplishment.

Next, they saw an old concrete garbage container, the kind of which had been built by the thousands in the early part of the twentieth century. They were about four feet tall, square with hinged metal lids on the tops that people lifted and tossed trash into. They had hinged metal lids on the bottom of the front sides that faced the alley, and when the garbage men flipped those lids back they were able to shovel garbage out of the containers and into their garbage trucks. Those containers were sort of indestructible, except when smashed with a sledgehammer, but it was always fun to try to damage them. For the concrete garbage containers, nothing but an M-80 would do.

The M-80 was sacred to the kids; it was the most powerful firework they could get, was truly dangerous, and to have even a couple of them was a sign that you were somebody. No one knew exactly how much gun powder an M-80 contained, but kids, always eager to exaggerate and believe what bigger guys said, told each other that it was the equivalent of an eighth to a quarter-stick of dynamite. The things looked menacing. They were red cardboard tubes an inch-and-a half-long and about a half-inch in diameter with a green, waxed wick coming out the middle of the tube. The wick was an inch-and-a-half-long, and when the thing was lit there wasn't much time to get away.

THE GREATEST FIREWORK EVER.

The guys lifted the lid to the garbage container, tossed in two M-80s and backed away slowly, knowing that they didn't have to run because the concrete walls of the garbage can would contain the blasts. When the M-80s exploded, the metal lid on top of the container blew back violently and the kids figured that three M-80s just might rip the lid off. They tried that, and the same thing happened. The lid blew back but wasn't ripped loose.

Next, they went to the house of a guy who a couple of years earlier had refused to pay them after he had agreed to a deal for them to shovel snow from his sidewalks. They had gotten a truly sweet revenge that cold winter day, and they had gotten it in a big way by shoveling the snow back onto the cheapskate's sidewalks. In fact, they put a lot more snow onto the sidewalks than they had taken off. The guys were still angry at the cheat, so they put a cherry bomb in the mailbox that was screwed into the front wall of his house, ran down the front steps and down the sidewalks and figured that when the bomb exploded the mailbox had been ripped from the wall.

Every guy had a model car or plane he no longer wanted, and so they went to an alley, put some regular firecrackers in the cars, lit the fuses and ran for cover. The plastic models were blown apart and the kids marveled at the destruction and at how many tiny bits the models had been blown into.

A thick Chicago phone book was next—laid open on top of a cherry bomb. The spine was ruptured and the alley was littered with thousands of pieces of confetti from the blown-apart pages. Then came one of the simplest but most satisfying efforts at making noise. The guys got out rolls of caps—long, thin red rolls of paper with dots of gunpowder or some other explosive on them that were put into toy guns—laid them on the concrete and then pounded them with baseball bats they had brought along. The noise from a single roll of caps exploding at once was simply spectacular. When two or three rolls went off at once, or in rapid succession, it was incredible, and the kids cheerfully claimed afterwards that the explosions had left them partially deaf.

Open apartment building and house windows, which were everywhere in hot, muggy July, presented the guys with targets for their bottle rockets. One guy would put a rocket in an empty glass soda bottle, aim it the best he could at an open window, usually across the street, another guy would light the wick and they'd both laugh as the rocket squiggled off toward its target. Almost none of the dozens of rockets they fired at windows ever made it in, but a few did, and when that happened the guys ran like hell, laughing all the time.

They walked to Koz Park where Steve reached into his shopping bag and pulled out their masterpiece: a homemade bomb that was as long as three M-80s and an inch in diameter. He, Dennis and Masciola had spent the previous night in their basement cutting open cherry bombs and silver salutes and emptying the explosive powder onto a work bench. When they had accumulated enough powder, they filled a long, thick and sturdy cardboard tube with it, packed it down and sealed the ends of the tube with wax. They then drilled a small hole in the top of the tube, inserted a long, waxed wick and sealed it with wax. The guys had no idea whether their homemade bomb would work, but they did consider the operation a major success because nothing had blown up while they were making it.

Steve taped the monster explosive to the wooden backstop of the green chain-link batting cage at one of the baseball diamonds and lit the fuse. The guys ran as fast as they could. Then, good god! The loudest, most terrifying explosion they had ever heard knocked them to the ground. They were dizzy, their ears were ringing, their vision was blurred, their heads were spinning and the world looked yellow. They were at once excited and scared. They had basically made a stick of dynamite and blown it up in a city park! That, they figured, could get them into big trouble. As they wobbled slowly to their feet the guys saw kids and adults streaming out of the park house and people coming out of their houses on the streets that bordered the park, apparently to see what had happened.

"I guess it worked," Steve said softly to the others.

"Man, that was boss," Masciola added. "We should make more of 'em."

THEIR HOMEMADE BOMB WORKED.

The guys were dying to see what damage their bomb had caused, but they didn't dare look right then because it seemed that half the neighborhood was out looking toward the park and trying to see what had happened. So the guys stumbled around the park a couple of times, trying to regain their balance and eyesight. When the commotion had died down and everyone was back inside, they headed to the batting cage. They had indeed made a real and powerful bomb! A big chunk of the wooden backstop was blown out and splintered, and several sections of the chain-link fence were twisted and bent and cut. They had caused real damage!

The guys worried that they would be blamed for the damage, but they calmed down after realizing that the evidence of their hard work—the bomb—was gone, exploded! No one could pin anything on them!

They headed to OLG and the church steps where they threw a few cherry bombs into the street close to the curb. One of the explosives rolled underneath a parked car. The guys didn't run because they figured the cherry bomb would blow up the car's gas tank, that they'd never be able to outrun such an explosion and that they were as good as dead. They waited, hoping their deaths wouldn't be too painful. Then the cherry bomb exploded, and nothing happened. The gas tank didn't explode, and the car didn't catch fire. The guys were relieved, but they ran like hell.

Shoes, schoolbags, toys, plastic and metal pails, more coffee cans, cardboard boxes and anything else the guys could find were blown apart that morning and afternoon as they roamed the neighborhood. One of the craziest things occurred when they saw a kid from another block in his back yard. The kid had strict, fun-hating parents who kept him sheltered and isolated and who had ordered him to stay in his yard by himself that day, which was pure cruelty and child abuse. He too wanted to blow stuff up, and when the guys came to his alley gate the kid showed them a model car and asked if he could buy a cherry bomb or two from them. They tried to explain that a cherry bomb was too powerful to be wasted on a model car, but the kid persisted and the guys, feeling bad for him, gave him three cherry bombs for free.

They hung around the alley behind his garage for a while to see whether the kid would escape his prison for at least a few minutes and get into the ally and blow up his car. They were about to move on, figuring the kid had wimped out, when they heard an enormous blast and the sound of shattering glass coming from the kid's garage. Then they saw smoke coming out of the broken windows. The kid had blown up his model car with a cherry bomb inside his closed garage and had blown out the windows! The guys didn't stick around to see what had happened to the kid. If he died or was maimed, they didn't want to catch the blame.

They met up with kids from other blocks and had a couple of firecracker fights, throwing lit crackers at each other. They lit four or five packs of firecrackers at once and pretended they were being shot at by enemy machine gunners, lobbed cherry bombs and silver salutes into vacant lots as if throwing hand grenades into enemy foxholes, and destroyed as much as they could and made as much noise as they could.

No one really cared about the noise because that's what was supposed to happen on the Fourth. Some adults complained, and those whose mailboxes were destroyed or whose windows got a bottle rocket weren't happy, but most remembered what they had done on the Fourth when they were kids, and what they were going to do that evening with their own fireworks. They approved of the mostly harmless destruction and the glorious racket.

How glorious that racket truly was. What began in the morning as scattered explosions as kids blew off their stuff built steadily throughout the afternoon and evening until by ten o'clock it was a nonstop roar of booms and pops and explosions as tens of thousands, maybe hundreds of thousands, of fireworks were going off in the city each moment. There were three-and-a-half-million people in Chicago, and it seemed like every one of them was lighting fireworks at the same time. There were massive booms everywhere from heavy-duty boomers that were part of official city, church, neighborhood and company fireworks shows. They came from thousands of aerial bombs that shot rockets into the sky that exploded into giant and beautiful starbursts. Those big boomers were exploding and creating dozens of red, white and blue starbursts every few minutes. It was like the sky was on fire and an entire city of three-and-a half-million people was being bombarded all at once.

After it got dark was when most of the real booming and bombing and fireworks began. There was nothing like the sensation and the primal thrill of illuminating and piercing the darkness with massive explosions. The darkness conveyed a sense of security in that it basically concealed one's identity so that if something did go wrong, well, no one could see who was responsible. Around eight, just as it was getting dark, the guys walked back to Koz Park to experience one of the neighborhood's great Fourth of July traditions: the burning of a small mountain of car tires. No one knew when the tradition began, but it had begun, and it was a thing to witness and to be part of.

All year long a group of older guys collected and stored old car tires, and at dusk they began rolling them out of their garages and basements to the middle of Koz's four baseball fields where they piled them up. The number of tires differed every year, but if they had forty or fifty tires it was a big deal. From about seven-thirty onward the park started to fill up with people who came to watch and celebrate the big fire and to speculate on how big it would really be.

After dark, the tires were torched, and within minutes they were fully engulfed, and a column of thick, black, oily, smelly smoke rose from the pile and stunk up the surrounding neighborhood. The fires lasted twenty minutes at the most because someone always called the fire department to come and put them out. When a fire truck arrived and began driving onto the field toward the blazing tires, a chorus of "Boos" arose from the spectators, most of whom wanted the fire to go on all night. In just a few minutes, a year's worth of work was extinguished under a high-pressure stream of water and the darkness closed in around the pile of smoldering rubber. Sometimes attempts were made to relight the tires after the firemen had left, but that was considered a dumb thing to do. If the fire guys had to come out a second time they would be sure to notify the cops and demand some official harassment of the perpetrators.

With the bonfire extinguished, the guys made their way to another of the neighborhood's great traditions: the fireworks extravaganza, party, celebration—whatever one wanted to call it—at the Malcheks' house on Lawndale. It was there that the four Malchek brothers and their dad, along with a couple of neighboring families, threw the biggest residential fireworks parties anyone had ever seen.

The fun began after dark when the Malcheks and their neighbors planted red railroad flares in their front lawns and lit them, their roaring tips of fire and orange glows acting as welcoming beacons to all who wanted to join in the fun. For about a quarter of a block the street-side curb in front of the Malcheks' and their neighbors' homes had been cleared of cars to make an area where any type of firework, bomb, rocket or other pyrotechnic could be blown up, launched or set on fire.

A constant stream of adults and kids flowed to and from the curb to the Malcheks' and the other wooden front porches as everyone took turns lighting things. There were Roman candles, rockets, aerial bombs, M-80s, cherry bombs, firecrackers, things that shot five feet into the air and twirled around, snakes, cracker balls and pretty much anything and everything that could explode and made noise.

The biggest thing was to see how much noise could be made at once, and so things were sort of synchronized with people at the curb lighting off pack after pack of firecrackers at once or in rapid succession. A dozen packs of crackers going off at once was astounding. Once, about ten kids and adults lined up and lit M-80s, and the subsequent Boom! Boom! Boom! Boom!Boom! Bu!Bu!Bu!Bu!Boom! was magnificent and surely could have woken the dead. After a half hour of massive and continuous explosions, a fog-like cloud of gunpowder smoke shrouded Lawndale, the sharp, acrid smoke stinging people's eyes, noses and throats. No one complained. That was the price of pure fun and joy.

The Malcheks' party was like thousands just like it that went on throughout the city and its two-hundred-and-twenty-seven square miles. After a few hours and hundreds of thousands of fireworks going off, the city itself was engulfed in a giant cloud of smoke.

The Malcheks' affair, as did the parties across the city, began to taper off at around eleven o'clock, and Dennis and Steve and the other guys headed home after nearly fifteen hours of adventure, excitement and fun. They were tired, but not weary or exhausted; they were too excited to be exhausted. When they climbed into their beds and pulled the covers over themselves, they drifted off to sleep to the sounds of tens of thousands of fireworks going off every moment.

CHAPTER 52

The Day After the Fourth

T HE DAY AFTER the Fourth was strange. The great party to which everyone had been invited, and to which almost everyone had come, was over and its energy and excitement gone. People were back to work in their stores, offices and factories, and everyone began to settle into summer routines. Families would be taking vacations and playmates would be gone for a couple of weeks, leaving kids without their best friends. The hot, stifling mugginess of July and August would descend on the city and seem to slow everything and everyone down. The long two-month slog without any holidays meant that kids were on their own to find things to celebrate and get excited about. They had no trouble doing that, and it began the day after the Fourth.

"Whaja hear? Anybody get fingers blown off?" Dennis, Steve and their pals asked each other as they gathered in the alley on the morning after the Fourth.

It was a routine and logical question that people asked each other after the Fourth because for days and weeks before the holiday, newspapers and TV news programs quoted so-called experts who warned of the dangers of fireworks, especially the possibility of severing fingers, and even hands. Although such accidents did occur, they were rare, and no one in Dennis's or Steve's circle of friends knew or had ever heard of anyone who had lost a finger to fireworks. Anyone who had had a finger or hand blown off or maimed would have been a hero to the kids.

The guys spent much of the morning walking the streets and alleys looking for unexploded fireworks. They usually found a handful or so, and when they did, as did kids in other neighborhoods who were doing the same thing, they blew the stuff up right away so that on the morning after the Fourth there was always a scattering of explosions all over the city.

By noon the hunt for unexploded ordnance was over and the kids moved on to new adventures. They walked to Koz, Milwaukee Avenue, and other places, and eventually made it to the junk-filled field that they liked to play at in the industrial area off Wrightwood. They sat on wooden crates and cans, chunks of concrete, discarded furniture and anything else that supported them and talked about their vacation and other summer plans. Dennis and Steve were going to spend a couple of weeks at the family's cottage in Wisconsin and at their aunt's dairy farm in Wisconsin. At the cottage they were going to sleep outside at night in homemade tents, get up before dawn and hunt and shoot raccoons with BB guns, all without the adults knowing. Other kids were going to Wisconsin, some to Michigan and a couple to Indiana. One kid said his family was going to some far-off place called Wyoming and Yellowstone National Park, and the guys wondered what it was, what it looked like and if it was as big as Riis or Humboldt parks.

WHAT IS YELLOWSTONE PARK?

They talked about the fun they'd have in the neighborhood and with each other: the games they'd play, places they'd go and the trouble they'd get in to. There'd be baseball, football, pinner, trips downtown, Cubs games at Wrigley Field, day-long L and bus rides, bike trips to Gompers Park and the forest preserves, water fights, movies to see, model cars to build, garage roofs to climb, light bulbs to steal, pizzas to eat, railroad tracks to explore, good kids to ridicule and everything and anything else. They'd cram a year's worth of fun into the next two months, of that they were sure. No one and nothing would stop them.

The end would come in the first week of September, after Labor Day and the final bash of the summer. School would resume and they'd have to once again deal with the starchy smell of the nuns' thick linen habits, with homework, report cards, hymn singing, having to attend mass and having to study instead of playing.

That was two months away, though, light years to kids. For now the only thing that mattered was that they were free.

CHAPTER 53

May Crowning and a Bleeding Host

THE KIDS' PLANS for summer vacation after seventh grade had to wait a few more weeks until school let out for the summer. Those weeks were pure agony. It was early May and the weather was warming, flowers were blooming, trees and roses and bushes were getting their full complement of leaves, the air was fresh and fragrant with new growth, birds were singing, and all any kid wanted, even the teachers' pets, was to be done with the school year and have three months of freedom and fun.

The students got some relief from the tedium that was made unbearable by the coming of spring because May was the month of OLG's May Crowning, a ceremony where a statue of the Virgin Mary was dressed in elaborate and expensive silk gowns and adorned with a crown that was painted gold. It was a big deal for all Catholic schools in the city, but especially big for OLG because the parish was named after the Virgin.

The relief from school the kids got was that for a month leading up to the May Crowning they were marched on Friday afternoons from the playground after the lunch hour into church where they practiced hymns and special prayers and where they were drilled about their roles in the upcoming ceremony, which would be a special mass. While being led in hymns and prayer in church by the nuns wasn't anyone's first choice for a fun time, it was better than being in a classroom. The ninety minutes a week the May Crowning practices took out of school for those four weeks provided solid relief from the misery of school.

The kids were seated in the pews according to their class levels and teachers so that if one group wasn't singing or praying with enough enthusiasm and passion the nuns would know who it was, demand the reason why and berate and beat them without waiting for an answer. Zita made the Disturbers sit in a pew by themselves so she and the other nuns would be able to spot the slightest violation of church rules and pounce and administer the most extreme discipline.

The opportunity to administer discipline came swiftly as the Disturbers immediately, blatantly and purposely violated the rules by doing two things that drove the nuns crazy. Instead of kneeling properly—knees on the padded kneelers, back straight, butt far away from the pew, hands folded together, fingers pointed upward and thumbs crossed—they slouched, leaned their butts back against the edge of the pew and folded their hands lazily with the fingers curled and intermingled, hands pointed forward, not skyward. It was pure sacrilege. Zita, DeLasalle and Yvonne moved quickly.

Kolba, who was closest to the aisle, got it first. The nuns yanked him out of the pew, stood him in the aisle and angrily demanded, "What is the meaning of this, mister?"

"Meaning of what, Sters?" Kolba replied.

"Of your disrespect for God in his own house? In his own house!"

They took turns beating Kolba, and the other Disturbers laughed, but not for long. They were quickly pulled out of the pew and beaten in their turn. Then they were marched to the front of the church where the nuns further berated and beat them and used them as an example to the other students.

"You will respect God in his house by kneeling properly and folding your hands correctly," Yvonne told the kids. "Anything less is disrespectful and a sign that you don't love God, and we will not tolerate that."

With that Yvonne and the other nuns slapped the Disturbers around again before sending them back to their pew. The Disturbers and many of the other kids wondered to themselves just how loving and respectful of God it was to violently beat up children in his sacred house. Kolba and the other Disturbers considered posing that question to the nuns right then and there, but that really would have been suicidal, and with only a few weeks of school left they figured it wasn't worth it.

BEATING UP KIDS IN GOD'S HOUSE

Whenever she had a large audience—and at May Crowning practice she had almost the entire school—Yvonne loved to show off how smart she thought she was. Even in church she'd pontificate about grammar and grammarians, Catholic theology and lots of other things almost none of the kids cared about. Yvonne always got everyone's attention when she talked about two of her favorite subjects: the evils of chewing the communion host and how the host would bleed if pricked with a pin.

The host was not to be chewed because one was supposed to show the utmost respect for Jesus—the host being his actual body—and chewing and mashing him to pieces before swallowing him was disrespectful. For kids who knew how to think, the theory and rule was idiotic, and, of course, illogical, because they figured that putting Christ's body into one's mouth was disrespectful to begin with. Whether you chewed Christ or let him slowly dissolve in your mouth before swallowing him, they figured it just wasn't a good way to treat Jesus or anyone else. They did amuse themselves, though, with the idea that there was a respectful way to eat a person.

Talking about drawing blood from a host by pricking it with a pin always ensured Yvonne that she'd have an attentive audience. The story fed every kid's hunger, whether it be for the macabre, the spiritual, the ridiculous or the humorous. The story was always the same, and Yvonne told it this Friday. A host had accidentally fallen to the floor one Sunday in church in a faraway parish—in Europe, the kids figured—when a priest was giving communion. The flour disc that was Christ's body was immediately covered with a white cloth that had been blessed by the priest, and the worshipers gave the covered host a wide berth, not wanting to disturb Jesus. After the mass had ended the priest and others went to carefully retrieve the piece of blessed sacrament. They uncovered it and were about to place it into a golden chalice when somebody accidentally pricked it with a pin. Upon being pricked, the host started bleeding! It was never clear if the host gushed blood or just oozed a few drops, but the fact that it bled was proof that it really was Christ's body and that it was sacred and worthy of the utmost respect and adoration.

Yvonne's story never had an ending because the kids were too amazed, awed, repelled or amused by it at that point, and they always erupted into a chaotic chatter. The nun always stopped it there so she could bask in the effect she had created. Kids never found out how much the host bled, whether it ever stopped bleeding, what the priest did with it, how it was pricked or why someone who was rescuing a fallen host had a pin in their hands. No matter what any kid thought about the story, whether they believed it or thought it ridiculous, one thing was certain: from the first time they heard it every kid had an urge to prick a host with a pin.

The May Crowning celebration was supposed to be just that, a celebration of hope, joy and salvation. For one OLG kid, though, it was just the opposite and amounted to years of pain, unanswered questions and torment. When the statue of the Virgin was crowned, all in the church were supposed to break into song and belt out a special tune to the Virgin that contained the chorus:

Mother of God,
Virgin most chaste,
Help us oh Mother,
Lady of Grace.

Whenever she heard or had to sing the song Nancy Gorski cried and felt a deep and horrible pain and sadness. Who, she constantly asked herself, is chasing the Virgin Mary, and why are they chasing her? Even in seventh grade, Nancy didn't know the answer.

CHAPTER 54

The Craziest Afternoon Ever

THAT SPRING, ZITA and the Disturbers were at each other as much as ever. The guys tried hard to get to the old nun, and she tried to ignore them, finally realizing that denying them attention was the greatest punishment of all. She was set in her ways, though, and as much as she knew that ignoring the guys and not responding to their provocations was the more effective way to deal with them, she couldn't quite do it. Every challenge to her authority, no matter how slight, set her off and triggered an instinct to respond. Plus, she still had the rest of the class to think about and she couldn't just let the Disturbers take control of the classroom. As punishment for what they had already done, and for what they certainly would do, she made the guys stand in the back of the room in the afternoons when they were in her classroom, figuring that would drain them of some of their mischievous energy. The Disturbers thought it unfair, especially on days when they hadn't really done anything, but they made the best of it.

Every day after coming in from the playground, the Disturbers, in direct violation of Zita's order that they were to stand in the afternoons, sat in their chairs in the back row. That they disobeyed the order was bad enough, the way they did it infuriated the nun. They marched together to the back row, stomping their feet loudly on the floor. When they got to their desks they pulled out their chairs in unison, stepped in front of them, and as loudly as possible plopped themselves into the chairs. Then they'd scoot the chairs forward, making sure to scrape the bottoms of the legs on the floor in order to make as much noise as possible.

That meant that Zita would have to order them to stand, which she did every afternoon. With every order to stand, the guys loudly protested about how unfair it was.

"Ster, this isn't fair," Kolba said one afternoon after Zita had issued her order. "Why isn't everyone else made to stand?"

"Because, sweetie, they're nice boys and girls who don't disrupt the class."

"That's not an excuse, Ster. They might be bad in the future, and you don't want that."

"So, sweetie, I should punish children who haven't caused trouble?"

"Yes, Ster, you should. Make the rest of them stand and make us sit down. That would be fair, and it would punish us because with all of them standing and us sitting we wouldn't be able to see you or the blackboard, Ster, and that would be awful."

Kurkowski was next. "Ster, my bunion is acting up. It's killing me. If I don't sit down I'll die! I'll die, Ster!"

"Well, sweetie, maybe you should have thought about your bunion when you were stomping your feet a few minutes ago. Did it hurt then?"

"No, Ster, it only hurts when I'm standing still."

"Well then, Mister Kookowski, you won't stand still. Starting now you will march in place where you are, and you will march in place until I tell you to stop. That will help your bunion, sweetie pie."

Then Ruchinski tried. "Oh Ster! I think that real punishment would be to make us stand on our heads, Ster. That would teach us!"

That suggestion stunned even Zita, who in more than forty years of teaching had heard everything, but never anything that dumb. She blinked slowly and thought briefly to herself, "This child really is disturbed."

Zita recovered and asked Ruchinski just why she should order him and the others to stand on their heads. Now it was Ruchinski who was flustered. He had made the suggestion just to say something, anything, and he had no real comprehension of what he had just said other than that he blurted it out.

He had no clever comeback to Zita's question, which was embarrassing. Even the good kids expected a funny reply—after all, that's what the Disturbers were there for—and at that second Ruchinski had none. The situation was dire. But the other Disturbers instinctively and immediately sensed his trouble and came to his rescue by shouting in unison as loud as they could:

"Because!"

The class erupted into laughter, Zita was mad, and the Disturbers were proud of themselves.

A blackboard spanned the length of the room's rear wall, and since they had to stand, the guys made use of the situation by drawing goofy pictures that were meant to anger Zita on it, and writing cuss words and things like, "Bernard Heller and Zita are crooks! Arrest them now!"

The antics had their desired effects, and whenever the offending images or words appeared, Zita would send a brigade of good kids who were armed with erasers and wet hand towels to wipe the blackboard clean.

The Disturbers found that one easy way to anger Zita was to plop themselves on the floor and refuse to stand. Occasionally Zita wobbled, pointer in hand, to the back row. The guys always scrambled away and never got hit and Zita gave up on trying to get them to participate in class. If they chose to refuse to learn the material and to flunk, well, that was their choice, she figured.

One day in mid-May when the kids didn't change classes and so had Zita all afternoon, Dennis and Kurkowski got tired of standing and sat on the floor, Kurkowski at one end of the room and Dennis at the other, and began rolling round, hard Jawbreakers candies across the wooden floor thinking the noise would upset Zita. It was around one-forty-five in the afternoon and once, when a Jawbreaker got away from Dennis, he lunged after it. In doing so he caught a glimpse of something that was underneath the chair of Arianna DeFranco, who had been banished to the back row earlier in the week as punishment for some minor infraction of Zita's rules.

What he had seen so shocked and overwhelmed Dennis's senses that he immediately started convulsing and hyperventilating. He tried talking but couldn't. Same thing with laughing. He was breathing heavily, deeply and rapidly, and sounding like a train locomotive, but it didn't seem like he was getting any air, and he thought he was going to faint. His jaw was trembling, his tongue was dry and his eyes were bulging. He had just discovered the most astonishing thing that any grade school kid anywhere had ever seen, and he couldn't tell anybody about it because he was spasming uncontrollably and couldn't talk.

The only thing Dennis could do was to start violently punching the leg of Ruchinski, who was standing next to him. Ruchinski had never been hit as hard or as often, and he was about to retaliate by kicking his comrade with as much force and violence as he had received when he looked down and saw that his pal had turned into a raging, spasming lunatic. Dennis's chest was heaving violently and uncontrollably, his face was turning blue, he kept trying to talk but couldn't, and his eyes, which really were about to pop out of his skull, had a pleading look which seemed to say, "Do you see what I see? It's real, ain't it?" All the while he kept pounding Ruchinski's leg with his right arm while pointing to DeFranco's chair with the other.

Finally, Dennis was able to get out a single word. "Look!" he stammered while continuing to point to DeFranco's chair. Ruchinski crouched down, looked under the chair and went into convulsions himself. All he could do was pound the leg of the guy next to him, point to the chair and stammer the same word: "Look!" The other Disturbers were notified of the situation the same way, and in a few moments all five were convulsing and looking at and pointing to the discovery that had sent Dennis into spasms: there was a pile of human excrement, or shit, as the guys called it, under Arianna's chair. Someone had taken a crap on the classroom floor! It was beyond astonishing and almost beyond comprehension. Who would do that, and why? Crapping anywhere was something bums, alcoholics, public school kids, communists, pagans, Lutherans, Protestants and the worst of the worst, the irredeemable, did, not Catholic school kids. How could it have happened?

How the shit got there, the guys didn't know. All that mattered right then was that it was there, that it was stinking up the back of the room and that it needed to be cleaned up.

After another few moments the shock wore off and the guys had regained their composure, even Dennis had calmed down, and they started in on what would be the craziest and most insane afternoon in OLG's history. They stood up and began trying to get Zita's attention by shouting things like "It stinks back here!" "It smells!" "We're gonna die from the stink!" and "Come back here and smell it!"

HOLY CRAP!

Strangely, Zita ignored them even though they were shouting and even though they were throwing the classroom into absolute chaos. Nothing the guys said or did got a response from the nun. Frustrated, the guys walked halfway to the front of the room and shouted to Zita, "Come back here and smell it! Smell it yourself!" Even dozens of demands like that got no response from the nun. The guys began walking among the rows of the other students asking if they smelled the stink and inviting them back to look at the pile. Many of the students took them up on the offer—Arianna had moved her desk and chair by then and the pile sat by itself in the vacated spot—and came to the back row and saw and smelled for themselves. When they returned to their seats they told the kids next to them what they had seen. Soon, the entire class knew that there was human shit on the floor, and many kids began demanding that Zita go back and see and smell it for herself.

Angry at being ignored, the Disturbers did something they had never dared do before: they shouted obscenities at the nun. "There's shit on the floor," Dennis yelled at her.

"Someone took a shit, as in s-h-i-t, on the floor," Ruchinski yelled out. The always-angry Bozeman said it better than anyone: "There's a filthy, stinking, vile piece of shit on the floor back here. Come back here and smell it, you witch!"

COME BACK HERE AND SMELL IT!

Feeling liberated and empowered now that the Disturbers had publicly sworn in class, and to the nun's face, at least a dozen other kids started shouting that there was shit on the floor and demanding that Zita go back and see it. Then, even some of the good kids took up the chant the Disturbers had started: "Come back and smell the shit! Come back and smell the shit! Come back and smell the shit!"

There had been riots in Zita's classroom before, but this was light years beyond those other disturbances. It was chaos, bedlam, anarchy, fury, rebellion, comedy, absurdity, tragedy and contempt all at once and packed into ninety minutes of class time. There was no authority in the room. Not only had Zita ceased to be an authority figure in her own classroom, she had, to many of the kids, ceased to be human as well. It was as if she had evaporated and no longer existed. Even the good kids wondered why she was ignoring what everybody knew was true, and why she didn't do a single thing to address the incredibly serious issue or try to impede and stop the chaos and anarchy.

Being unable to bear the chants and torment any longer, Zita finally relented, hobbled to the back row at around three o'clock, saw for herself and ordered Dennis to clean it up. Dennis protested, the other Disturbers laughed, and Dennis relented because the crap and the stench had to go. Dennis walked down the hall to the janitor's closet to get a broom, dustpan, and some throw-up powder—colored and scented sawdust—to throw over the pile. The school's janitor, Mr. Letart, was there and asked Dennis why he needed the stuff.

"Looks like a girl took a dump on the floor," Dennis answered.

Mr. Letart rolled his eyes and said with a sort of pained, sad voice, "What, did nun refuse to let her go to the bathroom?"

Then Dennis understood what had happened. He remembered that shortly after the class came in from the playground, Arianna had been furiously raising her hand trying to get Zita's attention. The nun ignored her, and she eventually gave up. She probably had to go bad, couldn't control herself, and when the load came, scooped it out of her underwear with a sheet of loose-leaf paper and deposited it on the floor hoping no one would notice it. Zita had ignored the Disturbers pleas because she knew that she herself had been the cause of it all.

The anarchy and chaos that incident produced—the madness that humiliated Arianna and destroyed Zita by making even the good kids dismiss her as someone to be pitied rather than respected—Zita had caused herself by refusing to let a twelve-year-old girl go to the bathroom. It was a hideous act of self-destruction, and even the Disturbers saw the tragedy in it. It was tragic, grotesque and reprehensible because it need not have happened. It was preventable. Yet it wasn't. If Zita had acknowledged Arianna's hand and let her go to the bathroom, none of what happened would have happened. But like the other nuns, Zita was inflexible. A rule was a rule and a trouble-making kid who was raising her hand was always up to no good, and that would never change.

There was little room in so many of those nuns for nuance, compassion, reality and a recognition and understanding that kids and society were changing, and changing quickly. Blind and absolute loyalty to authority, especially religious authority, was disappearing as people had more access to information and became more educated and less fearful and superstitious. TV, newspapers, news and satirical magazines, scientific journals, comic books, encyclopedias and so much more were everywhere and available to anyone who was interested.

Kids dreamed of doing something other than what their parents and aunts and uncles had done. Many wanted careers that didn't involve working in factories or staying home to raise kids and cook and clean and sew. There was a true revolution going on, and kids were helping lead it by refusing to follow the old rules. They were challenging authority, especially mindless, illogical and abusive authority. They wanted the freedom to think for themselves and to make their own rules. Society, led in part by kids, was trying to bust out of the straitjacket that had confined, stunted and imprisoned people for decades. Every time a kid loosened and tried to break out of that straitjacket by telling a joke, disobeying a rule or challenging Church doctrine, the nuns pulled the laces tighter and tighter until the resentment at being confined and abused exploded into open and gleeful insurrection. Things were changing, and the nuns either couldn't see that change as it played out in their classrooms, or they saw it and tried to kill it because they knew it would greatly and permanently diminish their power, authority and status in society. For whatever reason, the nuns were rigid and incapable of adapting or changing, and that's what led to the insanity of that school year. By being unwilling or unable to change, the nuns and lay teachers undermined their own authority and hastened its decline. The Disturbers were the beneficiaries of that inflexibility. They would have been troublemakers in years and decades past, because they were, well, natural instigators. In this case they were elevated to elite status by the insanity and intransigence of the nuns.

Dennis returned to the classroom, cleaned up the smelly mess and told the guys what Mr. Letart had said. Over the next few days the Disturbers spread the word about what really had happened, and Arianna didn't feel quite as bad as she had on that horrible May afternoon.

CHAPTER 55

The Last Day and One Final Victory

I T HAD COME at last and after nine truly long months: the last day of school. For all kids it was a joyous day because summer vacation was at hand. For the Disturbers it was both joyous and sad. Their wild, exhilarating, extraordinary and unbelievable nine-month-long rule was over. The school had never seen anything like them before and never would again. The fun and the camaraderie they had, and the circumstances that converged to create these Disturbers were exceptional and rare, kind of like a hundred-year flood. No other nun on the planet would have let them get away with what Zita did. Sister Mary Zita, at that stage in her life, never should have been in a classroom. But fewer women were entering convents and there was beginning to be a shortage of nuns. So Zita, even in her diminished capacity, was allowed to continue teaching. The nuns, with their self-destructive inflexibility and insistence on subservience and conformity, fueled the Disturbers. Each and every overreaction by the nuns was met with a more forceful counter-reaction by the Disturbers. The nuns couldn't see that if they had just calmed down, most of the disturbances would not have happened. The societal rebellion that crashed head-on into OLG that year had been building for years, but the nuns never reacted intelligently to it. The rebellion peaked that year with these five Disturbers, and with Zita's help. Even children knew that putting a group of troublemakers together in a row in the back of a classroom by themselves and giving them a silly title in an attempt to shame them was lunacy. Zita did it anyway, and the other nuns approved. Nuns constantly beat kids (in a few years it would be called child abuse for an adult to hit a kid), but they never realized that each beating fueled, not respect or fear, but a deep resentment and a thirst for revenge. They never considered that their over-the-top threats of eternal damnation, Hell and calling the cops for minor infractions of rules weren't credible anymore and made them look foolish, weak and inept. Older nuns were retiring, and the younger ones who took their places weren't as authoritarian or as abusive. In a few years, there would be no beatings and no abusing children. Like the knife sharpeners and the junk men with horse-drawn wagons, the era of abusive nuns who could beat children at will was closing quickly. Never again would what happened to the Disturbers and generations of kids before them be allowed. The days of clipping clothespins to the ears of first graders, shooting them with rubber bands and hanging them on coat hooks were ending.

Seventh grade had been a kind of limbo, a transitional time and place between childhood and the very beginnings of adulthood. It allowed kids to have a final and glorious fling with childhood and irresponsibility, and the Disturbers took full advantage of it. But it was over now, and they would have to start growing up. Eighth grade would be more serious and harder. They would have to start thinking about high school and college and careers instead of what they could do to torment an aging, hapless nun and make other kids laugh. They would never have as much fun in school as they had had in seventh grade, and they knew it.

Right now, though, there were still four hours of school left and anything could happen. Report cards were passed out early, and everyone, even the Disturbers, had been promoted to eighth grade. The room was all joy, and the kids were busy cleaning the room, sweeping the floor, washing the blackboards and their desktops and taking cans of trash to the school's incinerator.

After the cleaning was done, Zita led the class in a few rounds of hymns, and then, in a sort of Sister Mary Zita Lovefest where she asked kids what they had liked most about seventh grade. Several of the suck-up kids gushed that they had liked her the most and that she was the best teacher they had ever had. The Disturbers declined to participate and drew pictures of battleships and bombers in their notebooks.

At about eleven fifteen, Zita realized that there was one piece of unfinished business to finish. There were still two pagan baby coffee cans half full of change on her desk, one for the boys and one for the girls. Neither can contained enough money to buy a pagan baby outright, so Zita decided to have one last class election. There were only two options: combine the boys' money with the girls' cash and buy a baby in the girls' name, or vice versa.

The Disturbers saw an opportunity and went to work lobbying boys and girls as to their preferred choice. While the kids were starting to vote and writing their choices on slips of paper, Zita made it loudly known that she wanted the boys' money to go into the girls' can. That, she said, would be the perfect end to a wonderful school year.

Bernard Heller and a good-kid girl were tasked with counting the forty-two votes. They finished at a few minutes before twelve and read the results. Putting the girls' money in the boys' can got five votes. Zita smiled approvingly. Putting the boys' money into the girls' can got thirteen votes. Zita was confused and asked Heller what was going on.

"Well, Sister, there are twenty-four votes that have another choice," Heller told the nun.

"What do they say?" Zita asked.

"Well, Sister," Heller said as a look of horror crossed his face. "They say, 'We want our money back.'"

Zita flew into a rage. She was about to rip into the Disturbers when the noon bell rang to let out school for the summer. The kids leaped out of their chairs and raced out the classroom's front door. On their way out, many of the kids reached into the pagan baby coffee cans on Zita's desk and took handfuls of change while Zita watched in horror and disbelief. In a few moments, the cans were empty. Zita was outraged, embarrassed and depressed. She wanted desperately to beat the guys, but they were gone. The Disturbers had beaten her one final time, and there wasn't a thing she could do about it.

SEE YA, STER!

ABOUT THE AUTHOR

Dennis Domrzalski is an expert at helping everyone he meets come to grips with their own glaring shortcomings. Born and raised in Chicago, he lives in Albuquerque, New Mexico. He has been a reporter and writer since the mid-1970s, including stints at City News Bureau of Chicago, The Albuquerque Tribune, and the Weekly Alibi.